"STAY ALERT"

It was an eerie sensation, knowing that the Xenos were there, swimming through solid rock a few hundred meters beneath the crater floor, but unreachable, untouchable. Dev and the other newbies had been shown recordings of the Xenophobe attack at the site seven weeks earlier—at just about the same time, he knew now, as the alert that had paralyzed communications during his first day on Loki.

In sims, Dev had watched streamlined Xenophobe snake-shapes emerge from the ground, nosing their way up through solid rock turned plastic by a technology humans didn't understand and couldn't copy. If HEMILCOM was tracking a Deep Seismic Anomaly here, now, it meant the Xenos could be rising toward the surface.

Why the hell wasn't anyone as scared as he was?

Other titles in the
WARSTRIDER *series*
by William H. Keith, Jr.
Coming Soon from Avon Books

WARSTRIDER: REBELLION

WARSTRIDER

WILLIAM H. KEITH, JR.

AVON BOOKS • NEW YORK

WARSTRIDER is an original publication of Avon Books. This work has never before appeared in book form. This work is a novel. Any similarity to actual persons or events is purely coincidental.

AVON BOOKS
A division of
The Hearst Corporation
1350 Avenue of the Americas
New York, New York 10019

Cover illustration by Dorian Vallejo
Published by arrangement with the author
Library of Congress Catalog Card Number: 92-90416
ISBN: 0-380-76879-8

First AvoNova Printing: February 1993

AVONOVA TRADEMARK REG. U.S. PAT. OFF. AND IN OTHER COUNTRIES, MARCA REGISTRADA, HECHO EN U.S.A.

Printed in the U.S.A.

RA 10 9 8 7 6 5 4 3 2 1

RS-64D Warlord

LaG-42 Ghostrider

RLN-90 Scoutstrider

Prologue

Eight years before he joined the Hegemony Guard, Devis Cameron knew little of interstellar politics and cared less. He knew next to nothing about the far-off threat Man called the Xenophobes, or why the Imperial and Hegemony fleets had been mobilized in Eagle Sector, or even where Eagle Sector was. He'd not heard of a world called Lung Chi—yet—and all he'd ever seen of the Emperor had been canned glimpses in ViRnews feeds.

And Dev most certainly did not understand why Imperial protocol demanded that Michal Andre Cameron divorce his wife and leave her and his family behind on Earth while he traveled up the Singapore Sky-el to assume his new post with the Imperial Staff at *Tenno Kyuden*, the Palace of Heaven. Politics, his father had called it, with a bitterness that astonished Dev. Damned, filthy extortion, his mother had called it, and then she'd burst into tears, because until the moment of that Imperial order, the Cameron family had been close and happy despite the fact that they were still non-Imperial citizens of Earth.

Dev was sixteen standard that spring of 2532, old enough, certainly, to know what was happening, but since he knew nothing of the tangled relationship of Hegemony with Empire, he couldn't understand why his father had to obey such a patently unjust command.

Why couldn't his father simply thank *Tenno-heika* for the honor but explain that he wanted to stay with his family?

"Tell them you can't do it!" Dev said, ashamed of the tears and unable to stop them. "Or, or tell them that you love Mom and that you want us to come along. I wouldn't mind leaving Earth, and I'll bet Mom wouldn't either."

Michal Cameron's eyes were moist as well. He was a big man, made bigger by the white and gold uniform of the Hegemony Navy he still wore. His shoulder boards and stiff collar bore the three cherry-blossom studs of *taisa*, a navy captain.

"It's just not that simple, son. I wish to God it were."

Dev's eyes fastened to the gleaming gold sunburst his father wore at his throat. *Teikokuno Hoshi*, the Star of the Empire, awarded for extraordinary service to the Emperor.

"It's all because of that medal, isn't it?"

His father sighed. "It's not just the medal, Dev. It's not just the promotion. They're transferring me to the Imperial Navy, giving me a slot on the Emperor's Staff. It is an . . . honor." His father's face twisted, saying otherwise.

Anger flared, edged with bitterness. "In other words, you had a choice between us and your career, right? And you chose your career!"

"Try to understand. It's not . . . not *proper* for an Imperial admiral to be married to someone who's not an Imperial citizen. There are political considerations." He looked away, shrugging helplessly. "So they have someone else for me to marry."

His father was silent for a long moment. They were sitting side by side on a park bench beneath an intensely blue, vibrant sky. Beyond the trees of Moosic Park, the West Scranton skyline gleamed, silver and transplas arcologies clustered about the blue-gray thrust of Bald Mountain. The city seemed to go on forever, tower upon tower, the high-tech anthill sprawl of the BosWash metroplex. A distant thunder rumbled, trailing far behind a fast-drawn scratch of white across the sky. Another ten hours and his father would be on one of those hypersonic suborbitals, on his way to the other side of the world . . . and to space.

"If I refuse, well, I would be insulting some very powerful people. *Gensui* Munimori. My patron, *Gensui* Yoshida. Even the Emperor, who agreed to let a *gaijin* like me join the Imperial staff. They would all lose face. It would be . . . very bad."

"You act like they own you!"

"Son, do you know the word *sepuku*?"

"Huh? Sure. You . . . you mean they'd make you kill yourself?"

"It's possible. If the insult to the Emperor was considered grave enough. Certainly I'd have to leave the navy. I might not be able to get decent work, and that would be hard on you and your mother and your brother. A lot harder than this separation is going to be.

"If I take the promotion, well, some things will still be the same. I'll still love you and Mom and Greg very much, and I'll visit you when I can. Not as much as we'd all like, maybe, but I'll come see you every chance I get. I promise you that.

"And lots of things'll be better. We'll have enough money to do things we couldn't think about before."

"I don't *care* about money—"

"For one thing, we'll be able to get you and Greg sockets."

"I don't want sockets." He held up his left hand, palm out, revealing the tracery of nano-grown metallic inlays in the skin at the base of his thumb. "I've got my interface."

"So does everyone else on the planet. Blast it, Dev, you need an education if you're going to get anywhere, and I mean something better than West Scranton Traditional! You need to go to a decent school where they feed you direct through a jack. BosWash Technic, maybe. Or MIT." He tapped the silvery ring of metal just visible in the short hair behind his right ear. He had another behind his left ear, and one at the base of his neck as well. Temporal sockets and cervical socket, T-sockets and C-socket, they connected directly with the cephlinkage plexus grown inside Michal Cameron's brain.

Few of Earth's citizens could afford a three-socket, full-interface set, but the elder Cameron had been born to a wealthy family, one with old ties to the Kyoto world banking complex. He'd never been able to afford sockets for his family, though, not on a Hegemony naval officer's pay. Dev's cephlink and palm interface, of course, had been implanted free when he was a child. It gave him access to ViR entertainment, even some of the simpler interactive programs, and it let him access the communications systems and the computers upon which the world's economy depended.

"Sockets are your passport out of the arcologies and off the Earth and out to where you can be yourself," his father told him. "This is the only way. Believe me."

"You're making all these decisions for me. Like I'm some kind of damned computer you can just program to suit yourself!"

"Your mom and I are programming you, as you put it, to be able to stand up for yourself. You know, an Earth kid these days doesn't have much of a chance. Especially if he's American and living in the HPAs."

"Doesn't seem so bad to me."

"Maybe. Something like a billion Americans live in the Hegemony Protectorate Arcologies. No cares, no worries . . . and no cephlink implants or sockets to let them tap into their own futures. They don't *have* futures, except what the Hegemony chooses to give them. Your mom and I want more for you. Lots more. In the outworlds you can still make something of yourself, but you'd damned well better have the hardware up here." He tapped one bony finger against his skull. "Otherwise you're just one of twelve billion other Earth kids with a bare minimum education and no useful skills. No employer, no shipping line, no survey agency, would even look at you."

Dev didn't want to accept that. "What about Mom? What does she think about it?"

"Actually, she's the one who suggested the divorce. She wants what's best for you kids. And this is best. For *all* of us."

Dev had enough of his father's vision and his mother's pragmatism to see that his father was right about the need for sockets. But the realities of politics, of a Japanese Empire that directly ruled only a small part of Earth, yet so dominated the Terran Hegemony that it could casually destroy a man's family in the name of propriety, were still utterly alien.

He wondered if he would ever understand. . . .

Chapter 1

To understand modern technic civilization, one must understand the significance of the intracephalic cybernetic linkage implant, the cephlink as it is more popularly known. A complex, membrane-thin webwork of nanotechnic circuitry, literally grown by programmed medical nano manipulating injected raw materials molecule by molecule deep within the brain's longitudinal sulcus, the cephlink serves as an extension of Man's intelligence, memory, and power, as well as serving as a direct link between organic brain functions and any appropriately equipped artificial intelligence, or AI.

In the course of the past three centuries, the cephlink has become the bridge between human and machine intelligence, and the means by which Man has at last stepped beyond the limitations of the flesh.

—*The Rise of Technic Man*
Fujiwara Naramoro
C.E. 2535

This, Dev thought as he stepped off the freighter's boarding ramp, *is my last chance.*

The steel-lined cavern, open to vacuum only moments earlier, was still cold, and Dev palmed the smartpatch on his suit to raise its thermostat. Steam spilled from *Mintaka*'s vents as port maintenance personnel and ten-meter cargo lifters moved in.

"Hey, look at the whitesuit!" a raucous voice called from the open hatchway at his back. Catcalls and laughter hooted in the chill air.

"Avast there, it be Fleet Admiral Cameron, the scourge of space!"

"Yah! Hey, Navy! Seen any Xenos?"

Ignoring the jibes of his former shipmates, Dev hoisted his shipbag and followed the glowing holosign proclaiming "Arrivals" in three languages. The docking bays and towers of Opptårn Havn starport unfolded from the tethered asteroid that kept Loki's space elevator taut; its greater-than-orbital velocity about the planet generated an out-is-down spin gravity of a third of a g, low enough to put a bounce in Dev's step as he headed toward customs.

The ribbing he'd been getting from *Mintaka*'s crew for the past week only underscored what he already knew. He *couldn't* go back, not now. If he couldn't make it out here, well . . .

Damn it, eighteen light-years ought to be far enough from Earth and the Palace of Heaven that the name Cameron no longer carried his father's shame. If he couldn't fulfill his promise to himself here at Loki, there wasn't much point in traveling farther.

The customs check didn't take long; he was wearing or carrying everything he owned. Beyond customs was the Starhigh Strip, a spiral corridor packed pressure-wall-to-wall with the businesses—or their high-tech successors—that have flourished around transport terminals for millennia. Bars, paycubes and flopcaps, locker rentals, and pawnshops jostled side by side in an endless, cluttered tangle with tattoo joints, uniform stores, and orjack houses, their gaudy come-on holosigns vying with one another in Norsk-Lokan, Nihongo, and Inglic.

Dev considered buying a RAM language implant for the Lokan dialect of Norsk but decided against it. He didn't expect to be here for more than a few days, and nearly everyone spoke Inglic, Nihongo, or both, the languages of trade and commerce throughout the Shichiju.

Hell, that was part of the problem. There was nowhere he could go without bumping into the Empire. Five minutes later he was aboard a transfer capsule with twenty other new arrivals to Loki, riding the tether in to Asgard Synchorbital.

Technically the Empire of Nihon ruled only Japan and Japan's assets on Earth and in Earth-Lunar space. It was the Terran Hegemony that represented the unified governments of fifty-seven sovereign nations on Earth, plus the colonial administrations of the Shichiju, The Seventy, as the scattering of colony worlds across known space was called, though their number was actually seventy-eight.

But everyone knew that the Terran Hegemony's power extended only so far as the Imperial Diet permitted. Japanese industrial might, first on Earth, later in orbit, had made *Dai Nihon* the single most powerful state in the history of Man. Three centuries after the Fall of the West, it was Nihon—through her control of Terran banking, shipbuilding, and nanotechnic engineering—that dominated the commerce between the stars and the spread of Man to new worlds.

It was Nihon that enforced the *Teikokuno Heiwa*, the Imperial Peace.

Imperial Peace. That, Dev thought bitterly, was a laugh. Seven planets, at last count, had been lost to the Xenophobes, and four more were infested. Neither Empire nor Hegemony had yet been able to organize a decent defense, or even to find out how the enemy spread from system to system, despite constant surveillance by orbiting Imperial Navy warships.

It wasn't that Dev hated the Empire. Michal Cameron's disgrace and suicide still weighed on Dev, of course, but he understood that there'd been nothing personal in what the Empire had done to the Cameron family. It had been politics, nothing more.

Politics, then, had led Dev to the outworlds after he'd finished five years at BosWash Technic. Politics had blocked his entrance into the Hegemony Naval Academy at Singapore, because the son of Admiral Michal Cameron slotted into a starship's helm might be a bad risk, and politics had decreed that the only off-world slot he could find was aboard an aging Orion Lines freighter.

He'd jacked aboard the *Mintaka* for almost three years, beginning as cargo officer and working his way to second helm. Dev was a starpilot, and a good one. The cephlink and sockets his father had arranged for him eight years earlier were among the best hardware implants available, and at BWT he'd learned how to interface with a wide range of equipment, from librarian AIs to heavy loaders to ascraft. Aboard the *Mintaka* he'd swum the godsea, as the Virtual Reality of a K-T drive link was known, and since his first interspace translation, he'd known with unshakable conviction that *this* was what he'd been born for.

But ever since Lung Chi, and Michal Cameron's death the following year, he'd promised himself that he would do it in his father's service. If he couldn't join the Hegemonic fleet through the Academy on Earth, he'd do it here, on one of the outworlds, where Cameron was just a name and Lung Chi did not carry the same political baggage it did on Earth.

The synchorbit city rotated about the Loki space elevator, multiple tori on a thread-thin axis. The transfer capsule let Dev and the other passengers off in the city's zero-g core, where he caught a spoke shuttle to his destination out in the one-g ring.

Emerging from the shuttle, Dev stepped into another world. Asgard's gleaming lightscape exploded around him in a cacophony of noise, color, and motion, a swirling confusion bewildering after months inside *Mintaka*'s tight and ordered microcommunity. Three-D displays and holosigns, storefronts and module entryways, tubecar ports and jacking booths, throbbing music and babbling crowd noise and an unending sea of humanity, bombarded him with light and images and an almost palpable sense of crowded urgency.

One entire, curving wall of Valhalla Concourse was transparent. Stars and the cloud-shrouded half disk of Loki rotated slowly beyond, the world's clouds dazzling in the ruddy light of the sun Loki's colonists called *Dagstjerne*, the Daystar. The sky-el was barely visible, a hair-thin slash of silver dwindling toward the planet's equator. Elsewhere, two brilliant orange stars, the brighter members of the 36 Ophiuchi triplet, marched in stately side-by-side procession.

Dev paid no attention to the view, focusing instead on the city's bustling confusion. He needed to find a public information kiosk. *There . . .*

Shouldering through the crowd, Dev approached the pillar rising from the middle of the Concourse. By pressing the network of gold and silver threads grown into the base of his left thumb against the interface panel and closing his eyes, he linked with the kiosk's AI, asking it where he was.

Words printed themselves in Dev's mind, requesting thirty yen from his personal RAM account and an access linkcode, an alphanumeric series keyed to a specific command. Dev approved the transfer, called up the code, and the AI began spilling data, a column of facts and figures, across his mind's eye.

Linkcode accepted. Datafeed commence—

Stellar Data: 36 Ophiuchi C

Type K5 V, mass .68 Sol, luminosity .18 Sol, radius .74 Sol . . .

Damn! He didn't want a full readout on the system. He'd given the wretched thing the wrong linkcode, one requesting general background instead of specific information. Unconcerned, the kiosk AI continued feeding to Dev's RAM.

Planetary Data: 36 Ophiuchi C II (Loki)

Mean orbital radius: .512 AU, period: 162.3d, planetary diameter: 10,120 km, mass: 3 x 10^{27}g, density: 5.528 *g/cm^3, surface gravity: .795 g, rotational period: 27h 32m 19.21s . . .*

"Cancel!" Dev brought the word to mind and focused on it, but the data kept coming, describing Loki's atmosphere. AI networks could be intelligent enough to qualify as self-aware under the Sentient Status Act of 2204, but that intelligence was usually restricted to rather narrow functional boundaries, "self-aware but of limited purview," as the legal definition described it. Which meant that they were sometimes difficult to argue with, once they'd been set in motion. This AI, working only through access codes, was more infuriatingly narrow-minded and literal than most.

Major terraforming efforts begun C.E. *2425 via nanotechnic resynthesis, using gas exchange towers to remove carbon dioxide, methane, and ammonia from the atmosphere and replace it with oxygen and nitrogen . . .*

"I know all this garbage," Dev thought. "Cancel!"

Synchorbital facilities: Single sky-el link, Asgard Synchorbital to Midgard Towerdown, height 31,750 km. Opptårn Havn starport is located on a trans-synchorbital tether at . . .

Dev yanked his hand off the interface, physically breaking the link. Upset and in a hurry, he'd fed the AI the wrong access code, then gotten flustered when the kiosk began feeding him the wrong data. He took a couple of deep breaths, forcing himself to relax, then tried again.

It cost him another thirty yen, but this time he accessed the right code and a map painted itself in his mind's eye. He was *here* . . . on the starlight concourse just off the tube-car station from the starport; the nearest ViRcom modules were in the Morokvarter, Asgard's fun strip.

He waited a blink as the AI fed specific directions to his cephlink RAM, then broke contact. He now knew where he wanted to go.

Stepping onto a slidewalk, he was whisked into another jumble of sex shops, clubs, and recjack centers. Loki and its star-dusted backdrop continued their slow pirouette to his right. Three minutes later he arrived at the communications center. He had a short wait in the lounge for an available booth, but at last he was able to squeeze himself into the padded embrace of a ViRcom module.

He could have used his palm interface again for a first-level call but elected instead to pay a bit more for a full-sensory link. The navy, after all, didn't take just anyone, and he wanted to make a good impression.

Most humans everywhere had cephlinks nowadays; life without them had been all but unthinkable since the governments of the Hegemony started making them available as a right of citizenship two or three centuries before. Where differences in social status and abilities appeared was in the access hardware. Palm implants were part of the basic package, allowing level-one access. Most people also had at least one temporal socket for receiving level-two entertainment and communications feeds. Dev had three sockets for full interface and feedback, an expensive gift from his father that had made the difference between his dreams of escaping Earth, and the reality.

He jacked twin leads into his temporal sockets, brought his left hand down on the interface to initiate the link . . .

. . . and found himself in an office of crystal and silver, facing a pretty girl who was almost certainly an AI construct. She parted perfect lips, revealing perfect teeth in a warm and perfect smile. Blond hair swirled at her shoulders. "Hello," she said, her Inglic flawless as the AI tailored its responses to Dev's native language. "How can I assist you?"

"Hi there," Dev said. "I'd like a full-sensory with the local Hegemony Service recruiter, please."

He glanced down, giving his own ViRpersona a quick once-over. His shipbag was gone, along with the old, gray and orange skintight he'd exchanged for one of *Mintaka*'s tan shipsuits. Instead he was wearing virtual clothing he'd bought and programmed into his cephlink three months ago on Rainbow, a stylish maroon bodysuit with a complex weave of gold down the left half of his torso, high collar, black shoulder cloak, and short-trimmed hair. Not the latest thing back on Earth, perhaps, but sophisticated, especially out here on the frontier. Since the maroon suit tended to give his light skin a pasty look, the package included lighter hair and a dark, even tan. He'd always felt that it was worth the extra yen to look his best in Virtual Reality.

The girl's eyes took on a not-here glaze, then focused on him again. "I'm terribly sorry, sir, but no one is available to speak to you at this time."

"Huh?" His persona's brows furrowed. "That's ridiculous!" The Hegemony Military Command for any colony synchorbital was a huge, sprawling affair employing tens of thousands of people, the most powerful AIs on or near the planet, and all of the resources necessary to terraform, police, and govern an entire world. To say that no one was available was like saying that the entire planet had just shut down.

"I will connect you with an analogue, sir."

And he was standing in the office of a Hegemony officer.

It was a virtual re-creation of some office within Asgard. A transparent wall looked out onto Loki, flooding the room with golden light. The man standing behind the desk wore a *shosa*'s collar tabs; the rank corresponded to a navy lieutenant commander or an army major. The army dress uniform was a two-toned blend of grays, light and dark, with gold piping. Three rows of ribbons decorated his upper left chest.

"I'm Major Kellerman," the figure said. It extended a hand and, reluctantly, Dev took it. It felt warm and dry. "What can we do for you?"

"I'm trying to get through to someone in Personnel, Major," Dev said. He would have preferred dealing with a human, of course. Analogues—AI simulations of a real person—were capable of independent thought to a certain extent, able even to make decisions within the AI's area of expertise, but they were generally restricted to routine business. "I'm here to enlist in the Hegemony Navy."

The image smiled, a slight upward twitch of thin lips. "I'm sorry, but we're having a bit of a crunch just now. I really don't think anyone will be able to see you. Next week, perhaps—"

"Next week!"

"I'm afraid—"

"Damn it, I want to talk to someone now!" Dev was aware of how petulant he sounded the moment the words were out. He stopped, swallowed, and took a moment to smooth the jagged snap of his temper. He'd been waiting for this moment for years. A delay of another few days would make little difference.

But damn it, HEMILCOM's entire administrative department couldn't have simply stepped out for lunch!

"I could take your application now," the major said. "But I have no way of knowing when someone will be able to process you."

Dev's eyes narrowed. "It's an alert, isn't it?"

"I cannot discuss military matters with civilians, sir."

Xenophobes. It had to be. They'd been on Loki for the past three or four years standard, and nothing else could tie up the whole HEMILCOM network. He grinned knowingly. "The Xenophobes giving your people some trouble, are they?"

"You don't expect me to comment on that one way or the other, surely." The major's eyes unfocused for a moment, then hardened, meeting Dev's gaze. "Let me suggest an alternative. I can induct you now. You'll be assigned to a holding company in Midgard, where you will take the usual battery of tests. From there, you'll be transferred to your training slot."

"Midgard. That's the towerdown? On the planet?"

"Yes, sir."

Dev considered this. There was certainly no point in waiting around in Asgard, paying high prices for hotels, food, and entertainment, not when Kellerman's option was at least a step in the right direction. "Okay," he said. "That sounds good."

"Fine. Preferred branch of service?"

"The *navy*," Dev said slowly. "Not the army." He managed to keep his voice neutral . . . barely.

"I see," Kellerman said. "Whitesuit, eh?"

"That's right. I've been jacking a freighter for the last couple of years. I figure it's time to plug into a real jobslot."

"Well, we can probably fix you up if that's what you really want. The navy'll take *anybody*."

Dev recognized the tone as banter, part of a tradition of interservice rivalry, but he pressed his lips together and said nothing. In fact, the divisions between military services within the Hegemony were far less than they'd been for the militaries of Earth's pre-Union past.

"What's your configuration?"

"Nippon Orbital Industries Cephimplant, Model 10,000. Left palm imbedded control interface. Twin T-sockets."

"Two temporal sockets. The ten-kay gives you a C-socket as well, doesn't it?"

"Yeah," he admitted, but reluctantly. The cervical socket was designed specifically for jacking heavy equipment and work machines, gear with leg-arm-hand correspondence like loaders, constructors, or . . .

Or warstriders.

The major regarded him for a moment. "If I might ask, sir, why the navy? Your C-socket would practically guarantee you a strider's slot."

"I'm a starship," Dev replied.

"May I ask why?"

"Just put me down for a navy slot, damn it!" He could feel his anger slithering out of control again, as it had at the information kiosk. The idea of slogging around a planet's surface, plugged into some great, lumbering combat machine when he could be plying the godsea, was frightening.

"Well, now, you must understand we can't promise you a particular slot, sir. Not before we run you through a standard MSE series and some other routine tests."

"I'm not palming anything if I can't have the navy."

The analogue shrugged. "The decision is yours. HEMILCOM personnel does make every effort to match inductees with their civilian specialties. Since you are an experienced starpilot, I feel sure you'll get what you want, contingent on those test results, of course."

Dev took a deep, steadying breath. "Okay. Where do I palm?"

Kellerman indicated an interface pad on his desk. "Right here."

Dev hesitated, then pressed his palm implant against the 'face. Waiting with a holding company at the towerdown was definitely preferable to crawling back to the *Mintaka*.

"Very well." Kellerman was brisk, all business. "You are now a provisionary recruit-trainee, assigned to Holding Company Three-One. Here is some information you'll need."

Dev opened his RAM for a data feed. Directions trickled past his awareness, along with a sky-el shuttle schedule, an understanding of Loki's system of keeping time, and a list of rules and regulations. Dev felt a momentary whirl of disorientation. Things were happening fast. He'd just joined the military!

"Your reservations on the next available Bifrost descent have been made and confirmed, sir. You have forty-seven minutes until your el-shuttle departs. Good luck."

"Thank you." The room and Major Kellerman dissolved, and Dev's hand broke contact with the interface pad. He was alone once more, inside the padded enclosure of the ViRcom module. Stepping out onto the deck once more, he took a moment to get his bearings. He'd just arrived in the one-g ring, and now he had to get back to the space elevator core. Spoke pods *that* way. He had forty-seven minutes.

He would have to hurry.

Chapter 2

Within cephlinked minds,
Ripples on the cosmic sea,
We find our greatness.

Imperial haiku
late twenty-fourth century

Seeming flimsy for its length, the thread of the Bifrost Bridge, ten meters thick, stretched thirty-one thousand kilometers from Loki's equator to Asgard Synchorbital, then well beyond to the tethered Opptårn Havn planetoid that kept the whole structure in balance. Sky-els were by far the most efficient means of transport between ground and orbit, the key on every world of the Shichiju to remaking the planet into Earth's image.

The twenty-eight-hour journey from Asgard to Midgard was made aboard a saucer-shaped el-shuttle riding down the tether on one of four magnetic rails. Arranged like the planetariums of precephlink days, the shuttle's passenger decks had reclining seats for a hundred people set in concentric circles beneath a broad dome, all comfortably padded and equipped with full sensory jacks. The passengers were provided with bodysuits that attended to their bodily needs and hygiene for the duration of the trip. The shuttle's library featured everything from elaborate participatory ViRdramas to virtual banquets that—if they added no calories to the jacker's diet—at least left him feeling pleasantly well fed when he unplugged at the elevator terminus. Hunger, after all, like so much of human experience, resides in the mind.

Dev passed much of the descent in a dream within a dream, wearing an orange bodysuit and jacked to the shuttle's entertainment network.

First, of course, he'd linked realtime with an external view. Not everyone could stand the dizzying spectacle of looking down that silver thread, one reason that the shuttle's walls were opaque. Before he'd initiated the linkage, a legal disclaimer appeared, warning those who had problems with vertigo from jacking in. Dev, experienced spacejack that he was, cheerfully ignored the warnings and spent ten minutes admiring the view, hanging in empty space above the cloud-brilliant swelling of the world below.

But the scene paled and Dev unplugged, not from vertigo but from boredom. He might have been hurtling toward Loki at fifteen hundred kph, but the view remained static, unchanging, with no trace of motion save the steady blur of the magnetic guiderail and, just once, a far-off flash as an elevator laser vaporized some speck of orbital debris that had strayed too close to the vulnerable tower.

Dev had returned to the library menu then, and there considered a selection of erotic programs. His anger at confronting HEMILCOM's bureaucracy had shaken him more than he wanted to admit, and he felt the need for a woman's gentle and confidence-building understanding.

He was tempted by an orgy scenario starring Lea Leanne, one of the hottest of the popular electronic sex partners, but he settled at last on a free-form fantasy of his own design with the pretty blond from the ViRcom. He gave her longer hair and larger breasts and named her Desirée after a girlfriend he'd had at BWT; they met in an isolated tropical grove with pink sand and three crescent moons hanging in a flame red sky. They'd undressed each other, shared an intimate, lingering caress . . .

. . . and then Dev had broken the circuit, shivering. Perhaps if he'd had a human recjack partner, it might have been different, but he found it impossible at the moment to become more than mechanically involved with a woman who had no reality at all outside of the shuttle's AI circuits and his own mind.

Besides, his father's face continued to haunt him, a cold presence on the edge of awareness that surfaced unexpectedly while he was kissing the girl. Not even Desirée's exaggerated mammalian charms could dispel it.

Angrily Dev opened the network menu again. He settled at last on a participatory ViRdrama space epic entitled *Battlefleet*. He was *Shosho* Devis Cameron of the Imperial Navy, commander of Battlegroup *Shori* and charged with the defense of Earth's solar system against the Xenophobe menace. The godsea flamed a glorious blue around him as he guided his titanic flagship *Mushashi* through the intricacies of the K-T plenum.

Two enemy fleets had broken through the outer defenses, one challenging his squadron of twelve line ships, the other sweeping out of the godsea, lancing toward Earth and the Palace of Heaven itself. In a desperate gamble, Dev divided his fleet, leaving half his squadron to deal with the first Xenophobe fleet while he raced Earthward with the rest, six ships against fifty.

He even found a part for Desirée in the story. She commanded Singapore Orbital's defenses, buying time for Mankind as Dev brought his dreadnought, the gigantic *Mushashi*, into the midst of the alien fleet, hammering away at the Xenophobe flagship at point-blank range. Ascraft fighters and warflyers filled the skies. Nuclear fury seared in terrifying proximity to the Singapore Sky-el. The Emperor himself was in grave danger. . . .

By the time the shuttle entered atmosphere, he was, of course, triumphant. The Xenophobe fleet was destroyed—the last ship seconds before it could crash into the Emperor's Palace of Heaven. Dev, his arm in a healsling after the fall he'd taken when the *Mushashi* rammed the enemy battleship, received the golden sunburst of the *Teikoku no Hoshi* from the Emperor himself as the adoring Desirée stood by his side. Even Dev's father was there, exonerated at last, proud and tall in his Imperial dress blacks, able at last to acknowledge Devis Cameron as his son. . . .

Dev had been sixteen when Captain Michal Cameron of the Hegemonic Navy had received the singular honor of promotion to *shosho*—rear admiral—and a transfer to the Imperial Navy. Few non-Japanese had ever been so distinguished.

The Terran Hegemony maintained small fleets of ships within each of the systems of the Shichiju, with each unit under the command of the local Hegemony Military Command. Opportunity was limited, though. The Imperial Navy outnumbered the vessels of all of the Hegemony fleets put together, and the biggest ships and best commands were to be found in the Emperor's service. For centuries, exceptional officers had been transferred from Hegemony to Imperial Navy; perhaps half of all Imperial Naval officers were *gaijin*—non-Japanese.

Cameron's skill at defusing the Chiron incident of 2529 without precipitating civil war had singled him out at a time when the Imperial service was being criticized for not advancing the *gaijin* within its ranks. Chuichi Munimori, *Gensui*-Admiral on the Imperial staff, had found Cameron a useful political foil, proof that non-Japanese *could* make good within the Imperial military.

He'd made good, all right, and it had destroyed his family.

An Imperial Navy admiral's wife was required to have the proper political connections. Mary Jean Pruitt, Cameron's wife of seventeen years, was a West Scranton girl, American to the core and somewhat technophobic. She didn't speak Nihongo, nor would she accept the nano-grown implant that would let her download the language. Even if she'd spoken fluent Japanese, however, it was unlikely that Cameron would have been permitted to keep her. A match was made for him with the Lady Kikuko Takagi, daughter of an important corporate representative of Mitsubishi Orbital.

As Cameron had explained to his son once, to refuse either promotion or marriage would have meant disgrace. Though the ritual of *sepuku* was no longer seen as the sole honorable way to resolve irreconcilable clashes of duty and honor and was rarely invoked, especially among *gaijin*, it might well have been Cameron's only way out of an impossible situation. At the very least, his professional career would have been at an end, with a dishonorable retirement his only option. Pensions, benefits, even insurance coverage, all would have been denied the man who had refused an Imperial command and a Takagi's daughter. His wife and two sons would have been left destitute.

In the end, Mary had suggested the divorce. There was, after all, no reason at all why a successful Imperial admiral couldn't keep a mistress on Earth, and his family would escape the onus of Imperial disgrace. Dev received his cephimplant and sockets, then spent the next five years at BWT, too busy to be unhappy.

Four weeks before Dev's graduation, Admiral Cameron had been ordered to Lung Chi.

The star DM+32° 2896, forty-five light-years from Sol and popularly known as Chien, was a G2 twin of Sol. Its fourth world was as Earthlike as any among the Shichiju. Most of its native life was still confined to broad, shallow seas, like Earth herself 350 million years before. Chien IV's sky-el had been started in 2320; terraforming required little more than bringing the atmospheric oxygen percentage up another few points and absorbing some of the excess carbon dioxide. By 2500 Lung Chi's population topped eight hundred thousand.

The first Xenophobe incursion on Lung Chi occurred thirty years later. Seven years after that, mass evacuations up Lung Chi's sky-el had begun, and Hegemony warstriders were fighting a desperate rearguard action in the foothills of the Xinjiang Shan Mountains. At Lung Synchorbital, a ragtag gaggle of liners, freighters, colony transports, even tugs and ore barges, began gathering to evacuate the colonists coming up the sky-el.

Cameron's squadron was ordered in. One of the great mysteries of the Xenophobes was how they spread from system to system, invading eleven worlds in the past forty years. Contrary to the fictions of popular ViRdramas like *Battlefleet*, no nonhuman vessel of any kind had ever been seen, despite fleet deployments, ground searches, satellite networks, and scanner arrays of every kind. Rumor had it that Xeno ships were invisible, though they'd never shown that kind of technological magic on the ground.

As always, there'd been no sign of Xenophobe ships. As always, the enemy had risen in shapeshifting hordes from underground, devouring buildings by the hundreds and panicked colonists by the thousands in deadly clouds of nanotech disassemblers. Evacuation efforts were redoubled. Half a million Manchurian colonists remained on Lung Chi, screened by ten thousand Hegemony infantrymen, an Imperial Marine assault battalion, and five regiments of lightly armored Lung Chi militia. With three elevator rails working full time on the ascent and one to send the empty shuttles back down for another load, with families packed into each shuttle to the limit of available life support, eight thousand refugees could be lifted to synchorbit every day. Conditions at Lung Orbital began to break down, as more and more terrified colonists arrived each hour.

Then the Xenophobes had tunneled up behind the marine perimeter, next to the base of the sky-el tower itself, slaughtering civilians waiting to board the shuttles. Communications with the surface were lost. Fragmentary reports from ascraft still transmitting indicated that the space elevator itself was somehow *changing*, transforming from carbon diaweave into something black and twisted, the change streaking skyward up the sky-el cable. . . .

Aboard his flagship, the Imperial fleet destroyer *Hatakaze*, Admiral Cameron had made the only decision possible. The Xenophobes might be merely destroying the sky-el, as they seemed to destroy all of the toys of civilization they encountered . . . or they might be using it as a bridge to reach synchorbit, where over three hundred thousand refugees and a hundred starships were crowded together in weightless, cheek-by-jowl horror.

According to the *Hatakaze*'s log, he'd not hesitated more than a few seconds before launching a Starhawk missile tipped with a twenty-kiloton warhead, teleoping the projectile into the slender target of the sky-el himself so that no one else in his command would be forced to live with the horror of that decision. The detonation severed the elevator at the 2,000-kilometer mark. Fragmenting, the upper part of the elevator tower whipcracked into space, spilling refugee-crammed shuttles in its wake. The lower portion, hundreds of kilometers of elevator cable, crashed to the surface in fiery reentry.

How many tens of thousands of people in the general towerdown area were killed by falling debris was never learned. Most of those remaining on the planet were trapped, with no way to reach orbit. A handful were evacuated by ascraft shuttle, including the Imperial general in command of the assault battalion, who accused Admiral Cameron of cowardice at his trial.

Half a million people died as the Xenophobes completed their destruction of every building, every vehicle, every trace of civilization existing on the planet. Cameron's defenders claimed he'd acted correctly. Had the Xenophobes reached synchorbit, had they captured that waiting fleet of transports, things might have been far worse. Humankind still did not understand how the Xenophobe infection spread from star system to system; those transports might well have become vectors, spreading the disease from Lung Chi to every world in the Shichiju.

Might have. The hard truth of the matter, carefully presented at Cameron's court-martial, was that yet again a Xenophobe landing force had slipped invisibly past blockading ships . . . and Cameron's missile shot had been directly responsible for the deaths of half a million Hegemony citizens. Manchuria, close ally of Japan and a powerful supporter of the Empire within the Hegemony Council, had demanded his execution.

Cameron had escaped that humiliation, at least. After the guilty verdict was handed down, he'd taken the so-called honorable way out—not through the painful and messy ritual of *sepuku*, but by means of poison smuggled to his cell by a loyal former member of his staff.

Not long afterward, Dev had decided to join the navy, the Hegemony Navy, but his application had been turned down by the Naval Academy at Singapore. Thinking that experience and a few light-years from Earth might give him a better chance, Dev had signed on with Orion Lines and begun his self-imposed exile from Earth.

His younger brother was still in school. His mother, the last he'd heard, was working for a ViRsoftware firm in Kyoto; she'd finally accepted an implant, but after her husband's death, she'd used it to take psychoreconstruction.

Dev had spoken with her once, months afterward. She remembered him and Greg—in a distant sort of way—but very little else remained of her own life. Autoamnesia, a deliberate memory dump, was widely considered one of the most effective means of treating severe mental trauma.

For Dev, though, it was as though she had died as well.

Dev was in bed with Desirée when the warning chime sounded. The shuttle had entered atmosphere some time before and was now ten minutes above Midgard Towerdown. He let himself come to a satisfying climax, then released his linkage, awakening in the shuttle with a hundred other orange-clad travelers.

Moments later, the shuttle grounded at Towerdown. Its magnetic grapples released the rail, and the arms of a port loader carried it to the debarkation bay. There Dev and the others were led to private cubicles where shuttlesuits were exchanged for personal clothing. Dev retrieved his luggage then, and stepped into the riot of color and noise that was Loki's first city.

Midgard was much like Asgard, louder and more crowded, perhaps, and dirtier, with a higher density of both holosigns and people. Midgard's population topped one hundred thousand, a third that of the entire planet, and the confines of pressure walls seemed to amplify the crowding, confining and compressing it within the city's cluster of forty-two domes. Loki's storm-lashed atmosphere was monotonous enough that Midgard's designers had not bothered with windows, and the gray-walled tunnels radiating out from Towerdown Dome looked grimly claustrophobic.

Here Dev noticed the first concrete signs of the military alert he'd suspected back in Asgard. Hegemony troopers in light, single-slot warstriders mounted guard at intervals around Towerdown Dome's perimeter. Three meters tall, they stood as motionless as statues, each coated by surface films set to show the gray of their surroundings.

Dev had never had much interest in the trivia of surface warfare and could not identify the different models. Still, it was obvious that they were on alert. So many war machines were rarely assembled in such numbers save for Emperor's Day or for formal reviews.

"Cameron?"

He turned. A big, hard-looking man in orange coveralls with a military look to them stepped out of the milling crowd.

"That's me."

"I'm Castellano. C'mon."

"Huh? Who are—"

"They sent me to collect you, hojie. Got any more gear? No? Okay, come with me."

Castellano was already walking away, and Dev had to hurry to catch up. "Where are we going?"

"HEMILCOM's dreamland, where else? Gok, man, you're gonna be sorry you ever palmed for enlistment in this hole."

"Why's that?"

"Take it from me, hojie. You've just grounded in a world of shit."

Chapter 3

Still, in all the towering, golden splendor of Man's technological achievements, one advance stands out from the rest, more significant than the advents of nuclear fusion or quantum power taps, of terraforming on a planetary scale, of industrial and medical nanotechnology or even of the K-T drive.

I refer, of course, to the direct cybernetic interface, "jacking" in everyday parlance, the means by which men no longer merely control their starships, terrain striders, or other heavy machinery, but in a very real sense actually become *ship, strider, or machine. . . .*

—*Man and the Stars: A History of Technology*
Ieyasu Sutsumi
C.E. 2531

Two VK-141 Stormwinds, Hegemony ascraft with stubby, down-canted wings amidships and twin V-stabilizers on the end of slender tail booms, howled northward through the black of the Lokan night. Locked into the number-one strider slot in the main hull, *Tai-i* Katya Alessandro fixed her attention on the feed coming down from the ascraft's AI and tried to ignore the darkness.

Katya hated the dark, hated it so much, it took an effort of will each time she squeezed her lanky frame into the commander's module of her sixty-ton warstrider and plugged herself in. Shifting her vision to infrared, she strained to make out some detail from the craggy cold-desert landscape sweeping past a hundred meters beneath her feet, but the surface was uniformly cold and masked by gusting swirls of snow, a patchwork of icy blues that only hinted at rugged, mountainous terrain.

Suspended by massive clamps within an open slot in the Stormwind's side, she was sheltered beneath one of the ascraft's canted wings. Rather, the warstrider she was jacking was in the slot; Katya, linked to the strider's on-board AI, was tucked away inside the combat machine's armored torso, probing the darkness below with electronic senses.

For Katya, "wearing" the strider was exactly like wearing her own body. She could feel the crisscross weave of the steel grating pressed against her back, feel the wind snapping past her legs. The nerve impulses that let her move her body's arms or legs were routed through her C-socket to move the strider's arms or legs instead.

Looking down—her primary optical sensors were set into a universal turret mounted below the Warlord's blunt snout—she could see her legs and the massive, flanged pads of her feet tucked up against the fuselage, and the black-gray-blue blur of the ground whipping past beneath the Stormwind's keel. Her external temperature sensors didn't relay the true, biting cold of the Lokan atmosphere, but she felt the chill and the wet nonetheless.

Inwardly she shivered. Midgard and a warm bunk lay eight hundred kilometers astern. Somewhere ahead was a mining colony called Schluter.

Schluter was an exception in the Lokan naming conventions, named after the valley, the Fossae Schluter, where it had been grown. Most names on Loki were drawn from Norse myth: Asgard, the heavenly city of the gods; Midgard, the realm of men; Bifrost, the Rainbow Bridge joining heaven and earth. Loki itself was named for the

Norse god of discord and strife.

Katya felt the buffeting of that methane gale and decided that the name had been well chosen. Someday the second world of 36 Ophiuchi C would change its name; Loki would become Freyr, god of peace, good weather, and harvest bounty. Now, though, the surface was still storm-wracked, the atmosphere unbreathable. The terraforming project had been under way for over a century; it would be two centuries more before temperatures rose above freezing and appreciable quantities of oxygen and nitrogen replaced the current mantle of carbon dioxide. The overcast was solid, and after sunset, the darkness became almost palpable.

"Temperature at minus two-eight, wind from the northwest at three-five," a woman's voice said, speaking in Katya's mind. "Great day for flying, ain't it?"

"Hell, Lara," Katya replied. "For you *every* day's good for flying."

She heard *Tai-i* Lara Anders's low chuckle. "Won't argue there, Kat. Born with wings, that's me."

With scarcely the pretense of streamlining, the ascraft gave a savage jolt as it plowed through bumpy air. The Stormwind was a true aerospace craft; in vacuum its fusorpaks heated cryo-H slush to a starhot plasma, expelling it as reaction mass; in atmosphere, gaping intakes gulped air and fed it through twin fusion furnaces, negating the need for large quantities of on-board fuel. It wasn't fast as ascraft went, strictly subsonic usually, but it could hit Mach 25 and orbit with a scramjet hotbox and a belly shell.

For orbit-to-surface insertions, an ablative shield covered the Stormwind's belly, enclosing its riders and protecting them from the blowtorch blast of atmospheric entry, but in normal ops the VK-141 had power enough to ignore such niceties. Katya's warstrider, an RS-64D Warlord, was securely held in magnetic clamps, but Katya felt vulnerable, exposed, as the wind plucked at her lower torso.

"We're coming up on the DZ, Captain," the pilot continued. "Seven minutes."

"Any more word from Schluter?"

"Not in the last ten minutes. HEMILCOM says the fighting seems to be spreading into the city. Sounds like things are pretty confused. They're still picking up DSAs, big ones, so the Xenos aren't all in the open yet."

"Damn." This was going to be a messy one. Hegemony Military Command, based in Asgard Orbital, was ideally placed to monitor events on the surface. If only they'd come down here and get their minds dirty once in a while . . .

"They said to set you down right outside the dome. There'll be local militia on the ground, and civilians, of course. Watch your shots."

"Hey, they want to send warstriders in there," Katya said, "they'd better keep their goking heads down. Something flops in my direction, Lara, I'm going to *burn* it!"

Hours ago, surface remotes had picked up a Deep Seismic Anomaly, subsurface tremors that could mean a Threat breakout at Fossae Schluter, a thousand kilometers north of Midgard, and HEMILCOM had put the Thorhammers, technically the Fifth Loki Warstrider Regiment, on alert. There were two important targets in the area, one of the big terraformer atmosphere plants and a mining colony. Colonel Gustav Varney, the Thorhammers' CO, had detailed the regiment's A Company, "Alessandro's Assassins," for a platoon-strength deployment to the threatened sector. Company Commander Katya Alessandro had picked First Platoon for the mission, and decided to lead the operation herself.

One platoon—theoretically that was eight warstriders. Alessandro's Assassins had a company TO calling for twenty-four warstriders organized into three platoons, but in fact, Katya had just thirteen operational striders under her command, plus, as of that morning, another five downgriped for battle damage or lack of spare parts. First Platoon fielded six of the operational machines, and her Warlord made seven.

She hoped that would be enough for the situation unfolding at Schluter.

"Five minutes," Anders reminded her. "HEMILCOM has given weapons clearance."

"Right." She shifted to the Assassins' tac channel. "Listen up, Hunters," she said, thinking the words and letting her implant transmit them over the link network. "This is Hunter Leader. We're three minutes from drop. We have weapons clearance, repeat, weapons are free. Final check, all systems."

She listened as the acknowledgements came back over the net, mingled with the usual soldiers' banter.

"Roger, Hunter Leader. Hunter One, ready to go."

"Hunter Two, ready and rarin' to go."

"Three's go. Let's odie!"

"Hunter Four. Armed and ready."

"Hunter Five. I think I left the water running in the barracks, Captain. No? Okay, Five's ready."

"Six, go."

She shifted to her strider's internal ICS. "Mitch? Junior? How's she wired?"

"Systems ready, Captain," *Chu-i* Mitch Dawson said over the intercom link.

"Weapons armed and ready," *Jun-i* Chris Kingfield added.

The RS-64D Warlord carried a crew of three, commander, pilot, and weapons tech, though in fact, any of the three of them could control the strider if necessary. The usual breakdown called for two *sho-i* junior lieutenants or a *sho-i* and a *chu-i* senior lieutenant in the commander and pilot modules; a *jun-i*, a warrant technical officer universally nicknamed "Junior," manned the teleop weapons. Commander and pilot could spell each other in running the strider, and the commander had the added responsibility of coordinating pilot and weapons tech in combat.

Katya's Warlord, nicknamed *Assassin's Blade*, had been modified to serve as a command strider, with extra comlink gear and a more powerful AI. In combat, Dawson handled the maneuvering while Katya ran the company or, in this case, a seven-strider platoon.

She was proud of her crew, and of her company. She'd been bossing them, firm and fair, since Rainbow two years earlier. They'd responded with an absolute loyalty that bordered at times on fanaticism.

"Katya?" It was Dawson's voice, speaking over their private ICS. "I, ah, I just wanted to say that last night was terrific."

"Don't say it, Mitch. It never happened, right?"

"If you say so, Captain." She could feel the hurt behind the words.

Life in the Hegemony Guard could be lonely . . . strangely so since there were few times when she wasn't surrounded by men and women in conditions that could only be described as claustrophobic. Frontier barracks rarely had the space for civilized amenities. Service men and women slept together in open dorms, shared communal showers, used the same toilets. The only privacy to be had was the privacy of the mind—lying in one's bunk and plugging into a good ViRdrama, for instance, or setting thoughts and soul adrift in a meditative trance.

Camaraderie in the service was intense; shared death, loss, and hardship quickly made brothers and sisters of total strangers. Romantic pairings were less common. Sometimes it seemed as if getting too close to someone special angered the gods of war. If nothing else, transfers and rotations were common enough that no relationship could ever be considered permanent.

But Katya had felt attracted to Mitch. Their encounter the night before had been purely recreational and purely electronic, a linked fantasy shared through a pair of ViRcom modules.

Though it was supposed to be impossible to tell the difference between full sensory linkage and the real thing, Katya preferred reality. The encounter with Mitch had been wonderful nonetheless, and much needed, a long-sought chance to relax, to blast free some of the tension of command that had been building for these past few months, a chance to share something beautiful with one close, special someone.

She hoped the gods of war hadn't noticed this time.

"Company commanders can't have friends, Mitch," she said. "And they can't play favorites. It didn't happen."

"I understand."

"But . . . I enjoyed it too."

"DZ in two minutes," Lara's voice interrupted over the regular channel. "Ready for a touch and dust-off. We're starting to pick up some static."

"Affirmative," Katya replied. Xenophobe machines employed powerful magnetic fields that blasted radio frequencies with intense static at short ranges. Human weapons—proton guns and electron cannons—had the same effect. Communications were often sharply limited during a close-in battle.

She called up a god's-eye view. Created by her Warlord's AI, the display revealed the surrounding terrain as a realistic three-D image of wrinkled hills and meandering valleys as seen from overhead. Fossae Schluter was a broad, flat valley carved by a vanished glacier. Schluter itself was a mining encampment nestled against one of the canyon's sheer slopes, part beneath a pressure dome, the rest built into tunnels laser-bored for kilometers into the layers of exposed black rock.

The two Stormwinds, marked by swiftly moving pinpoints of green light above the desert floor, were just entering the valley's mouth. Schluter was marked in blue, ten kilometers ahead. Across the valley, Terraform Facility Baldur rose from the badlands, a four-sided pyramid larger than the Great Pyramid of Giza.

Was it coincidence the Xenos had surfaced here? So far, Threat sightings and raids had been confined to the far side of Loki. The Xenos' target might be the mining facility, but the proximity of the terraforming tower was worrisome. The shapeshifters seemed to home on large masses of engineering and technology—like cities and sky-els.

Katya nulled the computer graphics, shifting back to hunorm vision. She could hear the whispered mental voices of Dawson and Kingfield as they went through their final checks, readying the Warlord for combat. No downcheck, no sysfails. Weapons powered up, safeties locked. *Chu-i* Hagan, First Platoon's commander, reported over the tacnet that the platoon was hot and ready.

The Stormwind jolted hard on some rough air, slowed, then skewed to the left in a gently drifting hover. Through her link with Anders, Katya could see the dome now, rain-swept and bathed in the glare of harsh external lights. There didn't appear to be much damage visually, but when she cut in her infrared again, Katya could see a heat plume spilling from a white-glowing rupture in the dome's face. On the horizon, Baldur squatted against rugged mountains, showing a heat plume like the mushroom cloud above a volcano.

No movement outside the Schluter dome. Where were they?

"Primary DZ coming up," Lara warned. "Cutting internals."

Katya lost her link with the ascraft module. All she could see now was the shadowy ground meters beneath her feet.

She opened the ICS again. "You've got control, Mitch."

"Rog." His voice was tight. "Jets hot."

Blade's AI was counting off the seconds to release: three . . . two . . . one . . .

Katya felt herself falling. An instant later she was jolted as *Blade*'s jump pack cut in with twin jets of screaming, superheated gas. Sand blasted from the ground beneath her feet, followed by a rush of fog as the heat melted the permafrost, then turned it into steam. The cloud blinded Katya, but her strider's radar kept ticking off the last few meters to the surface.

Contact!

Assassin's Blade rested on folded legs, then rose, torso and arms deploying from drop mode to combat mode. The warstrider's body looked like a lumpy, misshapen aircraft fuselage, toad-ugly with a blunt snout. Its two legs were longer than the hull slung between them, heavily armored and digitigrade, articulated with the "knees" angled sharply toward the rear. It gave the strider a mincing, birdlike walk, a light-footed gait surprising for a sixty-ton bird.

Blade's AI automatically established a laser line of sight with each of the other striders unfolding from their grounding spots, linking them together in a lasercom tacnet.

"*Move-move-move!*" she called. "Everybody! Spread out!"

Katya was out of the control circuit, so she was only along for the ride, but she could sense the feedback of the Warlord's sense of balance as Mitch leaned into a long-legged stride. She concentrated on the deployment. To left and right, the other warstriders of the platoon fanned out, putting distance between them. Victor Hagan's KR-9 Manta *'Phobe Eater,* flat-bodied and horned like its namesake, moved toward the Schluter dome. *Deus Irae, Sho-i* Guiterrez's Battlewraith, followed. Two smaller, roughly humanoid warstriders, LaG-42 Ghostriders, took up flanking positions. Nicholsson's Battlewraith and Chung's Skorpiaad heavy-weapons carrier brought up the rear.

She sensed movement in the darkness.

"Guiterrez!" she called. "Bandit, left ten, range four-zero!"

Guiterrez's Battlewraith dropped into a crouch, pivoting on the threat like a gunfighter, bringing its massive right-arm electron cannon into line with a shadow rolling across the rocky ground.

Man-made lightning seared down a laser-tunneled vacuum, accompanied by a boom of thunder and the searing hiss of static over the open radio channels. The flash banished the shadows, and Katya saw the Xenophobe machine.

It was torpedo-shaped—Xenos always were when first emerging from underground. Its surface gleamed like quicksilver in the alien light.

"Target lock!" Kingfield yelled in Katya's mind. "Primaries charged! Firing *now*!"

The RS-64 shuddered as the weapon tech triggered the left arm gun. Warlord mounted two proton guns, its primary weapons, heavy-bodied particle cannons that swung from the elbow mounts like blunt, oversize forearms. Katya felt the blast of raw heat as it fired, saw the eye-searing flash as megajoule energies channeled down a laser-bored tunnel in the air. Lightnings played across the Xenophobe, twisting in the alien machine's magnetic fields.

Guiterrez added his electron cannon's whipcrack flash to the fury clawing at the Xeno's silver hull. Dawson swung the Warlord's torso slightly, aiming the dual chin lasers that extended from the blunt snout like the mandibles of some great insect. The Xeno loomed huge in Katya's vision, fifty meters distant now, embraced in the red glow of targeting reticles. The lasers fired, scattering from the quicksilver surface even as that surface began changing shape.

Like a hideous silver flower, the Xeno killer began unfolding into something new. . . .

Chapter 4

The Xenophobe War is like no other conflict in Man's bloody history because, for the first time, his opponent is a complete unknown. In past wars, at least, the enemy was human, his science known, his reasons for fighting rational or at least intelligible, his worldview comprehensible.

After four decades of war, however, the only motive we can ascribe to the Xenophobes is hatred or fear of other life forms—hence their name. Some researchers go so far as to suggest that their thought processes may be so alien to ours that we may never understand their reasoning.

—*The Xeno Foe*
HEMILCOM Military ViRdocumentary
C.E. 2537

Flares popped in the sky, illuminating the landscape in eerie silver light. Its surface flowing like molten metal, the Xenophobe machine was morphing into a chunkier, nightmarish shape, a flattened polyhedron sprouting half a dozen weaving, snakelike tentacles. It seemed to grow legs as it needed them, flowing across the ground with a rolling, almost amoebic motion, advancing on pseudopods of mercury-bright metal that shifted from fluid-soft to diamond-hard at will.

Hegemony Military Command had classified the primary Xenos based on mass and on the types of weapons each most often used, naming them after poisonous Earth reptiles. This particular design, massing ten to twelve tons and armed with mag-fired nano-D projectiles, had been code-named *Krait*.

"I've got more targets," Kingfield warned. "Bearing one-seven-one, range four point five thousand! Looks like their tunnel mouth! Recommend Starhawk CMP!"

Katya saw them, points of light on a window called up on her visual display. The Krait was the immediate threat, but those other targets, emerging now from underground, would be problems damned soon. Better to stop them now, at a distance. A CMP—a Cluster Munitions Package—ought to do the trick.

"Do it!" Katya replied over the intercom. "I'll take the CPGs! You handle the teleops!"

"Rog!"

She felt the inner click, the *completion*, as control of *Blade*'s main weapons shifted to her linkage. An instant later, the Warlord shuddered as Kingfield triggered one of the strider's two dorsal-rack Starhawk missiles. The weapons tech was gone, his mind riding the teleoperated missile to the target on a beam of laser light.

Dawson, meanwhile, continued to operate the Warlord's legs and body motions, dodging to the right as the Xeno horror closed in a blur of silver spikes and tentacles. And Katya took aim.

A kind of mist or cloud flickered between Katya and the apparition—a shield. Many Xenos could suspend clouds of metallic dust motes in magnetic fields, clouds that could absorb laser and particle cannon energy enough to blunt an attack.

As long as that shield was up, though, the Xeno couldn't fire at her. She raised both arms, and twin green targeting reticles slid across her visual field, centering over the hazy outline of the Krait's body. She clenched her fists right . . . left . . . right . . . left.

Each flash was dazzling, banishing the night. The Xeno's shield could absorb only a fraction of each bolt, and by the third shot, the cloud had dissipated. With the fourth shot there was an explosion, a sharp report that tore two of the weaving tentacles off with a splatter of liquid metal and left a red-glowing scar.

The Xeno, stricken, seemed to collapse upon itself, melting, surface blurring . . . and then it reformed, growing new legs, and kept on coming.

Humans called them stalkers, shapeshifters, and snakes. Presumably they were combat machines, analogous to human warstriders, but how the Xenophobes got them to change their shape, to *morph*, was still a mystery.

So were the means by which they traveled underground, like enormous land-going submarines, and the way they could repair battle damage in seconds. Nanotechnics were at least part of their magic; that much was obvious. Human engineering, construction, materials processing, computers, and medicine had all been transformed by the nanotechnic revolution, and there was promise of more and greater wonders to come.

The Xenophobes, however, seemed to be able to apply nanotechnology on a far grander scale than human science had yet dreamed of. It seemed—*seemed*—that the alien machines were composed entirely of separate, bacteria-sized elements locked together by internally generated magnetic fields. Control of those fields appeared to be the key to how Xeno machines could change shape, grow legs or tentacles like metallic pseudopods, fill in battle damage, or even fragment into dozens of separate, individually mobile fragments.

"Watch it!" Dawson warned. "He's going to fire!"

Katya had already seen the buildup of a powerful gauss field in the stalker's shell. There was a flash, just as Dawson jacked the Warlord to the side, and something slammed into Katya's left shoulder.

There was no pain, of course, but it felt like a hard, numbing shock. Warnings flashed across her visual field.

"Mitch!" she yelled. "Nano count at point eight-seven, left shoulder!"

"Firing NCMs!"

The Xenos' principal weapons were nano disassemblers, clouds of molecule-sized machines that dissolved solid matter literally atom by atom, picking it apart and carrying it off in a stream of white fog so quickly that durasheath armor could be eaten away in seconds. They could be dispersed in clouds like an insidious, corrosive gas, loaded into shells, or incorporated into surface layers that made a Xenophobe's touch deadly. NCMs—Nano Counter Measures—were submicroscopic machines shot like fire extinguisher blasts from nozzles set into a warstrider's hull, programmed to hunt down and fuse with nano-Ds before they could cause significant damage.

White vapor gushed from a nozzle inset in Katya's left pauldron, the heavy curve of armor protecting the Warlord's shoulder. The nano count registering on her visual display dropped. *Blade*'s armor was down eighteen percent in the damaged area . . . a scratch.

She fired the Warlord's main weapons again, carving off one of the Krait's stumpy legs in a flash that left sand and gravel fused and glowing. A second later, light flared on Katya's inset data window. "Got them!" Kingfield exulted in her mind, his link with the Starhawk broken. "That's three down! The other two are hurting. . . ."

"Take the hivel!" Katya ordered. Her own hands were full, literally, handling the big CPGs. "Hit the Krait at zero-one-five!"

"Got it!"

Hivels—the acronym was drawn from the words *high velocity*—were the descendants of twentieth- and twenty-first-century Gatling cannons. Firing 8-mm rounds of depleted uranium at better than 150 rounds per second, the hivel's rotary barrels loosed a stream of projectiles traveling virtually nose to tail, streaking toward the enemy at a kilometer per second.

Katya heard the whine of the hivel's eight rotating barrels as they came up to speed, felt the shift in mass as the turret tracked the target. There was a shriek as Kingfield triggered the weapon, and Katya felt the savage recoil. The silver polyhedron of the Xeno machine *splashed* with the close-range impact.

"Hit!" Kingfield exulted. "That's another down!"

Down, but not out of the fight. The burst had torn the Krait in two, but both halves were still very much alive . . . still moving, still deadly.

Humans divided Xeno machines into three basic types. Alphas were their main weapons, snakelike when they emerged from underground, spiked and tentacled in their combat mode. Betas were something else entirely—*Xeno-zombies*, human machines, warstriders, or transports partly replaced by shape-shifting nanotechnics.

Deadliest of all were the Gammas, fragments of Alphas ranging in size from two or three meters long to the size of a man's hand, individually mobile, and coated with nano-D layers that let them eat through the hardest armor like acid through skin.

An Alpha could be torn to pieces, and the individual pieces, the Gammas, simply kept on fighting—less mobile, perhaps, and unable to kill at a distance, but deadly in their small size, great numbers, and ability to kill with a touch.

Heat was the best weapon against Gammas. Katya brought her CPGs into play again, firing bolt after bolt into the shattered Krait. Alarm tones keened in her ears, and blocks of red text wrote themselves across the periphery of her vision. Her particle cannons were overheating, the massive drain on her fusorpak critical. Her power systems would fail any second now if she kept driving them this way.

Movement scissored on her left. *Sho-i* Rudi Carlsson, a native Lokan newly commissioned in the Thorhammers, guided his dual-seater LaG-42 close to the churning ruin of the Krait, hammering at the glowing fragments with the Ghostrider's 100-megawatt chin turret laser in an eruption of light and hurtling shrapnel and glassy bits of heat-fused sand.

Katya shifted to her Warlord's lasers, twin 50-megawatt projectors extending on either side of the Warlord's snout like the jaws of some hugely improbable insect. Each delivered half the energy of an exploding stick of dynamite in a pulse lasting a hundredth of a second. Katya aimed by looking at what she wanted to hit, fired by clenching the muscles of her left and right eyes in a savage squint.

Dipping the Warlord's torso and swinging left to bring both lasers into action, she focused and fired, loosing twin bolts. The silvery metal scattered much of the light, but enough energy was absorbed within the still rough surface where it had broken off to blast the piece into a hundred smaller fragments. Once the fragments were small enough, they became harmless.

"Hunter Leader! Please, Hunter Leader, come in!" a woman's voice called over the tacnet. "This is Schluter Control. We need help inside the colony dome!"

"This is Hunter Leader," Katya replied. "What's your situation?"

"We've got a Xeno Alpha inside the main dome! We've lost integrity in the main section. Most of our people are pulling into the shafts and sealing them off behind them, but we've got thirty or forty trapped up here on the top level! Nano count . . . We've got a nano-D count of point two-two in the main dome level!"

Damn! It would be a death trap for warstriders inside the narrow confines of a colony dome, but she couldn't ignore that call.

"Sit tight, Schluter Control. Help is on the way. Keep your heads down! Carlsson! Stick with me!"

"Affirmative, *Tai-i*!"

Shifting to the ICS, she added, "Let's haul it, Mitch!"

"I'm with you, boss. Hang on!" The Warlord's legs scissored in a ground-eating stride toward the dome.

Calls rasped through radio static, or sounded clear as the Warlord picked up spills from tight-beamed laser transmissions. "Hunter Four!" a voice cried, quavering on the ragged edge of panic. "This is Four! I'm taking fire! Help me! Help me!"

"I'm on it, Nick! Come right ten!"

"Xeno down! Hit him! Hit him again! Use your flamers!"

"Watch it, Harald! On your right, one-five-zero!"

"I'm hit, God, I'm hit! Get them off! Get them off!"

"This is Hunter Two! Four's in trouble!"

Four was *Sho-i* Harald Nicholsson, another Lokan. Katya shifted optics, scanning the entire area. There he was, his Battlewraith spilling a stream of white vapor from its side that cascaded, heavier than air, across the ground at his feet. Thirty meters away, a Xeno, a squat, sea urchin–spined Adder, continued to hurl nano-D shells into the stricken warstrider.

"Hold it, Mitch," Katya said. "Swing right forty!"

The Warlord stopped, then turned. Her particle cannons were still hot, and the bow lasers weren't powerful enough to seriously hurt something as big as an Adder. Taking control of the strider's torso from Dawson, Katya lined up the sleek Mark III weapons pod recessed into the machine's fuselage. The pod could carry various munitions; for this patrol, Katya had ordered her machine armed with M-22 laser-guided rockets.

"Target lock!" Kingfield yelled in her mind. "Take it, Captain!"

She could see the dazzling point of reflected laser light where Kingfield was painting the target. "Trigger hot! *Fire!*"

Rockets slammed from the weapons pod in a rippling cascade of flame and smoke. Thunder erupted downrange; the first rocket homed on a spot of laser light thrown on the target by Kingfield. Nine more homed on the detonation of the warhead in front of it. The crag-broken Lokan plain lit up with the barrage, as pieces of Xeno machine, white-hot and trailing smoke, arced through the sky.

Katya glanced at the damaged Battlewraith. Two other striders were already dousing Nicholsson's machine with NCM fog, as a third began burning fragments of shattered stalker.

"Let's move," she told Dawson. The dome was just ahead.

The hole in the side of the dome was large enough to admit a warstrider the size of an RS-64, though Dawson had to flex the knees sharply, stooping to maneuver through the tight and jagged-edged entrance. It was as dark inside as out, though infrared showed a lot more color and detail. The dome's interior glowed in an eerie mosaic of colors painted in Katya's head. The stilting, two-legged form of Carlsson's Ghostrider glowed in oranges and yellows, with dazzling white patches marking hot weapon muzzles, exhaust ports, and leakage from the power plant. Together the two striders plunged into a cavern of ghostlike, nightmare shapes, lost in a blue-green murk that had the wavering, surrealistic feel of an undersea landscape.

"Nano count going up, Captain!" Mitch warned.

She glanced at her own readouts. Point four-three and climbing, with some erosion on the Warlord's armor. "I see it. Keep moving!"

In combat, nanotechnic disassemblers drifted free in the air by the tens of billions. Concentrations could be especially high in craters, hanging above nano-damaged wreckage, or, as in this case, inside confined spaces.

"Hit the lights!" she ordered. The infrared image of the dome interior was confusing, tangled and deceptive. The Warlord's external lights snapped on, and she stared into rawest nightmare.

The dome was open to Loki's carbon dioxide atmosphere, and any colonists still on this main level must be dead by now. But the bodies were still *moving*. . . .

They'd been caught in poses of horror, dozens of people, men, mostly, but several women as well, struck down and strewn across the room like rag dolls. The steel deck, the roof support pillars, the walls, the tables and chairs, all looked deformed, softened, as though they'd been carved from plastic and were melting now in blast furnace heat. The bodies, too, were melting, blending into deck and furniture as though becoming a part of it.

Katya knew what was happening. The intense concentration of nano-disassemblers in that room was dissolving everything—deck, walls, bodies—and as they disintegrated, they tended to run together. Directly in front of her, Katya saw a man's upper body settling into the deck, his head thrown back, his face locked in a soundless shriek of agony. *Thank God he's dead. . . .*

"Katya!" Dawson cried. "Threat! Left nine-five!"

She sensed the danger in the same instant as Dawson's warning. A nightmare shape lunged forward, vast, flat-headed, somehow dragonish in form, trailing tentacles and flame. That weaving, discoid head identified it as a Cobra.

Katya fired, both CPGs searing the air with crackling blue flame. The Cobra's hazy, soft-glowing shield absorbed the bolts as bodies and furniture flared and shriveled in white heat. Katya fired again, hoping to cripple the monster before it could fire. Lightning arced, snapping between the weaving Cobra head and the ground. The protective shield dissipated in a swirl of vapor. Flakes of silver metal scattered, burning.

Then the Cobra fired, and the sound was the screech of some hideously wounded animal. Lumps of metal hurled by gaussfields from the thing's sinuous body melted in their brief flight through resisting air, then struck Katya's Warlord with a *slam-slam-slam* that toppled her backward in a flailing tangle of metal legs and arms, a shrill, echoing scream ringing in her brain.

Dazed, she wondered if it had been she who'd screamed. She felt pain, a dim and distant ache enfolding her arms and chest, but she could not at first decide whether it was the Warlord's autonomous systems alerting her to severe damage to the strider, or leakage from her real body, strapped and wired in the Warlord's commander's module. Her flesh-and-blood body wasn't *supposed* to hurt while she was linked, but she'd heard stories. . . .

Ignoring the pain, she waited for Dawson to bring the Warlord back to its feet. It took her a full second to realize that one small part of her mind, which had been occupied moments before by Mitch's cephlink feed, was empty now, an aching, black void that might mean equipment failure . . . or something worse.

"Mitch!" she called over the ICS. "Damn it, Mitch, talk to me!"

The Cobra struck again. Warnings scrolled across the edge of her vision, telling of systems failures, power overloads, circuits cut. Lying on her back, she levered her left arm up and fired as the Cobra unfolded above her, slashing across the Cobra's relatively slender neck. Kingfield triggered the hivel Gatling in the same instant, sending a stream of deplur slugs into the drifting body. The Cobra staggered, then dropped writhing to the ground, its flat head separated from the body and flopping helplessly on the steel floor a few meters away.

And then Carlsson's Ghostrider was next to her, firing his chin turret laser into the smoking pieces, slagging down Xeno nano-metal and steel deck into smoking, molten puddles. Swinging around, he doused the fallen Warlord with NCM fog. Huge chunks of armor had already been eaten clean through.

Shakily Katya took over control of the Warlord. Levering its feet beneath the fuselage, she managed to rise, feeling the tug of the gyro as she wobbled unsteadily. "Mitch!" she tried again.

"I'm sorry, Captain," Kingfield told her. "He's dead."

Outside the dome, the battle was sputtering to an end. Streaks on the ground glared white-hot radiance where lasers or charged particle bolts had turned sand and gravel molten. Warstriders moved in pairs across the ground, hunting down bits and pieces of Xeno war machines and incinerating them with lasers or chemical flamers.

An hour later, six big Typhoon combat carriers from Asgard Orbital settled to the valley floor beyond the killing ground, disembarking a full company of Imperial Marine striders. The gleaming machines, lumbering Katanas and Samurais and nimble recon Tachis and Tantos, all jet black and bearing the rising-sun emblem of the Empire, swiftly secured the perimeter. A *tai-i* in a black Daimyo command strider curtly relieved Katya and ordered her to assemble her platoon and board the VK-141s. No thank-you, no well-done . . . just a sharp "I relieve you," and a brief string of orders.

Right, Katya thought. *Where were you when we needed you?*

In the valley, men in combat armor were probing the wreckage of the enemy machines, searching for the clues to the Xenophobe psychology and biology that never seemed to be there after a fight. Katya doubted that they would find more than the inevitable mysterious technology and rotting organics this time; the remains of Xenophobe battle machines were rarely very helpful in the human quest to understand the enemy.

The gods of war had noticed after all. Mitch was dead.

Never again, she promised herself. *Never again am I going to get close to a living soul!*

Chapter 5

After three centuries, we're still coming to grips with what it means to have machines smarter than ourselves, in some cases, as symbiotic partners. Lots of people never do learn to handle it.

—*Man and His Works*
Dr. Karl Gunther Fielding
C.E. 2488

"Hey, Suresh!" Dev called out as he entered the barracks lounge. "I hear you're not the only Nihonjin on Loki anymore!"

Suresh Gupta grinned, his teeth startlingly white against the black skin of his face. "About time," he replied. Somberly he placed one hand over his heart. "To think, a man of my culture and breeding, alone on a world of barbarians."

Cynthine Dole kicked him. "Just remember, Americans made it to the Moon *first*!"

"You *were* the first," Gupta replied. "But that was before we Japanese grabbed the space-industrial high ground."

The others in the room laughed. Gupta was Terran, a native of Andhra Pradesh, a state that had been part of the Japanese Empire ever since the Indian Federation's self-destruction in the mid-twenty-first century, but which was no more ethnically or culturally Japanese than Singapore or Hong Kong.

Still, a running joke pretended he was the only Japanese in Holding Company 3/1, and he affected a good-natured sense of racial superiority over his barracks mates.

Planetography and history had brought the six of them together, out of the forty-two men and women who currently occupied Barracks Three of the Midgard Hegemony Guard Receiving Station. Dole and Castellano, both originally from New America, Gaffet, who was from Rainbow, and Jacobsen of Liberty were all of North American descent, while Gupta and Dev both were from Earth itself. The fact that Dev was both Terran *and* American had made him an instant celebrity with the outworlders; New America, Rainbow, and Liberty all had strong cultural ties with an America that no longer existed on Earth, save in romantic ViRdrama.

"So what are Imperials doing on Loki?" Erica Jacobsen asked, brushing a strand of gloriously long, blond hair back from her face. "Slumming?"

"Kuso!" Castellano swore. "Didn't you guys hear? Friend of mine up in commo gave me the straight hont."

"Yeah, right," Dole said. *Hont* was military slang, stolen from the Nihongo *honto no koto,* the word of truth. The recruits had already learned that the "straight hont" was anything from exaggeration to wild fabrication.

"No, I mean it! There was a breakout at a place called Schluter, not very far from here. The Imperials pulled a hot landing and sealed it off."

"C'mon, Castellano," Ran Garret said. "We'd've heard if the Xenos were anywhere within ten thousand klicks of Bifrost."

"Ha!" Castellano grinned. "You think they're going to tell *you* goking anything?"

"Why not?" Dole asked. "After Lung Chi, if the Xenies came anywhere near a sky-el, word would spread damned fast."

Dev shifted uncomfortably in his seat. The conversation was hitting just a little too close to home.

He'd been in Company 3/1 for four days. Subject to

the petty tyranny of military discipline, marched to meals, marched to the evaluation center where they were put through batteries of cephlink testing, he found the routine more boring than anything else. Mostly the hojies—the name was a corruption of the Nihongo word for "recruits"—were left alone, "until," as Cynthine Dole had pointed out, "they figure out what we're good for."

The one person in the group not awaiting assignment to a training slot was Phil Castellano, a five-year veteran who was waiting now for his release. The rest were new recruits, native Lokans, most of them. A few were newcomers to Loki, people who'd emigrated to the colony looking for work and ended up enlisting in the Hegemony Guard; or, like Dev and Ran Garret, they'd been shipcrew paid off at Asgard Orbital.

The vast majority of the holding company's recruits had signed on for technical service training—communications, ViR processing, AI systems, maintenance, or meditechnics. A few, including both Suresh Gupta and Erica Jacobsen, had palmed for a hitch in the strider forces, strange as that seemed to Dev. Why would anyone actually *volunteer* to extend their five-standard-year service requirement to seven and risk a washout to the infantry, all for the privilege of becoming a large and unwieldy target in a battle? Warstriders, Dev thought, were patently silly, lumbering, clanking brutes that were expected to get *close* to an enemy to fight him.

Give him the navy any day!

Of the others in the company, Ranan Garret was closest to a kindred spirit. A small, intense black from Crystalsea on Rainbow, he was determined to join the Hegemony Navy. Like Dev, he'd linked for several years aboard an independent freighter, and he saw a fleet hitch as a static-free line to a slot with a passenger carrier like Nipponspace. During the past few days, Dev and Garret had openly speculated about whether or not they'd be assigned to the same ship for training.

"Hey, Lung Chi can't happen again," Garret said, replying

to Dole's earlier comment. "The navy's got it covered from orbit."

"*Kichigai!*" Jacobsen said, shaking her head. "You're crazy! They 'had it covered' at Lung Chi, too, didn't they? And what do they do on a hellhole like Loki? You can't laser targets through a cloud deck, friend!"

Garret snickered. "I suppose you think striders are the answer? Hey, the whitesuits provide the *real* firepower. You striderjacks are obsolete, right, Dev?"

"I guess so." He wanted to change the subject. "Anyway, Ran's right about them telling us if the Xenos get close. Something was going on four days ago—"

"Probably a drill," Dole said.

"Probably. But if Xenos had been anywhere close to the el, it would've been big news."

Castellano laughed, a sharp, harsh bark. "*Kuso*, Navy! You norkin' stupid or what?"

Dev frowned. Phil Castellano was the most enigmatic member of the little group. After five years with the Guard, he only held the rank of *gocho*, corporal, which meant he'd been busted at least once. Tough, arrogant, swaggering, he turned evasive when questioned about his experiences in the Guard. He had plenty of war stories, but he could never be pinned down on particulars. Dev didn't like him.

"What do you mean?"

"You really think you're going to get a navy slot? You'll be lucky to get the PBI."

"PBI?" Garret asked.

"The poor bloody infantry, sonny. Crunchies, the striderjacks call 'em,'cause that's the sound they make when their CAs get stepped on by the big five-meter jobs." He grinned. "Or maybe you'll be tapped for the striders, God help you. Get to stomp around in a dual-podder with a great big target painted on your chest!"

"I've been promised my slot," Dev said, with more conviction than he felt. "By this time next week, Ran and me'll be *navy*."

Castellano laughed. "You've been living too many ViRdramas, kid. You need a reality test!"

With slow deliberation Dev stood up. "You care to explain that?"

"Yeah, sure." Castellano rose, topping Dev's 182 by a couple of centimeters. He was more massive, too, with muscle behind a layer of fat. "Yeah, I'll explain it, hojie. You think anybody gives a rusty jack about you? The bastards upstairs'll stick you wherever they've got a slot . . . and if you don't fit just right, they'll bend you until you do! And when they're done with you, they'll discard you like a spent casing." He snapped his fingers. "Just like that."

"Sounds like you're talking from experience."

"Maybe I am. At least I'm on my way out of this hellhole, eight more days and a wake-up. But you, boys and girls, have landed in a world of shit. Five standard years." His grin stretched his face, but his eyes were hard and cold. "Maybe more, if they decide you're dumb enough for *shoko*-school."

"I've got the sockets for officer school," Dev said evenly. "But I'll be a navy officer, not a muckgrubber grunt like you."

"Ah, you're nothing but fresh meat on the block for the *shiseiji* to feed to the 'Phobes." He looked Dev up and down, his mouth pulling into a sneer. "You ask me, the 'Phobes'll spit you back!"

Dev's hands balled into fists. He'd fought his share of battles in the grimy street canyons of West Scranton, where a challenge as sharp as this one was answered by an immediate attack. Dev took a step forward, his right fist drawing back . . .

"Psst, hold it!" Garret snapped. "Attention!"

Dev whirled, thinking for an instant that someone had just entered the lounge. At the far end of the lounge, the life-size, 3-D image of a Hegemony Navy lieutenant commander was materializing into near-solidity.

"Recruit Cameron," the officer said. He did not look up from his desk, and sounded bored. "Report in person to Office

50-A. Execute immediate." The image faded out again.

At first, Dev wondered if someone had seen the near-fight. It wasn't impossible that surveillance devices monitored all of the barracks spaces. Then he realized that the speaker's being a naval officer meant that it probably had to do with his assignment. He glared at Castellano.

"We'll finish this later."

"It'll be a pleasure, hojie."

Dev checked the location of Office 50-A on the information 'face panel at the front of the barracks, then headed across the dome compound at a trot.

The pressurized habitat on the eastern outskirts of Midgard known as Tristankuppel, one of the city's forty-one interconnected domes, housed most of the local military facilities, including barracks, administration and support buildings, recruit training center, and technical schools. Most of the buildings were drab, Rogan-grown structures shouldering one another beneath the transplas sky, arrayed in a two-hundred-meter circle around a barren central field still called the grinder, a name backed by long centuries of military tradition.

Office 50-A was in Scandia Hall, the sleekest and most modern of the Tristankuppel's buildings. The lieutenant commander Dev had seen in the holoprojection was waiting for him in a windowless work space in the Personnel Office on the first level.

Another officer was there as well, tall, long-legged, and sexy in a hard-bodied way despite her brush-cut hair. She wore collar tabs on her skintights identifying her as a *tai-i*—the same as a navy lieutenant or an army captain. He started to grin appreciatively but was stopped by the emotionless appraisal of those hard, dark eyes.

"Sir!" Dev said, snapping to attention as his latest feed in military courtesy had instructed him. "Recruit Cameron reporting as ordered, *sir*!"

"At ease, recruit," the man said, looking up. He gestured to a chair next to the desk. "Dock yourself."

Dev was surprised at the informality. "Thank you, sir."

"I'm Commander Fisher. This is Captain Alessandro. She's company commander of one of Midgard's strider units." He tapped a small, flat screen reader on his desktop. "I've been going through your records, son. I see you want to follow in your father's footsteps."

"That's right, sir."

"Good God," the woman said. "Why?"

Dev stiffened. "I'm qualified to ceph the K-T jobs. I want to be a starship—"

"Glitter and gold, pretty uniforms, and a jackin' Jill on every planet," Alessandro said, her words biting. "Tradition and glory! What makes you think the navy'd have you?"

Dev bristled, stung by her scorn. "They'll have me, ma'am. I'm good."

"The correct form of address for all senior officers is 'sir,' " Fisher reminded him. "Cameron, I'm afraid I have bad news. Your MSE threw a flag, point four on your TM rating. The navy can't use you."

He seemed to wait for a response, but Dev had none to give. The shock of Fisher's quiet bombshell twisted his gut, leaving throat dry and brain numb. He gaped at the two of them. "Sir, I—" He stopped. "That's impossible!" he finished.

"There's nothing personal in a Mental Stability Evaluation," Fisher said. He paused, as though considering what to say. "And a Psychotechnic Disorder flag isn't necessarily a downcheck. But it is something that anyone who employs you as a linker is going to have to take into consideration."

He met Fisher's level gaze. "That point four . . . is that bad?"

"Not necessarily. Not for most jobs. If it was technophobia, now, that could be a problem, but TM? Hell, all of us have a touch of that. But it does rule you out for starships."

Dev opened his mouth, realized he was gaping foolishly again, and snapped it shut. *"Kichigai!"* The word was one he'd picked up in the barracks. Literally it meant "you're crazy," but in Nihongo it came close to being a fighting word. "I've been jacking a freighter for two years!"

"I'll ask you to control yourself, Cameron," Fisher said coldly. "With your TM rating, I'm surprised even a civilian merchant line would offer you a job. The navy won't take anyone with a TM higher than point two."

Orion Line, Dev thought grimly, was not exactly in the same league as Nipponspace, but this was the first time he'd even considered the possibility that the navy wouldn't take him.

"Look," he said. "It's got to be a mistake. I was second helm on the *Mintaka*. She's still at Asgard. Call and talk to Captain DeWitt!"

"Tell me, Cameron," the woman said suddenly. "What do you feel when you're in the godsea?"

"Huh?" The sudden change of subject had caught him off guard. "It's like . . . like nothing I could describe. Not in words. It's flying . . . and power—"

"Ah." She nodded. "There's the magic word. Power. You feel big when you're linked, don't you? Powerful. Invulnerable."

"I guess so."

"Like you could take on the universe. That's why jackers flagged for TM are pretty carefully scrutinized when they're bucking for lead helm. Think you could pass muster?"

Dev didn't answer at once. Second helm aboard a merchant ship was a reserve position, basically little more than a training slot. He'd passed his shipboard tests and qualified for all watch-standing duties, but twice he'd been passed over for promotion to first helm.

He'd assumed that DeWitt had downchecked him because of petty dislike, or, more likely, because of who his father was. Now, for the first time, he was considering the possibility that it was an MSE result that had blocked his advancement. Captain DeWitt had never said anything, one way or the other, but . . .

"So what are you saying, sir? That the Hegemony Guard

won't have me?" He was already wondering if DeWitt would take him back. He doubted it, especially if there was something in his MSE. "It's like I was a criminal or something."

"Not quite," Alessandro said. "We've got plenty of slots for someone aggressive like you. Someone who doesn't mind taking chances when he's jacked."

"But I'm a *starpilot*!"

"Not anymore," Fisher said. "You know, son, with your jack configuration, you'd be a natural with heavy ViRface equipment. You ever jack transports, loaders, anything like that?"

"No." Dev saw where the conversation was headed.

"With a TM of point four, you'd be perfect for striders," Alessandro said. "I'm short some people, and your stats look pretty good to me."

That was the second time someone had told him that. "No way! I don't *want* to be a striderjack!"

Fisher turned tired eyes on Dev. "Look, son, here's the straight hont. If you don't want striders, you can go to the line infantry, or you can try for a tech rating. Meditech. Maybe ViRtech. If you wash out of school, though, you head straight for the combat pool. They'll be fitting you for your CA."

CA—Combat Armor—lightweight, nano-grown hardshells little heavier than a standard environmental suit. *Crunchies*. The word, and Castellano's mockery, burned in Dev's memory.

"If you choose striders," Fisher continued, "you'll be king of the stack. An officer with a solid career and a good future."

"A grounder?" he said, deliberately, bitingly sarcastic. "Kicking up dirt clods with a combat walker? The navy's where the real action is, anyway. All you striderjacks're good for is—"

"Kid, you've been living too many ViRdramas," Alessandro said, cutting in.

"Well, why do *you* want me?"

"There's no shame in having a high TM," Fisher said,

answering before Alessandro could. "Hell, some of the psychotechnic disorders are lots worse. Technophobia . . . the fear of technic society. Technic Depression. That's when you know the AIs have left you in the dust and you're never going to catch up. Compared to those, technomegalomania's nothing."

"I have a TM rating of point three," Alessandro added. She favored him with a cold grin. "You *have* to think you're a god if you're jacking sixty tons of walking death."

It all seemed too cut-and-dried for Dev, a soulless shuffling of numbers that left him, and what he wanted, out of the equation entirely.

"Frankly, son," Fisher continued, "with your MSE scores and your implants, I'd jump at the chance. The navy's not going to look twice at you with a point four TM. They want cold, calm, and steady people guiding their billion-yen babies through the godsea. Not *warriors.*"

"Hell," Alessandro said. "I doubt that the tech services would be that thrilled to get you either. Looks to me like you can put in for striders, or stick with the line infantry."

This was some kind of nightmare, a horror ViRdrama without an exit code. "What kind of goddamned choice is that?"

"No choice at all, I'd say. You don't want to be an enlisted grunt, do you?"

"But I have to palm for more than five years if I want striderjack!"

"Two extra years," Fisher agreed. "But think of the benefits . . ."

Dev scarcely listened as Fisher ran through the litany of higher pay, faster promotion, and brighter glory. Fisher had been right on one point. He didn't want to be an enlisted man if he had a chance at wearing gold. Better to give orders than to take them, and as a striderjack, at least he'd have some decent armor around him.

"And you might get another crack at the navy," Fisher concluded. "After you qualify as a cadet."

"How do I do that?"

"Take another MSE. Your score could change with training, with discipline, or just because your attitude changes. It's possible to reprogram your own selfware, you know."

"Selfware?"

He pointed at Dev's head. "Your brain is wetware, the organic counterpart to your implant hardware. Selfware is the program your wetware runs. You know, most people have several distinct sets of overlapping selfware that they run at different times. There's Cameron the freighter pilot. Cameron the lover, out on the town for a bit of RJ. Cameron the son of Admiral Cameron—"

"What's the point?" he snapped, angry now.

"In most people, there's a fair amount of overlap between selfware programs. If there's no overlap, you get multiple personalities, severe mental disorders, stuff like that. Too much overlap, and you're inflexible, rigid, unable to adapt. Your scores suggest the latter."

"He's saying you have a bad attitude, Cameron. Rigid. Set in ferrocrete. But *I* can fix that."

He glanced at her suspiciously, then looked back at Fisher. "But I might be able to transfer to the navy later?"

"Possibly." Fisher shrugged. "We've been hardwiring humans to machines for four centuries. Hardware, software, that's no problem. It's the selfware that's still the mystery. Mostly it's what you make of it yourself."

In the end Dev agreed. It was the only thing he could do.

Dev returned to Barracks Three to pick up his gear and was thankful to find that the entire company had been marched off for more evaluations. The only one left in the building was Castellano.

"PBI," Castellano said, rising from his bunk. "Am I right? I can see it just from your face."

"Shows what you know," Dev said, putting as much of a sneer into the words as he could manage. He was tempted to save face, but Castellano had a way of finding things out, and Dev didn't want to give the guy the satisfaction of seeing through a lie. "They made me an officer."

"Hah! I should've known! A goddamn clanker!"

An hour before, Dev had wanted to pound Castellano's face in, but he found himself not caring now. He was still digesting a one-eighty course change in what had been a carefully planned career.

"Beats being a crunchie," Dev said.

"Sure it does," Castellano agreed. "Until they wash you out. When you can't handle the shit they're dumping on you, they'll fit you for a CA-suit so fast, your head'll swim."

Dev looked at the older man with new insight. "That's what happened to you, isn't it?"

He shrugged. "I screwed up once, and they dropped me in the infantry. Six months later I saw my best friend grabbed by a Xeno stalker and goddamned *eaten*, his legs, anyway, and he was there on the ground screaming for me to shoot him, and I couldn't do anything but run 'cause the thing was reaching for *me*! . . ."

Castellano stood there, his hands working at his sides, his eyes wild, as though he were still seeing some invisible horror. Then he relaxed, pulling back that part of self he'd never shown the others in the barracks.

"Hey." And the voice was gentle now. "I'm sorry. Don't mind me. Good luck, okay?"

Stiff-backed, he turned on his heel and strode off, whistling tunelessly. Dev packed his gear, checked out at the front desk, and reported to Recruit Training Command.

He tried not to think about Castellano's eyes.

Chapter 6

Now all you recruities what's drafted to-day
You shut up your rag-box an' 'ark to my lay,
An' I'll sing you a soldier as far as I may:
A soldier what's fit for a soldier.

—"The Young British Soldier"
Rudyard Kipling
early twentieth century

"Toes on the line! On the *line*, you norking brain-burned slugs! That's the long, straight white thing painted on the floor! Eyes front! We're going to *pretend* you assholes are soldiers and *pretend* you know how to stand at attention!"

Dev stumbled into line with the others. The night had been a short one, ended at an obscene hour.

The drill instructor paced before them as they shuffled into line, head erect, back and shoulders as rigid as duralloy, khakis spotless and razor-creased, with more ribbons on his left chest than Dev had known existed.

"I am *Socho* John Randolph Maxwell," the DI thundered. "But as far as you are concerned, I am *God*! Do you understand?"

There was a mumble of assent from the ragged line of men and women, some of whom were still tucking civilian shirts or tunics into trousers. Most looked blank, dazed, or simply confused.

"*When* I ask you if you understand," Maxwell continued with scarcely a pause, "you will answer, in unison, 'Linked, sir!' *Do* you understand?"

"Yes, sir!" "Linked, sir!" "Yessir! . . ."

"What was that?"

"Linked, sir!"

"God*damn* my audio feed must be out! I *still* didn't hear that!"

"LINKED, SIR!"

Maxwell was not a large man, no more than 172 centimeters, and he had the build of a comjacker, small and compact and lean. But his throat must have had built-in amplifiers, for Maxwell could roar orders and insults without seeming to raise his voice, delivering a whipcrack of precision and authority that captured the recruits' attention as completely as a full sensory feed. He had a cadence to the way he spoke that was fascinating, a way of stressing key words that put tremendous feeling into them. Dev wondered if Maxwell really meant what he said, or if he was simply a consummate actor.

"You have been assigned to me for six weeks of basic military indoctrination, after which you will be assigned to field training with an active unit. Ladies and gentlemen, during this next six weeks you will come to hate me, but that's okay because all I have to do is weed out those of you who are unfit to be officers and striderjacks. What the infantry does with you after I am finished with you, I don't care.

"My job is to find those few of you who might make halfway decent officers for the Guard warstrider regiments. It is a difficult and demanding job, requiring as it does the sifting of several tons of worthless rock for a few grams of gold. Sometimes the job is impossible, and having seen the bunch of you this morning, I am very much afraid that that is the case with *this* company of miserable, scuzzbutt recruits! Never, *ever* in all my career seen such a batch of misbegotten rejects and genetic mistakes!

Officers! God *help* me, I never realized our side was this desperate!"

Maxwell continued his pace from one end of the barracks line to the other. Two corporals stood impassively at parade rest by the door.

"This, people, and I use that term with extreme reluctance, is Company Six-forty-five, Third Battalion, Second Regiment of the Midgard Recruit Training Brigade, First Hegemony Guard. Do you understand?"

"LINKED, SIR!"

"I am God. Do you understand?"

"LINKED, SIR!"

"*Gocho* Vincetti and *Gocho* Delaney are my assistants. You will obey their orders as you would obey me. Understand?"

"LINKED, SIR!"

"You! Scumface. What's your name?"

"Uh, Hal Morley, sir," a scared-looking kid four down the line to Dev's left said.

"*No,* Uh-hal Morley. You are *Seito-recruit* Morley, and if you have something to say to me, the first word I want to hear out of your scumface is the word *sir*! Do you understand?"

"Linked, sir!"

"What?"

"SIR, LINKED, SIR!"

"You are *all* seito-recruits! *Seito-hojohei*, for those of you with any Nihongo. Seito means 'officer cadet.' Seito-recruit means that someday, maybe, *maybe*, you will have a chance to be a cadet officer and drive warstriders . . . but only *if* you make it past me!

"This morning there are thirty-five of you. Normally I would expect ten or twelve of you to make it as far as a field training assignment, but now that I've seen this pathetic lot of NORC-Socket cripples, I have to say that I'm going to be lucky to get one! You! With the hair! What's your name?"

"Sir, Seito-recruit Jacobsen, sir!"

"Why are you here?"

"Sir, I want to jack warstriders, sir!"

"Bull*shit*! You couldn't jack a flatloader down a cargo ramp!" Maxwell turned sharply, his finger jabbing at Dev's face. "You! Why are you here?"

Dev swallowed, forcing himself to keep his eyes riveted on the wall he was facing, knowing that to meet the eyes of this wiry monster in uniform would invite attack. "Sir, I . . . I'm not really sure, sir!"

"Ha! Honest, at least. You're too *stupid* to know why you're here! You're *all* too stupid to know. Well, I'm gonna tell you why you're here! You're here because each and every one of you just made the biggest goddamned mistake of your miserable lives by thinking that any of you could possibly be officers! Could possibly be *soldiers*! You *could* have joined the techies! You *could* have joined the goddamned *navy*! But no, you decided to come here and play soldier!"

He stopped, hands on hips, shaking his close-cropped head for dramatic effect. "Maybe they'll be able to find a place for you in a labor battalion once you wash out of here. I don't know, and I don't much care, because once you people wash out, you'll be someone else's nightmare!

"But for right now, we're going to make sure you're healthy while I'm doing my very best to kill you! I want you out of those civvie clothes! Now! Everything! Lay 'em out in front of you, neat pile, footgear on top. C'mon, move it! Move it! Get it *off*!"

Reluctantly at first, then faster as Maxwell continued his tirade, Dev stripped off boots, coverall, and underwear, arranging them on the floor as directed.

"I'm *waiting*, people! Don't be shy! Ain't none of you got one damned thing I ain't seen plenty of before! Okay, right face! That's *right* face, you numbskull! Follow *Gocho* Vincetti out that door! C'mon, c'mon, single file, nuts to butts! Nuts to butts! You seito-recruits of the female persuasion'll just have to make do the best you can without nuts, and close it up!"

They shuffled ahead, Maxwell goading them along with sarcasm and scorn. "Aw, don't tell me you scuzzbutts're embarrassed! Let me tell you something! You people are *not* people. You are not men. You are not women. You are *scuzz*butts, and you will be treated as such until you convince me otherwise or I kick your asses out of here! Close it up tight! All of you! Make the guy in front of you smile!"

Dev learned later that the processional was called the recruits' parade, a seemingly endless single-file shuffle through chill-floored corridors and drafty rooms that would have seemed a lot worse if they hadn't already been in shock from the early reveille and the verbal abuse. Each recruit in turn was probed, prodded, scanned, and repeatedly air-injected in shoulders and buttocks with blood-cell-sized antigenics programmed to hunt down and destroy everything from mutyphant bacilli to malarial parasites.

After the meditechs were through with them, they were made to stand, one at a time, on a platform with arms and legs spread, as lasers painted their bodies with glowing contour lines. The laserscan theoretically measured them for custom-fitted uniforms, but Dev decided there'd been a mistake when he stepped into his bright yellow coveralls fifteen minutes later and pressed the seal closed. The slick-surfaced garment was at least a size too large for him. The corporal handing out the uniforms just grinned when he complained. "You'll grow," was all she said.

By then it was time for breakfast, and Dev had long since decided that he didn't care much for the Guard.

After a meal where they took trays, filed through the mess line, sat, and ate by the numbers, they were marched to still another building. There their heads were shaved . . . a tragedy in the case of Jacobsen, Dev thought, as he stood waiting his turn, watching her luxurious blond hair drop to the floor a handful at a time. Their stubble-darkened scalps and exposed T-sockets made them all look more naked than they'd been before, and far less like individuals.

And that, of course, was the idea, the reasoning behind the humiliation, the shaving, the loss of personal identity. From that moment on, they ceased to be individuals.

They were on their way to becoming soldiers.

The first few days were called orientation, though Dev and the other seito-recruits universally referred to that hell of sleeplessness and steady harassment as *dis*orientation. They ran everywhere. The exercise regimen was intended partly to toughen them, partly to get them used to moving and working as a unit, but mostly it was designed to make them work up appetites for five meals a day. The medical nano in their bodies was working round the clock to rebuild their systems, and food was the necessary raw material for the construction.

Existence become a hazy blur of standing in line, filling out forms, plugging into AI evaluation programs, and dazedly responding to orders that seemed to make no sense at all. Much of each day was spent on the grinder, either marching senselessly back and forth in a ragged pretense of drilling or performing calisthenics en masse, listening all the while to Maxwell's nonstop harangue as he continued to list in exacting, precise, and improbable detail their mental, physical, and moral shortcomings, individually and as a group.

Even more than marching and calisthenics, though, was the time spent "under instruction," the cadets lying in long lines on narrow cots, their brains plugged into AI programs that fed them a seemingly endless mass of data, information on tactics and strategy, military history, nanotechnics, machine repair, tool making, electronics, AI diagnostics, systems analysis, nanomedical theory and first aid, survival, planetography, and even exobiology—at least to the point of downloading what little was known about the Xenophobe enemy. Since all of this information was transmitted through direct AI to cephlink RAM, it was difficult each evening to even be sure what had been learned that day. Most of the cadets spent the hour or so before lights out lying motionless on their bunks, retrieving and cataloging the day's feeds.

His disappointment at having failed to get a navy slot was keen, but he had little time to think about it those first few weeks. Life swiftly settled into a routine of linking, eating, drilling, and sleeping, with a two-hour stint on fire-and-security watch every third night. By the morning of Day Four the company had its first attrition. A surprise middle-of-the-night barracks check by *Gocho* Delaney had caught Seito-recruit Gehrling asleep in the wrong bunk.

The girl was transferred to a tech support company as soon as it was determined that she'd been an active participant—a self-evident conclusion given the proximity of over thirty sleeping recruits and the fact that the double-tiered bunks tended to rattle and squeak with all but the gentlest movements. While there were no specific rules against sexual fraternization among the recruits, the unspoken assumption was that if you had the time or the energy for extracurricular pursuits, you simply didn't have the dedication necessary to be an officer.

For Gehrling, the situation was much worse. He'd been on fire-and-security watch at the time, and sleeping on watch was *the* unforgivable transgression. There was talk at first of a court-martial and hard time with a prison battalion, but he agreed instead to transfer to the leg infantry, and that was the last Dev heard of him.

Leg infantry. That quickly became the terror, the personal bugbear of each of the recruits in Company 645. Within the Guard there were two classes of infantry. At the top were the strider forces, highly mobile, heavily armed and armored, powerful units answering to the tank units or attack helicopters of twentieth- and twenty-first-century warfare.

Then there was the leg infantry, enlisted personnel considered unsuitable for link-jacked machinery. Most were men and women who, because of poverty or technophobia or religious conviction, had never received the interfaces that let them control full-sensory sockets. Too, the leggers had long since become a dumping ground for undesirables and untrainables from the other branches of the Guard. For a strider recruit to be sent to the leggers was considered the ultimate humiliation, a public acknowledgement that the man simply could not be trained to serve in any useful capacity on the modern battlefield.

Unofficially the average life expectancy of a leg trooper, wearing nothing but combat armor against the deadly environment of the modern battlefield, was measured in minutes.

Dev decided that he would have been terrified if they hadn't kept him and the other recruits so busy. It was Day Six before the enormity of what had happened to him actually struck home. That was the day that two men and three women were cut from the company for no better reason than that they were the last to complete a running ten-times circuit of the grinder. The leg infantry, Maxwell told them, might be able to find a place for them, but the warstriders needed sterner stuff. An hour later they were gone.

Dev later learned they'd ended up as techies, but the dread of transfer to the leggers continued to hang like a shadow over the seito-recruits. The incident escalated Dev's disappointment to an impotent rage. For no better reason than a blown psych test result, his life had been rewritten by someone else. It wasn't fair!

His survival seemed to depend on remaining unnoticed in the ranks of seito-recruits. "You might get another crack at the navy," Lieutenant Commander Fisher had said. "After you qualify as a cadet." Dev clung to those words with an unreasoning hope that bordered on desperation. Six weeks! He could endure anything for six weeks, even this. All he needed to do was follow directions and stay out of trouble.

He would stick it out, then put in for transfer to the navy. Things *couldn't* get much worse than they were by Day Six.

On Day Seven the company began simulator training, painfully simplistic, basic stuff at first for someone who'd jacked thousand-ton freighters into Orbital Dock, but quickly growing more detailed . . . and more difficult. Dev began to think he might be in his element.

But they still had to run everywhere.

"God!" he panted, late on the afternoon of the eighth day. They'd just finished running four kilometers, twelve times around the grinder, and he was stooped over, hands braced on knees, trying to beat down the fire consuming his lungs. Suresh Gupta panted next to him. "God," he said again. "I thought they were training us for warstriders. What does running have t'do with jacking?"

"Quite . . . a bit," Gupta replied, catching his breath. The air was chilly, but both were coated with sweat. "We have to be ready physically before they start working on our minds."

"I'm not sure I want them goking around with my mind." A part of Dev realized that his language had become rougher during this past week, rougher and more bitter. "Kuso, what do they expect us to do, carry the goking striders into battle on our backs?"

"If we have to. Haven't you noticed? We're getting stronger."

"After only a week? No way!"

"Remember those shots on Day One?"

Dev straightened and rubbed his left arm, which was still a bit sore. Most of the recruits still bore traces of bruises on arms and buttocks from those injections. "The antigenics, yeah. How could I forget?"

"Some of them weren't antigenics. Meteffectors, man. They're rebuilding us. Haven't you noticed? You're putting on mass."

The information was part of a data feed from several days earlier, but Dev somehow hadn't applied it to himself. Meteffectors, though, were the only way that HEMILCOM Training Command could hope to turn over- and under-weight, understrengthed civilians into soldiers in a scant six weeks. Rather than hunting down bacteria like the antigenics, nanotechnic metabolic effectors increased the efficiency of his metabolism, turning fat to energy and food into muscle. Since muscle tissue, gram for gram, was denser than fat, he'd put on some weight as muscle replaced fat. It was the same for the others in the company. The fat ones were slimming down, the skinny ones building up.

"What," he said, still gulping for air. "They want us to live forever?"

"Hardly that, Dev." Gupta's white teeth flashed against his dark skin. "Haven't you heard? Life extension's just for us Japanese."

"Wouldn't want to live forever," Dev said. "Not if it means running around this grinder again!"

"All right, you two scuzzbutts!" Maxwell's voice rasped across the panting, sweating mob of recruits. "If you can still work your mouths, you haven't had enough yet. You've just bought another twelve circuits for the whole company!"

A chorus of groans rose from the yellow-clad recruits as they started to hit the track again in ragged formation. Someone punched Dev hard enough on his sore shoulder to make him curse through clenched teeth.

Company 645, down now to twenty-five recruits, began circling the field again.

Chapter 7

When an army is being trained to fight, it must begin by weeding out those whose character or temperament makes them incapable of fighting.

—*The Anatomy of Courage*
Lord Moran
mid-twentieth century

The line of war machines worked its way up the slope. The landscape was barren and uninviting, a sameness of gravel, rock, and sand beneath a burning, featureless sky; the only terrain feature visible was the hill itself, a cone-shaped peak with the triangular silhouette of an atmosphere generator one hundred meters high, flattened at the top.

That was where the second line of warstriders awaited the first.

The defending line atop the hill consisted of four two-man LaG-42 Ghostriders and four RLN-90 Scoutstrider one-man recon machines, their nanofilm colors glowing a dazzling red. Opposing them were five Ghostriders and two Scoutstriders, all showing blue colors, carrying more firepower but disadvantaged by being forced to attack uphill. Each step kicked more dust into the crystal air, dust that blurred the striders' legs and clung to bare metal like mud.

Laser light flared from the hilltop, striking a blue LaG-42. Armor splattered like water as the left weapons pack was blown away. Smoke boiled from exposed circuitry, but the Ghostrider, taking a backward step to steady itself, shrugged off the blow, then kept advancing, the massive flanges of its feet scrabbling for purchase on the loose gravel.

"Smoke!" came the shouted command. Canisters arced from the advancing blue line, bursting on impact. Cottony blossoms of white smoke expanded in smothering clouds, blocking visibility for both sides. Lasers continued to flash and snap, visible now as dazzling traceries in the fog and attenuated by the drifting aerosol. Another blue strider was hit, but the armor on one slender leg merely glowed briefly.

"Blue Leader to Blue Scouts!" The voice was Suresh Gupta's, pitched a bit high with excitement but otherwise steady and clear. "Break left and right! Flank 'em! Blue Ghosts, follow me, up the center!"

The Scoutstriders, looking like squat men in bulky, headless full-armor suits standing three and a half meters tall, angled to either side through the fog, cutting across the slope to get on the enemy's flanks. The Ghostriders, over four meters tall and looking more like enormous, flightless birds with their long legs and strutting gait, moved in a ragged V straight up the hill. The defenders, unable to halt the attackers with laser fire, switched to machine guns, grenades, and rockets, fired in staccato bursts from the Kv-70 weapons packs that served as arms for the Ghostriders.

Katya watched the battle unfold through a godview, looking down unseen from the air just above the blue formation with a gaze that penetrated fog and dust alike. "A frontal assault on a prepared position?" she asked in her mind.

"They haven't been fed much in the way of formal tactics yet," *Shosa* Karl Rassmussen's voice replied. She couldn't see the training battalion commander but knew he shared her aerial viewpoint. "All we're looking for now is initiative, quick thinking, and raw guts. This is a rough simulation for both sides. No cover, poor footing, and limited weapons.

Red's got some cover with the hillcrest, of course, but he's got to stay put to cover the flag. Blue's completely exposed but has room to maneuver."

Abruptly the blue Ghostriders emerged from the drifting smoke, twenty meters below the Red line. Red immediately shifted to laser fire from the turrets mounted beneath their blunt torsos. Unguided rockets and laser-guided missiles scratched white trails across the hilltop, and the thunder of explosions drowned the squeak and clank of machinery. The *thud-thud-thud* of a heavy machine gun hammered away at advancing armor. Rocket grenades arced high into the sky, then fell, detonating with sharp bangs and actinic flashes of light.

"Who's the Blue team leader?" Katya asked as a blue strider's right leg was blasted from its body. The machine toppled, its left leg clawing at the hillside as it struggled to right itself.

"Gupta. Earth kid."

Another blue strider took a hit, a near-miss that gouged armor from its back in a long, jagged furrow. "Looks like he's learning about frontal attacks from experience."

But the rush had carried the Blue wedge to the crest of the hill, and now there was no advantage for either side. Smoke canisters popped, adding to the confusion. A red LaG-42 was down, both legs burned away by laser fire. Magically the color faded to steel grey, indicating that both pilots aboard had been tagged "dead" by the AI running the simulation. Smoke continued to pour from the crater that had peeled open the pilot's module like the unfolding petals of a flower.

It was, Katya reflected, a fair simulation of combat. The entire battle existed only in the mind of the AI creating it—and in the linked brains of the twenty-five seito-recruits taking part and the dozen-odd instructors, monitors, and observers. The warstriders were a bit too clean to be mistaken for the real thing, too gleaming, too lacking in dents, nicks, grime, and patched-over hits to be believable.

Like the landscape—too perfect, too neat, too clean. A battle in virtual reality, with none of the blood or agony.

But the recruits were conducting themselves as though the fight were a real one, a battle to the death between two halves of Company 645.

One of the blue RLN-90 recon Scouts, identified by a white number twelve on its upper left chest, came in from the flank. It carried a 100-megawatt laser mounted on its right arm. It fired, sending a flash of coherent light into the back of a red Scoutstrider, melting steel and duralloy and dropping the machine to its knees.

The blue Scout panned the weapon to the right, sending bolt after bolt of laser light into the red Ghostriders. Blue and red striders were mingling now, a colorful melee, smashing at one another with rockets at point-blank range. The Scout sidestepped as a red LaG-42 opened fire with a rocket barrage, sending a trio of laser bolts snapping into the Ghostrider's torso in return.

One hundred megawatts was enough to crack a Ghostrider's armor, but it took several hits to pierce the duralloy shell and cause any real damage. The RLN-90 fired with deadly accuracy, aiming not for the LaG's main hull, but for the joints that mounted legs and weapons pods to the hull.

"Who's in the blue Scout?" Katya asked. "Number twelve."

"Name's Cameron," Rassmussen said. "Another Earth kid."

Katya remembered him well, the tall, bitter-sounding young man, one of the new batch of recruits she'd met in Fisher's office three weeks earlier. The one so determined to join the navy, whose father had been some kind of hero. She watched him maneuver with approval. The guy was good, surprisingly good for a kid in his third week of Basic.

The Scoutstrider stepped in close, inside the reach of the Ghostrider's chin laser, and fired a quick succession of bolts into the same spot in the bigger machine's armor, eliciting a flash and a curl of black smoke from its left hip. The LaG took another step, hydraulics straining to keep it balanced as the left leg sagged. Then the joint gave way, pitching the twenty-five-ton combat machine nose-first into the gravel. Swiftly the RLN crouched behind the wreckage, as another red Ghostrider, aiming for the Scout, slammed four bolts into the downed LaG instead. The Scoutstrider returned fire with a cool deliberation that made Katya want to sing.

"He looks good," she said.

"I'm not sure he's going to make it," Rassmussen said. "He's a loner. I think he's nursing a grudge."

"What about?"

"Here. Scan his records."

With half her mind, Katya absorbed the flow of data from the training command's data stores. With the rest, she continued to watch the number-twelve Scoutstrider.

The melee on the hilltop had claimed more casualties. The second blue Scoutstrider was down, the gray color of the wreckage showing that the pilot had been declared KIA. One blue Ghostrider—Gupta's machine, battered and missing its right weapons pod—remained on its feet, squared off against two red striders almost as badly damaged as it was. The last remaining red RLN-90 struck number twelve with a burst of laser fire, and the light recon strider toppled, its torso armor gashed and torn. Another red LaG-42 went down, savaged by Gupta's hammering rocket fire. The surviving red LaG and RLN closed in on the Blue leader's mangled strider. At their backs, the red flag snapped in a nonexistent breeze.

Katya took in Cameron's bio. She'd gone through his records once before, in Fisher's office, but she scanned them again now. BosWash . . . yeah. Unusual for a kid from one of old North America's crowded metroplexes to get the socket and link hardware that would take him off planet. Gupta was from Earth, too, she remembered, but he'd come from a province of *Dai Nihon*. There were advantages to being a citizen of Greater Japan, even a second-class citizen, and one of them was easier access to Japanese nanotechnology.

She came to the notation about Admiral Cameron . . . *the* Admiral Cameron. So that was how a metroplex kid had gotten a nano-grown implant. And Dev Cameron's father wasn't a hero, as she'd half remembered. That tended to explain what the son was doing out here on the frontier.

Most inhabitants of the outworlds tended to ignore the political tug-of-war between Japanese Empire and Terran Hegemony. In general, the farther away a colony world was from Earth, the less meaningful Solar politics were. Katya's own New America, 26 Draconis IV, was a case in point. Her home system was thirty-five light-years from Loki, but over forty-eight lights from Sol, one of the most distant of all the human-colonized worlds. A Colonial Authority governor kept his office and residence in the capital at Jefferson, and the Hegemony seal appeared on the world flag, but few of the Terran Hegemony's pronouncements, debates, or laws had much bearing on the day-to-day lives of the colonists, not when the travel time, Earth to New America, was over seven weeks.

Everyone on New America knew about Lung Chi, and most knew about the young Imperial admiral who had destroyed the Manchurian colony's sky-el rather than risking the evacuation fleet parked at synchorbit. Life on the frontier, making an inhospitable world habitable, was a daily parade of tough decisions; in New American ViRdrama, the hero was often the person faced with disaster who tried to do *something*, even if that something ended in failure.

Admiral Michal Cameron would have been ideal cast as a New American ViRdrama hero.

Katya was realist enough to know that there was another factor in her distinctly New American feelings about Michal Cameron. Chien, Lung Chi's sun, was less than twenty light-years from 26 Draconis. The reality of Xenophobe attacks on human colony worlds was far sharper in most New Americans' minds than the rather remote theory of Hegemony legislation and Shichiju frontiers.

She wondered if young Dev Cameron's determination to join the Hegemony Navy had anything to do with his father. It had to, she reasoned. She wondered if Dev Cameron himself knew why he'd sought to follow in his father's footsteps.

Perhaps more to the point, though, was what he thought about ending up in the strider infantry.

"Ah," Rassmussen said suddenly, interrupting her thoughts. "Looks like we have two Reds ganging up on that last blue. I'd say Red's got this one sewed up."

"Cameron's strider is still showing color," Katya said. She called up a window overlaying the scene in her mind. The display let her tap into the blue RLN's system controller. "Damage doesn't look too bad, actually," she said. "He could be . . . yes! There!"

On the hilltop, Cameron's Scoutstrider stirred, then rose unsteadily to its feet. It appeared to hesitate, staring at the backs of the two surviving red machines, then broke into a ground-eating lope *away* from the showdown between Red and Blue.

Gupta's strider was down now, its torso torn open and its internal wiring spilling onto the ground like ghastly intestinal coils. Alerted by their all-round scanners, the red LaG and RLN both spun, weapons tracking, but it took a precious second to acquire the rapidly moving target. The blue Scoutstrider vaulted a crumpled pile of wreckage, whipped around, then hoisted the limp ruin of the second Blue Team RLN-90, holding it in front of its body like a shield.

The second Scoutstrider had been declared a kill, its blue coloring dissolved to gray. Red Ghostrider and Scoutstrider opened fire together, but their laser bolts struck the wrecked RLN, burning off chunks of armor and one of the limp-dangling arms. Cameron's Scoutstrider began moving backward step by step, edging toward the fluttering Red flag and dragging the dead RLN with him. The two Red machines advanced, splitting up to hit him from opposite flanks, but they were too late. Still supporting the wrecked Scoutstrider in front of him with one arm, Cameron reached behind him and brought down the Red flag.

A warning klaxon sounded, and the simulation ended. Katya found herself lying in a comfortable recliner, temporal feeds in place. She broke contact with the palm 'face and unjacked. Across the room, Rassmussen unplugged as well and sat up. He was a tall man, a native of Loki with yellow hair and intensely blue eyes.

"You see?" he said. "A loner. Faked critical damage while his teammates were getting mopped up. Then he used one of them as a shield while he sprinted for the flag."

"What were the op orders?"

"To seize the flag—"

"And the other blue RLN was already dead. He showed initiative."

"In a real battle he wouldn't have known that Jacobsen was dead. Damn it, she might have been trapped inside the wreckage, wounded or unconscious. His action would have killed her. You don't *do* that to squad mates."

"But he fulfilled the conditions of the op. Sometimes you have to make tough decisions."

Rassmussen spread his hands. "Hey. I just call 'em as I see 'em. I think he's going to be trouble."

"With a TM of point four, he could be a hell of a problem," she conceded. "He could also be the hottest damned striderjack we've seen in a while. Put a tag on him, Major. He's mine."

"As you say, Katya. Your company. Anybody else?"

"That Blue leader, certainly. What was his name? Gupta. He's got some things to learn about strategy, but he was steady right to the end. Now, I *need* eight people—"

"But so do three other companies, Katya, and we only have this one crop of recruits at the moment. I can promise you those two guys, at least. Maybe one or two more."

"I'll be back in two, three weeks and see how they're getting on."

"If they're still here."

If *any* of us are still here, Katya thought. There'd been no more sightings or breakthroughs since the Battle of Schluter, but HEMILCOM had been picking up strange noises and seismic disturbances ever since, most of them within a couple of hundred klicks of Midgard and Bifrost. Something was happening out there in those methane-lashed wastes, that was for damned sure. Nobody knew how the Xenos perceived humans or their cities, but it was a sure bet that they knew the city and the sky-el were there. It couldn't be much longer before they made some kind of move against them.

Katya just hoped her people would be ready for them when they did.

Chapter 8

Cephlinkage was the great nanomedical breakthrough opening the science of the mind. With teleopsychology and neopsychometrics, the mind, at last, became quantifiable. Though critics deny that numeric values quantify the man, it is upon this rock that all modern psychological research is founded.

—*Man and His Works*
Dr. Karl Gunther Fielding
C.E. 2488

From his steel-caged vantage point four meters above the deck, Dev stared from an access gantry platform across the cluttered expanse of the company's maintenance bay. The dome, adjacent to the Tristankuppel and joined to it by a pressurized, hundred-meter walkway, was called Mjolnirkuppel, and it was home and workplace to the three platoons that comprised A Company, First Battalion of the Fifth Loki Thorhammer Regiment.

Cacophony assaulted his ears. The maintenance bay, a domed-over expanse the size of a sports arena, was a rattling, clanking, booming confusion of men, women, and machines, of towering gantries, massive carryalls, and heavy equipment, and everywhere the hulking steel and carbocomposite armor of warstriders. Sun-bright flares dazzled and showered sparks where teleop welders touched plasma arcs to metal. Elsewhere, white fog roiled from cryo-H storage tanks, and a massive sheet of armor released from a carryall's meter-long duralloy grippers struck the dome's deck with a ringing crash of durasheath plate on steel.

The fog boiling off cryo-H tanks added a chill to the air that reminded Dev of the minus-eighty temperatures and sleeting, poisonous winds outside. The sharp bite of ammonia—some of the stuff crept inside the pressure dome every time the big, ten-meter airlock doors at one end of the bay were opened, no matter how thorough the decon wash afterward—still brought tears to Dev's eyes, though he'd been told he'd get used to it after a while. He palmed the smartpatch on his coveralls, turning up the garment's heat.

Four days earlier, Dev and twelve other survivors of Company 645 had completed their final recruit exercises, and four of them had been assigned to field training slots with Company A of the 1/5. Recruit trainees no longer, they were now full-fledged *seitos*, officer cadets, entitled to wear brown coveralls instead of yellow during their day-to-day duties, and dress gray uniforms bearing the cadet's one slender gold stripe on sleeve and shoulder board. But the architecture designed for giants rather than humans, the massive shapes of the warstriders themselves embraced by their service gantries and power feed cables, the noise, stink, and orderly confusion, were all still strange and a bit overwhelming.

For the past three days Cadets Dev Cameron, Erica Jacobsen, Suresh Gupta, and a young, blond Lokan named Torolf Bondevik had been discovering that the *real* training started now, as they sought to apply the data feeds of the past six weeks to the realities of operating, maintaining, and repairing the huge and complex link-operated machines called warstriders. Each had been assigned to a different machine, Jacobsen to Hagan's *'Phobe Eater*, Bondevik to Nicholsson's Battlewraith *Pacifier*, and Gupta to the Company Commander's Warlord *Assassin's Blade*.

Dev's assignment was with *Sho-i* Tami Lanier's Ghostrider, a two-slot recon strider named *High Stepper*.

Warstriders were large and complex machines, virtually solid masses of wiring, pumps, circuits, hydraulic systems, and the myotensor bundles that imitated the muscular action of a living organism, all encased in durasheath armor shells and layered nanotechnic films. Lots could go wrong with them, as Dev was beginning to find out. He'd spent most of the last three days submerged in the wiring and dry-slick silicarb used as a strider internal lubricant, learning mechanical systems, diagnostics, and repair with a thoroughness that his training feeds in boot camp hadn't even attempted.

"Cameron!" Lanier's voice snapped at him from above.

Clinging to the gantry platform's guardrail alongside one massive leg actuator, he turned, suppressing the burned-in instinct to respond with a shouted "Linked, Sir!" That recruit nonsense, he'd been told several times already, was no longer required. Spit and polish in the field was virtually nonexistent.

"Yes, sir!"

A chunky, heavy-set woman with sandy hair peeking from beneath her vehicle link helmet appeared, squeezing her head and shoulders from the narrow commander's access hatch. "Git yourself up here, newbie. It's about time we got you and *Stepper* formally acquainted."

"On my way." He'd been working at the acetabular myocircuitry, and his hands and arms were slick with black silicarb. Pausing only to wipe off what he could on an already blackened rag, Dev grasped a rung welded to the warstrider's curved hull, then stepped off the gantry and started pulling himself toward the pilot's access.

High Stepper was armed with a 100-megawatt chin laser and a pair of Kv-70 weapons pods on either side of the fuselage, like stubby, handless arms. *Stepper*'s hull was currently a glossy black but patchy, showing scars where combat had blasted away some of the nanoflage film, inactive now, that covered all exposed surfaces. The access hatches were on the dorsal hull, one on each side of the centerline, the commander module to the right, the pilot module to the left.

Squeezing through the pod hatch, he dropped into the embrace of a padded, horizontal couch that all but filled the cramped pilot's module. Normally, as soon as he entered the strider, his first task would be to hook a web of control and monitor cables into his vehicle skinsuit, which took care of such pedestrian necessities as monitoring his heart rate and breathing, eliminating body wastes, and controlling bleeding. Since this linkage would only be for a few minutes, he didn't bother.

Instead, he pulled a VCH, the Vehicle Cephlink Helmet, from a recess in the bulkhead to his right and settled it over his head. Reaching up beneath the helmet's rim, he snapped the interior jack cables home in each of his three sockets, then locked the unit in place.

"Okay, newbie," Lanier's voice said over the VCH speaker. "Let's get 'er revved up. Switch on."

The manual control panel was a small console set above Dev's face next to the access hatch. "Power on," he said, as he touched a series of contact pads. Beneath him, the warstrider's massive Ishikawajima-Harima Y-70A fusorpak came to life with a low hum that built slowly to a muted whine. The strider's on-board computer, a series 7-K manufactured by IBM-Toshiba, signaled readiness to link with the steady pulse of a green indicator light. Another touch pad closed the access hatch. He was alone now, cloaked by darkness save for the glow of pinhead-sized indicators on the manual console.

Wiggling in the seat so that he could reach above and behind his head, Dev extracted his three cephlink leads and snapped them home, one after another, into his VCH external sockets.

"Make sure the link setting's on neutral," Lanier warned.

"Neutral," he repeated, checking the light display. "Got it."

He pressed his palm implant against the interface contact to the left of his couch. Something like light flashed behind his eyes, accompanied by a hissing ache between his ears. The strider's Artificial Intelligence had to be tuned to his cerebral patterns, a process that would take several moments.

Carefully he thought the alphanumeric sequence that unlocked the AI access codes stored in his cephlink RAM. Numbers and letters flickered against the static. A sense of inner completion, of rightness, indicated that he was linked.

"Pilot replacement," he thought, concentrating on the words. "Reconfiguration, Code Three-Green-One."

"Think of the color blue," the strider's voice said in his mind. It was a bland, neutral voice, recognizable as neither male nor female. "Picture a red sunset, viewed from a beach on the shore of an ocean. . . ."

Dev had never seen an ocean, but part of his training had included downloaded images keyed to generate the appropriate responses in his mind as he brought them again to mind. The AI continued asking for specific thoughts—numbers, colors, simple mental images. The process was largely automatic, and Dev performed effortlessly, just as he had dozens of times before in simulation. Next time, *High Stepper* would have his cerebral patterns stored in memory, and this break-in process would not be necessary.

"Reconfiguration is complete," the AI said several minutes and many questions later. "Enabling cephlink, full control to Module Two."

The familiar flash of linkage, a tiny explosion of light and static, filled his brain, and the narrow confines of the pilot module, the lights, and the primitive, hard-wired board vanished. He was standing in the company maintenance bay, braced by the zigzagging struts and braces of the gantry, surrounded by the dangling power cables and cryo-H pipes and electronic data feeds that wired him to the base complex like the strings on a puppet.

He was aware of another presence, a watcher sharing a small, bright part of his mind. Power flow brought a second pod in the strider to life.

"Well done, Cameron," Lanier's voice said in his mind. "Now that *Stepper* knows you, I'm sure you'll be the best of friends."

Dev scarcely heard her. He was tingling now to the familiar thrill of full linkage.

Though he could never have explained the difference, linking with a jack-bossed machine, whether it was a warstrider or a starship, felt different, more real, more solid than a ViR communications or entertainment feed, even a feed with full sensory feedback. He felt large, powerful, and more alive than he ever had before. *This* was reality, and no matter what the engineers and designers said, it was not the same as a ViRsimulation. You weren't supposed to be able to tell the difference; sensation, after all—whether it was the feel of the metal deck beneath his feet, the sound of hissing steam and shouted commands, or the sight of Victor Hagan's squat, black KR-9 Manta shrouded in the maintenance gantry opposite his—manifested itself in the brain and ought to be the same whether the incoming nerve impulses carrying that sensation were from the body's organs of touch, sound, and sight, or generated by an AI and fed through sockets and cephlink.

Power. A movement of his left foot would topple the fragile crisscrossings of his own gantry, would send him striding out across the maintenance bay deck. A battery of weapons—100-megawatt laser, Kv-70 weapons pods, chemical flamer—were his to command.

Not the same as swimming the *Kamisamano Taiyo*, the godsea of the K-T Plenum, perhaps. Still, Dev felt purpose, order, and strength, just as he did when he was linked to a starship's AI.

"Hey, newbie!" Lanier's voice cut through his thoughts, knife-edged. "Wake up in there! I said let's begin the weapons system check."

"Uh . . . right." Pulling new access codes from his RAM, Dev engaged the Ghostrider's left and right Kv-70 weapons pods. Those mounts could accommodate rockets, a variety of tube-launched 30-mm grenades, heavy machine guns, or a combination of the three, though neither was loaded yet. Dev read the data scrolling past his mind's eye, however, as he'd done countless times in ViRsim. "Both Kv-70s show full function," he said. "Acquisition, tracking, and firing systems are go."

"Chin laser."

"Check."

"Wait one." There was a moment's hesitation. "Cameron, you have an outside call. Channel one."

He accessed the communications code, felt the click of a completed circuit. "Cameron here. Go ahead."

"Cameron, this is Captain Alessandro. I need to see you ASAP, my office."

Now what?

"On my way, sir. Five minutes."

"What did you do now, newbie?" Lanier asked.

"I don't know. I've been doing my best to stay clear of trouble. I'll be back soon as I can."

"You do that. We still need to go through the on-board stores."

Calling up the codes to break link, he felt again the slickness of the interface plate beneath his left palm. Lifting his hand sharply, he broke the connection. He lay again inside the narrow confines of the pilot's module.

He stabbed at the touch pad, and his access hatch hissed open. Wiggling back into the light, he squeezed out of the module, dropped to the gantry deck, and started down. The captain's office was at the back of the dome, past the gantries shrouding a line of strider hulks, corpses kept for spares. The damage evident in those shattered, half-melted frames—and the mild depression that always set in when he emerged from full-sense link—always made Dev feel a little cold.

But he didn't turn up his coveralls' heat again.

He touched the door annunciator. "Enter," Alessandro's voice called from inside.

"You wanted to see me, sir," he said, stepping into her office. It was small and utilitarian, rather spartan save for a framed holoview on one wall, a tropical-looking landscape of feathery trees and white buildings under a golden sun.

"Yes, Cameron." She gestured to the room's only other chair. "Come in and dock yourself. How are you getting settled in?"

"Fine, I guess. There's a lot to learn they never fed us in boot camp."

She smiled at that. "Welcome to reality. Always a shock." She hesitated, as though wondering how to put what she had to say into words. "I guess the best way to do this is to give it to you straight. I'm turning down your request for a retest."

He felt the anger rising, the protest at the blind unfairness of it all, but bit it back.

When he said nothing, Alessandro continued. "I was impressed with what I saw of your simulations in Basic. You have the makings of a terrific striderjack. Now, I know Mr. Fisher said you could retest and put in for a transfer as soon as you were out of basic training, but our reasoning still stands. The numbers on your MSE still say the navy won't want you."

"I guess I wasn't expecting any different."

That was true enough. He'd put in the request the day he'd checked in with the 1/5, but with no hope that he'd get what he wanted. He extracted a memory from his implant RAM. A tiny window opened in his mind, Castellano's arrogant face grinning at him. *You think anybody gives a rusty jack about you? The bastards upstairs'll stick you wherever they've got a slot. . . .*

Castellano was right. They—the ubiquitous and all-powerful *They* of HEMILCOM Training Command, and Alessandro herself—would all do as they damn pleased to make their numbers balance.

"I want you to give us a try for a while. In, say, six months we'll talk about it again. Who knows? Maybe with some experience, your MSE scores will change."

She didn't sound as though she believed that. "Will that be all, Captain?"

"No. I want the straight hont from you. I want to know how you feel, right now, about winding up here instead of in a navy slot."

"The truth? I'm not happy about it. I'm beginning to think I made the wrong choice when I palmed up." He shrugged. "I'll do what I'm told, take it a day at a time, and try to stay out of trouble." He stopped. He wasn't sure what the woman wanted from him.

"Why were you so set on the navy, anyway?" When he didn't answer right away, she added, "Was it your father?"

"I guess so. You know about him?"

"I don't think there's a New American who doesn't. If it's any help, I think he did exactly the right thing at Lung Chi. He had a couple of seconds to make a decision no man should ever have to face. He made it, and I for one think it was the right one."

Dev nodded. "You know, I always thought I could . . . I don't know, prove something, I guess, if I could join the navy."

"What? That he knew what he was doing? How could *you* prove something like that?"

"Sounds pretty silly when you put it that way. I know. Maybe I just wanted to prove something to myself." He leaned back in the chair, crossing his legs. "For as far back as I can remember, I wanted to be a starship. First helm. Once I got a taste of it with the Orion Lines—"

"Swimming the godsea."

He caught the look in her eye, the note of . . . wistfulness? And wonder. "You . . . know?"

"I used to link starships too, Dev. Back in my youth, I jacked a little fifty-meter racing yacht. So later, of course, when I palmed for Hegemony service, they slotted me in an I-4000."

Dev whistled. Ishikawajima 4Ks were the largest interstellar carriers in human space, kilometer-long monsters usually used as colonization transports. The military used them for moving whole regiments and their equipment from system to system.

"I'm impressed," Dev said. Memory clicked. "Hey, you said you had a high TM rating. How—"

"Boring story," she replied. "Tell me what you would do if you had a chance at starships."

"I don't know anymore. Maybe nothing. Once I thought I'd be, I don't know, able to set the record straight, somehow. Now . . . well, I'm not so sure."

"What's changed?"

"That goking TM rating," Dev said. His fists, resting on his legs, clenched hard. "Captain, I always thought that a man was something more than just numbers. But there are damned numbers on everything today. Psychotechnic disorders." He worked his mouth around the phrase as though it tasted bad. "It's like they have us programmed. Download our RAM and they know everything about us, right down to when we use our finger to pick food from our teeth." He stopped, then looked up at Katya. "Captain, do you think my father could have screwed up because of *his* TM rating? That he, I don't know, miscalculated, maybe tried to cowboy things and made a bad call?"

Katya shook her head. "I told you I thought he made the right choice. More than that, I can't tell you. Look, I've seen Xenophobes in action. You haven't, not for real. Once the Xenos were in the sky-el, nothing could have saved the colonists still on Lung Chi. You have my promise on that."

"I keep wondering if I would have done things any differently if I'd been on the *Hatakaze*. Hell, who am I kidding? I've seen Xenos in training sims, and . . . I'll tell you the truth, Captain, I'm scared. I don't know how I'll do out there, realworld." His mouth pulled back in a rueful grin. "It's not quite the same as jacking star freighters."

"You're good, Dev. I've watched you."

"In sims—"

"They're as real as reality. I think what you need to do is stop being so damned introspective."

"Huh? What—"

"Stop worrying about it so much. If you stop to think about it in combat, you're dead. Believe me, I *know*."

Dev saw pain in her dark eyes. "You're not going to leave me hanging there, are you, Captain? What's the story?"

She appeared to consider it, then shrugged. "Let's just say that my first time under stress, I screwed up, okay? And it was because I was thinking too much. I damn near bought it, too."

"What happened?"

"I fought it. I'm *still* fighting it, every day." She paused for a moment, quietly studying her hands folded on her desk. "Dev, you told me you think you're more than a number. If that's true, you won't let the numbers back you into a corner. When I lost it as a starship, everybody figured I'd quit and go home. I could have, too." She tapped the side of her head. "I was pretty badly dinged up in here. I think maybe the fact that I knew they expected me to quit was what made me keep going."

"Are you telling me to fight your decision to keep me in the Assassins?" He managed a smile. "Wouldn't that be mutiny?"

"No. I'm telling you to make the best of it, don't dump program over the MSEs, and try again in six months. I think you're more than a number, too, Dev. And that means you can be whatever you want to be."

More than a number.

Ever since his father's promotion to admiral, Dev realized, he'd been fighting the impersonal and faceless system that transformed humans into ciphers, statistics to evaluate, numbers to shuffle, equations to balance.

Funny. He'd been furious at Alessandro, furious with the whole system, but the anger was gone now. And all because this captain with the brush-cut hair had actually treated him like an individual.

It was an unusual feeling.

Chapter 9

In combat, man and machine must become one, the machine taking on the man's life and vitality, the man assuming a machine's emotionless and unwavering purpose. There can be no thought of fear.

—*Kokorodo: Discipline of Warriors*
Ieyasu Sutsumi
C.E. 2529

"C-Three, this is Gold Seven," Dev reported. "We're at the crater and moving into position."

"Roger that, Seven. Stand by to copy new orders."

"We're ready, C-Three."

"Transmitting, Seven." Data flickered across Dev's awareness, an illegible muddle of alphanumerics without the necessary decryption codes. He shunted it into the strider's AI.

It was snowing heavily, the wind swirling flakes of mingled ice and frozen CO_2 past the Ghostrider as it moved along the crater rim. It was midmorning, but the thick and leaden overcast kept the tortured landscape under a gloomy, gray-green dusk. Several times Dev had considered switching on the LaG-42's external lights but settled instead on increasing the sensitivity of his optical scanners. There was no need to call any more attention to *High Stepper* than was necessary. The strider's surface nanoflage mimicked the gray-white-brown gloom of the Lokan surroundings. In the snow, at ranges of more than a few tens of meters, the strider was quite difficult to see, a fuzzy, gray ghost.

He wondered if the camouflage made any difference to the Xenos.

"Okay, newbie," Tami Lanier told him. "I'll take it now."

The Ghostrider's commander had been running her own check of the strider's weapons, leaving him to communicate with HEMILCOM C^3 and navigate the strider up the crater slope. Now, though, she was relegating him again to passenger status. He wondered if that was because she didn't trust him.

"Orders just in from C-Three," he said. "I parked them in *Stepper*'s RAM."

"I saw 'em. HEMILCOM probably wants another inspection, full kit, just to impress the Imps." She brought the strider to a halt, overlooking the twenty-meter expanse of snow-covered crater floor. "Keep watch while I see what they want."

"Right, Lieutenant."

Dev panned the twin stereoptic cameras mounted in the chin laser turret housing, scanning his surroundings. To his left, the dome of the Schluter mining facility emerged from its hillside, barely visible through the blowing snow. C^3—militarese for command, control, and communications—was watching over the deployment from there. Straight ahead, well beyond the crater and present only as a shadow behind a curtain of snow, the pyramid of the atmospheric plant rose above the more distant mountains. To his right, a kilometer away, stripping and fractionating towers vanished into the low, churning overcast of the sky.

Few signs of the Xenophobe attack at the Schluter facility remained, except for the crater itself, the tunnel mouth through which the attackers had emerged seven weeks earlier. The facility dome had been repaired, and constructors had cleared away most of the blast-shattered wreckage. Line soldiers, crunchies in gray and black combat armor, were helping to position huge Rogan molds slung from the bellies of lumbering four-legged constructors. Inside the molds, engineering nano was converting rock and dirt into fabricrete, growing defensive walls in position.

The rest of the company's striders were gathered near the dome, but the two recon machines—*High Stepper* and Rudi Carlsson's LaG-42 *Snake Stomper*—had been deployed to the crater rim, where a half dozen Rogan-grown gun towers thrust like teeth from the broken rock, maintaining their robotic vigilance.

The Imperial Marine unit that had relieved the Assassins at the Schluter facility was still at the site, but fresh signs of Xenophobe activity—the ground-transmitted rumblings of movements deep beneath the ground—had been detected, and HEMILCOM had ordered the Assassins to redeploy back to the crater at Schluter to reinforce the marines against the possibility of another Xeno attack.

Dev focused on a squad of Imperial Marines, six hulking Daimyo striders protecting the facility's small landing strip two kilometers away, their surface films jet black even through distance and snow. Those, Dev thought, were the *real* machine-warriors, men trained in the martial art called *kokorodo*—the Way of the Mind—to control their striders with an almost inhuman speed and efficiency. There weren't many of them available, but it was said that their presence alone had turned the tide against a Xeno assault more than once.

He knew he should feel better seeing the Impie Marines close by, but watching the motionless Imperial squad, he could only wonder why, if the Impies were so good, the Assassins had been deployed to Schluter at all.

Dev had joined a few of the late night talk sessions in the Assassins' barracks, even though he was still a newbie and an outsider. The Imperials thought of the Hegemony units as cannon fodder, some of the other 1/5 pilots were saying. After all, why risk highly trained marines and their pretty black machines when the locals were available to blunt the enemy's attack? Strangely, such comments didn't appear to carry any bitterness or anger. Their nature was closer to the inter-service rivalry between navy and army, joking and almost good-natured. Dev was willing to admit that, in his current frame of mind, he couldn't really appreciate the banter.

Why the hell weren't they as scared as he was?

"Right, newbie," Lanier said, interrupting dark thoughts. "Stay alert. HEMILCOM Asgard's called a Class-Two alert. They've tracked a solid DSA, right beneath our feet."

"A Deep Seismic Anomaly? Here?"

"Yup. Looks like the Xenies're coming back for seconds."

It was an eerie sensation, knowing that the Xenos were there, swimming through solid rock a few hundred meters beneath the crater floor, but unreachable, untouchable. Dev and the other newbies had been shown recordings of the Xenophobe attack at the site seven weeks earlier—at just about the same time, he knew now, as the alert that had paralyzed communications during his first day on Loki.

Like so much else about the Xenophobes, exactly how they performed their subsurface movement trick was unknown. It was assumed that they were able to turn rock plastic or even fluid by manipulating it somehow with intense, focused magnetic fields and clouds of nanotechnic tunnelers. In sims, Dev had watched streamlined Xenophobe snake-shapes emerge from the ground, nosing their way up through solid rock turned plastic by a technology humans didn't understand and could not copy.

The rock did not remain plastic after a Xenophobe passed through it, nor was an actual tunnel excavated. However, the rock was certainly weakened by the machine's passage, creating what was known as an SDT, or Subsurface Deformation Track. HEMILCOM theorized that the Xenophobe forces might well use existing SDTs as underground highways. Possibly it took less power to force a path through rock that had been deformed once before. If HEMILCOM was tracking a Deep Seismic Anomaly here, now, it meant the Xenos could be rising toward the surface.

"What are we supposed to be doing out here, Lieutenant?" Dev asked.

"We're a recon strider, newbie. We recon."

"Why the hell don't they just nuke the tunnel mouth and be done with it?"

"Maybe someone's sentimental about Schluter and doesn't want the place incinerated."

"If they know the Xenophobes are coming back, they ought to evacuate it," Dev said. "How many people are here, anyway?"

"Five, maybe six thousand. It's Mitsubishi's biggest ore-processing plant on Loki. I don't think they're going to let it go without a fight."

The argument made no sense to Dev. In seven weeks, surely they could have evacuated six thousand people to Asgard. Which was more important, the people or Mitsubishi's investment?

Numbers again.

"Gold Seven, Gold Seven," Katya Alessandro's voice called over the tacnet. "This is Gold Leader."

"Gold Leader, Gold Seven," Lanier replied. "Go ahead."

"Looks like this might be it. Sensors have a hot spot triangulated at Bravo three-seven, Hotel one-niner. That puts them smack under your feet, Tami. Back off and let the towers take the first rush."

"Don't see anything happening yet," Lanier replied. "It looks dead."

Which is what we'll be if you don't do what Alessandro says and get us out of here, Dev thought. He kept the thought off the ICS, however, and focused his optics on the crater floor. He could almost imagine that he was sensing a deep-down vibration, transmitting itself through the ground and the Ghostrider's legs. He tried lowering his audio range. In Basic he'd learned that it was sometimes possible to detect a Xeno approach through infrasonics—

the low-pitched grumble of rocks yielding far below the surface.

"Gold Seven, we've got a plus five on IR at your coordinates," another voice said. "Local magnetic now at point three gauss, with a flux of point two five. Data feed on Channel Five."

The data from C-Three began scrolling down one side of Dev's visual display. He shifted his own vision to infrared and overlaid it with computer graphics representing the local magnetic field. The ground *was* warmer inside the crater, glowing now in shades of green that contrasted with the blues and purples of the surrounding rock and snow, and there was a vague node of magnetic force in the crater's center.

"Gold Seven, Gold Leader. Suggest you pull back. *Now!*"

"Sounds like a good idea to me, Lieutenant," Dev added. He hoped that his voice didn't sound as scared as he felt. Sometimes cephlinked transmissions could carry a lot more emotion than the sender intended.

"Copy, Gold Leader. There's no danger yet. Maybe I can get off a shot or two when the bastard rears its ugly head."

Damn it, Dev thought. *That's what the gun towers are for! I don't want to be a hero!*

"All units, go to combat alert!" Alessandro's voice barked. "Weapons free!"

"IR at plus six," the emotionless voice of C-Three added. "Centered on Schluter Crater. Mag now at point three-two, flux point three-seven."

"Back off the crater rim, Gold Seven. That's an order!"

"Roger, Gold Leader." Lanier actually sounded disappointed. The Ghostrider turned and, gingerly on the uneven footing, began picking its way back down the crater slope. Dev was certain that he could feel a trembling now underfoot. The gun towers appeared to have come to life, their movements urgent as the muzzles of paired heavy lasers twitched back and forth. "Let us have a visual feed from one of the towers."

"You got it, Gold Seven. Patched in."

A window opened on Dev's field of view, an inset of the crater floor from the vantage point of one of the robot sentry towers.

Something was happening there, but it was becoming harder to see. The snow was melting, vanishing into a swirl of fog obscuring the ground. The continuing data feed from C-Three showed that the crater floor temperature had risen ten degrees Celsius in the last fifteen seconds.

And then something burst through the cloaking fog.

Gravel sprayed into the overcast, like cinders from a volcanic eruption. The fog billowed into the sky as something struck Dev's legs from behind, a savage blow that nearly toppled him. He cursed as he tried to balance himself . . . then realized that his reactions were still out of the circuit. Tami Lanier was in control of the strider, and all he could do was watch as the crater interior exploded in hurtling fragments of rock. Gravel pelted the Ghostrider like hailstones, and the ground continued to lurch underfoot. On the inset picture from the sentry tower, a blunt-nosed worm or snake five meters thick was squeezing out of the ground and into full view.

All six laser towers fired at the same instant, and the clouds above the crater lit blue-white with their reflected glare. Other warstriders were advancing across the valley now, a staggered line rushing to put themselves between the dome and the emerging Xenophobes. *Stepper* and *Snake Stomper*, the other LaG-42, were closest to the eruption. Dev glimpsed Carlsson's strider, blurred and indistinct by its nano film, dropped into a gunfighter's crouch atop the ridge, loosing a salvo of rockets. Explosions masked the crater's center for a thunderous moment. Dev caught a glimpse of a silvery fragment spinning end over end as it arced through the dirty air.

More elongated shapes were forcing their way up through the ground now. Shock waves rippled through the fog, and across those patches of bare rock and gravel Dev could see. It looked as though the ground was writhing.

Then the visibility grew worse. Heavy, white smoke was boiling from the ground, a mist that could have been mistaken for fog except that it had a milky texture that made it seem almost liquid. Almost immediately the outside nano count began to soar.

"Lieutenant!" Dev yelled. "We're picking up nano-D on our hull! Point three-one . . . no, three-two, and rising!"

"I see it." Lanier cut loose with a rocket salvo of her own, sending a rippling barrage of M-22s searing into the crater. Dev saw something like a huge, silver worm shuddering as the LaG-42's volley smashed into it, the detonations flashing and snapping and hurling smoke and dirt into the air. With startling suddenness the Xeno machine's sinuous body changed, lengthening, extruding silvery whiplash tentacles. Dev had seen recordings of Xenos morphing during Basic, but seeing it *this* way was different. This was no AI-simulated graphic, but the real thing, transforming itself from traveler to killer. Dev recognized the new shape—a flattened sphere studded with slender spines and tentacles, a Fer-de-Lance in combat mode. The thing was jet black until a beam from one of the gun towers touched it, and then it flashed silver, scattering light in a rainbow cascade.

"Cameron!" Lanier shouted over the ICS. "Take the chin laser!"

Dev felt the inner chunk of relays slamming home, saw the target reticle for the 100-megawatt laser drop onto his field of view. The lieutenant was now handling both the strider's movement and its left and right weapons pods; Dev had control of the heavy Toshiba Arms laser mounted beneath the Ghostrider's blunt prow.

For several seconds, all was chaos and raw, thundering noise. Dev saw pieces of Xenophobe machine on the ground, most of them inching forward with a horrible, blindly searching life of their own. On either side, other Assassin striders were coming up the ridge in support. Something roughly the size and shape of a beach towel leaped through the air and hit Carlsson's Ghostrider, clinging wetly to the right leg.

Dev stared in horror as the strider's leg began to dissolve, streams of white smoke gushing from visibly enlarging holes in the armor. Large patches of surface film had eroded away as nano disassemblers attacked it. No longer reflecting the colors of the strider's surroundings, the affected areas looked like crumbling patches of rust.

"*Damn* it, Cameron!" his partner yelled against the muddled background of his thoughts. "Shoot! Shoot!"

He stared, unable to find the coded thoughts that would let him engage the Ghostrider's laser. Things seemed to be happening around him in slow motion. Directly in front of him, ten meters away, a disk-shaped head balanced on a slender snake of a neck rose from the smoke.

"Cobra!" Lanier shouted, naming the Xeno machine. "Lase it, Cameron!"

He tried, but the codes, the numbers, would not come. Helplessly Dev watched as the flat head opened lengthwise, exposing a deep groove extending from a hole that gave the machine a sinister, one-eyed look. The opening glowed red, and a stream of high-velocity slugs howled into the Ghostrider's left weapons pod with a sound like tearing sheet metal.

Something slammed into Dev with pile-driver force. The shock surprised him; despite training sessions, feeds, and lectures, he hadn't realized that he would feel the impact of enemy rounds when he was not actually in control of the strider. A second blow struck his side, spinning him partway around. Glancing down, he could see the left Kv-70 pod dangling from the wreckage of its ball-and-socket mount. The pod's upper surface had been opened from front to back, and loops of interior wiring were spilling from the tear, smoking and sparking in the cold air.

"Left arm's gone, Dev!" Lanier called. "Fire, damn you, fire!"

Shifting the focus of his eyes, he brought the targeting reticle into line with that flat, deadly head, willing the main laser to fire, desperate now, still unable to make the thing work. Tami was still firing with the right arm pod, sending a long burst of high-velocity rounds into the rapidly descending horror that appeared to be coming apart even as he watched.

Then the Cobra's main hull slammed into the Ghostrider, sending him toppling over backward in a spray of sand, gravel, and glittering fragments. A three-meter tentacle slashed across the cameras transmitting his visual feed. There was a flash of static, and then his vision was gone.

Gone! Desperately he tried to switch to another camera group on the LaG-42's hull, but the entire visual feed network was down. He could still sense the warstrider's position; he was on his back, a heavy, squirming weight across his chest, but he couldn't see to fight back. A shrill scream filled his mind, going on and on and on for an eternity before he realized that the scream was his.

His hand came off the palm contact, and suddenly he was strapped to a narrow couch in a dark and fear-stinking space, surrounded by metal and feed cables and the lonely amber and green lights of the strider's manual power-up system. His breath came in short, shallow gasps that rasped in his ears through the confines of his helmet. The metal walls reverberated as something hit the strider outside and rocked it to one side. He grabbed for support, his fist striking cold steel.

He slapped his palm back on the contact panel, but nothing happened. Lights winked at him, baleful eyes in the darkness warning of system shutdowns and failing power. The strider shuddered again, with a shriek like that of a damned soul. Dimly, with his ears rather than his mind, he thought he heard a far-off, muffled scream, not his scream this time, but someone else. A woman's scream.

The lieutenant was sealed into the command pod, and he had no way of reaching her. He was trapped, and a Xeno Cobra had them in its deadly embrace.

He had to get out! Out!

Dev tried to interface with the strider AI again, and this time succeeded. The feeling of pressure on his chest and legs was terrible, suffocating, and he still couldn't see.

Words flowed across the emptiness: power was down to twenty-seven percent, left leg hydraulics were gone, massive damage to imaging and control systems, command module dead . . .

Dead! He tried to get more information, tried to open the ICS link, and failed. Either Tami Lanier was dead or the strider's internal communications were completely shot. A red square flashed insistently at the corner of his vision. The Ghostrider's AI was trying to pass control to him.

The darkness enveloping him was more terrifying than the sight of the oncoming Cobra. "Eject sequence!" he commanded. "Code . . . uh . . . red, seven, three . . . *Eject! Eject! Eject!*"

Nothing! Dev didn't know whether the failure was in the eject sequence or in him. Breaking the linkage, he woke again to the darkness of the pilot's module. Groping above his head, he found the manual controls, flipped up a guard shield, and grasped the ejection handle inside its recess.

He twisted it to the right. A thunderclap of sound and pressure battered Dev into unconsciousness.

Chapter 10

. . . it is left to war itself to strip the mask from the man of straw, which it will do with a quite ruthless precision of its own.

—*The Anatomy of Courage*
Lord Moran
mid-twentieth century

Katya spoke up for Dev at the inquest, but there was very little that she could do. The young Terran was doomed from the very start.

The review board included her, as Dev's company commander; her own 1st Platoon Leader, *Chu-i* Victor Hagan; the Thorhammers' CO, *Taisa* Gustav Varney; commanding officer of the Midgard Training Command, *Shosa* Karl Rassmussen; and an Imperial, the Adept Ieyasu Sutsumi. They sat behind a long table covered by a green cloth, while Cameron, still looking somewhat dazed, stood before them and answered their questions.

Sutsumi was not, strictly speaking, a military man, nor was the inquest a court-martial. The Imperial Adept—he was addressed by the title *Sensei*—was a master of the mind-control art called *kokorodo*. He'd designed several of the AI routines that oversaw the training of Hegemony recruits in managing implanted links. Rather than trying to punish Devis Cameron, it was the board's duty to review his case and determine whether or not he could be of any further use to the Hegemony strider forces, and *Sensei* Sutsumi was present as an expert in neopsychometrics. He'd been asked to come down from Asgard and attend the inquest because the young striderjack's problems appeared to be primarily psychological.

"Did you ever have trouble accessing weapons codes during your training?" Karl Rassmussen asked.

"No, sir," Dev replied. His voice was, not cold, exactly, but distant, almost as though he didn't care what was happening to him anymore.

As the questioning continued, Katya remembered the look on his face when she'd told him that once, years before, she'd been a starpilot, too.

New America was a raw frontier world, so new that it didn't even have a sky-el yet. Like Lung Chi, 26 Draconis IV had already developed an ecosystem of its own when human explorers first discovered it in the early 2400s. All that it had needed was a slight decrease in the atmospheric CO_2 and the genetic tailoring of several microbion species to help the native life adjust to the change.

Life in the young colony was hard; modern equipment and industrial nanomolds were hard to come by, the costs of shipping, say, farm machinery from Earth prohibitive.

Katya, the third daughter of a Greek-American father and a Ukrainian mother, had grown up hating that farm. Attending New America's only technic university, at Jefferson, she'd mortgaged her expected income over the next eight years for a three-socket implant; her first job had been as a panel rigger aboard New America's single tiny space station.

From there, however, she'd managed to get better slots, first as shuttle transport pilot, then crewing aboard the *Golden Aphrodite*, the fifty-meter interstellar yacht belonging to Prestis Chadwick, one of the major shareholders in the New American Corporation, and a vice-president of the colony's local branch of Bank Nakasone-America.

She hadn't cared for life among the New American elite, not when keeping that job demanded hours and activities not listed in her job description. At her first opportunity, she'd tendered her resignation and visited the Hegemony service recruiter in Jefferson. With her experience jacking the *Aphrodite*, she'd been immediately slotted into interstellar transports.

Starting as reserve helm aboard the 12,000-ton *Kosen Maru*, she'd swiftly worked her way up to first pilot on a monster I-4K, the 1,900,000-ton *Kaibutsu Maru*. She'd paid off her socket loan in two years, after just one New-America-to-Earth-and-back run.

During that whole time, there'd been no indication at all that she had a TM rating of point three.

Much later, she figured out what must have happened. Working conditions aboard the *Aphrodite* had been unsettling enough, unpleasant enough, that her emotions had overshadowed some of her MSE responses.

In fact, she'd been very nearly emotionally dead when she tested for her slot with the service. Maybe someone in the evaluations section had been sloppy. Maybe the scores themselves didn't matter as much as the way they were interpreted. But Katya was glorying in the raw power and wonder of the godsea, guiding her lumbering charge through the swirling blue currents that ViRsimulated the interface between normal four-space and the Quantum Sea, the K-T Plenum.

Katya knew exactly what Devis Cameron had experienced there, where energy came into existence from nothing, free for the taking, where the reality of fourspace became a fragile bubble adrift on an unimagined, unimaginable flux of quantum energy. It was so easy to ride that feeling of invincibility, to stretch the odds and take that extra chance, riding on the edge of the godsea tide. . . .

A quantum flux shunt circuit had burned out as the *Kaibutsu Maru* rode the blue currents between Sol and 26 Draconis. She'd felt the power levels fluctuating, felt her control slipping, but had *known* she could ride the crest and maintain control.

An entire damper rack had burned out, and *Kaibutsu*'s AI had jettisoned the starboard engine seconds before a power cascade had transformed five thousand tons of complex technology into starcore-hot plasma. The *Kaibutsu* had dropped out of the K-T Plenum, power systems dead, drives fused, the freighter ten light-years from home.

Still linked, Katya had stared into a star-dusted immensity, Blackness Absolute, an emptiness that she'd never had to cope with before. She'd viewed space directly, of course, aboard the space station and every time she'd maneuvered *Aphrodite* or one of her cargo haulers into or out of orbit. Always before, though, there'd been sun and planet filling part of the sky, convenient anchors that gave her particular location in space an identity, an address, with light enough to keep those lonely stars at bay.

This, however, was something completely different. Through the starship's senses, she'd seen nothing but stars and the faint frost-dusting of the Milky Way describing an unimaginably vast circle about the sky. For a horrible moment—it might have been seconds or hours or days—she'd felt as if she were falling into that horror of emptiness, and all the while the Dark was closing in. . . .

Their rescue had been a million-to-one shot. Ships could be detected within the godsea by the pulse-regular interference patterns their passage left against the random noise of the quantum energy fluctuations, a kind of orderly wake against chaos. The watchstanders of another ship, the free trader *Andrew St. James*, noticed when the *Kaibutsu*'s wake vanished. They logged the incident and reported it to New American space traffic control when they arrived at 26 Draconis ten days later. The Imperial destroyer *Asagiri* dropped into fourspace and picked up *Kaibutsu*'s distress beacon two weeks after that, while quartering the area with a small fleet of search and rescue vessels.

Katya had spent another week in the hospital. There'd been talk about psychoreconstruction and deliberate, selective amnesia. She'd been subjected to a hell of a shock, and dumping some of those memories might be the only way she'd be able to face the world again.

But she'd fought back.

She'd told Dev the truth that day in her office. Everyone had expected her to quit the service and go back to the farm.

Katya had refused, choosing instead to transfer to the infantry. With three sockets and experience jacking starships, she'd been accepted into the 2nd New American Minutemen.

Six months later, the Minutemen had been transferred. The Hegemony had a policy—one encouraged by the Imperials—of not letting a military unit remain too long attached to one world, a way of preventing too great an attachment between soldiers and civilians. Besides, Xenophobes had appeared on 36 Ophiuchi C II—Loki—and the Empire wanted to reinforce the local forces. The 2nd New American Minutemen became the 5th Loki Thorhammers, arriving just in time to take part in the campaign at Jotunheim.

Katya had been happy since, working up through the ranks, first to platoon leader, then to company commander just six months earlier. But she still remembered her unshielded look at the stars, enough that she was glad the nights on Loki were always cloudy.

And she still hated the dark.

She became aware that someone had spoken her name.

"I beg your pardon?"

Varney looked at Katya, one eyebrow creeping higher on his forehead. "I asked if there was anything you had to add in this case, Captain Alessandro."

She paused, gathering her thoughts, retracing her memories of the proceedings so far. "Yes, Colonel. I'd like to remind the board that even if Cadet Cameron had been able to lock and fire, the outcome would not have been different. As you know very well, LaG-42 Ghostriders are no match for Cobras in combat mode. If anything, the fault was mine.

Those two light striders should not have been so close to the tunnel mouth."

"According to the action debriefs," Varney said, "you had already twice ordered Lieutenant Lanier's strider back off the crater rim. The other Ghostrider, commanded by Lieutenant Carlsson, did manage to escape, did it not?"

"*Stomper* sustained considerable damage, sir. But yes. Rudi managed to get clear. The rest of the company came up in support and destroyed both the Cobra and the Gamma attacking Rudi's machine."

"Cadet Cameron?" Varney said. "Is there anything you'd like to add to the record?"

"I have no excuse, sir." His eyes locked with Katya's. His voice sounded dead. "I screwed up. I'm sorry."

"I remind you, Cadet, that we're not here to judge you. I tend to agree with Captain Alessandro that the outcome would have been the same in regard to Lieutenant Lanier's death even if you'd been able to access your weapons. In fact, you would almost certainly have died as well if you'd tried to fight the Cobra, rather than ejecting as you did. Once you discovered that you could not control your warstrider's systems, you acted correctly.

"But it is not the correctness of your actions that we are discussing here. Sensei? Can you add anything?"

"Yes," the Japanese Adept said. He was an old man, though the age resided more in and around his eyes than in wrinkled skin or sagging features. "If you would each palm your interface?" Katya laid her palm on the 'face panel in the table in front of her. Data began scrolling past her mind's eye, as Sutsumi discussed the findings point by point.

"I have reviewed Cadet Cameron's latest battery of tests. Rather than the technomegalomania rating that he exhibited before, he now seems to show a distinct tendency toward technophobia, point one, up from point zero two. His insecurity index is up three points, and that is coupled with a growing sense of persecution and an innate distrust of those in authority. I would guess that he feels as though his life is no longer his, that those in authority over him are arbitrarily interfering with it. Note, particularly, ambivalent feelings toward his father, pride and admiration on one hand, disappointment and a sense of being manipulated on the other. . . ."

Katya listened with growing embarrassment as the psychometrician continued to list his findings with a bluntness that seemed to assume that the subject of his analysis was not even in the room.

"It seems apparent," Sutsumi concluded, "that Cadet Cameron has extreme difficulty concentrating under stress, that while he operates well under simulated conditions of reality, he may always, ah, 'freeze up,' in the vernacular, when faced with severe stress and the need to access data through his implanted linkage. He may now fear cephlinkage. He certainly feels alienation, persecution, and mistrust for authority figures. I, for one, would hesitate to allow him to link again, in any capacity."

"Cadet Cameron? What do you have to say to that?"

Dev looked tired, so tired it seemed he might sway forward and collapse on the floor before them. Though his chair had a 'face pad on one arm, he'd not bothered palming it when Sutsumi had reviewed his test results.

"I have nothing else to say, Colonel," he said. "I guess this pretty much finishes me, huh?"

"That remains to be seen." But Varney did not sound confident.

The final vote was three to two, with Katya and Senior Lieutenant Hagan in the minority. The decision was to transfer Dev to the leg infantry rather than risk another incident with him linked to a warstrider. He would be assigned to the Second Regiment of the Ulvenvakt, the Wolfguard, stationed at Midgard. If possible, a noncombat position would be found for him. Varney suggested the regimental motor pool. He'd been good working on the silicarb-slicked guts of warstriders.

Dev Cameron accepted the verdict without expression, though his face was very pale. What's he thinking? Katya wondered.

She was confused by her own reaction, her hurt and her sense of loss. Tami Lanier had been a friend, and she'd died a nightmare death when the Xenophobe had eaten through the armor surrounding her module and gotten to her before she could eject. Katya had been furiously angry with the man who'd panicked and ejected and left her to die alone.

Now, though, her anger had drained away. It was, she supposed, one of her failings, this concern for the strays and the orphans. Maybe Dev Cameron had nudged her mother's instinct; maybe it was the shared memory of the godsea, the blue light that held the Dark at arm's length.

Or maybe—she forced herself to look at the possibility—maybe she genuinely liked the guy and wanted him to succeed.

She caught him in the passageway outside, shortly after the inquiry was closed. "Dev? Are you okay?"

He looked at her without expression.

"Look, Dev. It's not over yet. I can still—"

"Forget it, Captain. I don't want your help."

"But—"

"I said forget it!" She glimpsed for a moment something behind his eyes, something dark and a little frightening. "I'm tired of fighting. Whatever you people want to do with me, that's fine."

You people. Suddenly he seemed so very much alone. "What will you do? What do you *want* to do?"

The word grated. "Survive."

Chapter 11

The sergeant came right down the line, he looked at us and swore,
A sorrier bunch of rag-assed scuts he'd never seen before.
He said we'd never make it and he said it was a shame,
But at the fight at Morgan's Hold, by God we won our name.

—"The Ballad of Morgan's Hold"
Popular military folk song
C.E. 2518

Dev sat on the thinly padded seat in the low-ceilinged, red-lit chamber, surrounded by other combat-armored troops. The chamber lurched and swayed with a gentle, rhythmic motion set in time to the muffled hiss, creak, and thump of enormous leg drivers.

"Man oh man, you hear the latest who-was?" Leading Private Hadley clung to the barrel of the Interdynamics PCR-28 wedged between his knees, a 4-mm high-velocity rifle with a stock magazine holding two hundred caseless, armor-piercing rounds. "The Xenies popped up today a hundred klicks from Midgard!"

"Suck methane, Had." A hard-looking woman opposite

Hadley grinned. "Ain't no Xenos within a thousand klicks of the place. Unless we count your brain."

Dev leaned back in his seat and joined the answering chorus of chuckles and catcalls. Who-was—a corruption of the Nihongo word for rumor—was, as ever, among the enlisted man's favorite pastimes, the topics monotonously predictable. *Where are we going? When are we leaving? What's happening in the world beyond our own tight circle?*

There were twelve of them, Third Squad, First Platoon, Bravo Company of the Second Ulvenvakt Regiment. The platoon's first, second, and fourth squads were packed away in separate chambers within the huge VbH Zo Armored Personnel Walker's belly. The Zo—the word was Nihongo for elephant—had a swaying, four-legged gait, uncomfortable, but far smoother than those of any wheeled or tracked vehicle covering rough terrain at fifty kilometers per hour.

His transfer to the Ulvenvakt's motor pool as a techie had lasted for just one week. He'd requested the assignment to a combat unit, for reasons that were only now becoming clear. Bravo Company had been only too glad to get him. Few of the men and women in the leg infantry had three-socket hardware, and C-sockets were necessary for jacking plasma guns.

Dev clung to his helmet and the long, complex bulk of his plasma gun and looked from face to face, studying his new companions, his *kamerats* as the native Lokans in the group called it. Fully armored except for helmets that they cradled in their laps, they sat in two rows of six facing one another, each trooper pressed against the legs and shoulders of the soldier to either side. Their faces showed a gamut of emotions, from fear to excitement to boredom to outright unconsciousness; two of his new squad mates were taking advantage of the experienced soldier's ability to sleep anywhere and anytime to catch up on some sack time.

The most common expression, Dev decided, visible on six of the eleven faces around him, was boredom, feigned or real, he couldn't tell. Two, Kulovskovic and Dahlke, looked excited, while one young man, Willis Falk, looked genuinely frightened.

Dev tried to analyze his own feelings. Fear, certainly, but excitement as well. And boredom. Mostly he wished they could get on with what had to be done. This tiny, steel-lined compartment would have been hell for a claustrophobe.

He took a deep breath of air tasting of oil, sweat, metal, and fear. It was strange. After four weeks, he felt more at ease, more at home, with the Wolfguard than he'd felt at any of his previous duty assignments. He'd been quickly accepted by the others in Bravo Company, by browns and greens alike. Browns were combat veterans, so-called for their khaki uniforms. The greens, who also wore khaki but were "green" by virtue of their lack of experience, were the trainees assigned to the company to complete their training and military indoctrination, newbies who would stay newbies until their first combat.

His position in this regard was unique; he'd been in combat—once—but he hadn't been in combat with the members of Bravo Company. As a result, he would be a green until he proved himself, but he already enjoyed a greater degree of acceptance among the company's old hands. The fact that he'd goked his one and only firefight seemed to matter not at all. *Everybody* screwed up their first time in combat, or so the old hands told him. He'd *been* there, and that was what counted.

For his part, Dev found the transfer carried with it a sense of profound relief. For two months, every part of his awareness had been focused on two primary concerns: Could he somehow manage to wangle a transfer to the navy, and could he survive the regimentation of Basic and avoid ending up as a legger?

He would never get his slot aboard a ship. He knew that now. Not only was his TM rating a problem, but the way he'd failed in harness when that Cobra had attacked had convinced him, once and for all, that he did not have what it took—call it discipline, the right stuff, grit, whatever—to jack a mobile canteen from Towerdown to Tristankuppel, much less a starship through the godsea.

And now he *was* a legger—though he'd quickly learned that his new comrades never referred to themselves by that name. Now that the raw and panicky edge of anticipation was gone, he was finding that life in the infantry was not nearly so bad as he'd imagined it. The striving for perfection, mental and physical, was over. He was a *nito hei*, a second-class private, and he was content. For the most part, Dev's daily routine had fallen into the eternally grumbling hurry-and-wait and make-work routines of the combat infantryman, a constant at least since the time of Sargon the Great. If he wasn't *happy*, at least Dev was at peace for the first time since his arrival on Loki.

Fear remained, of course, and guilt. He'd watched as they'd pulled Tami Lanier's body from the wreckage of the *High Stepper*. Not much had been left—her upper torso, some scraps of clothing and bone, part of one leg fused with the padding of her couch; a piece of the Xeno had eaten its way into her compartment and turned most of her into smoke.

The shock of what had happened had so numbed him that he'd not even been able to speak in his own defense at the inquest. The facts—and the data downloaded from his own RAM—had spoken for themselves. Even after three weeks, it was still hard to remember the sight and the smell without gagging.

He'd reached a point where, intellectually at least, he did not blame himself for Lanier's death, but the knowledge that he'd panicked and abandoned her to a hideous death, then ended up safe and secure in a stridertink techie platoon, was simply too much to face. Even knowing that he couldn't have done a thing to save her didn't help.

Only after volunteering for combat had the guilt been appeased somewhat. Somehow, accepting his worst fears had helped exorcise Lanier's ghost.

Someone forward was humming something, a familiar tune. Dev tried to remember the words.

The who-was had been flying about the barracks for two days. A major Xeno breakout had occurred, it was said, somewhere to the north of Midgard. An attempt to stop them by another Lokan strider regiment, the Odinspears, had been brushed aside. The Xenos were said to be heading for Midgard and the sky-el, and attempts to hit them with heavily armed ascraft and hastily assembled strider teams had all failed. A series of defensive positions was being thrown up in the Xenophobes' path. Farthest north, twenty kilometers from Asgard, was the Norway Line, supported by an airfield and nano manufacturing center called Norway Base. Ten klicks south of that was the Sweden Line. And behind that were the defenses at Midgard itself.

The big question, of course, was why foot soldiers were being thrown into it. So far, there'd been little use for leg infantry in a war that required the strength, speed, and firepower of warstriders.

Superior Private Lipinsky, a pretty, dark-haired girl, started singing the song aloud. By the second line, half of the men and women in the compartment had joined her.

The Xenos came from underground, they swarmed toward Argos town.
By God the plain was black with them, and Nagai had withdrawn.
But Morgan called us to his side, Hegemon infantry
And let us choose to stand and die, or choose instead to flee.

"The Ballad of Morgan's Hold." That was the name of it. He'd heard it a time or two before during Basic, though no striderjack would ever have sung the thing. Dev noticed that Falk, wide-eyed and with sweat beading his forehead, was singing along.

Morgan's Hold was a battle fought against the Xenos years before, on Herakles. The third planet of Mu Herculis had been the site of a terraforming colony for three centuries. A Xenophobe incursion in 2515 had wiped out several outlying settlements and a nearby atmosphere plant. At that time, the Xenophobe menace was still new, and few worlds of the Shichiju had the troops or equipment to make a serious attempt at stopping them. The only military forces on Herakles were an Imperial Marine battalion and two companies of the 62nd Hegemony Infantry, foot soldiers from Earth tasked with keeping order in the panicked planetary capital of Argos.

As the song told it, the warstriders withdrew before the battle, loading their heavy equipment onto the sky-el and shuttling up to synchorbit, leaving the colony on its own. Their commander, a Colonel Nagai, had ordered the foot soldiers under Captain David Morgan to withdraw as well.

But Morgan and most of his men had refused the order, electing instead to stand and fight.

We disobeyed our orders when they said to sound retreat
And Morgan laughed and said "My God, we'll see who's the elite!"
For fighting steel had broken faith, the samurai had fled.
But Morgan's men defied Nagai, they stood and fought and bled.

Argos was a classic infantry holding action against superior numbers. Three hundred eighty-eight infantrymen had dug in on Mount Athos at the peninsula's base and waited for the enemy to come to them.

Warstriders did not make that stand, it was the infantry
Who stood and fought and died and paid the price of mutiny.
We took our stand on Argos Hill, four hundred fighting men.
And when the smoke had cleared away, sixteen walked down again.

Morgan's Hold had taken its place in the annals of military history next to Thermopylae and the Alamo. For two bloody weeks the men and women of the 62nd held out against wave upon wave of Xenophobe Alphas and Gammas surging toward Argos. Though a few Xenophobes did break out inside the capital toward the end, the defenders bought precious time for the city to complete its evacuation. At the end of the siege, the last sixteen of Morgan's unwounded men departed up the sky-el, the last humans to leave Herakles. An hour later, the 500-megaton thermonuclear device they'd left behind vaporized Argos and kept the Xenophobes from following them to synchorbit.

Morgan had died on the third day.

At golden Tenno Kyuden they cannot begin to see
That honor's price is paid in full while glory can be free.
So give a cheer for Morgan's crew, the God-damned infantry,
The men who fought the Xenophobes, the grunts like you and me.

Hegemony Command did not approve of the "Ballad of Morgan's Hold." It rubbed the Japanese the wrong way, reminding them of their part at Herakles. There were plenty of horror stories floating around of men and whole Hegemony units disciplined for singing it, or even for possessing a recording in their personal RAM.

But soldiers from the beginning of history considered it a God-given right to grumble at those higher up the ladder. Perhaps because they knew that troops needed to have some outlet for their frustrations, most small unit commanders turned a deaf ear. Twenty-five years after the battle it recalled, "Morgan's Hold" continued to enjoy an underground popularity quite out of proportion to any musical virtue it might have had.

The deck of the APW jolted with a rapid-fire string of concussions. "That's thirty mike-mike AC," a dirty-looking private said from the rear of the compartment. He looked up toward the compartment's low ceiling. "Dorsal turret's got a target."

The APW was a boxy, headless beast with a flat turret mounted on its dorsal surface. If the turret's 30-mm autocannon was firing, the enemy must be damned close. For a long moment, every person in the squad sat deathly still, straining to hear past the thud of the cannon. Dev desperately wished he could see. The lack of jack connections in this primitive vehicle was going to drive him crazy yet.

There was a clatter from the front of the compartment, and *Socho* Gunnar Anderson, the platoon sergeant, dropped down the ladder, bulky in his armor and combat harness. "Listen up, people!" He had to yell to be heard above the thunder of the cannon. "We've reached our assigned area on the Norway Line. Prepared positions have been established along the crest of a ridge. When the ramp goes down, you will move to those positions, take cover, and engage the enemy on your front. Take time now to check your weapons and gear." He then repeated his instructions in Norsk-Lokan.

Dev lifted his Mark XIV plasma gun and slipped the pintle into the steadimount socket at his right hip and locked it home. The heavy weapon floated in front of him, muzzle up, its weight taken up by the complex harness Dev wore over his armor.

"Hey, Strider-man," Superior Private Rosen said from the seat opposite his. "Hope you're better jacking that thing than you were striders!"

The others laughed, and Dev managed a good-natured grin. Anyone with three sockets was assumed to have failed with either striders or the navy. Three-jackers, as they were known, were usually assigned the squad's heavy, link-adapted weapons like the Mark XIV.

"Don't forget to keep monitoring your nano count," Anderson told them. He held up a small gray canister in one gauntleted hand. "If you get hit, remember your AND canisters. They contain a counter-nano agent. Use it fast enough and you'll save yourself the muss and fuss of a breached suit."

There was another, heavier jolt, then silence. "We've

stopped moving," Falk said, staring at the ceiling. "We've stopped moving, guys!"

"Easy, kid," Lipinsky said. "There's plenty of 'Phobes to go around."

"Okay, people," Anderson continued. "Welcome to Norway Base. Helmets on!"

With a clattering sound, the troopers donned their helmets, sliding them over their heads, sealing the gorget assemblies to their cuirass locking rings. Dev made sure the helmet's internal jack was snapped home into his right T-socket.

"Communications check," Anderson said, his voice even louder now inside Dev's helmet. "Squad, by the numbers, sound off!"

One by one, each trooper called off his number.

Then, "Stand up!"

As he rose, Dev felt a peculiar sinking feeling, as though he were descending in an elevator. The APW was lowering its body to the ground. He adjusted his Mark XIV's harness; even in Loki's .8 g gravity, the weapon weighed over eight and a half kilos, and his armor added another fifteen. He felt awkward and clumsy.

"Every man, check your neighbor!"

Dev studied the readouts on Rosen's chest panel, as Rosen studied his. Combat Armor served as a full environmental suit, with life support for up to eight hours. The readouts showed suit systems readiness and the condition of the wearer. All green. He gave Rosen a thumbs up and received one in return. He could see Rosen grinning at him through his helmet visor. "You'll do okay, Strider," the brown said over the squad net.

Two troopers clashed gauntlets, a noisy high-five. "Let's odie!" someone else called. *Odie* was soldier's slang, twisted from the Nihongo word for "dance." Morale was high, the troops ready to go.

Movement stopped, and a warning light on the ceiling winked red. A section of the deck split open, admitting a swirl of cold and dusty air. Dev caught a glimpse of snow-covered ground below as the ramp lowered itself from the walker's belly.

"Squad!" Anderson called. "Let's hit it!"

In a rush, the two men in the rear of the compartment pounded down the ramp and into the dusty light. The rest followed after, two tight columns filing down the ramp and into the light.

It seemed bright outside, though the sky was the usual dirty gray overcast of Loki. Norway Base was little more than a newly grown landing pad and a few RoProcess huts and storage buildings. Directly in front of him, the Norway Line stretched along the crest of the ridge like the walls and towers of some medieval fortress. The Rogan process allowed combat nangineers to grow fabricrete structures in a matter of hours wherever there was a plentiful supply of stone and dirt. Jogging across uneven ground toward the wall, Dev had a blurred impression of men, of vehicles and heavy machinery, of swirling confusion.

Crack-*thud!*

The ground lurched beneath his feet, nearly throwing him. Smoke boiled into the sky from the far side of the ridge. The squad reached the shelter of a two-meter-tall Rogan wall near the crest of the ridge and dropped to the ground. Behind them, their hulking APW rose on tree-trunk legs, its turret sweeping back and forth in quick, nervous jerks. A laser tower twenty meters to their right shifted, then fired at some unseen enemy toward the north with an eye-searing flash.

Crack-*thud!*

"Steady, people," Anderson's voice said, cool and unhurried. "Those're ours. They're calling in railgun packages on 'em from orbit."

That was reassuring . . . and frightening. With Loki's cloud cover, lasers and most other orbital weapons were useless, but spotter drones could call in railgun fire with pinpoint accuracy. The crack he'd heard was the sonic boom of a high-velocity artificial meteor piercing the atmosphere from almost straight overhead; the thud was the concussion as the meteor liberated its considerable payload of kinetic energy into the planet's crust.

But the barrage sounded awfully close.

Crack-*thud!*

"God damn!" an unidentified voice said over the tactical frequency. "Where are the goking striders?"

"Morgan's Hold!" another voice called. "The bastards're pulling a Morgan's Hold on us!"

"Okay, okay, people," Anderson snapped. "Can the comments. Lock and load."

Dev's external mike picked up the harsh clatter and snick of weapons as full magazines were snapped home, as charging levers were pulled, chambering rounds. He checked the play of his weapon in the steadimount, then pulled a cable from the weapon's side and jacked it into his helmet's external socket. Static flickered in his brain, then cleared, leaving red-glowing cross hairs superimposed on his vision.

Suddenly the ground struck him and he was on his back. He didn't hear an explosion, though he assumed there must have been one, because he was half-buried by dirt and gravel and shattered chunks of fabricrete.

"Xenos!" someone screamed over the tacnet. "Xenos! They're coming through the wall!"

Chapter 12

Squad Support Plasma Guns, SSPGs, fire slivers of cobalt, vaporized, stripped of electrons, and ejected by an intense magfield as finger-sized bolts of plasma, hot as the core of a sun. Cyclic rates are variable, ranging up to five hundred rounds per minute. Unfortunately, the gun is bulky enough that a level-two linkage is necessary to handle the targeting feedback, limiting its use to gunners with appropriate hardware.

—*Modern Military Hardware*
HEMILCOM Military ViRdocumentary
C.E. 2537

Dev lay on his back, half-buried in mud and rubble. A black, churning pillar of smoke mushroomed from the far side of the wall, the crown unfolding toward the overcast zenith like the mushroom of a nuclear detonation. His first thought was that the Xenos were using nukes, something they'd never done before. His second was that something had gone wrong, that Asgard had accidentally dropped a railgun load too close to the Wolfguard position.

Friendly fire or hostile, it didn't matter much. *Something* was pushing through the wall three meters in front of him, something with a surface like quicksilver, flowing over the splintered remnants of the RoPro wall, dissolving solid fabricrete in currents of milky white fog. It slapped a flattened pseudopod across Hadley's back, and Dev heard the man scream in sudden, wild panic.

Dev dragged his plasma gun around, swinging the muzzle until the glowing reticle in his vision centered on what seemed to be the silvershifter's center of mass as it bulked its way through the hole in the wall. His right hand squeezed the trigger grip, sending white fire blazing into the Xeno.

Each burst of plasma flame left a dancing trail of purple spots on Dev's retinas, despite the automatic polarization of his visor. Under that deadly barrage, the Xeno machine twisted, form morphing into monstrous form as it tried to escape that searing hellfire.

It was an awkward shot from a sprawled, seated position, but the stream of fire convulsed the Gamma's body, splattering droplets of molten metal. The pseudopod released the struggling trooper, lashing the air. Then the life seemed to drain from the thing and it literally fell apart, pieces of smoking slag hitting the snow and mud with a sputtering hiss.

"Nice shooting, Cameron!" Dahlke said.

"Way to go, Strider-man!" Rosen added.

The thing's surface was blackening, dissolving as he watched, its edges curling away in streamers of heavy white smoke. Someone sprayed the back of Hadley's armor with an AND aerosol canister, hosing down the crinkled scar on the ceramic surface with anti-nano; the nano-D count was high, point twenty-eight, and seemed to be coming from the disintegrating Gamma.

"C'mon, c'mon, people!" Anderson bellowed. "Clear the hot spot!"

The squad shifted right, following the wall in single file, moving away from the nano-D-contaminated area at a slow jog. The wall was too high for Dev to see beyond it to the north, but elsewhere, the landscape was a crawling confusion of men and machines.

There was furious activity everywhere. Troops manned weapons behind RoPro walls, moved about Norway Base in platoon-sized bands, or spilled down the ramps of four-legged APWs. Lightly armored hovercraft shrieked along on wakes of splattering mud and snow. On the towers, the twin barrels of heavy robotic lasers dipped and turned and flashed. It looked as if the whole Wolfguard regiment—eighteen hundred men in all—had been deployed along this section of wall.

"Gok, Sarge, where are the striders?" Lipinsky called. "What're they thinking of, throwing light infantry against Xenos?"

"Can it, Lipinsky," Anderson replied. "You got your flamer. Use it."

"Yeah, and if we run into a stalker?"

"Striders're on the way," Anderson replied. "If you want to live long enough to see 'em, keep the damned Xenos off this hill!"

Lipinsky had a point. The squad was armed with a collection of light weapons, from combat rifles to the barely man-portable SSPGs carried by Dev and a big-shouldered trooper named Bronson. Lipinsky and Rosen had been issued Taimatsu Type-21s, squat, large-bored weapons that the troops called flamers.

Mark XIVs and flamers *might* be able to damage a Xenophobe Alpha—with luck and concentrated fire—but throwing infantry against stalkers made as much sense as throwing them against warstriders, an exchange of many men for a few machines, a shocking waste of good infantry.

Dev flinched from the thought. The idea of meeting a Xeno Alpha face-to-face without the relative safety of forty centimeters of nanofilmed durasheath and ceramic armor surrounding him was horrific, conjuring the memory of Tami Lanier's body in the pilot's module of her half-eaten Ghostrider. It conjured, too, Phil Castellano's bitterness, his insistence that the brass simply didn't care for the enlisted men and combat-rank officers.

"Spread out, people!" Anderson yelled, gesturing with an armored hand. "Take your positions!"

They'd reached a low point along the wall. Swiftly they fanned out, leaning their weapons across the gray-white parapets. For the first time, Dev had a clear look at the terrain to the north, across a stretch of flat valley to another snow-patched ridgeline two kilometers away. Black pillars of smoke churned skyward from hundred-meter craters scattered across the landscape, and everywhere, everywhere, the ground was *crawling*, as though it had taken on a life of its own. Lasers and plasma gun bolts were striking and flashing at hundreds of Xenophobe Gammas, raising gouts of earth and vaporizing snow in swirling puffs of steam. Dev saw no Alphas or Betas anywhere, only the small and slithering Gammas, fragments of quicksilver and tar. The orbital bombardment and the steady barrage from the robot laser towers, Dev reasoned, must have shattered all of the Alphas.

Good. Gammas were deadly up close and they attacked in huge numbers, but infantry, which also relied on numbers, stood a better chance against them than did warstriders. He locked on to a meter-long crumpled-rag shape crawling up the ridge twenty meters downslope and loosed a burst of plasma flame. Gleaming metal exploded in quicksilver gobbets that steamed when they hit the mud.

Fire swept the slope from the entire length of the Norway Line wall, burning down the advancing Xenos. Dev tracked left, acquired another target, then loosed a stream of bolts that tore the Gamma into hurtling flecks of liquid metal.

The valley flashed and glowed in the actinic glare of manmade lightnings. Fires were impossible in the oxygen-poor atmosphere, but wrecked and half-melted Gammas lay smoldering everywhere on the ground.

Dev glimpsed movement on the far ridge. A touch of a button set into his left forearm dropped foam-padded eyepieces over his eyes. Leaning into the helmet optics, he engaged the telescopic zoom. Movement became distinct shapes moving across the crest of the ridge on amorphous, shapeshifting legs.

He recognized the combat mode of a Mamba, a Fer-de-Lance, a Copperhead, the weaving neck of a King Cobra.

Alpha stalkers. But it would take some time for them to cross the two-kilometer valley. Dev raised his optics out of the way. The Gammas close at hand were a more urgent problem.

"The striders!" someone yelled. Dev thought the voice was Falk's. "Here come the striders!"

Four ascraft were drifting out of the sky above Norway Base, blunt-nosed Stormwinds with stubby wings and Y-tail stabilizers. His external mikes caught the shrill whine of approaching fusion jet intakes. God, HEMILCOM couldn't have cut things much closer than that. The Alphas were well into the valley now, and more hulking shapes were silhouetted against the far skyline. Dev dropped his attention back to the killing ground to the north, frying a meter-long fragment that was humping toward him like a demented inchworm.

Somebody was shouting over Dev's helmet phones, but he couldn't make out the words. Static induced by the Xenophobe magnetics was so bad, Dev could scarcely hear the hiss and thunderclap of the big tower lasers, or the volleyed clatter of automatic rifle fire. Bolts of living flame keened overhead, deafening, filling the air with mind-numbing thunder, a sheer, elemental violence so raw that movement, that thought itself, was all but impossible.

Most of thc Gammas were dead. The human forces were winning! The line was holding! If the striders could deal with the advancing Alphas . . .

Behind him, all four Stormwinds were on the base landing pad, each releasing its cargo of warstriders, then lifting again in a swirl of dust and steam. Dev wondered which unit it was. The striders were anonymous in their reflective nanoflage, but the blue and white markings on the ascraft looked like those of the Thorhammers. Dev wondered if Katya was down there.

"Attention, First Platoon!" Anderson snapped, his voice carried over the laser tacnet. "By squads, fall back to Norway Base! One and Three, lay down cover! Two and Four, move out!"

Dev had never heard such warm and welcome words. When the big boys arrived, leg infantry was best pulled back and kept out of the way. Dev stayed where he was as half of the platoon moved back from the wall and started slipping and sliding back down the south slope of the ridge toward the base and the waiting APWs.

A Gamma as large as a groundcar was gliding up the north face of the ridge faster than a man could walk, flowing like a rippling, living blanket. Sergeant Anderson raised his laser rifle and fired into the shape, and Dev brought his SSPG up to assist.

An orange line of fire pierced the clouds and struck in the valley, a piece of star suddenly released. Dev stared into the expanding fireball, then realized he could see nothing at all as his helmet visor's polarizers cut in. A heartbeat later there was a shock like a full-speed collision with a RoPro wall, and he was lying on his face in the mud ten meters down the slope, blinking away light-dazzled blotches of visual purple that were dancing before his tearing eyes. Again, he'd heard nothing. His armor's speakers had cut out, a safety measure to keep him from being deafened. As his vision returned, he could make out the red-lit underbelly of a new cloud mushrooming above him.

He rose, stunned and dizzy but otherwise unhurt. *That* railgun package had been entirely too close!

At the top of the ridge, the Gamma he'd been aiming at had flowed over the shattered ruin of the wall, had knocked Sergeant Anderson down and was pinning him to the ground. Dev heard Anderson's scream in spite of the static.

Frantically Dev reached for his plasma gun, but his gloved hands groped empty air. Looking down, he saw that the steadimount had been sheared off as cleanly as if sliced through by a laser. Anderson screamed again, not in fear but in mind-tearing agony.

Nearby, a body lay sprawled on its back, a flamer still clutched in gauntlet-clad hands. Stooping, Dev retrieved the flamer, trying to avoid seeing Lipinsky's bloody, staring-eyed face behind the shattered helmet visor. He aimed the stubby weapon and loosed a burst of incendiary rounds that blossomed into a golden stream of chemical flame washing across the Gamma, which writhed and twisted and cycled from black to silver in pulsing waves.

Suddenly it released its prey and turned, slithering down the ridge toward Dev in a suicidal rush. Dev clamped down on the trigger until the flamer was empty and the Gamma lay two meters from his feet, a blackened, smoking corpse.

Platoon Sergeant Anderson was dead. His armor had been opened up the front as though cut by a knife. What remained inside did not look human anymore. Skin and muscle, bone and teeth, had melted into the inside of the armor, which smoked as though it had been sprayed with hot acid. Biting back his rising gorge, Dev stumbled back a step, then looked around helplessly. Where was the rest of his squad? Lipinsky's body lay a few meters away . . . and farther along the slope, Falk sprawled like a broken doll, white smoke steaming from corroded patches on his armor. That railgun load had landed squarely on the ridge less than a hundred meters away, shattering the Norway Line wall and spilling troops about in every direction.

Spotting movement farther down the slope, Dev hurried forward. It was Bronson, lying on his back, half of his SSPG beside him on the ground. The plasma gunner was clawing wildly at his helmet, and as Dev stepped closer, he could see the man's visor turning opaque as the transplas crazed in myriad tiny cracks. A viscous white smoke curled off the helmet, as fluid as a lighter-than-air liquid. Bronson's gloved fingertips began smoking as he scrabbled wildly at his invisible attackers.

Dev's knees almost gave way as he fought to control a paralyzing fear. The Xeno that had killed Anderson had released a cloud of nano disassemblers that was attacking every piece of artificial material within reach.

The only way to fight a nanotechnic weapon was with nanotechnics. Dev fumbled at his belt for his aerosol, aimed it at Bronson, and pressed the trigger. One burst should have released enough N-tech hunter-killers to neutralize the Xeno nano-Ds, *if* Dev had gotten there in time. Dev's external speakers could pick up Bronson's helmet-muffled screams.

God, part of Bronson's suit was softening into swirls of white mist. His chest armor was crumbling away into black char as the nano-D ate through ceramic and durasheath. Twinkles of light played across his chest armor, energy released by snapping chemical bonds.

Dev heard the pop-hiss of escaping air and dropped to his knees, digging into a side pouch for a nano sealpad, but it was too late. Through the visor, the man's eyes bulged, his mouth gaped and filled with blood, and his screams turned to ghastly, drawn-out shrieks as his air mix became contaminated with the lung-searing flame of ammonia. An instant later, Bronson's helmet visor blew in a spray of glass and blood.

Dev's helmet buzzed warning, as words appeared on his HUD. His right arm had been contaminated, and both legs. The count stood at point six-three. Nano disassemblers were eating their way through his suit.

Desperate now, Dev stumbled back out of the contaminated area, tripped on something unseen, and fell heavily to the ground. Frantically he used the aerosol to dust his arm and legs and the front of his armor, praying all the while that he hadn't picked up such a heavy dose of Xeno nano-Ds that countermeasures wouldn't work. A dozen meters away, he saw a manlike shape struggling to free itself from ground gone suddenly soft. One gloved hand clawed at the air, then froze into immobility.

They were dead, all of them. Dev was still alive, so the aerosol must have worked in time for him. He thought about going back to look for more survivors, but couldn't bring himself to move toward the sprawled horrors of Anderson, Bronson, and the others. Besides, the area was completely contaminated now and would remain deadly until the nano-Ds' internal clocks ran out and they started to break down.

Rising, replacing the aerosol canister in its pouch, he started running, a heavy-footed slog, actually, moving down the slope and away from those mangled, motionless forms. Smoke filled the air, reducing visibility to a few tens of meters. He couldn't see the APWs, but he knew they were not far from Norway Base. He switched on his radio. "Bravo Company! Bravo Company! Can anybody hear me?"

Static was his only answer. All radio channels were out. He stopped for a moment, checking the compass reading in his HUD to get his bearings. The horror and confusion of the last few moments had really twisted him around. Which way was south?

That way.

Panic grew, a throbbing urgency beneath his chestplate, a heavy rasp of his suit respirator as he dragged at each breath. Damn it, where was the base? His boot hit something hard and he glanced down. A piece of Gamma lay there, a blackened twist of dead metal. Nearby was another . . . and another. . . .

Then Dev knew a fresh horror. Somehow he *had* gotten turned around. The railgun blast had flung him onto the north side of the ridge; he was in the valley north of the Norway Line, with the ridge between him and the base and the rest of Bravo Company.

Alone . . . except for those advancing Xenophobe stalkers.

Chapter 13

Our lack of understanding of Xenophobe tactics and strategy, the fact that we didn't even know if they did think, lost us some major battles that we should have won. At Norway Ridge, for instance, our warstrider units were kept back because certain Hegemony senior commanders thought the main Xeno wave was a diversion.

—Testimony before the Imperial Staff
Shosho Minoru Nagumo
C.E. 2540

Katya was not thinking of Dev Cameron as she guided the *Assassin's Blade* up the ridge toward the Norway Line. She was thinking that whoever was directing this null-headed *hema* of a battle at HEMILCOM Command ought to be shot for gross stupidity. For three hours, an eternity in modern battle, she'd been waiting with rising fury for the orders releasing the Thorhammers from their Midgard barracks. A battle was being fought within twenty kilometers of Midgard, a battle that could well mark the beginning of a major assault on Loki's capital city and sky-el, but the Thorhammers, put on alert the day before, had been left hanging at Midgard's airfield.

Colonel Varney had told her the reason. A new DSA had

been detected very close to the chain of fortifications called the Norway Line, evidence, possibly, of a new Xenophobe breakthrough. Was this evidence of a new Xenophobe strategy, a frontal attack on human defenses followed by a swift strike in the rear or flank from underground? Or was it coincidence in the seemingly blind probings of Xenophobe forces? Where and when would the new Xeno force surface?

No one on or off Loki was even willing to take a guess, and HEMILCOM was waffling, unwilling to commit the warstriders until the situation had been clarified.

The problem was that nearly two thousand foot soldiers had already been committed. The Second Loki Infantry, the Wolfguard, was fighting a desperate delaying action against an advancing wave of Xenophobes that had surfaced earlier that morning nearly one hundred kilometers to the north.

Katya had never thought much one way or the other about the leg infantry. Certainly she didn't share the disdain some of her brother striderjacks had for the "crunchies." They were useful for patrols and for standing guard duty, for house-to-house searches and in-dome security and other tasks that warstriders were simply too bulky or clumsy to handle. In most combat, however, striders were so clearly superior to line infantry that it seemed silly to think of the two as separate branches of the same infantry.

But they *were* people, and flinging them against Xenophobes without adequate weapons or armor or strider support was nothing short of murder.

The orders had come through at last, but even then, the commitment had been piecemeal. The Thorhammers' First Battalion would be deployed to the Norway Line, while Second Battalion reinforced the Sweden Line. The two remaining Loki warstrider regiments, the Heimdal Guard and the Odinspears, prepared the last-ditch defense of Midgard itself.

On a three-D holomap the deployment might look good, but Katya's own company, now numbering sixteen operational warstriders, would have to cover twelve kilometers of the Norway Line defenses. Her First Platoon, six striders on two ascraft, had set down at Norway Base, at the point where the Xenophobes were pushing hardest.

Disaster had struck only moments after their arrival.

Asgard had been bombarding the advancing Xenos for hours, pounding the enemy until few of their Alphas remained intact. Unfortunately, the communications between ground and Asgard Orbital were ragged and on the point of breaking down. Several railgun projectiles had fallen close enough to the human lines to cause casualties. As Katya guided her Warlord up the slope, another artificial meteor had thundered out of the sky, striking the ridge a few hundred meters to the west.

The concussion flung her strider off its feet. The legger infantry manning the line had been in the process of falling back from the RoPro fortifications. The sudden detonation almost on top of the ridge had thrown an orderly retreat into complete chaos.

Carefully Katya levered the *Blade* upright. Armored soldiers ran past her down the hill, sliding and falling in the well-churned ice and mud. To her left, mud-covered soldiers were filing up the ramp of a big APW, which was squatting between folded legs like a large and improbable-looking spider.

"Close one," Chris Kingfield said over the net. "I think Asgard Orbital forgot to allow for the wind on that last one."

"Maybe so. Let's see if we can cover these people."

"How can we do that without burning them, too?" her pilot asked. "The Xenos are already coming through the wall."

Suresh Gupta was one of the newbies fresh from the Training Command. He was eager, but inexperienced.

"We help by getting behind the Xeno lines and making a pain of ourselves. The Xenos might act crazy sometimes, but they do respond to threats. If we kill enough of them, they'll slow their advance while they take care of us."

"I love the way this woman thinks," Kingfield said. "Don't you, Suresh? A laugh a minute."

"Quiet, Junior," she replied. "You take the hivel and the belly pod. Leave the arms to me." Shifting her optics for a three-sixty scan of her surroundings, she spotted another strider at her five o'clock position, two hundred meters off, shimmering and fuzzy in its nanoflage as it slogged up the hill. Tagging it with her communications laser, she opened a static-free channel. "Guiterrez!"

"I hear you, Captain," *Sho-i* Raul Guiterrez replied. His strider was a big fifty-four-ton Battlewraith, the *Deus Irae*.

"Stay with me," she ordered. "Extended formation."

Footing was treacherous. Mud clung to the strider's feet with each step, and Katya found herself leaning hard into the balancing gyros to keep them from skidding on the hillside. At the top of the ridge, the RoPro wall was a temporary obstacle, too high to step across. Delivering three quick kicks, she reduced a three-meter section to rubble. The works, she noticed, were deserted. The last defenders had pulled back within moments of that last railgun bolt from the sky.

Scanning the terrain to the north, she picked up numerous targets with motion sensors and infrared. Heat sources were everywhere, picked out, framed in glowing reticles, and IDed by the Warlord's AI; the brightest were the fresh-blasted craters, courtesy of Asgard Orbital, but other sources smoldered, unmoving, or advanced across the open plain singly or in small groups. Less than a kilometer away, Katya saw a trio of large heat sources, almost certainly Xenophobe Alphas . . . and they were moving toward her at a steady pace.

"Three targets," she said, alerting Kingfield. "Bearing three-five-one, range nine hundred and closing."

"Got them," the weapons tech replied. "Striker missiles, firing *one!* And *two!* And *three!*"

One after the other, the three Mitsubishi DkV laser-guided missiles hissed from their dorsal launch tubes, then arrowed toward the north on white contrails. Explosions strobed and flashed in the valley.

"More stalkers on the way," Suresh warned. "I have six

bandits, bearing zero-one-five, range fifteen hundred."

"I've got four bandits at zero-two-five, range two thousand," Guiterrez added. "Engaging . . ."

Data from *Blade*'s AI scrolled past her visual display. The nano count in the valley was fierce, up to point sixty or seventy in some hot spots, and nowhere less than point fifteen. Worse, her motion sensors were picking up movement all around the Warlord, and close. The ground was alive with Gammas, and they were closing in on the lumbering Warlord from all directions. "Guiterrez!" she called. "Watch the Gammas!"

Before Guiterrez could respond, something large and black detached itself from the ground and struck the Battlewraith's legs. He turned a point-defense flamer on it, and it dropped away, but the Battlewraith's lower left leg was smoking, the armor under attack by invisible clouds of nano disassemblers.

A second Gamma rippled across the ground, as quick as thought, and heading for the *Blade* . . . followed by a third. The hivel cannon on her back spat brief buzzsaw shrieks, tearing the Gammas to shreds in rapid succession. Gammas were everywhere. Twice she fired her CPGs, shriveling attackers in searing bolts of electric flame. Twisting her torso left and right, she began picking off the Gammas with precisely targeted bursts of coherent light from her bow lasers.

Movement was a slow agony of step—wrench—step. Hours of combat and orbital bombardment had melted water ice and churned the ground to mud half a meter deep. Many of the Gammas were actually hidden under the mud, alerted to the warstrider's passing by vibration or heat or some unknown Xeno sense. Slogging forward, she kept her attention on the Gammas and the ground within ten meters of the *Blade,* leaving Gupta and Kingfield to watch the approaching Alpha stalkers. More missiles slashed from the *Blade*'s dorsal tubes. The flash of their detonations seemed unnaturally dark under the pall of smoke and soot that stained the darkening sky.

Something moved. . . .

She swiveled the Warlord's torso, locking on the target, then bit off a savage curse as she recognized the clumsy humanoid shape of a soldier in combat armor. That armor, gray and black and splattered boots to helmet with mud, was hard to see in hunorm vision; under IR, he glowed with the heat of overworked servomotors and power pack.

Under the cold double stare of her lasers, the figure stood for a moment as though transfixed, then lifted one arm and waved. Angry at the distraction, she kept the strider moving forward, ignoring the lonely figure.

God, what was he doing out here? In this mud, with so many Gammas about, the poor bastard wouldn't last another five minutes.

Well, there was nothing she could do for him. Two Alphas, a Copperhead and a Cobra, were less than five hundred meters off. She increased the strider's gait, closing the range.

The Copperhead was in the lead, moving so quickly now that each step threw a spray of freezing mud to either side as it galloped ahead on shifting silver legs. Katya stopped, bracing herself, then opened fire with both CPGs and her lasers. The Copperhead crumpled under the assault, great slashes torn in its body, its charge stopped, but the Xeno was morphing as Katya watched, filling in the molten holes. Katya fired again, missed. . . . The Xeno unfolded a gleaming pseudopod, and she sensed the gathering of an intense magnetic field. Too late, she tried to shift her aiming point, then staggered under the impact of five hard-driven blows against her chest that slammed her back a step.

Warnings shrilled in her mind. Nanotech projectiles had pierced her armor in three places, damaging her right arm, tearing away her belly weapons pod, smashing armor on leg and torso. Nano-contaminated hot spots glowed against her hull. She was initiating anti-nano-D countermeasures when the Copperhead splashed toward her out of the gathering smoke, a vaguely octopuslike shape, though without the body, a rubbery sprawl of broad tentacles that engulfed Katya in black and silver coils.

With a sharp slashing motion, Katya knocked the Xeno down and fired both CPGs at point-blank range. Lightning arced, blue-white and dazzling, carving through the Copperhead's core in a splatter of molten droplets. Two tentacles fell away, followed by three more, the pieces huge and smoking on the ground. Lightning flared again, and what was left of the Copperhead fell away, shriveling.

"Suresh!" she called. She felt uncertain of the strider's balance, as though she were teetering, about to fall. The landscape wobbled around her. "Chris!"

Data from the Warlord's AI indicated that Chris Kingfield was dead. One of those nano shells had torn through the Warlord's lateral armor and exploded inside his module. Internal nano-D countermeasures had been released. Would they be enough?

Suresh Gupta wasn't answering either, but she couldn't tell if he was dead or simply knocked out of the circuit. She was having trouble with her own link, too. Static crashed in her brain, blinding her. The interference cleared, briefly, giving her a glimpse of tortured ground and the smoking hulk of the Copperhead, and then her link failed and she was back in her body, her human body, lying inside the dark and stinking coffin of the strider's command module.

She felt herself falling. When the Warlord's body hit the ground, the concussion exploded like a galaxy of stars in Katya's mind, a dazzling light that engulfed her, then carried her into blackness. . . .

Chapter 14

If you are in a tight place and feel fear, recognize it. Then get control over it and make it work for you. Fear stimulates the body processes. You can actually fight harder, and for a longer time, when you are scared. . . .

—*Guidebook for Marines*
Fifteenth revised edition
late twentieth century

Alone on a battlefield of giants.

Dev stood in shin-deep mud that was already starting to refreeze around his feet, staring after the towering apparition. The Warlord had advanced ponderously out of the gloom, its surfaces distorted by nanoflage, each step a measured concussion, a titan's footfall. He'd held his breath as it paused, so close he could hear the hiss of its hydraulics and pressure bearings, the grating chirp of metal on metal in a worn articulator. It was an RS-64D, powerful, magnificent, a storm god astride the wind of the battle's storm. He could see the name picked out on the hull against the reflective nano, *Assassin's Blade*.

Katya Alessandro's Warlord.

Had Katya seen him? Or Suresh? Idiot, he told himself. Of course they had. Little happened within range of a warstrider's senses that the commander and crew *weren't* aware of, and as if in answer, the machine's blunt nose angled sharply with a whine of servos, bringing the twin bow lasers to bear on him. He waved, but the big machine's torso angled up almost disdainfully, the right leg swept past, and the *Blade* moved on, ignoring him.

He let his arm drop, feeling foolish. Hell, the only thought striderjacks gave to infantry was their nickname for them—crunchies—and they certainly wouldn't have recognized a lone grunt in combat armor. Dev had been lucky the *Blade* hadn't walked him down.

One thing the strider had done was confirm his guess that he'd gotten turned around, that he was north of the Norway Line. His helmet, he realized, was only lightly shielded, and the powerful Xeno magfields had hopelessly scrambled his field sensors. Trusting to intuition, then, he started to move up the slope in the direction from which the Warlord had come. He just hoped the APWs hadn't already packed up and left.

Thunder crashed, and lightning painted the smoke clouds and billowing dust with savage hues of blue and green. Turning, Dev saw the Warlord clashing with something huge, a Copperhead, he thought, bolt following crashing bolt. Feeling small and alone and terribly naked on this no-man's-land of giants, he started running up the ridge, his boots slipping and scrabbling in the mud. He stopped when his HUD warned of N-tech disassemblers, a count of point thirty-two and rising. Eight meters away, the ground was writhing and changing as he watched, stones dissolving into steam.

Dev stepped back, lost his balance, and began sliding down the hill. At the bottom the nano count stood at point twenty-one. Better, but his helmet electronics identified hot spots on his gloves and arms. He used the AND spray on them, wondering how much longer the canister would last.

The clash of metal, the thunderous discharge of lightning and a flash that lit up the sky, grabbed his attention. Through drifting smoke and the deepening gloom, he could see the Warlord, lying on its side fifty meters away.

Dev started running then, straining to reach the fallen strider. The mud was quickly freezing, and with each step he had to struggle to pull his foot free as the slop steadily assumed a nightmare's consistency of thickening tar. He wasn't sure what he could do, but he knew the *Blade*'s crew was in trouble. They might have ejected, or they might still be trapped inside. Either way, he had to get down there fast.

Smoke curled from a gash in the armored flank. His helmet warned of a nano count of point fifty, and everywhere he looked, pieces of the shattered Copperhead lay twitching on the ground. He grabbed a handhold and pulled himself up the curving side of the Warlord's hull . . . then another, then two more. No one had ejected. The explosive hatches were still sealed and intact.

In moments, Dev found what he was looking for, a maintenance panel set into the external hull near the commander's hatch, with a readout for techs who needed to check the machine's systems when it was powered up and in the field. He slapped the release, and the cover slid back. A constellation of green, red, and amber lights winked at him, and he frowned, puzzling out their meaning.

The commander's module showed definite life signs. Captain Alessandro was alive but unconscious, possibly hurt, and there was class-three damage to her control circuitry, a nano burn-through, it looked like, in the primary computer link node. The Warlord's AI had cut her out of the circuit to isolate the damage, shifting primary control to the pilot.

But the pilot's module showed a mix of red and green, and Dev winced. Suresh—if he was the guy in the pilot's compartment—was dead, though his systems were still powered up and operational. The weapons tech was dead as well.

Clinging to the rough, nano-pitted hull of the Warlord, Dev considered his options. He wouldn't last long alone on this hellfield, and Katya Alessandro would be easy meat for the first Xeno to come along. He tried to push away the image that came too easily to mind, as a Xeno absorbed her Warlord and she became a screaming, living part of the horror closing around her.

He couldn't let that happen . . . he *couldn't*. She'd tried to help him, had spoken up for him at the inquiry. Dev couldn't leave her to face the nightmare of Xeno assimilation.

Scrambling up the handholds, avoiding the worst of the nano hot spots, Dev worked his way to the primary core maintenance access hatch, a circular plate set into what had been the upper surface of the main hull, just in front of the hivel cannon mount, but which now, with the Warlord on its side, was sunken into a vertical wall. Flipping open a cover marked in red and white stripes, he reached into the recess and grabbed a handle marked EMERGENCY RELEASE, and twisted hard. There was a sharp hiss of equalizing pressures and the round hatch slid aside, exposing the coffin-tight interior.

The narrow tube served as internal access for pilot, commander, and weapons tech, as well as a way to reach the strider's AI core and primary circuitry. It also served as airlock, a way to get in and out of the strider without opening the operating modules to a hostile outside environment. Lights glimmered in the darkness. His shoulders hunched to avoid snagging his backpack, he wiggled around until he could stab at the pressure plates on the small control board, sealing the hatch and flooding the compartment with anti-nano-D. The local count dropped to zero, and he keyed in the sequence that would replace the chamber's air with something breathable.

Come on . . . come *on*! Impatiently he counted off the seconds, waiting for the atmosphere indicator to change from red to green. He was completely blind in here, and he didn't like to think about what might be moving around outside the crippled warstrider. *Green!*

Awkwardly in the tight compartment, Dev removed his helmet and shrugged out of his life support pack. The air burned with the acrid taint of ammonia, making his eyes water, but it was breathable. He found the pilot's module hatch—with the Warlord on its side, it was beneath him—and unsealed it.

The chamber beyond was tight and cramped and dark; Suresh lay on his side, at right angles to the airlock tube. He hung in his restraint harness like a puppet, the jackfeeds still plugged into his helmet. The helmet was twisted back, almost beneath the body. It looked to Dev as though Suresh had been slammed against one end of the module, and the impact had snapped his neck. A quick inspection of Gupta's medisensor on his chest confirmed that he was dead.

If Dev could get him to a medical station, there was a chance. Nanosurgical techniques could reconnect or regrow severed spinal cords as easily as they could reattach a severed arm, but if his brain went many more minutes without a blood supply, so many cerebral connections would decay that nothing would bring the Earther back.

At the moment, Dev had to worry about getting the Warlord on its feet again. Suresh would have to wait.

With unsteady fingers he unsealed Gupta's cephlink helmet and slipped it off, then struggled for several moments more to release the harness straps and drag the body out of the module. What followed was a contortionist's nightmare. Gupta's body was a dead weight, the effort like wrestling with a bag of sand while lying on his side in a steel pipe as wide as the reach of his arm. He tried to be gentle—the less he damaged the already broken body, the more likely Suresh might be brought back later—but at the moment, speed was more important than finesse. For now, at least, Dev and Katya were both definitely alive, while Gupta was not. Any second now a Xeno would sense them, and then they all would be dead for certain.

At last Dev dropped into the narrow space occupied by Gupta moments earlier and, bracing the body above him with one hand, hit the hatch close switch. He was sealed off from the access tube now; lights, red, amber, and green, glowed eerily at him in the darkness, and he sensed the warm hum of the Warlord's systems all around him.

He studied the controls, finding he'd forgotten nothing. Had it only been a month since he'd jacked one of these armored monsters? He removed his glove to reveal the left palm implant, then donned Gupta's helmet, reaching up beneath his chin to snap the jacks into his sockets, one—two—three. His palm sought the interface board. Light exploded behind his closed eyes . . . and *pain*.

Groggily Dev fought the confused cascade of sensations surging through his brain. The Warlord's AI was configured to Suresh Gupta's cerebral patterns, not his, and it would take moments more to reset the system.

Concentrating, he unlocked the AI access codes still stored in his cephlink RAM. "Pilot replacement," he thought. "Reconfiguration, Code Three-Green-One."

"Think of a field of yellow grain," the strider's voice said in the back of his mind. "Concentrate on a flock of birds flying overhead, left to right."

He did so. Urgency gnawed at him. The mental image wavered, and he thought for a moment he was going to lose it.

No!

"Red," the AI voice told him, and he pictured the color. "Orange . . . blue . . . white . . . square . . . triangle . . ."

The list of words droned on, each a stimulus triggering an image received and recorded by the Warlord's artificial intelligence. Distantly he felt a shudder pass through his body, a heavy, rolling sensation as though the Warlord had been struck by something very large, very massive. Fear rose, a clawing darkness behind the clarity of his thoughts, urging him to reach for the manual eject key . . . but he fought it down.

" . . . the number fourteen . . . Picture a wild and rocky seacoast beneath a gray sky, with waves crashing against the rocks. . . .

"Reconfiguration is complete. Enabling cephlink, full control to Module Two."

Pause, and then, with a satisfying inner snap, light flared again in Dev's eyes, but this time it was like waking from a sound sleep. He was lying on his side, his face close to a gel of ice and mud. Something large and shaggy stood above him on silver pseudopods, its bulk obscenely distended and alive with the twist and wiggle of snakelike appendages. Dev recognized the amorphous shape, a King Cobra, slow and a bit clumsy, but one of the largest and most deadly of all the Xenophobe killer machines.

The cascade of data through Dev's senses was numbing in its length and in its complexity. He'd not handled a direct sensory link for a month, and the shock was like stepping into the thunder of a waterfall. The Warlord's AI confirmed what he already knew: Katya was alive but unable to link, *Jun-i* Kingfield was dead; the strider itself had sustained damage—the list of failed or failing systems was the bulk of the data cascade—but it could still move and it could still fight.

Nanotechnic disassemblers were storming at the Warlord's outer hull, degrading the armor in an invisible molecular storm. The exterior nano count was approaching point eight-four. The behemoth standing above the fallen Warlord extended one broad pseudopod like a rippling black tongue, and where it touched the strider's left weapons pod, the nano-D count shrieked into the point-nineties, approaching the one-point-oh that marked complete molecular breakdown.

Lifting a fallen strider to its feet was difficult at the best of times, especially when it had weapons instead of true arms and hands. While under attack, it was nearly impossible. Dev thrust his left arm out, levering the hull far enough off the ground that he could tuck his left leg beneath his body. At the same time, he swiveled his torso and snapped his right arm up, bringing the right-hand CPG into linc with the looming King Cobra.

Lightning flashed, and the amorphous hull of the Cobra flattened beneath the assault. Dev triggered a second blast, and a pair of ropy, lancet-tipped appendages as thick as elephants' trunks broke free in a splatter of silver droplets. The King Cobra drifted back a step, and Dev used the pause to straighten his left leg, raising the bulk of the damaged warstrider shakily erect.

The nano count on his right pod registered point six-two, point six-one on his right leg. With a thought, he triggered a countermeasures release. Smoke, like a fire extinguisher's blast, enveloped the strider, cooling the hot spots before his armor began dissolving.

Twisting right, he triggered his twin bow lasers. Red warnings flashed across his visual field. The laser circuits were out, mud-clogged and shock-damaged, and so was his left-arm CPG. The fall had broken a power feed. With peripheral vision, he saw the blue-white snap and flash of an electrical discharge at the elbow connector, and he could feel the slow but steady drain on his power reserves.

The King Cobra drifted forward with a curious rolling motion that slid the damaged areas out of the warstrider's line of fire. A black pseudopod grew like a slender head from obscenely bunched and writhing shoulders. Dev started to fire his right CPG, noted temperature warnings and a threat of power shutdown to his right pod, and reset the fire command before he'd completed it. Shifting control instead to his dorsal hivel cannon, he loosed a point-blank stream of depleted uranium, hosing the Cobra with the hammering impact of fifty rounds per second.

The King Cobra, its mantle spread to enclose the Warlord in a deadly embrace, was caught, vulnerable and exposed. The flattened pseudopod shredded in a whirling storm of fragments.

Another tentacle groped toward him from the left. Sensing its approach, Dev twisted, bringing the arcing flare of the damaged power lead between him and the enemy, then lunging sideways. The Xeno machine flinched under the sputtering crackle of Dev's impromptu electric stun gun, part of its surface sloughing off as internal magfields were disrupted. Dev fired another hivel burst, then, noting that the right CPG bore temperature had dropped almost into safe levels, he loosed another burst of protons.

The Cobra's surface crackled and sparked, part of its mass smoking into vapor as the Xeno lost control of its N-tech surface. An explosion strobed at the thing's core, sleeting Dev with Xeno fragments and tearing the alien machine into molten pieces. The largest fragments twisted and snaked across the smoking ground until, one by one, Dev fried them in bursts of nuclear flame.

Power levels at seventy-four percent . . .

Patches of armor on left side and leg depleted by twenty-seven percent . . .

Temperature warning, right CPG, nine hundred degrees . . .

New warnings flashed, and the line breakers in his right arm tripped out again. Smoke was pouring from the right Mark III—not the viscous white smoke of nano-Ds dissolving armor, but a sputtering, greasy black cloud from melting plastic and burning lubricants, mingled with green fumes from a ruptured coolant line somewhere. He tried to move his right arm and felt the mechanism grind and seize, rigidly locked and probably ruined.

Dev was rapidly running out of weapons. His systems readout indicated he could still fire the CPG, but he would have to aim it by turning his whole body, a slow and clumsy way to fight an enemy that was already quicker and more maneuverable than he was.

A wink of light on his visual display caught his attention, the electronic equivalent of his Warlord's AI tapping his shoulder and pointing. Swiveling his primary optics toward the black and ominous sky, he glimpsed a fast-moving speck skimming just beneath the overcast, crossing the ridge from south to north.

Dev engaged his telescopics, enlarging the image until he could recognize the lean-tailed shape of a VK-141 Stormwind at a range of eight kilometers.

Relief flooded Dev's mind. A Stormwind! He wasn't alone after all! He triggered the Warlord's communications laser before the ascraft could vanish into the overcast. "Stormwind, this is Assassin Leader!" It felt strange identifying himself with a company commander's call sign, but he was in the command strider, and there was no time to cxplain things.

"This is Stormwind Thor-Two," a woman's voice replied over the laser comm. "*Tai-i* Anders. Who the hell is this? What happened to Captain Alessandro?"

"I think she's okay," Dev replied. "Her link with the AI is down. I've taken over."

"I have you in sight, Assassin Leader." Anders probably assumed that he was Gupta or the Warlord's weapons tech. There was a moment's hesitation. "And someone else does, too. Bandits at your four o'clock, range three hundred!"

Dev turned, his optics zeroing in on the black and silver shapes flowing toward him across the ground. A Fer-de-Lance, an Adder, and a Mamba, all swift and deadly, were closing in for the kill.

Chapter 15

The science of information—the storage, retrieval, transmission, and exchange of data—has done more to broaden the scope and reach of Man's mastery of both his physical universe and the dark mystery of his own soul than all previous discoveries, technologies, and philosophies combined. Knowledge, as ever, is power; ignorance is damnation. Perhaps this is why we still dread that which we don't know.

—*The Golden Apples of the Stars*
Shelly Westegren
C.E. 2457

"Stormwind, I need ground support!" Dev yelled. "Now!"

"Get clear, Assassin Leader! I'm on them!"

Dev was already in motion as the Stormwind dipped toward the battle-torn ground, sending the Warlord lunging up the ridge with long, scissoring steps. The Fer-de-Lance put a trio of nano disassembler projectiles into his back, but he fired his nano countermeasures and kept moving. An instant later, the Xeno turned away, focusing on the approaching Stormwind.

Ascraft could not risk close passes over Xeno units. Their airspeed made AND clouds useless, and though most had layers of anti-nano-D sandwiched between sheets of armor, a hit by Threat nano could usually bring the ascraft down. For that reason, ascraft like the Stormwind relied on standoff weapons for ground support.

Dev's telescopic vision tracked the projectile as it detached from the Stormwind's hull. Then rocket engines kicked in and sent the pod arrowing toward the Xeno. He recognized it, an SK3-7E Skyray air-to-ground missile. The fat, elongated snout was a Cluster Munitions Package.

Anders hadn't been kidding when she'd told Dev to get clear.

Dev kept climbing, feeling the slushy yield of dirt and loose gravel beneath the flanges of his feet. Halfway up the slope, he turned, positioning his body so that he could bring his CPG to bear on the Fer-de-Lance, which was firing nano weapons at the approaching Skyray. Dev fired, the bolt staggering the hovering Xeno, bringing its attention back toward the escaping Warlord.

Then the Skyray was overhead, flashing eighteen meters above the Mamba and Death Adder as its dim-witted brain computed that it was now as close to the target as it would get on this trajectory.

The warhead detonated.

To Dev, it seemed that there were two simultaneous explosions, one a fireball in the sky, the second a volcanic eruption on the ground. The Skyray's micronuke warhead vaporized ten thousand cobalt slugs sealed in rhenium-tungstide cartridges; the same detonation powered a brief-lived magnetic field that stripped the cobalt of electrons and hurled the resulting plasma bolts on precisely aligned paths, filling a ten-by-one-hundred-meter footprint with white-hot bolts from the sky.

The ground beneath the fireball shuddered in a thunderous eruption of flame and pulverized rock. Caught in the center of that deadly footprint, the Mamba and the Adder were shredded; the Fer-de-Lance was holed thirty times by searing lances of starcore heat; writhing fragments twisted in white heat and died.

Dev felt the throb of the micronuke's electromagnetic pulse. A tenth second later, a hailstorm of molten fragments slashed across his back, and the twin concussions—one from the explosions, and the second caused by the thunderclap of air blasting into the vacuum left by the fireball—hurled the sixty-ton strider facedown against the hillside. Dust sucked into that hellfury boiled skyward in a roiling mushroom cloud.

Slowly Dev brought the Warlord to its feet, checking the RS-64D's damage readouts. Power reserves were down to forty-eight percent, and there were holes in his armor where the nano-Ds had eaten clear through to the internal support struts. The CMP blast had peeled armor from the dorsal surface of the fuselage across an area one meter square. The left weapons pod was gone now, the broken joint still sparking fitfully from severed power leads.

But the Xenophobes were destroyed, their fragments smoldering in the CMP's charred and heat-blasted killzone.

He let his AI scan the sky and acquire again the distant, circling Stormwind. "Thanks, Thor-Two," Dev said. "Clean sweep. Targets destroyed."

"Copy, Assassin Leader. Listen, I don't know if Xenies talk to each other, but I'd say now would be a good time for you to hightail it out of there. I'm picking up a lot of activity in your area."

"Ay-firmative, Thor-Two. Can you link me up with other striders?" He'd not seen any other human combat machines since he'd climbed aboard the *Assassin's Blade*.

"They're pulling back to the second line. Didn't you get the word?"

"Negative. I was . . . ah . . . out of the circuit." He wondered what Anders would think if she knew a legger was jacking the stranded Warlord.

"Okay, no static. Here's the tacsit. The Xenos hit the Norway Line hard. The Thorhammers lost four striders in seven minutes . . . uh, make that three striders, now that you've been found. The rest boarded the transports and are falling back to the Sweden Line. The Xenos are still moving toward Midgard. They're between you and your friends now."

"Great. I don't suppose I could impose on you for a ride."

"Sorry, I can't," Anders replied. "My ship's configured for ground attack. But I'll put through a call and have a transport out here in ten minutes."

"Understood." Dev swiveled his primary optics skyward as the Stormwind passed a hundred meters overhead with a shriek of intake fans and plasma jets. He could see the strider slots beneath the stubby, canted wings, and the bulky cargo of snap-in weapons pods that occupied them. Stormwinds were designed as multiple-role ascraft, but they needed time on the ground with a maintenance crew to switch from one role to another.

He could manage ten more minutes, especially with a heavily armed ally circling overhead.

"Ah, Assassin Leader, I have to leave you for a second," Anders said.

"Why?" The thought of being left alone out here again was not pleasant. "Where are you going?"

"Just up above the cloud deck. Radio's still blanked by static. I need to establish a solid L-LOS if I'm going to call in that transport."

"Hurry back," Dev said. "It's kind of lonely down here."

"Copy that, Assassin. Back in thirty seconds." The shrieking engines throbbed to a roar, and the Stormwind was gone, swallowed in the overcast.

Thirty seconds. He could survive that, too.

Only then, as he stood on that flame-scorched hillside, did full realization hit Dev. For the past half hour, he'd been patched into a warstrider, accessing, aiming, and firing his weapons; coordinating link communications with a Stormwind; engaging in hand-to-hand combat with the strangest, most deadly enemies Man had ever faced . . . and not once had fear or uncertainty blocked his access to the strider AI. Stress. He'd handled it as smoothly and as effortlessly as he would have handled the downloading of a comm number from his RAM . . . or calling to mind his father's face.

The surprise, the sheer exultation numbed him for a moment. Whatever had stopped him from making full use of his linkages in his first battle was gone.

Maybe Katya had been right. For those past thirty minutes, he'd been too busy to think, responding on instinct and training alone.

Another crackle of static sizzled in Dev's brain, and he ordered the AI to trace the damage. If he lost his control link with the machine's computer, the strider would become a useless mountain of junk. His AI reported back almost at once, describing damage to the primary feed line. Backups were in place, and the AI was now programming internal repair nano to reroute the connections and restore a clean feed.

Good. Better still, the AI had finally tapped into Katya's medisensors. Dev still couldn't talk to her, but the medsystems indicated that she was awake. High pulse rate and respiration suggested that she was under considerable stress. That wasn't surprising. Dev could imagine what she was feeling, sealed inside a coffin-sized box, unable to see out or even to receive data. She would be able to feel the strider's movements, but that was about all.

At least she was alive. Dev ordered the AI to accelerate its attempts to repair Katya's link. He'd gotten this far on luck and by not thinking about what he was doing. He would much rather that someone experienced jack in and take over.

In the meantime, though, all he could do was find a good spot for pickup by the transport. The uneven ground blurred beneath his four-meter stride.

Minutes later, he'd reached the top of the ridge and found himself overlooking a horror of death and devastation. The

Norway Line's battlements looked like they'd been assaulted by a hurricane. Walls had been torn down or pushed over; in places, solid RoPro constructions had melted like sugar in hot water.

Signs of the battle were scattered everywhere. The shell of a Battlewraith lay faceup, torso splintered, weapons skewed, greasy smoke streaming from its engine compartment. Dev recognized the name on the blackened hull: *Deus Irae*.

Across the ridgetop, human bodies and pieces of bodies were heaped about in twisted, hideous clumps where Xeno nano-D clouds had lingered. Many corpses had already partially merged with the ground or with the wreckage of vehicles or RoPro walls, grinning skulls and clutching hands straining from their fabricrete embrace, combat armor in mangled, twisted postures that spoke of agony and death.

Dev scanned the area carefully. A check of the radio bands proved that there were Xenos nearby. Every channel was blasted by white noise. But there was no sign of motion anywhere, no Alphas, no Gammas, nothing moving at all save the smoke streaming from scattered, burning wreckage. He picked his way past the shattered RoPro barrier until he could overlook the plain to the south.

Norway Base lay in the valley four hundred meters to the southeast. The infantry transporters were gone now, but the fabricrete landing pad remained, along with some quick-grown shelters and fuel storage spheres, all curiously intact despite the devastation along the top of the ridge. The temporary base looked lifeless and abandoned. Evidently the Xeno wave had swept on toward Midgard without pausing to destroy the facility. Dev started down the southern slope of the ridge, angling toward the landing pad. That would be as good a spot as any to await pickup by a strider transport.

Laser light pinged on his communication receptors. "Assassin Leader, this is Thor-Two."

Anders was back below the flight deck, circling five kilometers to the west. Three more Stormwinds and a pair of Lightning gunships were in the area as well, just arrived from Midgard.

"I hear you, Thor-Two. Good to see you again."

"Roger that. We have a transporter on the way. They say to hang on."

"No static. I'll be waiting at the Norway Base LZ. There's no sign of Threat activity here at all."

There was a hesitation from the other. "I'm afraid that's not entirely true, Assassin Leader. HEMILCOM reports a force five-one DSA centered at your location."

Dev had to call up data fed to his cephlink RAM over a month before. DSA . . . a Deep Seismic Anomaly, and force five-one was pretty hefty. The Xenos might be tunneling just beneath the surface.

Chilling thought. Dev felt a juvenile and completely instinctive twitch in the phantom soles of his feet, the remembered fear of a child dangling bare feet in the dark beside a bed that might harbor unseen monsters. These monsters were real, and only a few hundred meters from the bottoms of his Warlord's feet.

"What do you recommend, Thor-Two? I can move to another location if you want."

"Negative, Assassin. HEMILCOM thinks we have time, if we move fast. Stand by. Your ride out of there is now eight minutes out."

Eight minutes. Not long at all. He could wait that long, no static.

And then the bottom dropped out of the world.

To Dev, it looked as though a circular patch of ground nearly a hundred meters across was sinking at the base of the ridge. The fabricrete landing pad, too tough to break in half, balanced above the deepening pit for a moment, then toppled in as bedrock eroded away beneath it. One of the pressure storage tanks fell into the abyss, then another, trailing with it a spaghetti of broken struts and braces.

Swiftly Dev moved sideways along the ridge, seeking shelter behind the war-shattered shell of a section of the ridgetop battlements. White smoke was filling the crater, swirling up from a relatively small central core. More quick-grow buildings fell into the pit as the circle of destruction deepened and expanded.

Dev shifted to infrared optics, trying to probe the heavy white mist swirling in the crater's depths. The stuff was hot, the core from which it was issuing hotter still, a blazing patch of white heat against the cooler reds and oranges surrounding it.

Then an explosion smacked Dev across the bottoms of his feet and sent the Warlord crashing to the trembling ground. The noise, a deep-throated, full-voiced roar of outraged earth and stone, was deafening despite his AI's intervention to prevent overloading Dev's temporal lobes. Grit and shattered bits of rock began pattering across the Warlord's armor like hot sleet; the ground itself bucked and shivered beneath him, and as Dev rolled onto his side, he could see a tongue of glowing lava extruding itself from the crater floor, white-hot under IR, a dull, throbbing orange crusted with black and red glowing within the fog when he switched back to normal vision.

"Thor-Two!" Dev called. "Thor-Two, come in!" But the lasercom link was lost, his L-LOS cut off by smoke and billowing clouds of debris. The nano count was rising, too . . . point five-five and going up. The fog was lapping beyond the rim of the pit now, ground-hugging, streaming past and through the RoPro structures still standing, causing them to slump and melt, as though that alien alchemy were returning them to the rock and dirt from which they'd been grown.

Meanwhile, at the eye of the storm, *things* were beginning to emerge.

At first Dev thought that he was seeing some new kind of Xeno Alpha or other war machine; this was the way they typically emerged from underground, after all. But these jagged and sharp-edged structures rising from the fog on the crater floor looked more like living crystal. Some were black, others a translucent pearl gray or silver. They speared the murky sky above the pit, like the teeth and claws of some vast and still unseen horror lurking beneath the fog. Were they buildings of some sort . . . or a weapon? Flashes of light glared and shimmered in the white fog depths, reminding Dev of the radiance from a great open-pit smelter or industrial furnace.

He made a quick check. The strider's AI had already shifted the Warlord's surface nano to imitate the cracked and mottled color of what was left of the RoPro wall, but enough of his armor had been melted away that less than half of the machine's surface was still nanoflaged. Holding himself motionless, though, he might escape notice, at least for a while, another piece of inert wreckage on the battle-blasted ridge. The outside nano count was now at point six-seven. He guessed that his outer armor would survive another ten minutes under the assault of that molecular storm, and stood his ground.

Damn it, though, what was he seeing down there? A building complex of some sort was his best guess, but that guess could be wildly wrong. Given that nothing was known of Xeno motives or science or even the way they thought, the guess probably *was* wrong.

Whatever he was looking at, Dev thought, it was different from anything he'd ever seen before, and HEMILCOM Intelligence would want to have a close and detailed look. Automatically his AI was recording every sight and sound and sensation. If he could establish a comlink with a Stormwind for even half a second, he'd be able to dump that recording to the ascraft's AI. HEMILCOM Intelligence would be able to share this experience in virtual reality later, *if* Dev could avoid being melted down with every other piece of human-manufactured scrap on this hillside in the next few minutes.

The eruption was continuing, but fitfully now, the shriek and roar of tortured rock dwindling away. As the Warlord's AI readjusted the sensitivity of Dev's audio sensors, he could hear a rising susurration, like ocean surf, but throbbing as though to the beat of an unseen pump.

The fog sea was thinning, revealing the crater floor. There solid rock had flowed like water, then frozen in weirdly carved, twisting pillars, arches, and towers. Strangest were the alien constructs rising in isolated clumps, eldritch shapes of nightmare, organic, surreal, and incomprehensible. Crystal-looking spires and pillars with geometric lines and topologies were still visibly growing minute by minute, their substance flowing up out of the earth itself. That fog was almost certainly Xenophobe nano, Dev thought, programmed to devour rock and sand and debris, and convert it into something else.

Dev felt the stirrings of awe. Human nanotechnology was still a slow and cumbersome thing compared to this. Except for isolated exceptions like AND aerosols, the human nanotech required growth vats and processing tanks, and large and complicated products—a warstrider, for example, or a laser rifle—still had to be assembled by macroengineering. Theoretically a cloud of programmed nano could go to work on a heap of earth, do their work, and leave behind a fully assembled, powered, and AI-programmed strider; in fact, even the most optimistic nanoengineers spoke of generations before that kind of technological magic could be realized.

The Xenophobes, obviously, possessed that magic now. They were growing their alien architecture before Dev's optics, using rock and wreckage as raw materials.

Dev could see the tunnel mouth clearly now, as the last of the fog dissipated in the crater's central core. The white sea continued to lap in a vast circle around the crater's perimeter, but the crater floor was exposed at the center. It looked like tar or liquid asphalt, jet black, liquid, but thick and viscous. IR showed that it was warmer than its surroundings, but not nearly as hot as the lava had been moments before. The lava itself seemed to have been converted into something else, the delicate tracery of crisscrossing spires and crystal shafts surrounding the core, perhaps.

A Death Adder emerged from the tar, blunt-nosed, sluglike, gleaming clean and gray-silver as if coated with liquid mercury. Sliding clear of the tunnel mouth, it began transforming into its combat mode, shapeshifting into a six-armed starfish armored in spines like black needles. Close behind it was the snake-shape of a Fer-de-Lance. Other shapes followed, a nightmare procession of alien geometries. They spread out around the crater perimeter, like sentries mounting guard.

Had he been seen? Apparently not. None of the invaders appeared to notice the lone, combat-savaged Warlord lying in the rubble of the fallen battlements three hundred meters from the tunnel mouth. Maybe the strider's protective coloration was camouflaging him after all, or maybe they'd dismissed him as another piece of wreckage, junk like that broken Battlewraith nearby.

He wouldn't be able to rely on their nearsightedness for long. If nothing else, there must be thousands of Gammas and hot-nano scraps all over the ridge, left over from the earlier fight. Sooner or later they would start gnawing on whatever they happened to find, and the Warlord would become a large and helpless hors d'oeuvre.

There was little more he could accomplish by staying where he was, and every second he remained increased the risk that he would be seen.

Dev started to turn away, then froze. Distinctly he could hear a heavy *thump-thump-thump*, a rhythmic pounding that was almost certainly coming from the Warlord's hull.

A Gamma, he thought. A Xeno Gamma had attached itself to his fuselage and was smashing its way inside!

Chapter 16

No one who, like me, conjures up the most evil of those half-tamed demons that inhabit the human breast, and seeks to wrestle with them, can expect to come through the struggle unscathed.

—*Complete Psychological Works*
Sigmund Freud
early twentieth century

For Katya Alessandro, the blackness surrounding her had become an intolerable hell. She lay in the coffin-sized niche of the command module, swaying in her support web, feeling the ungainly lurch-swing-lurch of the Warlord's long-legged gait.

Her AI link was still completely dead, and even the module's manual controls appeared to have shorted out. She'd long since given up trying to eject. Not a single gleam of light came from the small console pad, which left her muffled in a terrifying, stifling cloak of darkness.

That darkness had brought her to the ragged edge of stark panic and held her there, held her as she battled the rising terror she'd felt once before, aboard the *Kaibutsu Maru*. She'd gone through a year of implant therapy before she could sleep without a light on at night, had come *that* close to submitting to voluntary amnesia. With a claustrophobe rating of point seven, she'd come within an ace of being rejected when she volunteered for warstrider training. During training, a simulated power failure had dropped her into a night much like this one, and she'd come damned close to washing out right then and there.

Somehow she'd managed to hang on, going through the rote procedure to restore link power manually and not giving in to panic. Those procedures hadn't worked this time, however—her fingers were bleeding from pounding at the control pad in the dark. She wanted to scream, and knew that if she did, she would lose all control, all reason, and possibly kill herself trying to batter through that hatch.

And what made it worse was the knowledge that *they* must be just outside her hatch.

They. The bogeyman, the horror in the dark, the monsters under the bed. She remembered what had happened to Mitch, and couldn't stop shaking. She could clearly remember the moments before the power failure during the fight with the Copperhead. Suresh Gupta and Chris Kingfield had both been dead, *dead* . . . and when she had recovered consciousness an unknown agony of minutes or hours later, she'd felt the Warlord moving and knew that Xenophobe Gammas must have infiltrated the machine, transforming it into a zombie.

Strange. She'd never seen a Xenozombie that still had its legs. Usually when the 'Phobes remade a human strider, they reworked the legs into a misshapen platform containing powerful magfield guides, letting it float a meter above the ground. She could definitely feel the thump of each foot as it hit the ground, could feel the swaying stop-and-go motion of the strider's birdlike walk.

But the *Blade* had to be a zombie. The AI couldn't run the strider by itself, and Gupta and Kingfield were both dead. That meant the monsters were all around her, inside the Warlord's armor, inside its power plant and weapons and hull, eating their way toward her compartment. And when they reached her . . .

Katya screamed, her fists pounding against the padded surface of the module's external hatch. The manual hatch release, like the eject handle, seemed to be jammed. She had to get out . . . *out!* . . .

Somehow Katya had managed to free herself from the support harness and unplug her helmet from the useless link feeds, then squirm about until she could double her legs above her body, knees to chest. Kicking hard, she thought she felt the hatch give slightly. She kicked again. *Thump!* And again. The manual release was still jammed, but she thought she'd felt the centimeter-thick sheet of nanomolecular armor give ever so slightly. A shock might free it, might force the locking mechanism open and unseal her prison.

She tried not to let herself think about what was going on in the Warlord around her. For a time, the strider's swaying motion had stopped, but then, over two minutes later by her internal clock, there'd been a savage explosion. The shock wave had made the walls of her metal coffin ring, there'd been the unmistakable stomach-twisting sensation of a fall, and then the Warlord had smashed into unyielding ground.

The crash slammed her against one end of the module and nearly returned her to unconsciousness, but though flashes of visual purple danced and sparked before her eyes, she clung to her awareness like a talisman, like a weapon, unwilling to lose it when the Xenos were eating their way through the darkness to reach her.

That thought bit, slick and panic-edged, like sharp ice twisting in her brain. Hysterical strength surged through her body, mingled with a throat-rasping scream of anger and defiance and stark terror. She kicked again, and this time she was sure she felt the hatch yield ever so slightly. Perhaps the shock of the fall had loosened the locking mechanism.

A thin, high whistle sounded in her ears, swelling quickly into the mindless shriek of escaping air. The pressure seal was broken!

Then the hatch snapped up and away from her coffin as a hurricane tugged and brawled against her skintight. In less than a second the pressures equalized. Cold bit the fingers of her ungloved hand as moisture turned to frost on her helmet visor. She groped in the darkness for her left glove, found it, and pulled it on. Her hands were shaking so badly, she had trouble pressing the wrist seal closed. Next she unhooked her helmet from the module's life support system and reconnected it to her skintight's PLSS. When she touched the test switch and got an answering green light gleaming in the dark, the relief was almost palpable. The pack was fully charged. How far would two hours get her? Not far enough, she suspected, but better than being trapped here in the dark, waiting to be eaten by Xenos.

Three final checks, all by touch: her laser pistol holstered to her right hip, a medikit strapped to her left, and, most important, an AND canister in a belt pouch. Her vehicle suit wasn't equipped to warn her of nano hot spots, so she would have to use the stuff as a prophylactic and pray it lasted until she got . . . where?

She didn't know and she didn't care. Bracing herself, she kicked up and out with both feet one last time. With no difference in atmospheric pressures to keep the hatch sealed, the outer hull access banged open, and light flooded her black prison cell.

Clinging to the rim of her hatch opening, she raised herself on trembling knees. Light, the eerie, shifting glare of fires banked behind thick clouds, gleamed through her helmet's visor. She saw . . . strangeness, and the movement of Xeno machines. *Assassin's Blade* was still on the ground, and the open hatch was less than two meters above the ground.

Where was she? What was this place? She was having trouble identifying the shapes looming from the swirling, light-charged fog, so alien were they, so far removed from anything familiar or recognizable.

The rasp of her indrawn breath sounded unnaturally loud in her helmet. She didn't know how long the skintight's PLSS would last her, and she didn't really care. She had to get out, to get away from this nightmare of black and crystal shapes and unearthly light and smoke boiling above a lake of smothered fires. Standing erect in the open module, she swung one leg over the side, clinging to the hatch for an easy slide to the ground.

Suddenly the Warlord stirred beneath her, a sleeping monster awakened to full awareness. The fuselage jerked up and back, throwing her forward. Katya screamed as the sharp motion catapulted her from the open hatch. Twisting, she grabbed the hatch combing, dangling by her arms as the combat machine rose on unsteady legs. The fuselage snapped forward with a piercing squeak of metal grating on metal, and her hands lost their grip. She fell, her gloved hand raking painfully across hull metal, grabbing at a foothold, then tearing free.

Katya was still screaming as she plunged five meters to the ground. She hit hard and awkwardly, bounced, then slithered down a loose scree of rock and gravel.

The pain when her right leg snapped was indescribable.

Chapter 17

Why does a man fight? Not for country or leader or ideology, despite what the ViRdramatists might say. He fights for his brothers and sisters who fight at his side.

—*A History of Human Warfare*
HEMILCOM Military ViRdocumentary
C.E. 2533

Dev was first aware that Katya was the cause of the ominous thumping that had convinced him the Xenos were on the Warlord's hull when his AI sent a cascade of data across his visual field, warning of a pressure loss in the command module, that the commander's strider PLSS had been taken off-line, and that the commander's access hatch had been blown.

At that point Dev had already started to lever the strider erect, leaning against the strider's gyros to maintain his balance. He tried to abort the mental command, but too late. The brief mental conflict of order and counterorder jarred the strider to motionless indecision just as Dev felt something bump against his left side.

He shifted visuals, switching from the main optics on the Warlord's blunt snout to sensors mounted high on the strider's left shoulder. From that angle, he could look forward and down across the hull and see the gaping maw of the commander's access hatch and two black-suited arms clinging to the opening from the outside. His audio sensors caught Katya's scream as she lost her grip and fell. Shifting optics again, he saw her hit the ground next to the Warlord's left foot, then bounce and slide down the ridge until she came to rest on a pile of loose gravel and snow ten meters below the Warlord's position.

She was still alive, trying to sit up, cradling her right thigh and rocking side to side in pain. *Damn!* He couldn't leave her, but if he stayed put much longer, the images he'd been recording for the past minutes would be melted down with the rest of the combat debris on the ridge crest, just as soon as the Xenos worked their way up the slope.

Dev checked again for one of the circling Stormwinds, but the smoke and steam from the tunnel eruption were still too thick to even let him glimpse the ascraft, much less tag them with a communications laser.

He had only one real choice. He couldn't leave Katya to the Xenos, but he couldn't risk losing the recording either. Carefully he folded the Warlord's legs, lowering the fuselage once again to within a couple of meters of the ground.

"AI," he thought, concentrating. "Robot mode. Receive programming."

"*Blade* ready to accept programming," the AI's voice replied.

He considered firing an AND round to shield himself and Katya from the nano count outside, but decided that the detonation would almost certainly alert the nearby Xeno machines. He'd have to trust in speed . . . and the last few shots in his hand-held AND dispenser.

Dev gave the computer its instructions, received an acknowledgment, then disconnected from the link. In a way, Dev had just transformed the Warlord into a rather simple-minded robot. He'd ordered the Warlord to continue to scan for any of the circling ascraft, to initiate a lasercom link when atmospheric conditions permitted, and to transmit all of the recorded imagery in the Warlord's RAM as soon as that link was open. If the Warlord was attacked, it would be able to fire back with the hivel cannon, which had been slaved to the AI.

But those simple-minded orders, with no room for interpretation, would leave it easy prey to an attacking Alpha, especially since Dev had also ordered it to remain in place.

Sensation returned to Dev's body, and he pulled his left hand from the contact pad. The interior of the pilot's module was stuffy and hot, the padding around him slick with condensation. He unhooked harness, helmet jacks, and life support, checked his combat armor PLSS and glove seals, then cracked his access hatch with a squeal-whoosh of equalizing pressures. A ladder was stowed in an external compartment below his hatch. He extended and locked it, swung out of his compartment, and clambered down to the ground.

Dev was scared as his boots crunched again on bare gravel. Leaving the safety of the Warlord was one of the hardest things he'd ever had to do in his life. He could feel his heart hammering beneath his sternum, and his mouth had gone vacuum-dry. From behind the tumbledown of the RoPro wall, he had an excellent and unobstructed view down the slope and into the steaming pit.

With an almost morbid fascination, he found himself rooted to the spot, staring into the pit. Something new was emerging from the tunnel mouth, something unlike anything he'd seen before. It looked like a pearl, a glistening silver-white sphere half a meter across, rising from the pool of tar at the crater's center. Other pearls followed the first, more and more of them. They hung in the air, supported, Dev supposed, by some sort of magnetic field. Hovering anywhere from just above the uppermost wisps of fog to fifteen meters in the air, they dispersed in every direction, drifting slowly, traveling in straight lines that took them through the new-grown crystalline architecture as though according to some complex plan. One by one, like soap bubbles, the spheres sank to the ground and vanished. Since he no longer had access to the strider's telescopic optics or AI enhancement, Dev could see no details, but it looked like the top of each sphere simply vanished, while the bottoms came to rest on the ground.

Tearing his gaze away, he leaped across the wall and scrambled down the gravel slope to Alessandro's side, rocks and loose sand scattering in a tiny avalanche. "Captain!" he yelled, not sure if her helmet radio was tuned to the tactical frequency. "Captain Alessandro! Can you hear me?"

Her eyes opened behind her visor, showing both recognition and a sharp edge of pain. "My God, what are *you* doing here?"

It was like an accusation. "Never mind that." His voice cracked from the fear-dryness, and from relief. "Let's get you back aboard the *Blade*. Where's your AND?"

"Lost it." An arm gestured weakly down the slope. "When I fell."

Glancing down the slope, Dev saw movement there. The deadly fog was creeping slowly up the ridge, and shapes, small and slithery shapes, moved there, half-visible in the gloom.

"Medikit?"

Katya grimaced. "I think I landed on it. Felt it smash. But I still have this." She patted the holstered lasgun with something like affection. "They won't get me alive, anyway. . . ."

"That's enough of that kind of talk, Captain. We're going to get you out of here."

Dev already had his AND dispenser out. Alessandro's skintight was dusted with patches of silver, like a fine, metallic flour, sticking to her shoulders and wrists and against the swell of her left breast. Nano-Ds adrift in the air were gathering in patches large enough to see. Her suit would be holed in seconds.

He sprayed the parts of her body he could reach thoroughly, but he had to coax the last few squirts from a near-empty canister. Unless there were more counter-nano applicators stored aboard the strider, he'd just used the last there was. Discarding the empty can, he knelt beside her. He could see the kink in her leg where it had broken. There was already quite a bit of swelling.

"How bad does it hurt?"

A grimace was her answer. She would be working on an anodyne block through her implant, but she wouldn't be able to hold it for long.

A wet clink nearby, metal on rock, convinced him there was no time to attach a splint. He had to move her *now*. Pulling his own medapplicator from his pouch, he slapped it against her thigh above the break, firing a stream of medical nano into her leg. It was strictly rough-and-ready field first aid, designed to prevent further damage, stop bleeding, and, most important if he was going to carry her back up that hill, help anesthetize the break.

"Come on, Captain. We've seen all we want to here."

As gently as he could, Dev slipped one arm beneath her shoulders, the other under her thighs, then scooped her up. She yelped once when the movement broke her concentration, but she clung tightly to his neck as he carried her back up the slope toward the looming gray shadow of the Warlord. Dev heard a shrill whine and glanced up. The hivel turret spun to the right, the barrel tracking something behind them. When the cannon fired, the flash was bright enough to throw shadows, and the thunder was as shrill as tearing steel. The stuttering thuds of high-speed rounds striking ground, the clatter of something scraping rock, sounded at his back, meters down the slope.

Dev spun, searching the murk. One of the silver spheres lay a few meters down the slope, half of it melted away, and the hollow interior exposed to Loki's air.

Inside, something moved.

His stomach twisted. This was the first time he'd seen anything associated with the Xenophobes that actually looked and acted alive, but he still couldn't be sure of what he was seeing. A glistening wet, gray-black mass was sliding from the open sphere. It looked like an animate glob of grease . . . or a slug the size of his fist.

Had that been the hivel's target? No. He caught the fluttering movement of a Gamma farther down the slope as it rippled toward him across the uneven ground.

Slinging Katya over his shoulder to free one arm for balance, he jogged up the slope, cursing as loose gravel skittered from beneath his feet and nearly threw them both to the ground. As he reached the top and paused to pick his way across the fallen rubble of the RoPro battlement, something closed on his left ankle.

Lurching off balance, he slammed his shoulder against the strider's hull and groped for the ladder to keep from falling. A Gamma, an amorphous mass the size and shape of a crumpled bath towel, jet black shot through with iridescent silver, clung to his foot, was working its way up his leg.

He screamed and kicked against that sickening pressure, hard, his boot sinking into the thing's formless body. The Gamma was more massive than he'd imagined, and he kicked again. This time it broke free with a sucking sound and dropped to the ground a meter away. Dev vaulted the first three rungs of the ladder despite his burden. "Below you!" Katya yelled, her helmet banging against his as the ladder lurched and swayed. "It's coming up after us!"

With her help, he managed to roll Katya off his shoulder and into the narrow hatch. The medical nano had not yet had time to do its work, and she must have been in agony, but she leaned out of the hatch and grabbed Dev's shoulder with one hand, drawing her laser pistol with the other.

Dev tried to squeeze past her into the compartment, but the heavy thing hit him from behind, molding itself to his legs and the ladder, pinning him. Dev could imagine the machine-creature's nano already eating at his armor and boots, could imagine his legs beginning to dissolve like the bodies he'd seen. Then he felt the first real pain, a searing, burning sensation, like flames licking at his calves and the backs of his knees. Panic rose like a whirling nightmare, fire and storm in his mind, but he clung to the strider's hull and twisted, prying his feet free from the monster's grasp.

The pain was unbearable, a searing liquid fire now flowing up his thighs. In his mind's eye, his legs were shriveling in the heat, his feet reduced to charred tendons taut across blackened bone. He'd seen recordings of people savaged by Xeno Gammas, seen the agony in their faces, and thought he understood now the hell those poor wretches had faced. He was screaming, screaming, but still clinging to the warstrider and fighting back with a near-hysterical strength, kicking with whatever was left of fire-shriveled legs.

"Don't move!" Katya ordered, lunging her upper body past his, arm extended as she trained her laser on the black and silver amoebic horror enveloping his legs. She fired, the 30-MJ handgun's beam invisible, but its effect immediately apparent, as a dazzling point of red light appeared on the Gamma's surface centimeters from Dev's knee. It spasmed under the assault, oily black smoke boiling from that part of the slick black surface that suddenly crinkled like burning paper.

Dev kicked again. "Damn it, I said hold still!" she yelled, but it was impossible not to thrash as agony continued to eat through his brain. The Gamma slipped, still clinging to his calves and feet but releasing his knees. Looking down, Dev could see the remnants of his armor, smoking globs of melted plastic imbedded in flesh that had the mottled look of raw, bloody hamburger. White smoke streamed from his legs, Xeno nano-Ds carrying away molecule-sized pieces of him. The sight, the realization, assaulted his mind; the emotional shock was as sharp and as deadly as any physical damage.

Closing his eyes, Dev tried to bring his cerebral implant into play. The pain lessened now as Dev went through the mental processes necessary to switch off part of his own nervous system. Next he concentrated on contracting blood vessels already starting to pool blood deep within his abdomen, and he elevated his blood pressure slightly to keep his circulation going. Shock, both physical and psychological, could kill him now just as surely as a plasma bolt through his skull.

Subjectively, he hung there battling his own body's reactions for an agony of time, despite the fact that his inner clock recorded the passing of less than four seconds. Suddenly the weight and pressure were gone, though the fire remained, and Katya was pulling him the rest of the way into the open hatch. Dev opened his eyes and looked down as he swayed precariously on the strider's hull. At the foot of the ladder, two flopping, severed pieces of Xenophobe tried to find each another again.

He also saw the ruin of his legs, his bare and mangled feet, and the shock hit him like an electric current. *Control!* . . . His body sagged, limp, and Katya nearly lost him.

Then he was sliding into the embrace of the command module. A jacking slot aboard a warstrider was cramped for one; for two it was nearly impossible. He landed on top of her. They were face-to-face, with no room to move and scarcely room enough to breathe. Somehow Katya managed to reach past him and stab at the manual panel, cycling the access hatch closed. Neither of them could reach his legs, so she pressed his medical nano dispenser against his shoulder to inject him.

Part of his mind continued to work on his own survival. Each breath was painful now, bringing with it an acrid, biting rasp in his nose and throat and lungs. Blearily he realized that his suit had been breached, that he was breathing a rather unhealthy concentration of methane and ammonia at half an atmosphere, that his combat armor PLSS was feeding enough oxygen into the mix to keep him going but that its O_2 charge must be nearly exhausted. Katya would need to hook into the Warlord's life support if she was going to jack them out of here; he damned sure couldn't do it, but he wondered if that meant he was going to suffocate.

There were worse ways to die. He remembered the horror outside the strider's hatch, shuddered, and nearly lost his anodyne block.

Katya must have already assumed that he couldn't pilot the strider. She'd grabbed the dangling jacks, plugged them into her helmet, then peeled off her glove to make contact with the interface plate.

She hesitated, though, before making contact, turning her helmet so that she could look into his face. The compartment's only light was from the tiny manual control board beside Dev's shoulder, and most of that was blocked by their bodies, but he could see her eyes, centimeters from his behind the two transplas layers of their visors.

"Thank you, Dev," she said. "You should have left me, though." He could hear both anger and gratitude in her voice.

"Hey, it could happen to anybody," he said. His own voice surprised him, thin, weak, and shaking. "I moved the *Blade* before I knew you were outside."

"Dev, I *panicked.*" Bitterness edged her voice. He thought he could tell what the admission had cost her.

Her helmet-framed face blurred in his vision, leaving only startlingly green eyes in focus. Was the medical nano taking effect? He couldn't tell. "Hey, 's'okay," he said, his words slurring. Her eyes were starting to grow fuzzy now. "Couldn't leave a buddy out there . . ."

He didn't know if she'd heard him or not. Her hand was on the interface, and her eyes were closed. Her body twitched once beneath his, then went limp as her brain patched into the strider's AI.

Was the Xenophobe nano still eating his legs? He couldn't tell and was afraid to relax the pain block to find out. He concentrated instead on controlling heart and breathing, and on subduing the panic that had so very nearly destroyed him. After a moment, he was dimly aware of a heavy, rolling motion, like a boat caught in a storm at sea. They were moving. Once he heard what sounded like an explosion, dim and distant, and he wondered if Katya had made contact with the Stormwinds, wondered if the Warlord would make it clear to a dust-off site, wondered . . . wondered . . .

In the swaying darkness, exhaustion and the ministrations of the medical nano in his system finally gained the upper hand. Dev fell fast asleep.

Chapter 18

Healing, like so much else of Man's endeavors, has been transformed by nanotechnics. Injuries once fatal can be erased in days, the body itself reshaped into new and more efficient vehicles of the spirit. It is when the spirit is wounded that even the god of nanotechnology may fail.

—*Introspections*
Ieyasu Sutsumi
C.E. 2538

The Hegemony Military Medical Center occupied most of a dome adjacent to the Tristankuppel. It was a doughnut-shaped RoPro building, the hole roofed over with transplas to create a pressurized central courtyard with a circular patio and garden.

Katya stopped at the HMMC's main entrance long enough to check with the patient information 'face, then followed a glowing holographic guide to the courtyard. Dev was in the garden, she learned, practicing with his new walker brace.

It was amazing that Dev was alive. It had been touch and go getting him back from Norway Ridge.

She'd attached her suit's PLSS to his helmet in the Warlord after shooting him full of emergency medical nano. After that, she'd had no time to spare for him as she submerged herself in the *Blade*'s linkage. There'd been a moment's terror there, when she realized Dev had recalibrated the pilot module's linkage to his own brain; her own calibrations were still stored in the AI's main access RAM, though, and a palm 'face command had set up the transfer and completed the linkage. She still remembered the dismay she'd felt as the data had flooded in, detailing the inventory of damage and systems failures the Warlord had already suffered. With energy weapons all but useless, with only fifty rounds remaining in the hivel cannon, all she'd been able to do was turn and run, Xeno Gammas writhing up the slope behind her like a living carpet.

Eight seconds later, she'd broken out from beneath the blanketing umbrella of ash and dust that had kept the Warlord from establishing a lasercom link with the Stormwinds and Lightnings circling the battle area. Dev had left the appropriate commands; as soon as a clear L-LOS appeared, the Warlord's AI established contact, transmitting all recorded data in a decisecond burst. Lara Anders's VK-141 had led the air-ground strike that shattered the pursuing column of Xenos, as a Stormwind with vacant striderslots had touched down and slotted her in. They'd unloaded Dev's mangled body at HMMC less than twelve minutes later.

They'd kept him unconscious while they worked on what was left of his legs. She'd glimpsed them as they pulled his body off of her; everything below his knees had been gone, and the rest was raw, bleeding tissue and white bone halfway up his thighs.

Katya had not seen him since then and wasn't sure what to expect.

She found Dev in the garden practicing with his personal walker, a lightweight frame of nanolayered alloys that did his walking for him. He was standing with his back to her, staring at the atrium's small Japanese garden.

"How are the new legs shaping up?" she asked.

Dev turned. A jack in his C-spine socket connected with the walker's tiny brain, mounted at the small of his back, translating his nervous system's commands and anticipating his movements. His legs, revealed by the hospital-issue briefs he was wearing, were full-grown, but still smooth-pink and hairless, like a child's. Try as she might, Katya could not detect a seam where new tissue had been woven into old.

"Hello, Captain!" he said. "I wasn't expecting you."

"Just making my rounds, Cadet," she said, watching his face closely. She caught the slight widening of his eyes, the tic of a muscle beneath his cheek. As she'd expected, he hadn't come to grips yet with what had happened to him in the last few days. "They told me you were trying out your new legs, so I thought I'd come down here and have a look. How are they?"

"A bit weak." One hand slapped the silver ribbon of his brace running down his thigh. "I can't stand up without this thing on." He looked down at her legs. "You seem to be getting around okay."

"Kuso," she said. "I didn't even need a brace. They had medical nano in me knitting the bone before they'd even finished cutting your legs off. I was walking on it again in twenty-four hours. But *gods,* you were a mess!" The words were calculated to shock, to probe for raw, hidden wounds.

"Yeah, that's what they told me." He looked away, shaking his head. "Did you hear about Suresh?"

She nodded. Suresh Gupta had lived, his spinal cord spliced together by HMMC's nanosomatic engineers. Unfortunately, large parts of his brain had been damaged during the twenty minutes or so when it had been deprived of a blood flow by his dead heart. It had been possible to repair the actual damage . . . but the neuronic pathways that defined memories, personality, even self-awareness, were gone. Traumatic amentia could not be corrected by nanotechnic surgery. Even with RAM feeds to reeducate him, it would be years before Suresh regained what he'd lost.

He would recover. Every newborn child went through the same process. But the new Suresh—or whatever name he eventually chose for himself—would never remember the old, identical to him genetically but with nothing in common with his original personality. It was as though he'd been reborn, with a twenty-four-year-old's body and a blank slate for a mind.

"I heard," she said. Was that what was gnawing at him? Gupta and Cameron had been friends in Basic. She decided to change the subject. "Did you hear the Xenos were beaten off? It took two days, but the Sweden Line held. Special team hit that tunnel you found. The word is, they picked up some damned useful stuff before they sealed it off. After that, it was just a mop-up."

He nodded. "I'm glad."

"So . . . how long you gonna be in that thing? Are the legs still growing?"

"They tell me they're full-grown. The nanosomes say I'll be in this thing for another week, until the muscles are strong enough to hold me up."

"You'll never know the difference." She held up her left hand and flexed it. "They grew this back on me two years ago."

"Really?" His eyes had a haunted look.

"They'll feel just like the old ones. They just won't have the same scars and blemishes."

"That's what they told me." He looked away. "I've been awfully hungry these last couple of days."

The medical nano Katya had injected into Dev in the strider had done little but keep him unconscious, stop the bleeding, and scour his body for any trace of invading Xeno nano. At HMMC the surgeons had amputated both legs, replacing them with force-grown, neutral tissue buds grafted in place by HMMC's best nanosomatic engineers. Full-grown in four days, the new legs were identical to the old, but they were still painfully weak, so weak, in fact, that he could not even stand or walk without the skeletal framework of the walker brace. Dev's system had been loaded with meteffectors busily converting raw materials to fresh muscle, which was why he always felt hungry. Soon he'd be on an exercise program that would leave him too tired to think about much else.

If his mind hadn't been damaged by what he'd gone through on that ridge. That was what Katya was trying to learn now.

"Glad to hear it." Katya smiled. "If you're hungry, it means you're on the mend. You know, when they pulled you out of the *Blade*, I thought they were going to have to take you out with a scraper and cutting torch."

Katya watched one corner of his mouth tug upward at that deliberately brutal probe. How would he respond? If his psychtechs knew what I was doing, she thought, amused, they'd toss me out of this dome without a suit.

But she *had* to know how he would react.

"I don't think I would have gone very well with her pilot's mod decor," Dev replied. "Late Army Spartan. Not my style at all."

"And what is your style, Lieutenant? Early Navy Romantic?"

"Definitely Romantic. Centuries out-of-date."

She laughed. "By God, Dev, I think you're going to be all right!"

He gave her a wry grin. "What, you thought I was going to null out?"

"It's been known to happen. Your mind can screw you over better than your body any day. And you got hit pretty bad."

Medical engineers could rebuild the body. In war, however, the most serious wounds often were those inflicted on the mind: shock at being wounded, shock at seeing friends die, the raw, destructive savagery of fear. Direct link counseling, psychiatric simulations, and sub-C therapy could all begin the healing, but the patient himself had to complete it.

Dev rubbed one leg thoughtfully. "Yeah. Maybe they got me patched up so fast, I never realized I'd lost anything. I'm okay, Captain. *Really* okay."

Katya agreed. She'd seen his preliminary psych studies but hadn't known how to pull the numbers together into a meaningful picture. His TM rating, for instance, was lower—down to point two—which might mean he'd lost some of his cockiness. There was some depression, of course. Claustrophobia was a bit higher, his suspicion of authority about the same. All in all, his attitude appeared to have improved.

"So how do you feel about coming back to work, Cadet?"

She caught the subtle twitch of facial muscles again. "I'd . . . like that, Captain. If you guys'll have me back."

"Like I said, you've got the makings of a great striderjack. I just have to know that what happened out there didn't permanently scramble your brains."

"They're no more scrambled than usual, Captain. I'm just . . . well, I don't know if I'll be able to handle it. It might be a better idea to bounce me back to the infantry."

She shook her head. "I played back the recorder, going through your fight with the Cobra after I got knocked off-line. You're good, a natural linker. You'd be wasted with the leggers."

"Infantry," he said, correcting her. "The trouble is that everybody's making out like I was some kind of hero. I wasn't. I was scared. When we were outside the *Blade*, trying to get up the ladder, I think I was more scared than I've ever been in my life."

So *that* was it. Burned once, he didn't know if he could face it again. He'd be reliving the nightmare for quite a while to come, despite everything the psychtechs could feed him.

"Kuso, Dev. The only people on a battlefield who *aren't* scared are dead or unconscious. You think you're something special?"

He gave her a lopsided grin. "Not me."

"You weren't the only one scared on that ridge."

"You, Captain?"

"Tell another living soul and I'll hang your brain out to dry. But the only reason I fell was the fact that I panicked. Blind, sick, run-away-and-hide panic. If I hadn't broken my leg, I'd still be running."

"That's a bit hard to believe. Sir."

"Don't jerk my strings, Cadet. I'm no different than you." She watched him for a moment, aware of the succession of emotions mingling with her thoughts. She, too, was lucky to be alive, and she had this unusual young striderjack to thank for that. She still couldn't remember her fall, worse, the fear, without a sharp inward wince.

There was guilt, too. During her debriefing, she'd realized that the lone trooper she'd encountered had been Dev. She'd passed him by, leaving him for the Gammas; he'd left the *Blade* and braved those Gammas to come after her.

She was realist enough to know that the two cases weren't parallel. There was nothing she could have done, nothing she could have been *expected* to do, to save him, but the realization could not diminish her gratitude.

Alive . . .

Aware of the flush rising in her face, she changed the subject again. "I, ah, noticed you weren't having trouble accessing codes up on that ridge."

"You noticed, huh?"

"Looks to me like you were trying too hard before. Or maybe you were letting your fear tangle your wires. Either way, you've got it licked now. You *know* it."

But just the same, I think I'll still put you in a one-slotter, she told herself. Just in case. There's stuff going on inside your head that'll never come out on a psych screening, and it might be better to let you find out about it on your own instead of teaming you with someone else. You certainly performed well on your own at Norway Ridge. "So you'll come back to the Assassins?"

"I guess so. Thanks." He seemed embarrassed. "I'll try not to let you down again."

"You ever do any horseback riding, Cadet?"

He shook his head. "I've heard about horses," he said. "On Earth. Never seen one, though."

"Some colonies still use them for transportation in the outback. They do on New America, where I come from. Big brutes. You can get hurt if you fall off."

The embarrassment was gone, replaced by a subtle, humorous twinkle. "Like falling off a strider?"

"Like falling off a strider. The number one rule, though, is to get back on as soon as you fall off. Before you have a chance to think about it."

"Makes sense. I think I'd like to, ah, get back on."

"It's still not the navy," she said, sticking out her hand. "But welcome aboard. Again."

Grinning, he shook her hand, and she felt the inner surge of something she'd promised herself she would not feel again. *I don't want to get close to anybody*, she thought. *Not again!*

She dismissed the thought almost at once. *Staticjack! You just get back on again!*

Chapter 19

Therefore I say: Know the enemy and know yourself; in a hundred battles you will never be in peril.

When you are ignorant of the enemy but know yourself, your chances of winning or losing are equal.

If ignorant of both the enemy and of yourself, you are certain in every battle to be in peril.

—*The Art of War*
Sun Tsu
fourth century B.C.

They floated in golden light, three men, with Loki a cloud-wreathed sphere swelling against the night above them. The office of Rear Admiral Kazuo Aiko was located on the Asgard Ring, one hundred kilometers east of the Bifrost Sky-el, but the AI that enhanced and projected the image had purged it of the clutter of the orbital ring, leaving only clean stars and space and the storm-wracked globe of Loki. The room had taken on the rose-warm hues of 36 Ophiuchi C, but the atmosphere seemed chilly.

None of the men in that room was happy.

General John Howard, immaculate in army grays, clung to a handline and regarded the two Nihonjin who had invited him to this conference with some apprehension. Technically Howard outranked Aiko, but the admiral was the *shosho* in command of all Imperial forces currently in Loki's system. Custom—and a healthy sense of career survival—dictated that even HEMILCOM lieutenant generals defer with respect and diplomatic courtesy to Imperial officers, whatever their rank.

And as for the third man, he held no military rank at all, but that would not help Howard's career if Shotaro Takahashi decided that a scapegoat was needed in the Loki affair. He was *Daihyo*, the Emperor's personal representative, and his word was the Emperor's command.

Appearances, Howard reflected, could be deceiving, for Takahashi did not look like an Imperial representative. He was obese, a sumo wrestler without the beef in legs and arms that hinted at strength beneath layers of fat. His clothing, little more than a white cloth wrapped around hips and loins, furthered the similarity to sumo, but his body adornment, nano-tailored feathers, baroque metallic inlays, and patchworks of jewel-like color winding across half of his exposed body, was like nothing Howard had ever seen.

The total effect was decadent . . . and threatening. Somehow the fabled human art of the Imperial Palace had crossed sixteen light-years to confront Howard here, in Aiko's office. The *Daihyo* floated cross-legged in the center of the room, ignoring the conventions of *up* and *down* imposed by the room's floor and meager furnishings. He seemed so at home in microgravity, and looked as if he would be so helpless on any world's surface, that Howard wondered if his body tailoring extended beyond the superficialities of feathering, skin color, and texture. Takahashi might well be more Freefaller than Earth-norm human, incapable of setting foot on Loki or Earth.

By contrast, Rear Admiral Aiko was completely human, as dour as ever in his severe Imperial Navy blacks, his bare feet slipped into footholds on the floor behind the silver-white console that served as comlink access and interface. Howard appreciated the gesture. He wasn't used to zero-g, and his vertigo was made worse by the room's rather unnerving background projection. Only floor, furniture, and Aiko's pretense at an upright posture existed to combat the disquieting illusion that the three of them were adrift in space. Howard, who left Loki's surface only when he had to, wondered if the projection was some kind of deliberate psychological ploy, a gimmick to keep groundpounder visitors like himself off balance.

"Your request is most irregular," Takahashi was saying, his voice a gentle and menacing rumble from beneath that massive chest. He spoke Nihongo, though Howard knew he always carried an excellent Inglic RAM feed. "And possibly illegal as well. You know the Imperial guidelines on this."

Howard's knuckles whitened as he gripped the handline. He was angry, but he didn't want his anger to turn this interview into a confrontation. He'd had experience enough with Imperial agents to know that he would never get what he needed through bluntness.

"Of course, *Daihyo* Takahashi," he replied evenly. "However, I feel compelled to point out that this new idea gives us our best chance to actually defeat the Xenophobes, rather than simply hold them at bay."

"We've not even been holding them," Aiko put in. "Norway Ridge was a victory, true, but the Xenophobes should never have gotten that close to Midgard in such numbers." He held up a thumb and forefinger, tips a centimeter apart. "We came *that* close to losing it all."

"Nuclear weaponry must remain the sole responsibility of Imperial forces," Takahashi said, reciting the old doctrinal line. "It's dangerous enough that Hegemony forces have access to tactical weapons in the fractional kiloton range. More powerful weapons require special training and handling. This new device your people have suggested has promise, but the Emperor will permit its deployment only under the control of his forces."

Special training, Howard thought. Right. A polite way of saying they don't trust us with the damned things . . .

especially if the Hegemony gets restless under the Empire's thumb.

"We're fighting the same enemy," Howard said, pointing out the obvious. "Four days ago, we acquired new intelligence, stuff no one's ever seen before. From this data, we've evolved an idea, a weapon. But as I stated in my report, we need nuclear weapons for the idea to be viable. I would estimate fifty devices in the one-hundred-kiloton range, for a start. . . ."

"Impossible," Takahashi rumbled.

Aiko gave the *Daihyo* a sidelong glance, then turned expressionless eyes back on Howard. "There is, in fact, no doctrinal conflict here, General. Hegemony forces rely on Imperial expertise whenever a Threat tunnel must be sealed. I imagine we could work out a similar arrangement here. We could provide nuclear warheads, but their deployment and activation would be under Imperial control." He looked again at Takahashi. "Would that be satisfactory to the Emperor?"

Solemnly Takahashi inclined his head, as though granting absolution.

Howard had expected this battle. The Japanese had maintained strict control of all nuclear warheads for five centuries—since the Central Asian War, in fact, when they'd been the ones to go in and disarm both the Kazakhis and the Uighurs of the West China Republic. The Treaty of Karaganda had led to the Hegemony's founding and implied—in what Howard thought was a deliciously ironic twist of history—that the Japanese Empire alone had the right to deploy weapons in the kiloton-or-larger category.

Officially, unregulated use of fission or fusion warheads could interfere with the terraforming of the Shichiju's worlds. That was true enough, Howard reflected . . . except that the Xenos had interfered with the t-form schedule of eleven worlds already far more completely than nukes ever could.

He wondered if the Imperial staff thought that civil war, the Hegemony against the Empire, was inevitable. Plenty of Hegemony officers he knew felt it was, Howard among them.

Between the Xenophobes and a restless Imperial Hegemony, the Emperor must be getting nervous.

"I'm sure that would be the best way to handle it," Howard said smoothly. "Of course, there is a lot of resentment in HEMILCOM already. They perceive . . . mistakenly, of course, but they perceive that we are carrying the brunt of the fight against the Xenos, that the Empire is standing in the background, out of harm's way—"

"Yoku iu-yo!" Takahashi spat. The Nihongo literally meant "How dare you say that," but in a culture where directness was insult, the phrase was as charged with anger as profanity. "You have no right to speak that way!"

"I merely report attitudes among the soldiers," Howard said, spreading his hands.

"A mutiny?" Aiko wanted to know. "A rebellion within the Hegemony forces?"

"Nothing so melodramatic, Admiral san. But there are bad feelings. How many Imperials died at Schluter?"

"Imperial forces did not arrive until after the battle was over."

"Precisely my point."

"But we are on the same side!" Takahashi insisted. "Humans, together against these monsters! Earth is in as great a danger as is Loki, at least until we understand how the Xenophobes traverse space. We must cooperate together, your people and mine."

"Tell us about this new data you mentioned," Aiko prompted.

"One of our striders became stranded behind Xeno lines during the battle. It happened to be in the right place at the right time. Everything the pilot witnessed was recorded by his strider's AI, broad spectrum, full sensory range. One of our combat engineers, when he saw the data and recognized its significance, came up with the idea for . . . our weapon."

"I would like to see this data for myself."

Howard nodded. "I thought you might, Admiral. Our comjacks assembled the sensory data from the warstrider to create a detailed Virtual Reality." He gestured at Aiko's desktop com unit. "If I may, sir?"

"Of course."

Howard pulled himself over, placed his palm on the contact plate, and made a connection. "Gentlemen?"

Aiko opened a panel on the desk and extracted three jack leads. Takahashi appeared reluctant to plug himself in at first, as though direct electronic contact would somehow contaminate him, but at last he extended a blunt-fingered hand, took a lead, and snicked the jack into a T-socket masked by a spread of white and scarlet feathers. Howard plugged himself in and then, exchanging glances with the others, brought his palm down on the desktop interface.

Room, gold-orange sun, and cloud-wreathed world were gone. In their place was a desolate and war-swept landscape under oily, angry-looking clouds. A warstrider crouched atop a ridge edged with broken battlements, the ruins sharp-edged and ragged, like a predator's teeth. Three hundred meters away, a column of smoke boiled from a fog-filled valley, where an alien, crystalline architecture grew from nothing. Dust and ash trickled from the bleak sky like rain, and a sound, like tinkling chimes, could be heard above a low and grumbling thunder. It looked as though it ought to be bitterly cold, but in fact, the surroundings actually felt comfortable.

"What is this place?" Takahashi demanded. Howard noticed with mild surprise that the *Daihyo*'s ViRpersona was different in the AI-moderated universe of virtual reality. Here he was stocky and muscular, but not fat, and he wore the armor of a feudal Japanese warrior, a samurai. The effect was as unnerving in its way as the feathers and skin art.

"A virtual simulation of the battlefield at Norway Ridge," Howard replied. "That's Cameron's warstrider up there on the ridge." Unlike a film recording, a ViRsim could be explored in three dimensions, with the AI filling in detail and hidden sides to create a simulated reality bounded only by the range and sensitivity of its senses.

"I gather that Cameron survived the action," Aiko said quietly. He looked the same as he had in the real world, stiff, erect, and immaculate. The ashfall stubbornly refused to touch his black uniform.

"Yes, Admiral-san. He was badly wounded, but both he and the company commander made it back. Cameron's still in the hospital undergoing nanosomatic reconstruction. He's become . . . quite the hero."

"So it would seem from the man's citation I received this morning," Aiko said. "The company commander put him in for the Imperial Star. I had to turn it down."

"May I ask why, Admiral-san?"

"There were . . . political considerations." Aiko paused, staring at a rounded shape lying nearby. "What is that?"

"This is what we found interesting, gentlemen," Howard said. He led them to the object, a pearl gray hemisphere, open at the flat side, lying on the gravel at the edge of a sea of fog. The smooth-surfaced hollow within was considerably smaller than the object's full volume.

"Empty," Takahashi said.

"This one is. Look. There's one coming up now."

He pointed. Thirty meters out in the fog-filled crater, another sphere was rising from the ground, shimmering, supported by the pale blue wings of a traveler magfield viewed through a warstrider's extended senses. It hesitated a moment, then began drifting toward the three watching men, hovering a meter above the mist.

"Did that just rise out of solid ground?" Aiko wanted to know.

"Essentially, Admiral-san, yes. We've known for a long time that the Xenos use powerful magnetic fields to warp rock."

"SDTs," Aiko put in.

"Yes, sir. They create paths where the rock has become plastic, almost fluid, and they can move along these paths the way a submarine moves through water." He nudged the empty shell with the toe of his boot. "Until we caught these babies in action, the only Xeno equipment we knew of that could perform that trick were Alphas—their equivalent of our warstriders—and Betas, which are human machines they've captured and reworked. But in all the battles fought on twelve worlds during the last forty-two years, we've never been able to capture a Xeno machine. Why? Because even pieces of them seem to have a life of their own. They change shape, move . . . and anything of ours they touch, they destroy, either by dissolving it with nano disassemblers, or by changing it into something else. None of our intelligence people, yours or mine, has ever had a close look at a genuine piece of Xeno technology."

As the floating bubble neared the edge of the crater, it slowed and descended. Touching solid ground, it rolled half over, then opened.

Half of the sphere vanished as completely as the bursting of a bubble. The other half lay inert on the ground, the squirming gray mass within exposed to Loki's chill air. Takahashi looked startled. Aiko's eyes narrowed as he watched the creatures begin to spill onto the ground.

"And this," Howard added, "may be our first close look at the Xenos themselves."

They were definitely *creatures*, organic life forms rather than machines. Each was the size of a man's hand, flattened slug shapes like large, shell-less snails or some of the free-swimming marine worms of Earth's ocean deeps. These were dark gray in color, but their surfaces glistened with prismatic displays of rainbow hues, like oil on water catching the light.

There must have been several hundred of them within the broken sphere. As soon as they were free, each began fanning out across the uneven ground with wet, pulsing movements of their bodies, half returning to the fog, the other half making their way across the rocks along geometrically perfect straight lines.

Aiko stooped, looking close. "They are connected."

"That's right. The detail at this range from the strider isn't sharp enough for us to be sure what's happening, but it looks like each slug is physically connected to those nearest to it by a slender strand."

"Are they separate creatures then?" Takahashi wanted to know. "Or a single organism?"

"Our bio people are still arguing that one." He nudged the empty shell again. "But this is what we found that was important."

Howard fed a command through his link to the AI controlling the simulation, and the landscape changed. The alien structures around the crater rim were more numerous now, competing with one another in jerky, angular thrusts into the lead gray sky. There were many more silvery hemispheres scattered about on the ground now. Some had the curiously melted look of objects being dissolved by nano disassemblers, but others were fresh and new. Spheres continued to rise from the crater floor like bubbles in an effervescent drink. The warstrider on the ridge was gone, but a dozen human ascraft circled the area at the very limits of visibility. An explosion thumped at the top of the ridge . . . then something streamed fire into the midst of the crater architecture and detonated with a shattering roar.

"This is four hours later," Howard said, raising his voice to be heard above the bombardment. "As soon as we saw what we had in the recording from Cameron's strider, we put together a special assault team. We're looking at a sim based on recordings made by a Stormwind in the area."

Shapes appeared along the ridge, the squat, deadly shapes of Hegemony warstriders. Answering shapes emerged from the crater, the dragonish uncoiling of a King Cobra, the spine-bristling threat of a combat mode Fer-de-Lance. Battle was joined. A plasma blast sheared whiplashing tentacles from the side of a drifting Copperhead, was answered by the rapid-fire *thud-thud-thud* of Xeno nano-D rounds hurled at the ridge. Drifting smoke obscured the battlefield.

Out of the haze, three armored, manlike shapes emerged, shepherded by a larger form. The shepherd was an LaG-42 Ghostrider. The humanoid forms were single-slot

Scoutstriders, with arms instead of paired weapons pods.

The Ghostrider took a covering position, blazing away into the smoke cover with missiles and laser. The Scoutstriders moved down the slope toward the empty hemispheres. Howard could hear the hollow fire-extinguisher *shoosh* as nano-countermeasures were sprayed over the area, the whine of servomotors as the recon striders stooped, grasped the Xeno artifacts in durasheathed hands, and picked them up.

"One of them didn't reach the recovery point," Howard explained as the warstriders began lugging their trophies back up the ridge. "Countermeasures failed. The other two spheres were brought back to a special containment area outside of Midgard. We've been picking them apart almost atom by atom since."

The battlefield faded from view as Howard broke the linkage. The three men floated again in Aiko's office in Asgard.

"As a result," he continued, "we now have the molecular pattern of a Xeno magfield projector. We know how they perform their little trick of moving through rock, and we're beginning to understand how they can manipulate the planet's magnetic field to float above the ground. We're programming construction nano to build replicas, as many as we need."

"To what purpose?" Takahashi, his pudgy legs still lotus-folded, was rotating slowly in the center of the room. Somehow his mass and the eye-grabbing details of his personal ornamentation tended to support the illusion that the *Daihyo* was stationary, and that Howard, Aiko, and the room all were rotating around him.

Howard fixed his eyes on Aiko, shifting again to Inglic. "We can duplicate their trick of sending payloads through solid rock."

"So?"

"Don't you see? We could create nuclear depth charges!"

Takahashi looked blank.

"Depth charges," Howard repeated. "Bombs that would sink into the ground and detonate at a preset depth!"

"Interesting idea, though I fail to see how such a weapon could be effective," Takahashi said. He shook his head, jowls wobbling in the zero-g. "In any case, I doubt that it would be feasible politically. There are not enough qualified Imperial officers at Asgard to supervise the deployment of so many nuclear warheads. Perhaps in time, with reinforcements from Earth, something could be worked out. . . ."

Howard released the handline, spreading his arms. "Admiral-san, we need your help. The *Empire's* help. Look, the people on Loki don't give a damn for the politics of the Empire and Hegemony. What we *do* know is that every time the Xenos stick their noses above ground, outposts disappear, mining facilities are destroyed, cities are smashed, and our people die. The Xenos are pushing us off the planet, and so far the Empire hasn't been giving us a rat's ass worth of real help!

"Well, now we have a way to fight back. Stop them cold and win back our world. We can't wait for things to thread their way through eighteen light-years of red tape to Earth and back." His eyes flicked to Takahashi, then back to Aiko. "The Xenos are as dangerous to Earth as they are to us. We could stop them for you, right here, right now, before they get anywhere near Earth. Isn't that worth something? A little help with the red tape, maybe? Or do we get nothing from the Emperor but promises and platitudes?"

He stopped, breathing hard. He'd gone over the diplomatic line with that little speech, he knew, but found he didn't care anymore. Fighting with the Imperial bureaucracy could be like arguing with a Lokan methane storm: lots of noise, fury, and confusion, with little accomplished.

Perhaps, though, if he made enough noise . . .

Aiko was silent for a long moment, and Howard wondered if he had, indeed, gone too far. Simply by questioning the bureaucracy's efficiency, he could have just ended his career. The Hegemony governor would hire or fire anyone in his command whom the Imperials told him to, including the commander-in-chief of the local armed forces.

"Tell me," Aiko said at last, "about depth charges that sink through solid rock."

Enthusiastically, Howard began outlining the idea.

Chapter 20

Decorations are for the purpose of raising the fighting value of troops; therefore they must be awarded promptly.

—Letter of Instruction
General George S. Patton, Jr.
mid-twentieth century

Tristankuppel was alive with the color and excitement of military pomp and ceremony. Tons of sand had been carted in from outside and RoProed into an elegantly curved and sunburst-graven reviewing stand set squarely in front of Scandia Hall. Bleachers had been grown to either side, forming silver wings that flanked stage and podium and masked the base's drab fabricrete barracks, classrooms, and equipment warehouses. Gayly colored banners representing each of Midgard's forty-one domes plus most of the outlying settlements hung from invisible struts crisscrossing the underside of the transplas sky.

As a very special touch, Asgard's lasers had gently nudged Loki's weather patterns the day before, creating a high-pressure zone that put all of the Midgard Plateau under a rare break in the perpetual cloud cover. Dagstjerne, Loki's orange Daystar set in a clear green sky, touched the dome's transplas with liquid ruby and bathed the parade ground in warm sunset colors.

The grinder had been kept clear, save for three ranks of warstriders, the First, Second, and Third Platoons of the Thorhammers' A Company, walked in through a specially grown airlock the evening before. Recoated with nano armor films in the Thorhammers' blue and white colors, they gleamed in the sunlight like brand-new machines. Only someone who knew combat striders and had a sharp eye could pick out the missing weapons or armor plates or sensor clusters that showed these machines had been in heavy fighting only days before.

Dev stood just inside a gold-decorated archway opening onto the parade ground. The ceremony was due to start in another few minutes, and the area inside the archway was crowded with the men and women of the Loki Fifth as they began to form up ranks for the processional march. Outside, the bleachers were nearly filled by those Midgarders with money or political rank or social pull enough to attend. Dev had heard that a fair-sized contingent from Asgard had descended Bifrost the day before. They would be in the special review stand seats, out of sight from his vantage point in the seats behind the speaker's podium.

He tugged at his collar with a forefinger. This was the first time he'd worn full dress army grays, and he was finding them damned uncomfortable despite the tailor-programmed fit. The crisply fashioned two-toned uniform had been fresh-grown in the base nanovats just that morning, and still it felt stiff, especially around the rigid collar. He didn't mind the formal discomfort in the least, though. His shoulder boards and collar both bore the thick gold stripe and single cherry blossom insignia of *sho-i*, sublieutenant.

Strangest of all, though, was his being accepted once again into the Fifth Loki Warstriders.

He checked his internal clock. Eight minutes to go. Yeah, no static. He could hold on another eight minutes. Outside, a crash of music announced the beginning of the festivities. The crowd cheered, creating the atmosphere of some mammoth sporting event.

Wryly, Dev shook his head. All this fuss. Victories against the Xenos were rare enough, so the Battle of Norway Ridge, as it was now being called, certainly deserved a celebration. The who-was, though, hinted at some sort of breakthrough, possibly a new discovery or weapon of some kind. Nobody knew any details, though, save that some mighty high-powered brass was coming down from Asgard for the awards ceremony today.

"Hello, Lieutenant."

Startled, he turned, still not used to the honorific that went with his new rank. Katya Alessandro stood there, slim and attractive in the female version of Hegemony dress grays, with a rack of medals and campaign ribbons above her left breast that made him do a double take. Above a rainbow collection of campaign ribbons and unit citations, she wore a silver star, three combat drop badges, a blood bar with one cluster . . . and the *Yukan no Kisho*, the Imperial Medal of Valor, fourth dan. His eyes widened. He'd not realized she carried that much show metal.

But then, he'd never seen her in full dress before. He saluted. "Good morning, Captain. You have this habit of sneaking up behind me."

"Stealth, Lieutenant. The secret of strider warfare. How are you feeling?"

He grimaced. "Sore. They've got me on the new exercise program. And the brace is hurting my legs worse than that damned Gamma. They say it's coming off tomorrow. I don't know if they mean the brace or one of my legs."

She laughed. Strange, he thought, how shared black humor could acknowledge *yujo,* the warriors' bond. He felt comfortable with Katya, despite the difference in rank and experience.

"So what do you think about all this?" The tilt of her head took in the arch and the stadium beyond, with its screaming thousands.

"Am I supposed to think something?"

"Well, it *is* in your honor, Dev. Your little exploit on Norway Ridge created quite a stir. Or hadn't you noticed?"

"I guess I did. I'm still trying to figure out why."

"Stop thinking. Give me your 'face."

He held out his palm, and she touched it with her own. Data passed from her RAM to his, a trickle of words and numbers. A place, a restaurant in Towerdown, and a time, that evening. "We're having a party. Be there."

"Why me?"

She grinned. "Because you're the guest of honor, newbie."

"Is that an order?"

"If it has to be."

"I'll be there," he said. "Hey, I hear you're getting some more show metal today to add to your collection. Congratulations."

She made a sour expression. "That and a *sen-en* will buy me lunch in Midgard."

"No big deal, eh?"

"Hey, I didn't mean to put *yours* down, Lieutenant. You did pretty good, first time up."

First time up. It was as though she'd forgotten his first ignominious experience under fire. Or was she telling him his first time didn't count?

He was about to ask, but her head cocked into a listening position. "They're calling me," she said. "Time to odie. Good luck, Lieutenant."

His own call came moments later, the official-sounding voice of the Ceremonies Master in his mind, relayed through the tiny radio/cephlink transceiver plugged into his right T-socket. He found his place in the waiting ranks of First Platoon, a solid block of men and women in two-toned grays, with full-dress epaulets and medals. A simulated band was blaring out the opening bars of "Earth's Hegemony" outside.

"Regiment, stand by!" the voice in his head called. "Ready . . . ten-*hut!* With the music, and *left!* . . . and *left!* . . . and *left!* . . ."

Dev had seen little use for drill during Basic, but he had to admit there was a martial thrill to the spectacle of over nine hundred men and women marching through the archway and into the center of that vast, circular coliseum. Perhaps it was nothing but showmanship, but for perhaps the first time since he'd volunteered for Hegemony service, he felt himself to be a part of something meaningful. *Sho-i* Devis Cameron might be a very small part of a vast and impersonal organization, but he did have a place, a slot that he'd made his own.

He *belonged.*

The Ceremonies Master continued to call cadence for the regimental formation as it turned onto the field and marched in review past a raised, temporary platform filled with the dignitaries and military brass. "Eyes *right,*" the CM called, and Dev had the opportunity to see them.

Most impressive of the visitors were the hundred men of Third Company, First Battalion of the Fifteenth Imperial Assault Guard, the *Zugaikotsu* regiment, dazzling in the full dress black and silver armor of the marines. Part of the Imperial garrison on Asgard, the 1/15 was arrayed in front of the review stand, blast rifles held at present arms. It was impossible to look at those spotless martial ranks and think of them as *crunchies.*

Behind them, on the stand itself . . . damn, it looked like half of the Asgard brass was present. Above and behind the stand, an enormous repeater screen had been raised, thirty meters tall and ten wide. At the moment it showed the regiment as it passed in review, endless blocks of marching color: officers in two-toned grays, technicians in green, ordnancemen in red, ascraft pilots in dark blue, enlisted troops in khaki or in dress black armor.

The men on the reviewing stand were divided about half and half, Japanese and *gaijin. Shosa* Fisher and *Shosa* Rassmussen, the HEMILCOM Training Command CO, were both there. A civilian, Piotr Klasst, the Hegemony governor on Loki, was present as well, a small, squat, self-important man in a purple jumpsuit and gold sash.

But Dev almost missed a step when he saw the man in Imperial black and gold standing at the podium, none other than *Shosho* Aiko himself, the commander of Asgard's Nihonjin contingent.

Aiko! *He* was making the presentation? The last time Dev had seen him, the man had been a captain, a member of the Imperial Staff. He'd been present at the ceremony when they'd awarded the Imperial Star to the newly commissioned Admiral Michal Cameron.

Dev wondered. Did his father's disgrace have something to do with Aiko being given a field command, eighteen light-years from the Imperial Palace? If so, it was astonishing that he'd agreed to preside at this particular ceremony. Behind Aiko was a ponderously fat civilian in nangineered feathers, scales, and inlays. Dev didn't know who he was, but his adornment suggested that he was from the Imperial Court. The who-was was right. This *was* a high-powered ceremony.

Marching rank by rank, the Thorhammers completed one turn about the stadium circuit, then took up their positions facing the review stand and the motionless line of Imperial Guardsmen. They numbered, all told, nearly nine hundred men and women, about sixty percent of their officially listed strength. From other archways around the stadium, troops from other units marched to their assigned places, techies and ordies by the hundreds, line infantry in newly grown combat armor, cadet-trainees in yellow. Only the Thorhammers and the training companies were represented in full, but both the Odinspears and the Heimdal Guards had sent colorfully uniformed contingents, each behind a staff-carried banner.

Music and marching ceased as Dev's implant noted that the eight minutes were up. There was a moment's silence, and then the band began playing the Imperial anthem. After that came the first of several speeches.

Dev stood at attention, watching the Lokan Governor's florid features on the giant repeater screen above the reviewing stand as the man talked about the utter necessity of pressing on, Empire and Hegemony, side by side until the job was done. Dev's mind wasn't on the speech, however. He was more interested in the data Katya had passed to him.

Yes . . . he'd thought so. Besides the date and time for the party, there was a small, closed file, marked personal so that it could not be picked up by a data feed scan without his express permission. He hadn't noticed it when she 'faced him the other information, but its presence had been subconsciously nagging at him.

Curious, he opened it, and heard her voice in his mind.

Dev, you're not even supposed to know this, but I originally put you in for the Imperial Star. I hear the recommendation made it all the way up the sky-el to Aiko's staff before the stiff-necked sheseiji finally squelched it.

Well, I doubt the Star would've passed without more witnesses anyway. The thing to remember is that it's the man who counts, not the show metal on his chest. Medals you can buy at any pawnshop on the Midgard Way; heroes, the genuine variety who don't wear their bravery like a medal, are damned hard to find.

Mostly I just wanted to say thanks again for not leaving me out there. I'm looking forward to seeing you at the party tonight.

—Katya Alessandro

The news rocked him. The Imperial Star? Gods of the K-T Sea, witnesses had nothing to do with it! The Imperials, who thought in terms of family and lineage and the responsibilities of sons for their fathers' names, did not like to be reminded of past failures. Awarding the *Teikoku no Hoshi* to the son of Admiral Cameron would be like confessing that his father had been a sacrifice to political necessity. Unthinkable!

For himself, he was just as happy he hadn't won that damned Star. Quite frankly Dev found it astonishing that they were even giving him a lesser award instead. The

Medal of Valor carried with it considerable prestige, but he'd done nothing to win it, after all, except rather foolishly risk important recon intel in order to drag a wounded buddy to safety . . . and it was his fault she'd been hurt in the first place. The instinct might have been brave, but damn it, he'd been *scared.* He was still ashamed of that mind-numbing fear, and of how Katya had had to yell to make herself heard above his screams.

He listened again to Katya's note, trying to reconcile it with what he knew was the truth. A hero? Him? Not likely!

The speeches were over at last, with Dev hearing scarcely a word. Later, perhaps, he would play the ceremony back for himself from his own RAM, but for now he was reduced to stumbling through the ceremony, piloting on automatic.

On signal from the voice within his mind, Dev marched forward, taking the corners at crisp right angles, ascended the steps to the review stand between motionless ranks of armored Imperial Guardsmen, saluted, and bowed. Expressionless, Aiko turned to an aide and took the medal from its box, a gold shield dangling from a crimson and yellow ribbon and bearing a holographic relief of the Emperor. The bar supporting the ribbon had a charged adhesive strip that would cling securely to Dev's tunic until he touched a contact point on the corner.

"Yukan no Kisho," Aiko said, pressing it to Dev's chest. "The Medal of Valor, for services to the Emperor above the call of duty." Turning, he reached for a second medal, this one silver and pearl on a scarlet ribbon. "*Shishi no Chi,* The Lion's Blood, awarded to those wounded in the Emperor's service."

Most *gaijin* simply called it the blood bar.

"Congratulations," Aiko added, still expressionless. Dev wondered what he was thinking now, wondered if he was remembering giving a medal to another *gaijin* a few years before. Did Aiko know he was Cameron's son? Of course he did. He would have reviewed Dev's records before seconding Katya's request. *The stiff-necked sheseiji,* she'd called him. The stiff-necked bastard. But there must be more to it than that.

"Thank you, Admiral-san."

"You have done great credit to your people, *Sho-i,*" he said, this time in heavily accented English, and with the voice circuit off, so that no one could hear but the two of them. "And to your family."

Now, what the gok did he mean by *that*? Dev wondered. The Japanese tended to be oblique, especially where politics and face were concerned, never saying things directly, avoiding any blunt statement that could carry insult.

Dev saluted, about-faced, and marched back to ranks with the Ceremonies Master calling cadence in his head. After that, it was Katya's turn—another order, or dan, to the Medal of Valor she already wore, and a blood bar, with no mention at all of just how she'd managed to break her leg. There was more to that story, too, he thought. He remembered her expression as she talked about her panic at Norway Ridge. There was something going on inside her, but he didn't know her well enough to even try to guess at what it was.

The thought led to another. He wished he could get to know her better. He knew he liked her, but wondered if it was because she'd treated him like a person back when he'd first joined the Thorhammers, or something more.

After Katya's award came a Medal of Valor for the Stormwind pilot who'd braved Xeno nano-D fire to land and retrieve the *Assassin's Blade*, and a Distinguished Service Star for a comjack technician who'd hit on the idea for an unnamed new weapon, something that promised to turn the tide against the Xenos. There were a lot of speeches after that, until it seemed that half of the brass and dignitaries on and over Loki were being given a chance to talk.

Finally, though, there were no more speeches to be made, no more parade or pageantry. Hidden speakers blared the "Imperial March," followed by "Earth's Hegemony." The Ceremonies Master gave his final, inaudible command. "Regiment . . . dis-*missed*!"

Dev was instantly surrounded by the men and women of the Assassins, who pounded him on his back, fingered his medal, and welcomed him back to the fraternity of the Thorhammers.

The *hero* . . .

That evening, as the party hit full swing in the officers' mess, Dev and Katya managed to sneak out, making their way to the Tristankuppel's recreational center and an unoccupied pair of comjack booths. Sealing themselves in, they linked with each other; Dev had already downloaded a visitor's sim from the base library, a moonlit evening on a deserted, palm-lined beach at a place on Earth called Tuvalu.

Isolated in separate modules, their sex was purely recreational, a shared erotic dream as detailed and as real and as intense as any physical coupling . . . more intense, even, since they used partial feedback loops that let Dev taste Katya's slow build to a fiery peak while she experienced his faster, harder, desperate hunger and explosive release. Their mental joining began as passion, naked legs moving in the wet sand, but ended in a warm and gentle embrace beneath a tropical, star-filled sky.

"Let's get out of here," she said at last, her voice small against his chest.

The illusion of sand and waves and moonlit sky was so perfect that Dev, still half-lost in the sexual afterglow, didn't know what she was talking about. "Out? Out where?"

"Out of these damned pods." She shivered. "I don't like to be alone in the dark."

He pulled back a little, blinking. Moonlight glistened off her skin. It wasn't that dark at all. "Would you like a sunrise? We can tell the sim—"

"No, I want *you*. Not a dream."

She couldn't possibly be aware of her physical body, locked away inside the comjack module, but he broke the linkage, then slipped out of his chamber to help her clamber out of hers. She hugged him for a long time, standing there on the comcenter's steel grating.

They spent the next several hours in each other's arms in an empty lounge in one of the barracks. There was no more lovemaking—real or virtual—but he enjoyed her closeness and their conversation and the way she explained how she'd won her first Medal of Valor at a place called Galahad, before she'd been transferred to Loki. Later, things turned technical as he described an idea he'd had, a way to merge ground troops and striders in a deployment that would let each support the other, and she listened with keen and intelligent interest, asking questions and pointing out flaws, helping him fine-tune the concept and encouraging him to submit a proposal to HEMILCOM.

But he never did find out why she was afraid of the dark.

Chapter 21

I ask you, what good are these research facilties? They cost billions of yen to build, millions to keep staffed and supplied. Handfuls of humans isolated for years at a time in the most godforsaken places imaginable. And for what conceivable purpose?

—Testimony before Terran Hegemony
Committee on Appropriations
François Dacres
C.E. 2512

The great wheel revolved slowly in the white glare of the star, providing spin gravity for the complement of thirty-two men and women aboard. Altair DESREF was one of fifty Deep Space Research Facilities scattered through human space to study astrophysical phenomena ranging from gravity waves to the tidal effects of Capella A and B.

Altair, a planetless A7 star only sixteen light-years from Earth, had been under close investigation since the 2360s. Its high rate of spin—its rotational speed at the equator was 160 miles per second—had warranted the construction of a DESREF to study rotational effects on Altair's magnetic field and solar wind. After nearly three centuries, Altair still had not divulged all its secrets.

"Odd," Dr. Jeanne Schofield said, looking up from her board with brown eyes focused on nothingness. A cephlink cable trailed from her left T-socket, feeding her raw data from the station's scanners. "That shouldn't be happening."

"What do you have?" For Dr. Paul Hernandez, life and work on the Altair DESREF had long ago settled into a comfortable routine. Statements like "odd" and "that shouldn't be happening" usually preceded a failure of some sort, equipment breakdown or an AI program crash, usually due to human error. A mathematician, he was a man who lived by order, reason, and the comforting predictability of numbers.

He did not like disruptions in the routine.

"Magnetic effects on the K-band," Schofield said, that faraway look still in her eyes. "Something's deflecting the solar wind, and I can't even guess what the hell it could be."

Hernandez set his coffee cup aside and frowned. "A ship?" Starships used powerful magnetic fields to deflect subatomic particles, dust, and stray molecules of gas that could pose a danger at high velocities. "We don't have a ship due in here for a week."

"No thermal effects," Schofield replied. Starships that had been locked away in the K-T Plenum tended to acquire large quantities of heat that could only be dumped in normal space. On infrared scanners they tended to glow like small suns for hours after emerging from the godsea. "No, nothing. Just a wake in the solar wind that looks . . . oh, God . . ."

"What is it?"

"Oh. My. God." The words were spaced and planted like a pronouncement of Armageddon. Schofield's thin face had gone white, eyes and jaw locked as her inner eye focused on . . . *something*.

"Damn it, what do you see?" He grabbed her wrist, trying to tug her palm from the interface, but he couldn't budge her, couldn't interrupt the trance that appeared to have her pinned immobile at the console.

A glance at the instrument readouts showed a solid target out there, something enormous, a kilometer long at least. He knew a thin, cold fear. There *should* be nothing out there. All he could imagine was that, at long last, someone had picked up the approach of a Xenophobe starship, and unfortunately, that someone was the crew of an unarmed research facility.

Paul Hernandez then performed the most heroic action of his fifty-eight standard years of life. Seating himself next to Jeanne Schofield, he sounded the station alarm, then pulled a linkjack from the console and, abandoning the predictable, plugged himself in.

"We have emerged, Lifemaster." The Third Controller secured itself to a branched projection emerging from a nearby wall. The words it chose signified completeness . . . and relief. "The Transit appears to have been successful."

"Appears?" That single, questioning word carried a great deal of meaning. "We cannot afford doubt in this mission, upon which so much depends."

"The Achievers have completed their assigned geometry and are now dead." The word would have as easily translated "empty." "We will not understand precisely what they have accomplished until we assimilate their remains.

"In the meantime, the Perceivers are attempting to confirm the new geometry. It is difficult, as always, to make sense of their initial observations. However, the target star is near and appears, as expected, to be a close match to our home sun. The Perceivers yet search for worlds. It is possible, however, that this star is barren."

The Lifemaster felt a pang of anticipatory disappointment. Barren! That word conveyed such aching loss, such futility and lack of purpose. So much had depended on discovering here the source of electromagnetic radiations that seemed to promise the presence of a starfaring civilization. Was it possible that those radiations were of natural origin after all, the product of a universe that seemed, increasingly, to mock the DalRiss philosophy that held Universe and Life to be one?

Its surroundings held no answer, filled and defined as they were by living processes. The very walls of the Ship's bridge were alive, revealed to the Lifemaster's delicate ri-sense as a pulsing, energetic enclosure. He could not perceive the Void beyond the Ship's walls, the Void that still defied DalRiss logic, belief, and experience after over eight thousand cycles. For that he relied upon the strange senses of the Perceivers, life forms designed to directly sense certain limited wavelengths of the electromagnetic spectrum. Perceived by those wavelengths, the Lifemaster knew, the universe was turned inside out, rendered more dead—empty—than alive.

"There remains one possibility," the Third Controller said. "A heat source that appears dead but which seems to be a source of electromagnetic radiation." Two of its upper appendages twitched open, an expression of concern. "There is strangeness here. The source could be artificial."

"Draw closer then. We will reach out and taste this source."

"And if it is Chaos?"

The Lifemaster stiffened. After coming so far, and with so much at stake, failure was unthinkable. "Then we die," it said. "As will our world."

Chapter 22

In war there is no substitute for victory.

—General Douglas MacArthur
mid-twentieth century

Eight months later, Dev was far around the curve of the planet from Midgard, his Scoutstrider *Dev's Destroyer* standing on what might one day be the bottom of the planet's deepest and widest ocean. Now the landscape was sere and barren, an unending, ocher flatness. Once, this plain had been a sea floor, a fact betrayed by the sparkle of various salts encrusting the ground like minute diamonds. Someday, when Loki became Freyr, salt water would cover this ground again, but without the ammonia and methane and frigid temperatures that had kept this world lifeless until the arrival of Man.

He was less concerned with Loki's past, however, than he was with the activity around him. Several ascraft transporters rested on the plain a kilometer away, while a four-legged cargo rig stood a few hundred meters in front of him. A dozen men in armor were guiding a pearl gray sphere from the walker's belly as it was gently lowered by monocable to the ground.

Other foot soldiers and warstriders had set up an armed perimeter about the cargo walker and transports. Hovercraft skimmed across the monotonous desert on plumes of wind-blasted salt, while striders of the First Platoon, Alessandro's Assassins, restlessly patrolled the area, weapons locked but ready for immediate release.

A familiar-looking Warlord stalked toward Dev. The *Assassin's Blade*'s nanoflage was inactive at the moment, and the big machine had reverted to the company's dress livery, blue with white trim.

"Hello, Lieutenant," Katya's voice said in his mind as her warstrider stalked closer. "How's number three?"

Dev gestured with *Destroyer*'s left arm, pointing with clenched duralloy fingers at the men positioning the gray sphere. "Almost ready, Captain," he replied. "We'll be ready to release in five minutes."

"Good. Numbers one and two are set. You're the last."

"Any update on the target?"

"Negative. No movement. It looks like we caught 'em napping."

Dev studied the bomb team. They were detaching the monocable now. Ponderously the cargo rig walked away, leaving the men alone with their deadly charge.

Operation Jigoku, they called it, though the Inglic-speaking troops in Dev's team had, perhaps inevitably, managed to corrupt it to Operation Chicago, Operation Gigolo, and even the rather unlikely Gee-goke-you. *Jigoku,* in fact, was the Nihongo word for Hades, the underworld of ancient myth. No one had explained whether that meant the Xenophobes were themselves denizens of an underground hell, or that this was an attempt to send them there, but the name was appropriate either way.

"We're set here, Lieutenant," another voice said in Dev's mind over the tactical channel. Across the dead sea bottom, one of the armored figures raised one arm. "Chicago Three, ready to drop."

"Roger that, Sergeant Wilkins," Dev replied. "Get your people clear."

Two new weapons were being demonstrated here, Dev thought, and he was getting at least partial credit for them both.

He still wasn't sure what he was supposed to have to do with the penetrators. He'd been told that the recordings he'd made at Norway Ridge had generated the idea, but Dev was pretty sure that someone would have hit upon the notion sooner or later. All he'd done at Norway Ridge was accidentally step in a Xeno nest.

But the crustal penetrators, as the new devices were called, promised to be the weapon that would stop the Xeno scourge at last. Each penetrator, nano-grown from sim replicants of the captured Xeno travel spheres, carried a one-hundred-kiloton fission bomb.

A nuclear depth charge. Dev didn't really want the credit for that one.

The second idea, however, he was proud of, for the rediscovery of combined arms warfare promised to be at least as important as crust-penetrating nukes in fighting the Xenos, and could well revolutionize the art of war entirely.

Combined arms was a concept that had surfaced time and time again through the course of human history. Cavalry working with foot soldiers, archers working with pikemen, tanks working with infantry, each advance in the science of war had brought together the strengths of separate military disciplines, and ultimately, each had become obsolete as technology or doctrine evolved.

Warstriders were the modern-day descendants of the great, hulking, tracked armored vehicles of the twentieth and twenty-first centuries, machines so heavily armed, so maneuverable, and so fast that infantry could do little to support them and, in fact, would only slow them down.

As a result, while armies still fielded line infantry regiments for certain restricted purposes, foot soldiers were almost universally despised as useless for serious combat. The modern battlefield, it was commonly said, was far too deadly for foot soldiers to survive on for more than a few minutes. Warstriders were the arm of decision in twenty-sixth-century combat.

But Dev had been both striderjack and infantryman, and seen the battlefield both from the vantage point of a warstrider linkage and from the dirt and blood and terror of a crunchie. One of the first things he'd done after being initiated once again into the Assassins had been to suggest the creation of special Combined Arms Groups, or CAGs.

Stalkers were deadly opponents in combat, but the greatest threat to striders were large numbers of Gammas. Men in combat armor could not face Alphas, but they could carry firepower enough to kill Gammas. Light striders, Dev had suggested in his report to HEMILCOM, machines like the LaG-42 Ghostrider or the RLN-90 Scoutstrider, could be assigned to work with line infantry platoons. To solve the mobility problem, the infantry could be transported in ascraft, Lightnings or Stormwinds, which were already part of a combined arms team when they flew close ground support with warstriders. Combat, Dev contended, might become a close-knit deployment of the three military arms—striders, ascraft, and ground troops.

HEMILCOM was still reviewing his concept, a notion that in some circles was considered heresy. In the meantime, Katya Alessandro had swung the temporary loan of an infantry platoon to the Assassins, put Dev in charge of them, and told him to give his CAG idea a try. They called themselves Cameron's Commandos.

For almost seven months he'd been working with Sergeant Wilkins and her troops, evolving tactics, and drilling, drilling, drilling. When the Thorhammers were assigned to Operation Jigoku, he'd found immediate employment for them, manhandling the new crustal penetrators into position as Assassin warstriders mounted guard.

He found it easy to work with them. They were First Platoon, Bravo Company, Second Loki Regiment, the Midgardian Ulvenvakt. Most of them, he'd already met.

The new team had already proven itself in combat, too. Dropping crust-penetrating depth charges on Xenophobe SDT complexes was safer than tangling with Xenos one on one, but it was not without a certain risk of its own.

The last of Dev's foot soldiers clambered aboard a grounded Stormwind, leaving the gray sphere alone on the ground three hundred meters away. With the shriek of turbines and intakes, the VK-141 lifted off in a swirling cloud of dust. "All personnel clear of the drop area, Lieutenant," Wilkins said in his mind.

Dev switched back to Katya's frequency. "Ready to drop, Captain. We're set for timed detonation at seventeen hundred meters."

"Thank you, Lieutenant. Stand by." Still tuned to her link frequency, he caught her side of a rapid dialogue with HEMILCOM. By agreement with the Imperials in Asgard, the penetrator warheads were inert. They could only be armed by a coded linkage initiated personally by Shotaro Takahashi, the Imperial *Daihyo.*

"We'd better move back ourselves, Captain," Dev pointed out when she was through. "The charts show a shallow tunnel layer here at five hundred meters. Could be a problem."

The warstriders began making their way north, toward a low ridge overlooking the plain. Other vehicles, striders, transports, and hoverscats, were already gathered there. A squad of infantry, wearing the black and red armor of Cameron's Commandos, stood and cheered as he stilted his way onto the top of the hill. He lifted his right arm, fist-heavy with its Cyclan-5K autocannon, in salute.

"Hey, Lieutenant!" Private Dahlke yelled, using his external speaker to send his voice booming through the thin Lokan air. "Let's drop it right down their damned throats this time!"

He thrilled again to the godlike power of man-become-machine, knew that it was more than the electronic TM-high of implant wired to AI.

He *belonged.*

"This is it, Lieutenant," Private Rosen yelled. "The big one!"

When Operation Jigoku had commenced months before, aiming the new crustal penetrators had been more art than science. Xenophobe subsurface deformation tracks could be plotted holographically by combining input from three or more DSA detector stations, but the data was fuzzy, the picture of the Xeno tunnel networks woefully incomplete.

Later, more detailed three-D maps had been AI generated, as the techs learned how to interpret the reflected shock waves from multiple nuclear detonations deep within the planet's crust. The destruction of a Xeno complex could actually yield far more information about tunnel complexes and SDTs in the area than had been known before the attack, and follow-up strikes could seal thousands of kilometers worth of underground passageways.

Now there was the promise of a whole new generation of weapons technology, meson scanners that could reveal the interior of a planet as easily as medical nanoprobes revealed the inside of the human body, and robot penetrators carrying warheads thousands of kilometers into the deepest and most inaccessible Xenophobe nests.

Well, those were still on the drawing boards, and the way things were going, they might not be needed at all. They hadn't been doing badly with echo mapping and straight-line penetration drops.

"Lieutenant Cameron?" Katya asked formally. "Will you do the honors?"

"Gladly, Captain." Code flickered past his vision. Takahashi was in the circuit, tied in through stationary orbit comsats since the Asgard Ring was below the horizon. The *Daihyo* was feeding down the code groups, changed daily, that would release three nuclear warheads to Hegemony forces on the surface. "I confirm weapons free. Warhead Three is now armed and ready for release."

"Stations One and Two report weapons free, armed and ready for release." The voice was that of a controller at

HEMILCOM HQ, relayed through the satellite net from Asgard. He had the self-important, pedantic tone of the technician reporting phenomena, rather than of the warrior dealing in death. "All stations, stand by."

Gently, in his mind, Dev found the frequency of the inert sphere. A particular code group would activate its penetrator fields.

"All stations," HEMILCOM said. "You are clear to initiate drop sequence."

"Right," Katya said. "Let 'er go!"

Dev triggered the activation sequence and sensed a single, powerful magnetic surge as the penetrator's fields switched on, pulsed once, then stabilized. In the desert, a kilometer away, the sphere vanished, sinking rapidly beneath the desert sands.

"Chicago Three," Katya reported to HEMILCOM. "On the way."

He waited out the seconds, watching them flicker past as his implant marked their passage. With their magnetic fields full on, penetrators tended to fall through distorted rock at a steady speed of about five meters per second. The Xenophobe DSA complex was seventeen hundred meters down, which meant a time delay of over five and a half minutes.

The problem, as it turned out, was that the Xenophobe complex was not a single underground path of distorted rock, but many of them, dozens of tangled mazes occurring in layers at different depths. The most shallow set of passageways, according to the three-D seismic maps, was only five hundred meters down. In less than two minutes, the crustal penetrator would pass that first Xeno nest.

No one in HEMILCOM knew what the Xenos thought about traveler spheres stolen from their own technology zipping through their subterranean realm; hell, they still couldn't agree on the question of whether or not Xenophobes *thought* at all, at least in ways that were meaningful to humans. What was known was that the spheres left behind a vertical highway of distorted rock. When this trick had been tried in the past, often the Xenos at the shallower layers followed the spheres' paths back to the surface, almost as if they were . . . curious.

Dev's internal clock registered two minutes.

"Ah, Station Three, we're picking up a DSA," HEMILCOM HQ reported. "Force four-three."

"The traveler?" Katya asked.

"That's negative, Three. Contact is rising, depth now approximately one-two-zero meters, force five-five."

"They're coming out to play, then," Dev said. "Stand ready, people." He ran a last check of his Scoutstrider's weapons systems, then activated the bolt on his right-arm autocannon, snicking home the first 27-mm shell.

On the sea bed, a plume of smoke erupted from the spot where the sphere had rested moments before. A shiver transmitted itself through the ground, and then the smoke grew thicker, a black pillar spreading toward Loki's perpetual overcast.

Something was moving within the smoke. "Spotter four-seven," a voice called. "I have a target."

"Captain?" Dev asked, deferring to the company commander.

"At your discretion, Lieutenant."

"Lieutenant Benson," Dev called. "The target is yours. *Fire!*"

To his right, a squat, four-legged Calliopede loosed a salvo of T-30 rockets, like white-hot flares streaming tails of smoke. They struck the half-glimpsed shape in a ripple of explosions that lit up the fuming, volcanic cloud and sent shock waves rippling through the ground.

More Xenos were appearing second by second, however, rising through the channel of distorted rock and scuttling out onto the surface. In moments, every warstrider in the line had joined the fire, sending volley after volley of rockets, shells, and energy into the eldritch shapes spreading out across the salt desert.

Radio became garbled; the hunters switched to lasers, maintaining a steady flow of coordinating communications that picked targets and brought them down, quickly, cleanly, efficiently. Large Xenophobe travelers were wrecked before they could shapeshift to combat mode. Pieces writhed and squirmed on the sand until they were fried by particle beams or lasers. Two Xenozombies, a Ghostrider and a Warlord, appeared and were immediately slagged into immovable junk. Overhead, a trio of AV-21 Lightnings darted and turned and stooped on shrill turbines, adding their deadly payloads to the killing ground in crashing cascades of flame. Communications relayed from Chicagos One and Two reported that there was fighting going on at both of the other sites as well.

Dev leaned into the recoil of his heavy autocannon as it slam-slam-slammed its rapid-fire stutter, hurling explosive shells into the chaos of the killzone. He concentrated on the Alphas. His CAG troops took up positions to either side of the Scoutstrider with practice-honed precision, ignoring the thunder of the striders' artillery overhead, burning down the Gammas as quickly as they appeared.

No Xeno machine came closer to the ridge position than fifty meters.

Internally, Dev's clock continued counting down the seconds. Five minutes, forty seconds after the penetrator vanished, Dev began listening with every sense his Scoutstrider possessed, straining to detect some sign that the warhead had detonated.

He heard nothing, of course. If the traveler had exploded on cue, then in the first millionth of a second, a gas bubble had been created over a mile beneath his feet, a cavity tens of meters across filled by a seething cloud of plasma at temperatures well over a million degrees, and pressures reaching millions of atmospheres. In the hydrodynamic phase, a stage lasting for a few tenths of a second, those temperatures and pressures created a shock wave racing out in all directions from the blast's center, traveling at or above the speed of sound in rock. Just how fast that would be depended on the density of the rock, but it would certainly be several seconds at least before the shock wave reached—

He felt it, a distant shiver at first, then a hard thump against the flanges of his Scoutstrider's feet. A visible shock wave flickered across the desert floor.

"Ladies and gentlemen," the voice of HEMILCOM HQ reported in his mind, "we have had positive detonation on all three devices."

Outside, the troops of the 2nd Loki broke into cheers. Dev tried to picture what had just happened far beneath the surface, and failed. Theoretically, the blast wave melted several meters of rock around the initial cavity and turned the rock for hundreds of meters farther plastic, or crushed it into rubble. The precise effect on the Xenos themselves was unknown, but nothing physical could survive overpressures of millions of tons per square centimeter, or the shearing action of solid rock flexing like a wave flicked down a length of rope.

Dev had gone through this operation fifteen times now, and each time he was surprised that the violence unleashed in the sunless depths of Loki's crust didn't break through to the surface. There was no crater, no plume of smoke, no leakage of heat or radiation, just that tremor . . . and a legacy of aftershocks over the next few days as the blast cavity collapsed and filled with rubble.

But a vast, labyrinthine maze of Xenophobe tunnels had just been trapped between three simultaneous nuclear blasts, and eliminated. If the picture of Loki's crust the tectonics boys had been assembling over the past couple of months was accurate, it was the last nest of Xenophobes on Loki.

The war was over.

"It's over. . . ." he thought, loudly enough that his AI transmitted the words.

Outside, the celebration was continuing, soldiers in red and black armor capering about like five-year-olds, even the striders gesticulating with their weapon-heavy arms as though they were waving and cheering. Dev was . . . numb.

"Say again, Lieutenant?" Katya said.

"Sorry, Captain. Thinking out loud. It's just hard to believe it's over."

"You think it is?"

"Isn't it? Our last precombat brief said this was the last major nest. You think there're enough survivors to reconnect?"

While the Xeno DSA tunnels could be mapped seismically, no one could be certain that all of the underground Xeno paths were being picked up. Too, if they were going to nuke every kilometer of tunnel, the task would take years and leave much of Loki's crust a battered, radioactive hell. The strategy so far had been to identify and nuke the major Xeno nests, the "cities," as they were called, destroying the big ones and isolating any that might have been in the tunnels between blast areas. Were those isolated Xenos still alive? Could they rejoin with other survivors and recreate their tunnel system?

The question had occupied HEMILCOM and Imperial strategic thinking for most of the past months, but there simply were no hard answers. Human forces on Loki would not be able to relax. Who was it, Dev wondered, who'd said once that eternal vigilance was the price of freedom? On Loki the prize would be not freedom, but survival.

"Hell, I don't know," Katya said. "But I do know the war's not over for us. Haven't you heard the latest who-was? We're being shipped out."

"Huh? Where?"

"Who knows? Maybe the powers that be figure that, if we were able to beat the Xenos here, maybe it's time to take back some of the other territory we've lost. Like Lung Chi."

Dev tried to examine his own feelings about that, but felt nothing. He still felt dazed. "I thought we belonged to Loki."

"We belong to the Hegemony Guard, Lieutenant. We go where they send us. Me, I bet it's Lung Chi."

"I think . . . I'd like that," Dev said. He remembered the last time he'd seen his father alive, and felt a new eagerness. "I'd like that a lot."

But military decisions have a logic of their own that rarely meshes with the likes or fears of the personnel who carry them out. Other events had been taking place far from Loki, events that demanded a far broader strategy.

Their destination was not Lung Chi.

Chapter 23

It is the Emperor's express wish that the astounding discovery made at Altair be followed up without delay. You are hereby requested and required to organize a military expeditionary force, to be placed under joint Imperial-Hegemony command, and to be composed of the following units . . .

—Orders to General John Howard
from Imperial *Daihyo* Takahashi
C.E. 2540

The ship was called *Yuduki*, a poetic Nihongo name for the evening moon. Classified as an Imperial armored troop transport, she was 330 meters long and massed 48,400 tons. Her hull was divided into three unequal sections. Running aft for half her length was the flat, bulky drives section, cluttered with sponsons, heat radiators, and K-T drive nacelles. Forward was the small, blunt wedge housing primary sensors and communications gear. Amidships, three flattened, pylon-mounted bricks, each sixty meters long by ten thick, rotated ponderously about a central core. Within the core were bridge, tactical center, life support, engineering, and cargo spaces, as well as all AI and linkage electronics; the slow-rotating spin modules, generating a carousel's out-is-down artificial gravity, had been divided into separate quarters for the ship's complement of forty-one and troop bays for her passengers.

No attempt had been made to streamline *Yuduki*'s cumbersome lines. She was designed to navigate from orbit to orbit and the godsea in between, not the turbulence of planetary atmospheres. Nor had much attention been paid to the comfort of her passengers. Each accommodations module was divided into three levels, and those decks reserved for the Thorhammers were crowded to the point of claustrophobia, over twelve hundred men and women packed into narrow compartments with bunk beds stacked four deep. Since getting rid of heat was the number one problem of ships in the godsea, and since the stomachs of many never did adjust to the odd sensations of spin gravity with its attendant Coriolis force and disorientation, the enlisted accommodations were widely viewed as a preview ViRsimulation of Hell.

Officers had a bit more personal space and the semiprivacy of thin-walled cubes, bunking four to a room. Most comfortable were the spaces reserved for regimental use, mess hall, Common Room, officers' lounge, and the equipment bay where the stridertechs continued to service and fine-tune their multiton charges. There was also the recreation deck, a space in the ship's zero-g core equipped with recjack slots. Since it could only accommodate fifty at a time, recjacking liberty was rationed out at four hours per person, one day in five, with officers allowed six hours of RJ every other day. The release of ViRdramas, games and sports, of mental strolls in wide-open spaces and electronic sex with partners real or imaginary, was the one factor that let so many people share so little space without going insane. The threat of curtailed recjack privileges was a better disciplinary motivation than the threat of court-martial.

Like every other soldier aboard, Dev was wearing shorts, deck shoes, and a T-shirt, but he was still hot. His clothing, fresh from the ship's nanovats that morning, clung to him unpleasantly. Why, he wondered, had he volunteered for this?

He *had* volunteered, he reminded himself. The day before being marched to the sky-el shuttles on Loki, the entire 5th Regiment had been addressed on parade by Colonel Varney, the Thorhammers' commanding officer. The regiment, Varney had told them all, was being redeployed—though he refused to say where or why—but anyone who wished to stay on Loki could do so, no questions asked. He wouldn't say where the 5th was being sent, or why, but he did say that the Xenophobe War was far from over, that the human success on Loki was only the first step in a very long road to victory.

Inspiring words, though Dev and the regiment's other old hands paid little attention to the speech. Rumors were circulating, each wilder than the last, and Varney's talk had not even mentioned them.

Why had he volunteered? The reason had nothing to do with bravery, that much was certain. He'd considered staying on Loki, but Katya was going, as were all of the other Assassin striderjacks. His own CAG infantry had volunteered for the deployment as well, as though they'd known that he was going.

How could he back down in front of all of them?

Besides, the 5th Loki Warstriders were far more home and family at this point than any world. Remaining on Loki would mean reassignment to the Heimdals or one of the local garrisons for the remainder of his hitch. Better, he thought, to stay with friends and family.

He wondered if he would have volunteered, though, if he'd remembered how hot it was aboard a ship in the godsea. Dev plucked his wet T-shirt away from his body, trying to air it out. He didn't remember ever being this uncomfortable during a K-T passage.

Possibly the fact that he'd never been locked up aboard a starship with over fifteen hundred other people had something to do with that.

He was standing in the Common Room, a precious enclosure of empty space that served as lounge, mess hall, and rec room for off-duty personnel. There was no furniture, but the decks were padded, and one entire bulkhead had been designed as a three-D screen for addressing the entire ship's complement. For the moment, though, it was projecting a giant, three-dimensional freeze-frame portrait of the Emperor.

The Common Room was slowly filling up. The men and women of the 5th Loki were filing in, taking seats on the padded deck *tatami*-fashion, row upon row facing the larger-than-life image of the *Fushi*-Emperor. Sitting close, side by side that way, the entire regiment could fit into the Common Room—just barely. It was used as an auditorium when announcements had to be made to the entire complement. Word had already been passed that there would be a special address at 0900 hours, ship's time. Dev consulted his inner clock. Another twelve minutes.

He studied again the motionless image at the front of the room. The Emperor's face was wizened, ancient with—some said—well over two hundred years, but either bionangineering or a flattering portraiturist had given him a strong, straight body, rigid in his navy dress blacks. His tunic was heavy with medals and gold braid; his own government's highest military decoration gleamed at his throat.

And you can keep that Star, Dev thought, remembering Katya's recommendation of months before. Wearing the Medal of Valor—the Emperor had one of those, too, Tenth Dan—had brought with it responsibility enough. He'd about decided that trying to live up to that damned medal had put him in this spot in the first place.

The Emperor's image was set against the glory of Earth as seen from orbit, white clouds twisted and feathering against the deep-heaven blue of the Pacific Ocean. That piercingly glorious backdrop reminded Dev of the godsea, and he sighed. Often he still wished he could get a chance to go up to *Yuduki*'s bridge and plug himself in as a pilot-observer. It had been over a year since he'd last dipped into the glory of the K-T Plenum, and he still felt a wistful yearning, almost a hunger, when he thought about it now.

But the Nihonjin crew didn't fraternize with their cargo, and Dev doubted that Minoru Shimazaki, *Yuduki*'s captain, would take kindly to any request by a hairy-chested striderjack to play tourist. Dev remembered his own opinion of striderjacks, back when he'd been convinced that he was bound for a ship's slot, and inwardly winced. It made a difference, having seen both sides.

Sometimes during the past two weeks, though, Dev had descended to Deck 3, the lowest, outermost deck of the A Mod spin habitat, and just put his hand against the gray paint of the bulkhead. There, faintly, he could feel the trembling vibration as the *Yuduki* made her way through the quantum sea. Katya's crew chief, Sergeant Reiderman, had laughed and told him he was just feeling the vibrations transmitted from the rotating sleeve that kept the quarters sections turning, but Dev had ridden the blue light of the K-T plenum, and he knew the feel of its muted thunders.

Dev couldn't detect the vibration now, though. Five hours earlier he'd felt the peculiar inner twist of the ship's K-T drive fields collapsing. The *Yuduki* was drifting in normal fourspace now, though where and why were still unknowns.

The Thorhammers had loaded their equipment aboard special cargo shuttle pods at Towerdown, then ridden the Bifrost Sky-el to Asgard, where they'd been herded aboard the *Yuduki* without even an hour's pass to visit the Moro. The who-was gained greater and wilder proportions: Xenos had appeared in Rainbow, and the 5th was heading there; the Fifth was preparing to invadc Lung Chi—or Herakles or An-Nur II—and take it back from the Xenos; a Xeno battlefleet had been encountered—at last!—near Loki, and the Fifth had been pulled off the planet to serve as a hidden force of reserves; the Xenos had invaded Earth, the Emperor was dead, Tokyo in ruins, and Hegemony forces from across the Shichiju were being rushed back to defend the Mother World.

They were part of a fleet. Dev was sure of that much. He'd glimpsed some of the other ships through a transparency in Asgard's curved wall—a big Kako-class cruiser and, hanging in the distance, the massive, wedge-shaped shadow of a Ryu-class dreadnought, one of the largest and most powerful warships in Human space. Smaller vessels, frigates, corvettes, and sleek Yari-class destroyers drifted in the leviathan's shadow in schools, like fish.

A thrilling, compelling sight . . . but all too soon Dev had been sealed away within *Yuduki*'s A Mod, and he could only wonder about the fleet gathering above Loki. Twenty hours later, *Yuduki* had ridden a tether out from Asgard and been released. An hour after that, the K-T drives had switched on and they were traveling faster than light.

That had been about two weeks ago—fifteen days to be exact. And now they were stopped. Where?

Fifteen days of travel meant—probably—about fifteen light-years, though the light-year-per-day estimate was rule of thumb only. Destroyers could travel faster, freighters and troopships were slower, and everything depended on the quality of the shipjack pilots.

Still, it was a starting point. He reached into his implant RAM, calling up data he'd not used for a year, navigational listings and X, Y, and Z coordinates for stars in the Eagle Sector. Scrolling swiftly through the columns of numbers, he added numbers, squared them, and extracted square roots from the results. He was looking for systems fifteen light-years or so from 36 Ophiuchi C. There were several possibilities. Earth itself, for instance, lay 17.8 lights from Loki. . . .

Got it. Dagstjerne/Loki to Altair, 14.9 lights.

Altair? There was nothing there. Altair was a hot A7 star . . . with a main sequence lifetime of less than two billion years and a rotation so fast, it was visibly flattened at the poles. There were no planets, only a thin accretion disk of dust and planetoids. Why would they stop there?

Dev could come up with only one answer that made sense. With an absolute magnitude of +2.2, Altair was one of the brighter stars within the boundaries of the Shichiju, an ideal beacon for a rendezvous. They were meeting someone here; they must be.

But who?

"So, Lieutenant. Why so serious?"

Dev turned and gave Katya a bemused grin. "Hi, Captain. Just wondering where we are. My guess is Altair."

Her eyebrows arched toward the line of her close-cropped hair. "Since when did Shimazaki put you on his planning staff?"

"That's the way the numbers work out." Dev looked away. Her appearance was . . . distracting. Like him, she wore ship's shorts and a pullover shirt which sweat had plastered to each curve and line of her torso. They'd never been able to repeat that evening in the comm center. Privacy had become nonexistent since they'd boarded ship.

In any case, platoon leaders could not afford to get emotionally involved with those in their command. Dev understood that, but it was hard to see her that way without remembering their linked romp on a simulated beach, or the shared tenderness afterward.

"Well, you're right," she said. He looked back at her and realized that what he'd thought was irony in her voice was surprise, and respect. "The word just came down. We're at Altair, and they're about to give us the straight hont. How the hell did you know?"

"Well, let's grab some mat and maybe they'll tell us why we're here," Dev said. "Altair's not exactly prime real estate."

"So I gather." They found space in one of the rows and knelt side by side. His hand brushed her thigh, and he was uncomfortably aware of her closeness.

At last the room was filled, and the Emperor's portrait dissolved. Facing them was another, much younger man, in his sixties, perhaps, wearing the two-toned grays of a Hegemony senior officer. Gold insignia on sleeves, shoulderboard, and collar indicated his rank was *chujo,* lieutenant general.

"Good morning, men and women of the Fifth," he said. "I am General John Howard, former commander of Hegemony military forces on Loki."

Former commander. Dev leaned forward, interest piqued. He'd only seen Howard two or three times during his tour on Loki. At the awards ceremony, of course, and at a formal review or two after that. Generals had little to do with mere *sho-i* striderjacks.

"It is my great honor," Howard continued, "to have been chosen to command Hegemony forces in what may well be the most important mission ever undertaken by our species. I now can tell you that which has been a carefully guarded secret for months now.

"Ladies and gentlemen, Mankind has made initial contact with another starfaring species. Their representatives are here, orbiting the star we call Altair. After detecting our civilization's radio emissions many years ago, they voyaged here to seek us out.

"It has taken a number of months just to learn to communicate with them, though we did have some unexpected help with their language. They are . . . different from us, with an evolutionary background quite alien to our own. Like us, they have been engaged for years in a war to the death with an enemy they call the *Chaos*. We believe, from what their representatives have told us, that that enemy is our own, the Xenophobes."

General Howard's image vanished, replaced by a camera view of space. Altair was visible in the lower left, an intensely bright disk, tiny compared to Sol from Earth or Dagstjerne from Loki, but large enough to show a discernible disk, flattened by rotation until it was twice as wide as it was thick.

Centered in the screen, backlit by that dazzling sun, was what must have been the alien ship. Most of the hull was in shadow, masking detail, but it looked to Dev like something organic. He was reminded of a tree or giant plant of some kind, with thick, branching masses on both ends and with a gnarled, ropy texture that looked like thick bark. There was no indication of scale, but it looked huge. The shadowed side was completely black; there were no lights, no ports or anticollision beacons as on a human ship, no way to tell bow from stern.

The overall effect was intensely *alien*. If this was their handiwork, Dev wondered, what were the builders themselves like?

"We have only begun to communicate with them," Howard continued. "Already we have had some . . . surprises. They call themselves the DalRiss." As he spoke the unfamiliar name, the word typed itself on the screen. "That name seems to be a compound word that refers to certain aspects of their biology. They are friendly, highly advanced . . . as their being here, some one hundred fifteen light-years from their homeworld, should tell us."

"C'mon, c'mon . . . show us what they look like!" a voice said from the line of watchers seated just behind Dev.

"What is significant is that we may have found an ally in our long war against the Xenophobes. I promise you that as more information becomes available, we will pass it along to all of you."

"My God," Katya was saying at Dev's side, over and over with a gentle rocking motion of her body. "My God, my God . . ."

"In the meantime, let me just say that the DalRiss have asked us to return with them to their homeworld, and we have agreed. Needless to say, this mission will be strictly a volunteers-only assignment. Those who don't want to go will be left with that part of the fleet that will be staying here, with the DalRiss ship.

"The rest of us, with DalRiss guides aboard, will be embarking on an historic voyage, to meet the DalRiss on their own world, to begin an exchange of technology and culture, to lay the foundations for interstellar, for interspecies, trade.

"Perhaps most important of all, we will be able to learn much from the DalRiss about our common foe. Possibly we will learn at last just what it is we are fighting . . . and why."

There was more, but Dev heard little of it, so great was the pandemonium that exploded in the Common Room. He was surprised to find that he had his arms around Katya. No one else seemed to care, or notice for that matter. Everyone was on their feet, shouting, questioning, all trying to talk at once.

Another intelligent species. The news took the ship by storm. Those aboard talked of nothing else, and as more information came through over the next few days, the excitement rose in pitch until Katya predicted that they were all about to fly to the DalRiss world without resorting to the quantum sea.

In centuries of space exploration, Man had met exactly three other species that might, *might* share with him the spark of intelligence. Dev had long ago committed the details to his permanent RAM.

On the hothouse world of Zeta Doradus IV, forty-eight light-years from Earth, an Imperial explorer had encountered the Maias—*Maiasedentis* species—massive organisms that communicated by organic radio and sheltered their motile/sexual/juvenile–stage offspring inside their own immobile bodies. The adults were *thought* to be intelligent . . . but even that was unproven, and so far unprovable. Completely atechnic, without even fire or simple tools, or hands for manipulating them if they did have them, the Maias were so different that it was possible they would never have anything in common with humans.

On the second world of a K3 sun designated DM -58° 5564, over thirty light-years from Earth, was a highly social species called the Communes. Like ants, bees, or termites on Earth, they showed a remarkable and extremely complex social order, apparently based on chemical communication.

So far, though, there was no way to demonstrate that they were self-aware.

And then there were the Xenophobes, a technical species that killed for no discernible reason, that might kill without even realizing that it was doing so.

Those three examples had raised an important question. For centuries man had speculated about someday meeting a nonhuman species, about learning to communicate with beings who might be of an entirely different order of intelligence, who certainly had a different history, cultural perspective, and way of looking at things in general. Studies of the Maia and the Communes—and attempted studies of the Xenophobes—had raised the possibility that any alien species, no matter how intelligent, might be so fundamentally different from humanity that any meaningful communication would simply never be possible.

Now there was the DalRiss . . . evidently communicating well enough with Howard and others in the fleet to make their name, their history, and their wishes known. What were they like? What did they know about the Xenophobes?

With every other person in the fleet, Dev waited hungrily for news.

Chapter 24

Until we met the DalRiss, we didn't know what the Xenos were. Afterward, well, we still didn't know what they were, but we were closer to understanding what they weren't.

—Dr. Samuel Gold
Senior Exobiologist, IRS *Charles Darwin*
C.E. 2541

At Altair the fleet was designated as Interstellar Expeditionary Force One.

Officially IEF-1 was a joint effort between Hegemony and Empire. The Imperial contribution in ground forces included the Imperial First and Third Assault Legions, both just arrived from Earth, and the Imperial Guard Striders from Loki, all under the command of General Aiko. General Howard commanded the Hegemony forces, the First and Fifth Loki Warstrider Regiments, the Twelfth and Eighteenth Rainbow Regiments, and several militia outfits, including the New American Brigade and the Chiron Centaurs.

The ships, however, were all Imperial Naval vessels, from the Ryu-class flagship *Shinryu* to the stores ship *Ginga Maru*. There were seventeen ships in all, pulled together from three separate task forces, and all under the command of *Taisho*-Admiral Masaru Yamagata and the civilian representative of the Emperor, Shotaro Takahashi.

While the Hegemony was certainly represented in the IEF, it was clear from the organization that Yamagata considered the force to be an Imperial war fleet, with himself its supreme commander.

None of that mattered as far as the Thorhammers were concerned. Volunteers already, all aboard the *Yuduki* volunteered again for what some were calling the Great Leap. Final preparations were made, several military vessels were detailed to remain at Altair with the DalRiss ship, and the fleet made ready to get under way. Three days after the *Yuduki* had arrived at Altair, the seventeen ships of IEF-1 accelerated outward, then made the translation into the K-T Plenum.

The Great Leap was an apt name. The world that DalRiss Translators called Home, it turned out, was well beyond the farthest regions explored thus far by Man—115 light years from Altair, 130 from Sol. Despite its distance, the DalRiss sun was a naked-eye star long known to Earth-based astronomers as Theta Serpentis; tenth-century Arabs had called it Al Haiyi, the serpent, and this had come down to modern sky watchers as Alya.

To be visible at all at such a range, Alya had to be bright. Dev felt an uncomfortable inner twist akin to disorientation when he learned that Alya was a double star, with Alya B a class A7 nearly identical to Altair save for its slower rotation, while Alya A was brighter still, an A5. It looked as though he was going to have to relearn much of what he'd thought he'd known. That such a star should have worlds and life, *intelligent* life, contradicted most of what Dev had assimilated on planetary bioevolution back in his starpilot days.

Fiercely radiating, white stars squandered their hydrogen reserves far more quickly than their more sedate F-, G-, and K-class brethren. Where a G-class star like Sol could expect to remain on the main sequence for ten billion years, stars like Altair or Alya A had less than two billion years before their spendthrift ways caught up with them and they collapsed, after a spectacular and planet-killing series of stellar pyrotechnics, into white dwarfs. On Earth, it was believed, life had appeared less than a billion years after the planet's crust formed, but it was another three billion years before those first primitive organisms learned to join into multicelled creatures. Another half billion years passed after that before those cells' remote descendants began clinking pieces of flint together to make tools and fire.

So how could intelligent life evolve on a world less than two billion years old?

The best guess any of the scientists who accompanied IEF-1 could manage was that evolution on such a planet proceeded at a frantic rate, at least compared with any of the life-bearing worlds so far investigated by Man. A-class stars, brighter and hotter than Sol, radiated far more energy. Ultraviolet and X-rays would be more intense in such a star system, as would the thin, hot proton soup of the solar wind. With lots more energy available for early biotic systems to draw on, mutations would appear more often, and natural selection, the great driver of evolution, would proceed far more quickly.

But it bothered Dev that his understanding of how things worked could have been so wrong. He wasn't alone. Two hundred astronomical, planetary, and biological scientists, half from Earth, half from other worlds of the Shichiju, were accompanying IEF-1 aboard the Imperial Research Ship *Charles Darwin*. Rumor had it that they all were in a collective state of near panic as they struggled to make sense of what the DalRiss emissaries had already revealed.

It was nearly ten more days before Dev and his companions aboard the *Yuduki* began to learn anything more about the DalRiss themselves. Most vessels capable of interstellar travel had an upper limit of two to three weeks before rising shipboard temperatures forced them to translate back to normal fourspace from the blue-fired fury of the godsea to radiate the excess heat. Since ship-to-ship communication was impossible within the K-T Plenum, *Yuduki*'s passengers could learn nothing about what was going on aboard the *Darwin* until both ships emerged into normal fourspace. The journey had been planned as a series of twelve ten-day hops, with a day of coasting between each hop for cool-down and data exchange.

Each scrap of new data was eagerly devoured by every one of *Yuduki*'s passengers as soon as it was available. Simulations beamed across from the *Darwin* allowed them to "meet" a DalRiss during their scheduled recjacking time and even question it, though most questions were turned aside by the simulation's AI with a polite "I'm sorry, but that information has not yet been made available to *Darwin*'s researchers."

Dev scheduled his first meeting with a DalRiss simulation so that he could share the experience with Katya. Linked to each other and *Yuduki*'s ViRsim AI, they entered Lab One aboard the *Darwin*, a gleaming room of sterile whites and silvers and mirrored surfaces. The atmosphere, Dev learned through his link, was predominantly carbon dioxide, with unhealthy percentages of sulfur dioxide, carbon monoxide, hydrogen sulfide, and suspended droplets of liquid sulfuric acid. The composition might have mimicked the runaway greenhouse effect on Venus, but the air pressure was low enough—less than one atmosphere—that the temperature hovered around a balmy forty degrees Celsius.

The heat, of course, was not accurately presented in the simulation, any more than was the corrosively poisonous air. As Dev and Katya stepped into the DalRiss habitat, the air felt dank and steamy, with just a trace of the rotten-egg smell of hydrogen sulfide, and the light was just harsh enough to make things unpleasantly bright. The air seemed to shimmer a bit, like the mirage above a hot stretch of ferrocrete, but it felt no more uncomfortable than a tropical bioenclave hothouse back on Earth.

There was little in that room that Dev could relate to anything on Earth. What waited for the two of them was definitely alive; it, no, *they* moved with a quivering, eager jerkiness. There were three of them, though at first they'd been so close together that Dev had trouble separating them in his mind.

"These are the DalRiss emissaries." The inner voice belonged to their AI guide, which would be there to lead them through the simulation. "If you wish to converse with them, you will need Translators."

A white-topped table appeared next to Dev. On it were two . . . creatures, black and glistening. He was reminded at first of the slugs he'd seen emerging from the travel spheres at Norway Ridge, but these were clearly something else.

What, he wasn't quite sure yet.

"The DalRiss create, through genetic and subcellular manipulation, life forms the way we create machines," the guide's voice said. "The organisms on the table are called *comels*. They are artificially created beings that the DalRiss call Translators. All you need do is touch one."

Dev hesitated, then, ashamed of his reluctance in front of Katya, stuck out his hand. The Translator's skin was wet but not slimy or unpleasant. It quivered, then began sliding up his fingers.

"The process is painless," Dev was told as he watched, morbidly fascinated. He was not reassured. The thing looked like a blunt, flat-bodied leech.

"Is it intelligent?" Katya asked, holding out her hand for the second Translator.

"Not in the way humans would understand the term. Like certain AI systems, it is intelligent but not self-aware. Its sole purpose is to serve as a bridge between a human and its makers by attuning itself to the human nervous system while at the same time maintaining communication with the DalRiss."

"Communication?" The creature had embraced Dev's hand now, a thin, translucent membrane that fit like a rubber glove. He looked from it to the patiently waiting . . . things a few meters away. "Telepathy?"

"Of a sort. The Translators consist of little more than modified DalRiss nervous tissue and an organic radio transmitter. An analogous organ exists in the Maias of Zeta Doradus IV."

"Consider them to be an extension of ourselves," another voice, high-pitched, almost feminine, said in his mind. "A way for our thoughts to touch."

Dev jumped. Katya, whose hand had not been fully engulfed yet, was startled. "Dev? What is it?"

He shook his head, unable to explain, unable to speak. A thousand questions chased one another through his head. How had these creatures acquired the symbology to understand him and to make themselves understood? How had they tapped into his implant? . . . For that, surely, was the only way they could speak in his mind. If the Translator was actually tapping his nervous system somehow, was there a danger of infection, or of an allergic reaction to alien tissue?

Dev's thoughts raced, stirred by fear of the unknown. He had to remind himself that this was a simulation, that he was not really aboard the *Darwin*, but still tucked away safe and sound in a link module aboard the *Yuduki*.

But the questions remained. Someone, obviously, had already gone through this for real.

"The comels are quite safe for your species," the voice continued. "Long ago we learned how to tailor servants such as the Translator to other body chemistries. There is no danger."

Dev's eyes were adjusting now to both the light and the strangeness. Picking the closest of the DalRiss towering above him, he focused on it alone. Working step by step, he began to recognize general anatomical features and relate them to things he knew.

Those, for instance, were legs. The lower body resembled a starfish, with six blunt, flexible appendages that held a spiny orange belly a meter or so off the deck, and a red-brown, leathery hide studded with bony lumps the size of Dev's thumb.

And *that* must be a head, an erect crescent on a slender, jointed neck rising from the center of the body, with fleshy, horizontal folds down the concave side that might have been a kind of face, and a pair of rubbery-looking protrusions to either side like those on a hammerhead shark. As Dev and Katya approached, the assembly swung their way as though it were watching them, a disconcerting effect because, so far as Dev could see, the thing possessed nothing like eyes.

An elongated casing that looked like hard leather extended back from behind the face, and Dev took that to be the DalRiss's braincase. Underneath, tucked in between the head and the starfish body, was a spidery complexity sprouting meter-long appendages, bone-hard on the outside, but with joints making them as flexible as whips. They ranged in size from finger-thick branches to flickering threads, always in motion and impossible to count.

Looking at the arrangement, Dev could not understand how the DalRiss could use those digits as fingers; they were fingers without arms, and much too short to reach past the thing's massive body. He said as much to Katya.

"I can demonstrate, if you wish," the voice in their minds said. There was neither accent nor inflection, and the Inglic grammar and vocabulary seemed perfect. "Give me something to pick up."

"Here," Katya said. She held out her hand and called a hundred-yen coin into being. The AI simulation picked up her thought and gave it reality within the simulation as she dropped it to the shiny deck.

One of the creatures shuffled forward—Dev estimated it must mass over three hundred kilos—with an incongruous grace. The upper body extended itself, body sections telescoping as fingers unfolded, reaching down and plucking up the coin between three hair-thin tips and handing it back to Katya. The movement was smooth, dextrous, and utterly inhuman. Even after the DalRiss repeated the act for Dev, he could not be sure of what he'd just seen.

Some aspects of the DalRiss, he decided, were *so* inhuman that the human mind had trouble grasping them.

Katya, bolder than Dev at this first encounter, stepped

closer, staring up into the folds of a DalRiss face. "I'd like to know how they see," she said. "It saw the coin. But I don't see anything like eyes."

"That is because mutation and natural selection on our homeworld never led to the evolution of light-perceiving organs," the DalRiss said. It was disconcerting talking about these beings as though they were a simulation—which they were, of course—and then being addressed by them as though they were physically present. Dev considered tailoring the sim so that the DalRiss were simply exhibits, but he decided not to. He enjoyed watching their movements, seemingly random, but lightning-quick and effortlessly precise.

"How do you sense your surroundings, then?" he asked.

"Sound," the DalRiss replied. "And other senses for which you have no corresponding name."

The whales and dolphins that once had swum Earth's oceans had navigated by sonar. Like them, the DalRiss could "see" reflected sound waves with detail enough to tell lead from copper, solid from hollow, rough from smooth. Like the dolphins, the DalRiss could actually see inside other organisms; they could look at Dev, both "see" and hear the beating of his heart, and know whether or not he'd eaten breakfast. The DalRiss "head" was mostly sound equipment; the crescent shape was filled with dense fluid that acted as a focusing lens for intense bursts of sound. The knobby extrusions to either side contained the receptors, widely spaced to give the being a stereo-audio, 3-D perspective.

But other senses came into play as well. Something like the lateral line in a fish sensed minute changes in air pressure, infrared sensors in the head detected subtle gradations in heat up to several kilometers away, and, most alien of all, the DalRiss seemed to somehow perceive the chemical and electrical processes of life itself.

Darwin's scientists were still arguing over just what that meant. Some felt that this "life sense" was simply a refinement of IR sensing or keen hearing. The DalRiss themselves insisted that their world, as they perceived it, was a blend of the *rischa*, the life fields of countless organisms, a kind of tapestry within which inorganic matter—rocks, say, or the spiky, metallic shape of a Xenophobe war machine—was dull, dark, sound-reflective voids.

They perceived the entire universe as life, and themselves as a small part of a larger whole. When Dev asked them to explain this, the AI stepped in. "I'm sorry, but that information has not yet been made available to *Darwin*'s researchers."

The scientists must be having trouble grasping that one, too.

But Dev was staggered. How could a species that could not perceive *light* have ever reached for the stars?

And that, Dev realized, was only the beginning of the mysteries surrounding the DalRiss.

Later, Dev downloaded all that was known about the DalRiss into his cephimplant RAM, then reviewed the data with Katya in the privacy of *Yuduki*'s com modules.

He was not surprised to learn that he'd misinterpreted much of what he'd seen aboard the *Darwin*.

The sac behind the crescent head housed, not a braincase, but digestive and storage organs; the brain was well protected in a bony shell close to the armored branching of the fingers. Perhaps Dev's biggest mistake was in the nature of the creature itself, which was not one organism, but two, living together in gene-manipulated symbiosis.

The six-legged starfish shape was called a *Dal,* an artificially engineered mount for the smaller creature that rode its back. The combination could be thought of as a partnership like that of horse and rider, save that in this case the rider was actually imbedded within the horse's flesh, tapping directly into its circulatory and nervous systems. At need, the riders could separate from their steeds, but the Dal had been custom-tailored for their role and could not live long independently.

As for the Riss—the word appeared to mean *masters*—they could plug themselves into dozens of other species engineered for the purpose over millennia. Evolving on a world defined by life, which they could sense all around them as a kind of translucent sea, the DalRiss had pursued the biological sciences almost to the exclusion of all else. Before they learned how to make fire, they'd begun domesticating other species; they'd never developed atomic fission, but they could tailor organisms to fulfill precise needs with a deftness that surpassed anything human biologists had even dreamed of.

Chemistry had grown out of biology. Life, all life, depends on chemical reactions to sustain them. The DalRiss studied these and eventually learned to gene-tailor organisms that would generate the reactions they wanted to study. Living factories produced chemicals, even manufactured goods in an organic approach to nanotechnic engineering. Earth technology had learned to manufacture submicroscopic machines, growing them in vats or assembling them through hierarchies of progressively smaller handlers. The DalRiss had ultimately learned to do much the same, but by controlling enzymes and biochemical processes.

Man and DalRiss had used two radically different approaches to arrive at the same destination.

The DalRiss did not build their cities, they *grew* them, as humans grew RoPro buildings, gene-tailoring large, energy-drinking, sessile organisms on their energy-rich homeworld to create the living spaces they desired. The Dal themselves were an example of an entirely new species created by the Riss as symbiotic legs and strength. For millennia the Riss had been able to directly tap the nervous systems of their artificial symbionts, feeling what they felt, knowing what they knew.

They were aware of radiation. Their planet was awash in energy from their sun—visible light, ultraviolet, infrared—and it was that energy that drove all organic processes on their homeworld. Requiring a way to further study this radiation, they addressed the problem in the only way they knew. They designed organisms that could sense light for them; where nature had never evolved eyes, the Riss had invented them.

Living, symbiotic eyes. The Riss called them "Perceivers." The DalRiss didn't need them for everyday activities any more than a human might need a portable radar, but they'd used them first to develop the science of biological microscopy . . . and later to look at the stars. Astronomy had led to an understanding of how the universe works—of the laws of gravity and motion.

Ultimately they'd learned how to grow huge creatures that used the explosive combustion of hydrogen and oxygen to reach planetary orbit.

And from there, the nearest star was right next door.

Their star was a double, an A5-A7 pair that orbited each other with a mean separation of 900 astronomical units—five light-days—more than enough distance for separate planetary systems to exist around each member of the system. The DalRiss homeworld, which they called GhegnuRish, circled the smaller of the two, which the Earth astronomers called Alya B. With no reason to think that planets orbiting A-class stars were rare, the DalRiss made the crossing to Alya A, a voyage that took many years.

Both stars, it turned out, had planets. Only GhegnuRish had life, but the sixth planet of Alya A, which they called ShraRish, had an atmosphere and surface conditions that might be molded to suit DalRiss tastes. They already had a history of growing life to meet their needs; now they proceeded to grow an entire ecology.

Although *Darwin*'s researchers were still working on understanding the DalRiss time scales, it appeared that ShraRish had been reworked in GhegnuRish's image nearly twenty thousand years ago. The DalRiss had been living on both worlds ever since.

Until recently.

According to the DalRiss emissaries, an enemy had appeared on GhegnuRish perhaps two centuries before, an enemy unlike anything ever encountered. They rose from solid ground in devices that could be sensed only by heat and sonar. Sometimes the enemy could be sensed directly, but vaguely, distantly, almost as though the life force was somehow diluted. Usually they remained undetectable behind walls of dead metal. The DalRiss called them *Gharku*—the Chaos.

The DalRiss had fought back, creating an arsenal of living weapons, creatures that sounded like heavily armored dinosaurs, living warstriders. But what the Chaos touched, it destroyed. The DalRiss of ShraRish had lost contact with the homeworld nearly fifty years before.

And now the enemy had appeared on ShraRish.

For centuries, the DalRiss had been aware of radiations coming from a certain part of the sky. They'd long been able to detect radio through living receivers—Dev thought of the Maias and their natural-occurring radio—and determined that the source must be a civilization spanning many stars so distant that the radio signals themselves had traveled over a century to reach GhegnuRish. At the time, the discovery had been hailed as one of the most incredible of DalRiss history. Life, as certain Riss philosophies had suggested, truly was universal!

But contacting that life directly seemed out of the question.

Then the Xenophobes had appeared, and contacting this other civilization became a matter of life or death. This civilization, it was argued, might know of the Xenophobes. Certainly their radio network appeared to indicate that they spanned many suns, while the DalRiss occupied the worlds of only two.

A special ship was grown, one employing a new theory of travel. Special creatures were evolved, semiintelligent forms called Achievers that could open space by force of mind, allowing travel from point to point simply by envisioning it.

As with nanotechnology, the DalRiss had achieved the same ends as had humans, but by totally different methods. Their means of traveling faster than light sounded more like magic to Dev than like science.

But it worked. The DalRiss ship had arrived at the star closest to the radio civilization that was also closest in mass and radiation to their own, home star.

And there they'd met the occupants of the Altair Deep Space Research Facility.

Five months later, Interstellar Expeditionary Force One had departed for ShraRish. Allies now in the fight against the Chaos, neither humans nor DalRiss knew where that alliance would lead.

But for the first time, there was hope of understanding that enemy, of *knowing* it as it had never been known before.

Chapter 25

It was a completely serendipitous event. If we'd not had the facility at Altair, a station, incidentally, devoted to pure research, we should in all probability never have encountered the DalRiss. After all, they had no way of knowing that we were native to the worlds of far milder suns.

—Dr. Paul Hernandez
Hearings on the DalRiss,
Terran Hegemony Space Council,
C.E. 2542

Four months later, IEF-1 dropped out of the godsea for the final fourspace leg of the voyage. For three days more the ships fell through space toward their destination, bathed in the arc-bright light of Alya A. ShraRish appeared first as a pinpoint of light almost lost in the star's fierce glare, but day by day it swelled from pinpoint to crescent, attended by a pair of mediocre moons.

Excitement aboard the troopship ran so high that heat, crowding, and discomfort all were forgotten. Most Thorhammer personnel had all but lost interest in the DalRiss during the grueling voyage out, but now that their destination was in sight, they again spent much of their allotted RJ time linked with *Yuduki*'s AI, gazing at the spectacle unfolding before them. Alya A was a tiny, dazzling disk nineteen times brighter than Sol, set like a jewel in a soft haze of zodiacal light. Alya B was a pinpoint beacon against the far stars, more brilliant than Venus at its brightest in Earth's night sky.

The Inglic-speakers had long since given up on the DalRiss transliterations of the two suns' names. They were simply Alya A and Alya B, names quickly shortened by familiarity to the letters alone. The worlds of ShraRish and GhegnuRish became, respectively, "the DalRiss colony" and the "DalRiss homeworld" or, simpler still, "A-VI" and "B-V," and the DalRiss themselves were often called Alyans . . . or Aliens, picking up on the coincidental Inglic pun.

Then for two days all RJ privileges were suspended and the Thorhammers were ordered to remain strapped in their bunks. The spin modules, no longer rotating, unfolded like the petals of a flower so that "down" remained "down" as the ship decelerated stern-first toward the destination at nearly two gravities. Men and women rose only to eat or use the toilets, moving carefully where a fall could break bones.

When deceleration ceased and spin gravity resumed, they were allowed to link for outside views again. The red-gold-violet-white glory of a world turned beneath them. They were in orbit.

ShraRish looked nothing like Earth or Loki. The local equivalent of plants utilized a complex sulfur compound to turn radiant energy into stored energy; instead of the familiar chlorophyll hues of Earth, the colors ranged from pale orange to deep red-brown. There were oceans, but they gleamed purple in the light of Alya A instead of blue, and reports from sampling probes sent down as scouts indicated that the seawater was mixed with sulfides as well as salt and included dilute solutions of carbonic and sulfuric acids. Over the night hemisphere, the polar areas shone forth with the shifting, ghostly dance of auroras, driven by solar radiations far more energetic than Sol's. The flash and spark of meteors was common as well, more common than the throb of lightning beneath aurora-lit night clouds; this was a young system, and a lot of dust and debris remained in the ecliptic. The impression was of a raw, new world still in the making and not yet tamed by the red-pigmented life that had taken hold of its surface from pole to iceless pole.

"Actually, we could survive on the surface of A-Six without a lot of protective gear," Dr. Phillip DuChamp's image said. He was a tall, lanky, blond man, one of the planetary scientists off the *Darwin*, and his ViRpersonality had been programmed as guide for the men and women who linked with *Yuduki*'s AI to explore the new world turning below the orbiting troopship's keel. "It's hotter than we normally like it, forty to fifty degrees on the average, and we'd need oxygen masks in order to breathe, and goggles of some sort to protect our eyes from the ultraviolet. But don't let anybody scare you about getting burned by all that acid. Swimming in the oceans would be a bad idea, but the actual concentration of corrosives in the atmosphere is quite low, less than a few parts per million. It wouldn't do your lungs any good . . . but I doubt that you'd even notice it on your bare skin."

"I think I'll stick with an environmental suit just the same," Sergeant Wilkins said over the link circuit.

"Yeah," Erica Jacobsen added. "Or a warstrider!"

"Will there be a problem with the striders?" Katya wanted to know. "Corrosion eating the hull, fouling circuits, that sort of thing?"

"Your ship factories ought to be cooking up nanofilms that will take care of that, Captain. Over a period of time, and without nanofilms to counteract the acid, yes, the environment could be pretty rough on machinery. That may be one reason why the DalRiss haven't done any building with, oh, steel, say. Ever hear the term 'acid rain'?"

"No, sir."

"One of the by-products of large-scale industrialism before the nanotechnic revolution. The rainwater on A-VI is acidic enough to dissolve zinc or tin over a period of months. On old Earth it was a man-made problem. Here, though, it's natural.

Sulfur and sulfur products—like H_2SO_4—are part of the life cycle."

"You mean life here is sulfur-based instead of carbon-based?" Rudi Carlsson wanted to know.

"No, it's carbon chemistry, like us. From the little we've learned so far, sulfur seems to play the same role in DalRissian biology that phosphorous plays in ours. I say 'seems.' The nucleic acids that make up our DNA are phosphates, but we don't bathe in the stuff the way the DalRiss bathe in sulfuric acid." DuChamp's image shrugged. "This is a whole new twist to carbon chemistry. We still have an awful lot to learn.

"In any case, the environment, though strange, shouldn't pose any special problems for you. Your machinery will corrode over a period of time, but then, wind-blown sand didn't do it that much good on Loki."

Dev caught Katya's sardonic murmur. "You got that right."

"On the whole, atmospheric conditions on ShraRish are mild compared to Loki. I imagine a suit breach was a rather serious event in Loki's atmosphere, with such a high concentration of ammonia."

Mental chuckles rippled through the audience, edged by dark, soldier's humor. Dev remembered the bite of ammonia when his own suit had been breached. A rather serious event? Yeah, you could say that. . . .

"If your suit is breached here," DuChamp said, pressing ahead, "the atmosphere CO_2 level is high enough to poison you, but the air won't burn your lungs the way Loki's atmosphere would. Air pressure at the surface is actually a bit below one bar. Keep your oxygen-nitrogen mix flowing in your helmet and you'll be okay until you can get to safety."

DuChamp paused, a lecturer surveying his class. "That concludes my discussion on DalRissian surface conditions," he said. "Are there questions?"

"How much longer are we going to have for precombat?" Dev asked.

The invisible audience chuckled again. For five days now they'd been in orbit, waiting as negotiations proceeded between members of the expedition's command staff and the DalRiss. Either no one in the military chain of command knew how much longer the negotiations might last, or they were unwilling to speculate.

By asking Dr. DuChamp's AI personality, Dev was trying to bypass the command staff and get some useful information from another source. There might be rumors among the science staff, for instance, that had not filtered across to the troopships yet. Even if he wasn't supposed to talk about it, he might make a slip. AIs often failed to recognize the significance of seemingly unimportant tidbits of information; one of the few things that separated human minds from AIs was the human ability to jump to conclusions—sometimes accurately—from some seemingly unrelated bit of data.

But DuChamp's AI image only smiled. "I'm afraid your guess is as good as mine, Lieutenant. The situation down there sounds pretty fluid. It may take a while to assess just where your troops and striders could do the most good."

Which was no fuzzier an answer than Dev had expected. From what he and the rest of the regiment had heard so far, IEF leadership was still divided over what they were going to do. Hell, there were rumors that Aiko and Howard had come to blows over the question, though Dev doubted that either the reserved John Howard or the imperturbable Kazuo Aiko could get that excited.

But the split between Imperial and Hegemony units was definitely a problem; Admiral Yamagata, insisting that the fleet represented the Emperor, had publicly suggested that the Hegemony *gaijin* remain in orbit. Their presence could upset the delicate diplomacy necessary to establishing relations with a new, starfaring species. His personal troops, the black-armored Imperial Guard, were better-disciplined, less likely to disrupt the negotiations.

General Howard and the other senior Hegemony staff officers, naturally enough, objected. They had not tagged along with the Japanese across 115 light years simply to remain in orbital reserve, and the consensus among the non-Nihonjin of the IEF was that Yamagata was trying to grab the benefits of DalRiss contact for Japan's Empire.

It was two more shipboard days before the waiting ended.

There'd been a sharp skirmish between Imperial troops and the mysterious enemy the Translators called the Chaos. It confirmed what everyone in the regiment had assumed ever since they'd first heard the name. The Chaos and the Xenophobes were the same. They'd appeared on ShraRish two standard years before, with different forms and different weapons than they'd used on the worlds of the Shichiju, but there was no doubt about the identification. Three Guards striders, two Tachis and a big Katana, had been lost in the skirmish, and an attempt to use a penetrator nuke had been botched. Though the reports from Aiko's HQ had claimed a victory, it looked as if the landing party had been lucky to get off as lightly as that.

The who-was spread through the Thorhammer modules at light speed. It would be a combat drop; they'd be going in to clear out Xeno surface structures, then plant penetrators where they would do the most good.

When the word came down officially through the ship's speakers, less than ten minutes after the rumors had begun circulating, the Assassins in A Module broke into ringing cheers. Dev cheered with them, then laughed when one of the Commandos observed that *anything* was better than dying of boredom in orbit.

After that, they were too busy to cheer. Final checks were run on each strider, and the big assault shuttles were prepped and given their final assessment: go, up-gripe, or down-gripe. Weapons were unpacked, stripped, cleaned, and reassembled in grim ritual. Power packs were charged, environmental systems tested, AIs queried and shunted into self-diagnostic routines.

Forty hours after the alert, a final mission briefing was held, a ViRconference of Platoon and Company COs and the Regimental command staff.

Dev was invited as well, somewhat to his surprise. Though he was not a platoon leader, his CAG ideas had received some attention at the higher echelons, thanks largely to Katya's intervention. The decision had been made to let the Commandos drop with the Thorhammers, tasking them with a special mission. Dev linked in with the meeting, said nothing, and took mental notes. This would be his opportunity to show what properly supported infantry could do.

The briefing was conducted by Major Gennani, the senior regimental intelligence officer. After laying out the planned deployment of the Thorhammers at a place the cartographers had dubbed Regio Aurorae, Gennani described what was expected of Cameron's Commandos.

Mindful of the benefits of the Xeno technology captured at Norway Ridge, the Commandos would enter the target area after it was secured by strider assault, searching for anything that the IEF's intelligence people might be able to use. Of special interest were the "greaseballs," the gray, sluglike organics that had been observed emerging from the ground in travel spheres.

Current thinking was that these were the Xenophobes themselves, though how they could manipulate technology like stalkers and Xenozombies was still not known. They seemed to be somehow intermingled with their technology, to the point where it was impossible to separate the two. Greaseballs had been discovered inside wrecked Xeno machines; they'd never been noticed before because they looked so much like lubricant or waste. Submicroscopic scans and N-tech probes had demonstrated that the greaseballs themselves were made of both organic and inorganic cells—part organism, part nanomachine. That seemed to explain their tolerance for a wide variety of environments—environments as mutually alien as Lung Chi, Loki, and ShraRish.

For centuries, most humans had been cybernetic blendings of man and machine. The Xenophobes had carried that meld much further, so far, in fact, that they probably had little in common with the full-organic creatures they had once been.

The DalRiss had never gotten close enough to the invaders to study the slugs. Xeno nano-Ds did nasty things to living tissue, no matter how well armored it was. With the Commandos' help, though, that would change. DalRiss biologists, their Lifemasters, were already growing organisms to receive and duplicate living Xenophobe specimens, a first step toward learning how to communicate with them.

The drop zone on ShraRish would be only a few kilometers from DalRiss lines, and local forces would be available for support. The new meson imaging gear aboard the science ship *Dirac* had begun mapping the Xenos' crustal lairs, and a large concentration of tunnels had been discovered close to the surface at Regio Aurorae.

The meson scans suggested an explanation for why, after almost two years, the Xenos weren't more widely established on ShraRish. Almost three billion years younger than Earth or Loki, with a thinner crust and a hotter interior, the planet was far more tectonically active than any world of the Shichiju. As the original infestation tunneled out from its first landing site, the SDTs must have been disrupted time after time by seismic quakes, slipping fault lines, and intrusions by pockets of magma. Now, according to the scanners, there were three main pockets of Xeno activity on the planet, and their expansion was still quite slow.

Not that that could save the Alyans in the long run. According to the DalRiss themselves, GhegnuRish, with conditions almost identical to ShraRish, had been completely overrun, slowly but inevitably, within a few hundred years. The knowledge that the same would happen to ShraRish had prompted the desperate search that had ended at distant Altair.

"Your force will be supported by A Company, Lieutenant," Major Gennani told Dev after laying out the overall plan. "Do you anticipate any special problems?"

"No, sir," Dev replied. A three-D graphic of the planned battlefield revolved slowly before his inner vision, showing subterranean tunnel complexes and company deployment zones on the surface. "We'll need enough airlift assets to get us off the ground fast, in case something goes wrong."

"Already arranged for. Three Stormwinds will be dedicated to your part of the assault. They'll put you down, fly air support, and take you off again afterward. Anything else?"

"Just the time for the assault, Major."

"Six hours," Gennani replied. His image grinned at the others. "I think the general's a bit anxious. Wants to show Aiko and Yamagata how it's really done."

"Just one more question, sir," Victor Hagan, First Platoon's CO, said. "That botched penetrator drop. Is anything more known about that?"

"Just that the thing didn't go off. We don't know why."

"Could have been a timer malfunction," Colonel Varney put in.

"Or it could be something else," Hagan said. "Back in the Shichiju, you know, the Xenos have a nasty habit of turning our own weapons against us. If they have an atomic warhead now . . ."

He didn't finish the thought. He didn't need to. The meeting ended on a somber and reflective note.

Chapter 26

Humans long for order, for rationality, for logic. Yet with each step in our understanding of the universe, somehow the universe persists in defying us.

—Hearings on the DalRiss
Terran Hegemony Space Council
Dr. Paul Hernandez
C.E. 2542

Katya found Dev in the spin module's number three equipment bay, as the Commandos were boarding their ascraft. He was standing next to his RLN-90 Scoutstrider, going over last-second instructions with Sergeant Wilkins and Corporal Bayer. The sergeant had a Hitachi Arms subgun slung over her back and a bulky flamer cradled in her arms. Bayer's plasma gun was folded in its steadimount, muzzle up. Above them, the ascraft crouched in the shadows like a huge, black insect.

"I'll want a fast dispersal," Dev was saying as Katya approached, "fast and clean. Tell your people that if they trip coming out the door, there won't be time to stop for them. We're supposed to be hitting a cleared DZ, but—"

"Don't trust us to do our job, Lieutenant?" Katya asked as she joined the trio.

Dev grinned at her. The self-confidence she saw there was reassuring. He'd gone through some major changes over the past few months. "Just taking Murphy's Law into account, Captain. Anything that can go wrong—"

"Will," she finished for him. "I approve. Lieutenant, can I talk to you for a moment?"

"We're about finished here," Dev said, looking at the others. "Any other questions? Okay. Get on board and check your people. I'll link with you soon as I jack in."

Katya waited as the two leggers saluted, then turned and headed up the ramp into the ascraft's brightly lit interior.

"You wanted to see me, Captain?"

She touched his arm lightly, and they started walking across the deck toward the line of First Platoon's warstriders. The combat machines were moving, one after another, into the waiting ascraft, where men in bright orange armor attached the clamps and feeder lines that connected them with the ascraft's systems. The equipment bay rang with the clatter of heavy equipment and metal striking metal. Technicians huddled over flaring torches as last-second repairs were made, and yellow-painted bugs scurried among the hulking striders and ascraft, carrying men, ammunition, and stores.

Katya nearly had to shout to make herself heard above the racket. "I wanted to tell you to be careful down there. This has all the markings of a real, old-fashioned *hema*." The word was another Inglic borrowing from Nihongo. It meant a bungled mess.

"Anything I should know about?"

"The Imperial-Hegemony politics are getting pretty bad. I gather Yamagata threatened to have General Howard relieved of command."

"That is bad. Who would replace him?"

"Aiko."

"Bad timing. My people are already upset about Yamagata's crack about us *gaijin* screwing up the diplomatic works. I don't think they'd like working for the Japanese one bit."

"Agreed." They reached Katya's Warlord. Sergeant Reiderman, Katya's crew chief, dropped off the access ladder next to them, wiped his hands on a rag tucked into his coveralls, then gave Katya a quick thumbs up. "She's hot, Captain."

"Thanks, Red." She turned again to Dev. "I guess I'm still not convinced you can count on the leg infantry," she said.

"*I'm* leg infantry," Dev said. "And strider. We'll get 'em what they need."

"Just so you get in fast and . . . get out safe. Promise me?"

He gave her a wry wink. "Promise. Just so I have First Platoon to keep the bastards busy."

"That's something I can promise you." Leaning forward swiftly, she brushed his lips with hers, then turned and started pulling herself up the Warlord's ladder, leaving him standing alone on the deck.

As always, she had to steel herself to slide into that narrow, black crypt in the Warlord's side. As soon as she'd jacked in, though, her crew welcomed her aboard. *Sho-i* Torolf Bondevik was in the pilot's module, and *Jun-i* Muhammed al-Badr was handling the weapons.

Engaging her external view, she picked out Dev Cameron's tall frame as he climbed aboard the single-slotter RLN-90.

Dev's Destroyer. The name made her smile. She remembered when he named his new strider, declaring that at last he had command of a ship of his own. He never had asked for a retest, or a transfer to the navy.

She still hadn't sorted out her own feelings for the man. He was sensitive, fun to be with, and superb recreation. She suspected that her first attraction had been less sexual than it had been her penchant for picking up strays. He'd seemed so vulnerable. . . .

Well, he wasn't vulnerable now, and she still felt . . .

Damn. As if she didn't have enough on her mind right now with a company to run.

"Status check," she called.

"Piloting systems green," Bondevik reported. "We're hooked into mother-bird and ready for drop."

"Weapons are safed and locked," al-Badr added. "But all checked out and go."

"Eagle-Three, this is Hammer One," she said, switching channels. "We're ready for hookup."

"Come to Mama, Hammer One." The ascraft was jacked by *Sho-i* Lena Obininova, a Russian national from Earth.

Technicians guided the Warlord into position as the ascraft's clamps descended and hooked on. Her view of the outside world was blocked off as power grippers slid a thin durasheath shell over the ascraft's belly, sealing the loaded strider slots off in the darkness.

Fear twisted in the back of Katya's mind for a moment. Then she went on-line with Lieutenant Obininova, watching the bay through her electronic eyes. *Easy, girl*, she told herself. *You've done this before. There's no call to lose it before you even get clear of the transport!*

She thought of Dev's easy grin, and that steadied her. Time dragged on, one long second after another. Eventually klaxons sounded and red lights flared, clearing the equipment bay of all personnel. Air was being bled from the deck into holding tanks, preparatory to drop. Finally there were only the strobing warning lights. The deck was in vacuum, rendering the klaxon voiceless.

"Coming up on the drop point," Obininova said. "Deck panels opening."

Silently in the hard vacuum, hinged panels beneath each of the waiting ascraft swung open. At first Katya saw only a giddily endless hole filled with wheeling stars. Then she was looking down at a mottled red and gold and white-streaked landscape swinging past the opening. Vertigo tugged at her. The spin module was still rotating; the open drop hatch alternately looked down onto planet and stars as it continued to turn.

"Everything's green," Katya said, as much to reassure herself as anyone else. "Power's up. Systems go."

"Release in five seconds," Obininova said. "And four . . . and three . . . two . . . one . . . *drop!*"

Clamps securing the ascraft released their hold. The habitat's spin gravity, assisted by a nudge from maneuvering thrusters, kicked the ascraft clear of the *Yuduki* and into space.

Then retros fired with silent thunder, and the long drop began.

For the next thirty minutes, Katya was too preoccupied with the steady flow of data from Obininova's control systems to worry. The ascraft hit atmosphere with a jolt like a kick in the pants, and soon the view outside was obscured by the pink-orange haze of reentry. When she could see beyond the ascraft's hull again, clouds were billowing toward her from the red-brown landscape, and the deep violet curve of the planet's far horizon was flattening out.

Lightning flared, illuminating rain-swollen thunderheads. A volcano brooded beneath a wind-scrawled track of white ash. Two other ascraft from the *Yuduki* dropped on parallel tracks, five kilometers to the north—Second and Third Platoons, on final approach. Obininova opened mental windows displaying flight corridors and surface detail in glowing, AI-generated graphics. Their destination was the gathering storm ahead.

The ascraft's reentry shields fell away and Katya corrected her earlier impression. It was not lightning that was illuminating the clouds ahead, but the steady stroke of lasers fired from orbit. They continued to fire until the entire target area was so masked by a spreading umbrella of smoke that the bolts were no longer getting through to the ground. With a hard jolt of wind-battered control surfaces, the ascraft flew into the cloud, and Katya was plunged into wet semidarkness. When she emerged, the land beneath the ascraft's belly was a fire-tortured hellscape. Katya saw the same sort of twisted architecture and crystalline growth she'd seen at Norway Base, but it appeared to be built here on a grander scale, and with greater complexity. The laser barrage from the orbiting fleet had slagged much of the alien-grown architecture to the ground, but enough remained to create the impression of an eldritch fairyland . . . a fairyland with just a taste of black nightmare hidden in the fantasy.

"Hang on," Obininova warned. "Ventral shields coming off!"

With a bang, the duralloy armor was whipped away, and Katya's Warlord was exposed for the first time to the local atmosphere. She checked her external sensors, watching the data fill block after block on her visual field. Temperature . . . atmospheric composition . . . acid levels . . . all as expected. Dust levels were high, but that was to be expected after the bombardment. There were no detectable traces of nano particles.

The ground was much closer now. They crossed a dry river valley, and a clump of what might have been trees—slender, compact cone shapes thirty meters tall and colored red-brown. Smaller, feather-shaped fronds waved nearby, pink and orange in the harsh white light.

"DZ coming up, Hammer," Obininova said. "Fifteen seconds."

Light-line graphics flickered across Katya's vision, painting out a bland strip of rolling ground three kilometers ahead. "I see it. Arming weapons." She shifted to the intercom. "Hey, Junior. You ready back there?"

"Safeties off, boss. We're set to odie."

Seconds later, the Warlord dropped from the ascraft's belly, then steadied on shrieking thrusters. Katya hit the ground in a swirl of dust, taking the shock with a groan of stressed hydraulics. First Platoon was down.

Where was she? More graphics overlay reality, showing strider icons scattered across half a kilometer. Blue outlines revealed Xeno structures hidden by the smoke. She shifted to infrared.

Better. Xenotown spread out around her, fairyland and nightmares mingled. Downtown, the mouth of a tunnel, was *that* way. "On me, Hammers!" she called. "Bearing two-five-oh. Snap it up!"

Over her link, she could hear the calls and commands of other units in the drop. "Third Platoon, down and moving!"

"Second Platoon, we're down. Lance, watch your six! I've got movement there!"

Magnetic interference crackled through her mind. "Bandits! Bandits!" a voice yelled. "Hammer Two-Three reporting bandits at Delta-Charlie-one-one . . ."

Katya put the Warlord into an easy, loping run. Light flared through the mist to her left, lighting up the smoke from inside. In a moment, she broke out of the cloud. Shafts of white sunlight lanced down through rents in the smoke staining the sky. Ahead, alien forms twisted and mushroomed like monstrous fungal growths among sponge-textured cones that might have been trees. DalRiss cities, she knew, were living creatures, grown rather than built; what she was seeing now was an alien perversion of an alien design, a city long dead and rotted, the shell reworked into the stuff of nightmare. There were crystal columns, like she'd seen at Norway Ridge, rearrangements, she thought, of sand into something like glass. Buildings like squat, red-capped mushrooms had unfolded, their walls spilling across the ground in heaps of pallid, wormlike tendrils, strangeness following strangeness until Katya felt a sharp inner vertigo. What was DalRiss, and what was Xenophobe? Nothing looked familiar save the clouds overhead and the occasional thrust of boulders through the carpet of alien biomass.

Something huge and monstrous turned on elephantine legs, wrinkled body slung between the hips, black above, gray-red below, with prongs or horns on one end, a balancing tail on the other. She hit it with her ranging laser; the AI computed size from range and angle and told her the creature was six meters tall—bigger than most warstriders—and massed at least fifty tons.

Katya noticed something else about that towering apparition. Chunks of pebble-rough hide dropped from its flanks with each step, revealing raw meat and purple-red blood.

Among striderjacks, *zombie* referred to a Beta, a warstrider or other human machine somehow taken over by the Xenos. This . . . *thing* gave new definition and horror to the word, a once-living organism now transformed into a decaying puppet two stories high.

There was a flash, and something hit the Warlord high on its left torso. The nano-D count soared, and Katya cut in the strider's external countermeasures.

Moving swiftly to sidestep the deadly, invisible cloud, she swung her left arm up and triggered the CPG. White light flared from the beast's shoulder, causing it to stumble. An instant later, al-Badr cut in with the dorsal hivel gun. Pieces of the giant beast splattered with the buzz-saw impact. The body took another step forward, then sagged in a bloody heap.

Other shapes were moving among the broken forest of pillars. Katya tracked something moving quickly on four legs and fired with her hull lasers, but the bolt flared against the side of a gnarled, organic column crowned with spikes, biting a chunk from it and sending it crashing to the ground.

"Hold steady!" al-Badr called. "I'm launching a Starhawk!"

She dug in the strider's armored heels, lurching to a halt. "Go!"

There was a hissing shriek and a jolt. A stub-finned missile streaked into the sky. She opened a window inset on her field of view. It showed the landscape ahead streaking past, the mind's-eye view from *Jun-i* al-Badr as he guided the teleoperated missile through a radio link. Katya's graphics showed more life-forms, closing from behind the encircling walls of smoke.

"We've got heavy targets at five kilometers," she told him over the link. Short range for a Starhawk, but they had to relieve some of the pressure in the immediate area of the DZ. "Moving this way."

"I'm on them."

Dots appeared on the ground, growing swiftly to shadows. Katya saw more alien life-forms, monstrous, already decaying in the thrall of the unseen creatures riding them. The Starhawk impacted one of the largest ones with a flash and a snowstorm of static.

"Scratch one zombie," al-Badr said, his point of view now back with the Warlord.

"Yeah, but we have lots more coming," Bondevik pointed out. He indicated an icon clear on the graphics display but not yet visible to hunorm optics. "I think we've got a Cobra over there."

A Cobra! So there *were* familiar Xeno types here. Katya had been wondering. The Xenos on ShraRish appeared to be using organic forms as their principal surrogates and mounts, and it seemed possible that the lack of any DalRiss steel or heavy manufacturing industry might be the reason for that. The Xenos needed processed metals and advanced materials to make combat vehicles of metal . . . though she'd always assumed they took what they needed from veins of ore underground.

But perhaps it wasn't that simple. Steel, for instance, was not found underground; it was iron, laboriously smelted from ore, then alloyed with carbon through one of several high-temperature processes. Other artificial materials came to mind: ceramics . . . plastics . . .

"Let's see what this Cobra is made out of, gentlemen," Katya said. She turned the Warlord onto a new heading, stalking the unseen Cobra.

Explosions erupted around them, pelting the strider with rock and shattered crystal. Katya engaged the ventral-mounted weapons pod when a starfish-shaped creature that looked like an overgrown DalRiss appeared fifty meters off, hurling fist-sized balls of flame from an unseen launcher implanted in its back. Rocket fire disintegrated the creature, or drove it under cover. Katya couldn't be sure which.

The EM spectrum was blocked now, the piercing hiss of Xeno electromagnetics as effective as any jamming. Katya scanned the skies, looking for the promised air support. Nothing yet.

Then the Cobra lunged at them from behind a low wall of toppled debris. It was in its combat mode, squat and lumpy and deadly-looking, but one blast from her CPG tore a piece from the gray hull as big as a Stormwind's wing. On a hunch she fired her bow lasers. Dazzling light flared from the thing's flank; metal vapor boiled into the air. Katya told the strider's AI to analyze the gas's spectrum.

Nickle-iron, raw and unrefined. Some lead, silver, gold, and copper . . . but mostly nickle-iron as pure as from any asteroid. Traces of silica, sulfur, magnesium . . . *rock!* The thing had worked slabs of stone into its hull.

Rock and nickle-iron. Stuff the Xenos could find deep within a planet's crust. The Xenos took what they could get, but they did little real manufacturing or metals processing of their own. For years it had been assumed that they had factories of some kind in their labyrinths deep in the crust, places where they could forge the scraps of demolished human technology they stole into something new.

Could it be possible that the nanotechnics they obviously used were their *only* technology?

She fired again, lasers and CPGs, and the Cobra started to morph, gray metal and stone flowing together like liquid mercury, gleaming silver in the sunlight. Taking control of the central weapons pod, al-Badr triggered a barrage of M-22 rockets. The multiple detonations shredded the damaged Cobra and scattered smoking lumps of the thing across a thousand square meters of ground.

In her mind, Katya chewed on an imaginary lip. She had a feeling she'd just pried back a small piece of the Xenophobe mystery.

Now if she could just get the data back! Damn, *where* were the ground-support ascraft?

Then the pace of the battle began picking up.

Chapter 27

. . . temperature range (equatorial): 40°C to 50°C; Atmospheric pressure (arbitrary sea level): .75 bar; composition: N_2 *83.7%,* O_2 *8.7%,* O_3 *3.6%,* SO_2 *2.4%, Ar 1.2%,* H_2O *(mean) .2%,* H_2SO_4 *(mean) 850 ppm,* CO_2 *540 ppm . . .*

—*Selected extracts from science log*
Alya A-VI
IRS *Charles Darwin*
C.E. 2541

Open flames were impossible in an atmosphere consisting of less than ten percent oxygen, but organic matter smoldered as intense heat broke it down, liberating choking clouds of greasy smoke, and chemical reactions precipitated liquid droplets out of the sky, a thin, wet mist. The ascraft's reentry shell had dropped clear moments before. Dev strained for a glimpse of the ground as the ascraft dropped through the pall.

There . . . an undulating landscape, streaked and broken by cloud-shadow. Trees—or something like trees—pink and orange spearpoints and curl-tipped feathers thirty meters tall rose from soft, red masses of ShraRishan life. Surreal spirals and twists and mushrooms carved from red foam matched descriptions of DalRiss living cities, but everywhere order had begun melting into disorder. No wonder the DalRiss called the Xenos the Chaos. Their city was at once both dead and horribly alive, with new and malevolent growths invading, penetrating, replacing, *changing* like a hideous cancer run amok.

Humans had added to the destruction, blasting craters, smashing delicate towers, slagging down once-living buildings, uprooting the geometric perfection of vast gardens. It was like a terrible, three-sided struggle, the life of the DalRiss pitted against the perversion of the Xenos, and the wholesale death delivered by the humans.

"Where are they?" Dev called, worried now. Somewhere in that hell, the Assassins should have secured a DZ where the Commandos could disembark. They'd been out of touch with regiment HQ for several minutes now, ever since the Commandos' ascraft had emerged from reentry blackout. Radio and laser communications both had been interrupted, and Dev could not establish a fix on any topological landmark with any certainty. This was certainly the right general area for the DZ, but nothing looked as it should have looked. His graphic overlays refused to mesh with reality as he was able to snatch it, a glimpse at a time, through the drifting islands of smoke and gas. Alessandro's Assassins could have been anywhere within two or three kilometers range, and he would never have seen them.

The ascraft jolted, hard, and Dev thought they'd been hit.

"No sweat," *Sho-i* Anders told him. "Rough air from a hot blast crater."

"Can you take us any lower?"

"Sure, but we won't be able to see as far. The higher we are, the better our chances of catching something through a hole in the sky junk."

But Dev had about given up on that. "Look, if we stay up here, your wings are going to fall off. You checked your hull integrity lately?"

He was watching the readouts from a battery of atmospheric sensors as he spoke. Those clouds were the product of an alien ecology, death-pallid fogs of sulfuric acid. As Anders guided the ascraft through the misty air, acid condensed on the wings and hull metal, streaming aft in corrosive rivulets. The nanofilm on the exposed portions of Dev's Scoutstrider had already been degraded by twenty percent in places. As Dev tapped into Anders's systems readouts, he felt the strain registering on the ascraft's intakes. How long would the turbine fans last?

"What's that over there?" Dev asked, using a cursor to indicate a circular, sunken field in the middle of the alien city. White mist spread like a milky sea across the terrain. Enhancing the view with telephoto optics, he could see what looked like balloons rising from the kilometer-wide swirl of barren earth and mist, and hovering above the ground.

Xeno travelers, emerging from underground by the thousands.

"Looks like our friends are coming up to play," Anders said.

A Xeno tunnel mouth. "Yeah. Let's set down over there." He indicated another spot, a flat area near the crater rim.

"We're starting to pick up a nano count," Anders warned him. "Point one-five."

"All the more reason to get this over with." He took another look about for Katya's company. Lightning flared and boomed to the north. That might be her . . . but here was the opportunity he'd been looking for. "Let's hit it!"

The ascraft flared out at twenty meters, releasing Dev's Scoutstrider from one side and a Mitsubishi Type 400 APC from the other. Dev tensed his shoulders, and the twin jets of his hotbox thrusters roared. Seconds later, *Dev's Destroyer* hit the ground with a crash, absorbing the shock on bent legs and whining stabilizers. At his side, the APW unfolded stiltlike legs.

Called the Kani—Nihongo for Crab—the Type 400 was a squat, humpbacked shape supported by four legs that folded against the hull during transport, but telescoped out from the sides on ball-and-socket joints to lift it clear of uneven terrain.

With a hull five meters long and two high, the Kani was a smaller version of the big VbH Zo walkers, carrying twenty armored men in motion-sickened discomfort. Hivel cannons in blister turrets to left and right provided fire support.

"How're you people doing, Sergeant?" Dev called.

The Crab lurched forward, sensor clusters tasting the air like sensitive antennae. "Down in one piece," Wilkins replied. A three-plug technician was jacking the APC, but Wilkins had linked into the comm system with her palm interface. "Where's our backup?"

"What backup?"

"Uh-oh. Things are getting interesting now."

An explosion gouged dirt and rock from the ground ten meters away. Dev pivoted, tracking the round. Two hundred meters away, something like a vast, convoluted sponge, roughly spherical but rising fifty meters into the air, was rolling ponderously and very slowly toward them.

Had it fired? The shapes surrounding him were so strange, so distorted, Dev was not sure just what he was seeing. He was glad now that the decision had been made to drop them deep in the Xeno-controlled area. If he'd had to worry about which of these alien shapes were friendly and which were hostile, he would have been unable to fight for fear of hitting an ally.

Another explosion ripped through ground and biomass, five meters away. Something hard clanged off Dev's light armor, staggering him. The nano count was rising.

With no DalRiss friendlies about, the simple rule was kill everything strange that moved. He aimed his right arm, heavy with the muzzle-heavy bulk of a Cyclan Arms CA-5000 autocannon. Codes flickered through his awareness, target track . . . lock . . . *fire!* High-velocity explosive shells ripped into the sphere, exploding deep inside with strobing flashes muffled by the creature's soft mass.

It fired back. This time his targeting radar caught the track of high-speed projectiles, but the thing was having trouble getting the range. Strange. It wasn't using an active radar lock, though Dev's external mikes picked up an ultrasonic squeal that might have been some kind of sonar. The APC's hivel cannons joined the thundering fury of Dev's autocannon. Pieces of the giant were hurled hundreds of meters into the air; white smoke streamed from the surface of the thing as the submicroscopic machines animating it lost their cohesion and flowed away by the billions.

Like they're abandoning ship, Dev thought, continuing to hose the living mountain with explosive shells. It was falling apart as he watched it.

Stranger and stranger. The Xenos on ShraRish had adapted the "technology" of the inhabitants, biological shapes and sonar, but ignoring such obvious and simple technical aids as radar or laser ranging. Why? The simplest answer was that they took what was at hand and adapted it to their own purposes . . . and those adaptations weren't carried from world to world. On Loki and Lung Chi and Herakles and the other invaded worlds of the Shichiju, they'd found steel and duralloy, glass and plastic, ferrocrete and duraminium . . . all products of advanced human manufacturing and materials technology. The Xenophobe weapons and vehicles on those worlds were made of metals and plastics, dissolved and re-formed in new and extremely fluid ways by Xeno nanotechnics.

Here, though, all the Xenos had to work with were organics, no match at all for durasheathed warstriders.

Legs scissoring, he ascended the low rise of the crater rim. Beyond, pearl-colored spheres drifted on shifting magnetic aurorae, some hanging together meters above the white fog like masses of glistening bubble-foam, others clustering along the creamy white shores of that alien sea and bursting, releasing their wet-slithering riders.

The slugs covered the ground within the crater rim. They were everywhere, woven into a glistening web of living tissue, crawling over one another, smothering one another as they oozed their way over the crater rim, clumping together into living sculptures, shapes of no certain form or purpose.

Strands of gray tissue stretched between crystal towers, like shreds of tissue clinging to bone.

If there was such a thing as evil, Dev thought wildly, this was it. There was a basic wrongness to this perversion of the ecology of an entire, living world. It felt unclean; *he* felt unclean, wading ankle-deep through that wetly shining mass of life-gone-berserk.

At least, though, there were plenty of samples available for the taking. "Okay, Sergeant," he said. "Come and get 'em!"

The Kani slewed to a stop at the base of the crater rim's gentle slope, its legs folding above its back as they lowered the hull to the ground. Clamshell doors at front and rear hissed open as ramps extended. Foot soldiers, ungainly in armor, pounded down the ramps and spread out in perfect combat deployment.

Six men carried bulky, insulated chests, two men on each. Inner layers of counter-nano films should keep the slugs from eating their way through if they had any nano-D capabilities themselves. Each two-man team lugged its chest to the edge of the gray, oozing mass, opened the top, and began snatching specimens with long-handled tongs.

An explosion gouted earth and rock to Dev's left. Three troopers went down, one screaming as his helmet started to dissolve. Dev pivoted, firing an AND round to blanket the area, then tracking the projectile back to its source.

Surprise stabbed at him. Just when he'd decided that the Xenos on ShraRish were all organics and relatively easy to deal with! Five hundred meters away, a huge, blunt snake-shape was morphing into the many-spined horror of a Fer-de-Lance.

Dev opened fire with both his autocannon and his left-shoulder Kv-48 weapons pack, crouching his strider to bring the rocket tubes to bear. M-22 rockets flashed and hissed, trailing white contrails through the wet air, then slamming home with a thundering barrage of detonations.

Spines and writhing tentacles snapped from the Fer-de-Lance's body. Gaping craters appeared in the soft gray of the hull beneath. Dev's strider did not possess a laser, so he couldn't analyze the Xeno's makeup, but it looked to Dev as though the core of the thing was alive . . . or at least made of something like meat. There was other material, too, rock, he thought, and possibly something like iron or lead. It was hard to make sense of it.

But sense or not, this Fer-de-Lance was easier to kill than its cousins on Loki. Dev swept the dying thing with another burst of explosive shells. Pieces were still moving, flopping on the ground like demented snakes, blindly questing like whip-slender worms.

"Wilkins!" he snapped. "Let's have some fire over here!"

"You got it, Lieutenant." Sergeant Wilkins yelled out orders. Corporal Bayer appeared, the long, heavy barrel of his steadimount plasma gun already tracking.

White-hot bolts shrieked from his weapon, blazing fire purifying everything its blowtorch breath touched. Dev continued to mount high guard from the crest of the crater rim, scanning the entire area for the approach of more Gammas. At his back, the six troops assigned to collect slugs were finishing their task. At an order from Sergeant Wilkins, the perimeter began to contract.

Gammas, organic-looking pieces of pseudolife like blindly struggling worms and rags and bloody scraps, flooded toward the top of the ridge, making for Dev and the Crab parked fifty meters away. Dev swung his hivel cannon across this new threat, but there was no way he could hit every one. Panic rose at the back of his mind. Those struggling shapes could cover the Scoutstrider, eat away nanofilms and armor, reduce the machine to a corroded skeleton in minutes.

But Sergeant Wilkins braced herself at his feet, training her heavy-duty flamer at that wriggling, living sea. Flamer chemical loads carried their own oxidizer; she triggered the weapon, sending flame searing into the Gamma horde.

"Thanks, Sarge."

"Any time, Lieutenant. Let's get the hell out of here, huh?"

"Right. Get on board." But something had caught his eye, something large and black, moving in the twisted, alien shapes on the far side of the crater. Another warstrider! Thinking it might be A Company, he engaged his telephoto optics and zoomed in for a closer look.

It was almost five kilometers away, but clearly visible as a stiff crosswind cleared the mists and acid clouds from above the white fog sea. Dev felt a shock of recognition: those curved power feeds like horns, the long and bulbous torso, the faded rising sun emblem on one armored pauldron. . . . It was an Imperial warstrider, a Katana, and it was emerging from the tortured cityscape like a vengeful demon from the mouth of Hell.

A zombie, one of the Imperial Guard striders lost in the first encounter days before. The upper works were relatively intact; the legs and lower torso had shapeshifted into something gleaming and metallic and horribly, nightmarishly other. . . .

But Dev's attention had focused on what the transformed Katana held clutched in its black-armored hands, a pearl gray sphere identical to the traveler spheres floating overhead and lining the fog sea by the thousands.

Why was the strider carrying it? . . .

Five kilometers—too far for autocannon. Targeting information flowed across his field of view . . . range, elevation, target lock . . . *now!* Stooping, he triggered his right-shoulder weapons pack, loosing an arrowing flight of M-22 rockets. As the last rocket cleared its launch tube, Dev whirled, throwing himself from the top of the ridge, hitting the ground in a spray of gravel and pulped, gray Xeno organics. "Cover!" he bellowed, using external speakers and radio simultaneously. "Everybody take cover behind me! . . ."

The sky lit up, outshining the white sun masked behind banks of clouds to the east. As the members of Cameron's Commandos dove for cover behind Dev's fallen, armored body, that white glare waxed brighter, stronger, in an absolute silence that had smothered every sound and dragged on and on and on. EMP surged through electrical circuits. Some failed, melted by the power surge. Others shut down to prevent damage. Dev's external view faltered, dissolved into static, then returned.

What was the speed of sound at slightly less than one atmosphere at a temperature of forty-eight degrees Celsius?

Dev's implant calculated the mathematics and fed him the answer just as the shock wave struck, a raw, howling hurricane of noise and overpressure that sheared off the upper meter of the crater rim at his back and struck him and raged at him and clawed at the armor of his hull. His nanofilm was gone in the first half second, stripped from his back by the sandblasting of heat and radiation and wind-borne grit, but he extended his arm above the huddled mass of armored troops that were snuggling against his torso. The ground shuddered beneath him; the hurricane roar filled the universe beneath a towering pillar of white cloud rising toward heaven.

Then Dev's external sensors were carried away, and he was left alone in a howling wind- and fire-swept blackness. He could sense the link systems shutting down around him as damaged circuits continued to fail. He began to initiate a disconnect. . . .

Too late. Total system shutdown engulfed his mind, plunging him into unconsciousness.

Chapter 28

There was a time when it was taken for granted that the sentient inhabitants of other worlds, if they existed, would be very much like us—different in form or color or size, perhaps, but sharing with us our perception of the universe.

Only now are we beginning to discover, once again, how very conceited our species is.

—Hearings on the DalRiss
Terran Hegemony Space Council
Dr. Paul Hernandez
C.E. 2542

Dev was surprised when he woke up aboard ship. To begin with, he was weightless, and the feeling of endlessly falling pervaded his dreams as he was brought slowly back to consciousness. *Yuduki*'s sick bay was located in the central core, and he nearly panicked when he opened his eyes to see a mass of colored tubing snaking above his face. It looked . . . *alive*, like the horrors he'd seen on ShraRish.

A Japanese nurse appeared almost at once, however, floating head-down a meter "above" him, reassuring him that he was safe, that an ascraft had brought him and his team back to the troopship, that his treatment was proceeding well and that he was already almost completely recovered.

He'd come close to being killed by radiation. While his Scoutstrider had screened him from alpha and beta particles and most direct gamma radiation, the atomic nuclei of steel, manganese, and silicon in the armor had trapped neutrons from the blast, creating a cascade of induced radiation that had poured through his module despite heavy screening and neutron-absorptive molecular layers.

He'd been sick, the nurse told him, almost dead, when Lara Anders had loaded him and his people aboard and dusted off from that hellfire desert five klicks from ground zero. But medical nano programmed to correct radiation damage on a subcellular scale had been filtering through his system for the past three days. His blood count was normal now, as were his bone marrow scans and thyroid levels. He now ran, he was told, a slightly increased chance of developing any of several cancers, all of which would easily be detected and treated automatically long before they became a threat. Even the higher risk of birth defects in any children he might one day have was negated by the medical nano watch now patrolling his body.

Dev's Destroyer had been so hot that it had been abandoned, as had the ascraft that had brought him and his troops back to orbit, the Kani APW, and the Commandos' battle armor. Of the twenty men in his command, three had died in the battle; the rest had been treated for minor radiation injuries and released.

And for the past three days the biological wizards of the DalRiss had been studying the specimens returned from Aurorae Regio with an interest that bordered on fanaticism.

"So you're a hero again," Katya said, drifting close. "What are you doing, trying for another medal?"

Dev had been nearly asleep. He started, then reached out, trying to shove the tubes aside so he could see her face. He was nude, held immobile by a webwork of restraints; the tubes, which carried nutrients for the medical nano in and a drainage system for wastes and scoured particles of radiation, branched from his neck, sides, belly, groin, and thighs, from hair-thin threads to pipelines the diameter of his thumb. He felt no pain, of course—the nerve endings around each insertion had been individually shut down—but he felt achingly hungry, as well as frustrated at his inability to move.

"I'd be happy just to get out of here," he said. "I can't tell where I stop and the plumbing begins."

"The nurse says another twenty hours and you're out of here. You'll be pulling barracks duty before you know it."

"Where? Is the regiment still on the ground?"

She made a sour face. "I wish. The Imperials have stepped in again. The Thorhammers are back in reserve. I think Aiko and Yamagata're afraid the DalRiss'll get the wrong idea if we go around detonating nukes on their planet."

"It wasn't us. Talk to the Xenos. They're the ones carrying around live nukes."

It had been pure intuition that had saved Dev and the others on the surface. There'd been no time to reason things through. But if the zombie Katana had been carrying the fission device captured earlier from the Imperials, and if the Xenos did only adapt captured equipment rather than remanufacturing it, then the chances were they'd tampered with the warhead's triggering mechanism, probably by dissolving the radio-controlled interlocks. Nuclear warheads were triggered by a conventional explosive that slammed two subcritical masses of plutonium together; by firing his salvo of M-22 rockets, Dev had induced a sympathetic detonation in the chemical explosives, and guaranteed that the warhead went off five kilometers from his command instead of closer. That zombie Katana had been heading their way.

Any closer and they all would have fried or been buried under the rubble from the blast crater.

"You know," Dev said after a moment, "I had a bit of a brainstorm down there. I think the Xenos are pretty badly limited by the stuff that they can capture. They can change its shape, but not what it's made of."

"I'm way ahead of you," Katya replied. "All that was in the report I filed with General Howard's staff two days ago."

"Hmph. Did you tell him about the opportunity this gives us?"

Her brow furrowed. "What opportunity?"

Dev thought a moment. He'd not worked all the details out himself. However . . .

"Look, GhegnuRish, the DalRiss homeworld, it's supposed to be just like ShraRish, right?"

"Sure. They . . . well, I guess 'terraformed' is the wrong word, but they modeled ShraRish after GhegnuRish."

"Then the Xeno war machines on GhegnuRish are going to be the same sorts of critters we're running up against here. Local animals that the Xenos have taken over, like those poor creatures we saw at Regio Aurorae. Maybe not even that much, if all the native life on GhegnuRish died off a couple of hundred years ago."

Katya blinked. "Say, that's a thought. The DalRiss have assumed that all life on their homeworld is extinct. They never had much in the way of machines. So what will the Xenos use for weapons?"

"Oh, there'll be something. Cobras made out of rock or crystal or the DalRiss equivalent of dead trees. They had stuff like that on ShraRish. But did you notice that it was easier to kill the Xenos down there?"

She nodded. "Back on Loki, you had to hit them eight or ten times before they'd start falling apart."

"That's because they were using RoPro fabricrete and high-tech alloys. I don't think we're dealing so much with superscience here as we are with the junk collectors of the Galaxy. They've got the tricks they pull with magnetic fields. That's probably connected somehow to their using nanotechnics to morph and repair damage. But when it comes to making alloys, layered armor—"

"Hang on a second, Dev. I want to bring some other people up here, get them in on this." Her eyes took on a glassy look as she used her link to tap into the ship's ICS.

Dev glanced down the tube-tangled length of his body. "I think I'd like to get a bit more presentable first."

The people she had in mind were Colonel Varney, the regimental commander, and Major Gennani, the regimental intelligence officer. While they were waiting, the nurse was able to provide Dev with a robe to afford him some measure of dignity, despite the tubes that sprouted from various seams and openings. She also released his hand and foot restraints so that he felt a little less like a victim of torture and a little more like a warstrider pilot undergoing debriefing.

Varney and Gennani both congratulated him on the success of his raid as soon as they swam into the sick bay cubicle. "That was fine work, son," Varney said. He was a lean, small man with hair turned silver at the temples and a white mustache. He looked as if he was in his fifties, though rumor had it that he was rich enough to have afforded the medical nano for advanced geriatric treatment. How true those stories were, Dev neither knew nor cared. Varney was wealthy, the son of a prominent Earth banking family with connections to Kyoto's financial institutions.

On the other hand, another rumor insisted that he'd passed up an inheritance to stay in the Hegemony army.

"Thank you, Colonel. We got lucky."

"I don't believe in luck. Never did. If I did, I'd have to insist that all my officers be lucky ones, and that'd look bad on the fitness reports." He pulled himself over alongside Dev's harness. Katya and Gennani floated near the door. "So. Captain Alessandro tells me you've got some ideas about GhegnuRish."

"Yes, sir." He'd been doing some hard thinking since his earlier conversation with Katya, but he still had to pause and marshal his thoughts. "I gather the Thorhammers are at loose ends at the moment."

"Hmph. You could call it that." The words were noncommittal. The expression was not.

"I would like to suggest a recon of the DalRiss homeworld, sir. This might be our best opportunity."

Varney folded his arms. "Okay. Why?"

"Point one. We still don't know how the Xenos get from world to world. Here we are, in contact with a civilization that was fighting them two hundred years ago, and they've never seen Xenophobe space fleets either."

"What's the point?"

"The DalRiss have had no contact with their own homeworld for one hundred eighty-some years. Presumably the Xenos have been at peace on that world for all that time. This might be the time to go pay them a visit."

Varney slowly unfolded his arms. "I'm not sure I see what you're getting at, son. What are you saying . . . attack them?"

Dev spread his hands. "Colonel, the one thing that's been hampering us ever since this damned war began was lack of intelligence on the enemy. We don't know how their technology works, we don't know how they think, we're not even sure we've seen a living Xenophobe. The grease blobs *could* be pets. Or slaves. Or juveniles, for God's sake."

"All of that's rather unlikely, given what we've seen so far," Gennani said. "But he's got a point, Colonel."

"Here's our chance to drop in unannounced and see how they really live," Dev continued. "If they have spacecraft, we'll see them. If they have large-scale manufacturing of their own, we'll see that, too. I mean, what have they been *doing* for two hundred years?"

"Attacking ShraRish," Varney said, his voice dry. "And the Shichiju."

"Not the Xenos on GhegnuRish, sir. As far as we can tell, every world grows its own crop of Xenos. We've still never seen a Xeno ship.

"Now we have DalRiss biologists who can grow and program Translators. Wouldn't it be worth the risk, just to see what a peaceful Xenophobe looked like?"

"If there *is* such a thing, yes."

"We've been assuming ever since the first Xeno attack that they attack humans on sight," Katya said. "That's the idea behind their name, right? They're afraid of strangers. Of aliens like us."

"That's never been proven, Captain," Gennani said. "We don't know why they attack us. In some cases, though, it's been hard to prove they were deliberately attacking us. They could perceive us as part of the landscape—"

"A source for raw materials, yeah," Katya interrupted. "I've heard that one."

"The DalRiss have given us a new example in that regard," Gennani pointed out. "Their picture of the universe, their worldview, if you will, is completely different from ours. We see . . ." He moved his arms, indicating the room, the space beyond. "We see space, mostly vacuum, some usable planetary surfaces, rather thinly populated by life-forms. They see the universe as an organic whole, a giant swimming pool chock-full of life, with inorganic matter as empty spaces in the water, and themselves as custodians doing the backstroke. If the Xenophobes are self-aware, their worldview may be more alien still."

"God, that's all we need," Varney said. "More cockeyed viewpoints."

"Who says *we* see things the way they really are, Colonel?" Katya asked him.

Varney ignored that. "So, you think we should zip off to Alya B to see the real Xenos. And if they attack us? Like they always do?"

"We take enough ships—as many ships as Yamagata lets us have—to cover us. If they have a fleet, well . . . isn't that worth knowing about? We still don't know what to look for when it comes to Xeno starships, if there even *is* anything to look for. This could give us some clues."

" 'If there's anything to look for,' " Varney repeated. He looked at Dev. "Are you one of those people who believe in invisible Xenophobe ships?"

"No, sir. But I wouldn't be surprised to find out that they send clouds of nano-sized ships to the stars, billions of machines a few microns across. Maybe those machines manufacture the organic components, the greaseballs, once they land. Or maybe the ships are larger—the size of 27-mm autocannon shells, maybe. We'd be hard-pressed to detect those. Or they ride on meteorites." He spread his hands. "I gather the DalRiss have a completely different way of crossing space."

"Achievers," Gennani put in.

"Magic, as far as our physicists can tell. Even with comels, they don't understand what the DalRiss are talking about. Well, maybe the Xenos have something else, a way of stepping directly from ShraRish to Loki without crossing all that empty space in between. There are *lots* of possibilities."

"Reasonable," Varney said. "Even if we don't see any Xeno ships at the DalRiss homeworld, the recon alone could tell us a lot about them. Just one problem. I doubt that Yamagata's going to buy in to this. Right now he's doing his best to convince our hosts that we're just along to carry the baggage. He won't like the idea of us nosing around the old DalRiss homeworld. Makes us look too important."

"Well, there are different ways of breaking it to them, Colonel."

"Such as?"

"Suppose we put it to them that, ah, we had reason to believe the Xenos were going to reinforce ShraRish from GhegnuRish? Volunteer to go check it out with a squadron of warships and the Thorhammers for recon. He can't very well refuse *that*."

Varney looked thoughtful. "No. No, he couldn't. There's sound military logic in that, son."

Katya grinned. "I told you about this guy, Colonel."

"So you did, Captain. So you did."

"I like it," the major said. "Yamagata won't want to risk a large part of his fleet, but I sure as hell wouldn't want to get caught in orbit by an unknown war fleet from God knows where. A patrol, a recon in force. That would do it."

"But your real idea is to try to talk with them?" Varney asked.

Dev managed a weightless shrug that set his plastic tubes swaying. "If we can. You know, sir, we've never seen any sign of cooperation between the Xenos on Loki, say, and the ones on Herakles or any of the others. That suggests that each invasion force is pretty much on its own. Well, it's a sure bet that the Xenos on ShraRish aren't going to talk to us. But maybe their relatives back on GhegnuRish will."

"Man oh man," Varney said, a sly grin tugging at the corner of his mouth. "What I wouldn't give to see Yamagata's face if we came back from the DalRiss homeworld with a Xeno peace treaty!"

Dev wondered if the Xenos understood the concept of "peace."

It took almost three weeks, with Yamagata stubbornly refusing even to consider the idea. After all, there were no indications that any hypothetical Xeno warfleet was making the crossing from GhegnuRish.

Still, Varney had planted a seed of worry in Yamagata's mind, and Admiral Aiko was far more willing to discuss matters of strategy with the Hegemony regimental commander than was the *taisho*. The *Daihyo* was unwilling to let the *gaijin* anywhere near the DalRiss homeworld, but patience—and Aiko's insistence that he had to know what he was facing in order to take proper precautions—won out in the end. Yamagata agreed at last, and Takahashi was overruled. Since the question was one of military strategy rather than politics, the Emperor's liaison could be courteously ignored.

The Emperor, after all, was a *long* way off.

The operation was called *Siranui*. The word referred to the phosphorescent foam stirred by a ship's wake at night, but literally meant "unknown fires," appropriate for a squadron reconnoitering the unknown fires of another star. It consisted of the cruiser *Sendai* as flag, with *Chosho* Yasunari Sato in overall command; the destroyers *Akatuki*, *Ikaduti*, and

Tatikaze: and the transport *Yuduki*. They would be accompanied by the *Darwin*, which numbered with her crew twelve DalRiss Lifemasters and a menagerie of bioengineered Alyan life-forms.

While Sato had the final say over the disposition of his ships, Colonel Varney was in command of the surface-recon element of the squadron, with orders instructing him to use his discretion insofar as whether or not to approach the planet or to attempt a landing.

His orders even included the possibility of establishing communications with the Xenos. Though Yamagata didn't relish the possibility of a political coup by the Hegemony, he was realist enough to know that a good military commander takes the chances that are offered him. A chance to meet the Xenos, to talk with them, or simply to learn about them, was simply not to be passed up.

Dev was surprised that Yamagata had been that open to the idea. Varney thought it likely that the Imperial admiral had weighed the possibility that the Xenophobes at GhegnuRish would be friendly, and discounted it.

Whatever the politics of the decision, three weeks after the battle at Regio Aurorae, Siranui Squadron entered the godsea for a short transit of just five light-days. They emerged in the A7 star's system and spent two days more maneuvering inward, surveying the planets and monitoring the electromagnetic spectrum for . . . anything, radio messages, radar, any evidence at all that the squadron had been sighted or that the system was even still inhabited.

There was nothing.

GhegnuRish did not look promising from space. As the squadron fell around the curve of the planet toward the sunlit side, the difference was striking. Absent were the reds and oranges and golds of ShraRishian vegetation. There were clouds here, and violet seas, but the land appeared barren, with an albedo far lower than expected. It was as though the entire land surface of the world had been scorched and blackened.

With no challenge, no sign of enemy ships, the five ships dropped closer, finally taking up orbit at two hundred kilometers.

And still there was no sign that the Xenophobes were aware of them, no sign that there was any life on the planet at all. Orbital scans showed that much of the land surface had been covered by complex shapes that seemed to rise out of the ground to engulf each former DalRiss population center, then spread out across the open ground like vast, malignant growths.

Those growths, black and dark gray, wrinkled, convoluted, drank the light of Alya B, and were responsible for the sharply decreased albedo.

Albedo was a measure of reflectivity, of how much light was bounced back into space by a given terrain feature. It used a scale of zero to one, with one indicating total reflectivity of light, and zero total absorption. *Darwin*'s astrophysical team reported that the blackened portions of GhegnuRish's land surface had an average albedo of .01, about the same as the maria of Earth's moon.

If GhegnuRish was absorbing a lot more light from its sun, however, it was also giving off a lot more heat. The planet glowed in the infrared bands, and the surface temperature averaged ten degrees Celsius higher than expected. Industrial waste heat, someone had suggested, but there was no sign of industry, of factories, of any life at all. Some of the expedition's officers speculated that the Xenos died off once they'd subjugated a world.

Dev doubted that. He *felt* the enemy down there, waiting. They'd never yet attacked a ship in orbit. Maybe they were waiting for the Thorhammers to land. Maybe . . . maybe . . .

After two days of orbiting, during which time survey teams completed their photo mapping of the surface and the DalRiss biologists aboard the *Darwin* completed work on a new species of Translator, the decision was made. The Thorhammers would attempt a landing on the DalRiss homeworld.

Final preparations were made, weapons, ascraft, and warstriders all checked and prepped for landing. Dev, fully recovered now, was issued a brand-new LaG-42 Ghostrider to replace the Scoutstrider abandoned at Regio Aurorae. The regiment was already shorthanded, though, which meant he would have to jack the two-slotter solo. He worked twenty-five hours straight with the Thorhammers' maintenance techs, breaking the machine out of storage, bringing its AI core on-line, powering up its fusion reactor, supervising the integration of a jet-pack hotbox, checking out the systems, and tuning its link hardware to his own.

The name *Dev's Destroyer* had been a wry joke, and for a time he considered naming the LaG-42 *Dev's Destroyer II*. Sergeant Wilkins suggested *Strider-man*, the nickname he'd been known by during his hitch with the Wolfguard, but he settled at last on *Morgan's Hold*. Not many of the other striderjacks caught the reference, but the members of Cameron's Commandos cheered when they heard.

After a too-short ceph-induced sleep, he was up again, briefing the Commandos on their part in the upcoming drop.

And to think, Dev thought wryly as the final moments before drop clicked away, *that this was all my idea!*

Chapter 29

. . . temperature range (equatorial): 45 °C to 55 °C; Atmospheric pressure (arbitrary sea level): .85 bar; composition: N_2 *82.3%,* O_2 *9.7%,* O_3 *2.1%,* SO_2 *3.5%, Ar 1.1%,* H_2O *(mean) .1%,* CO_2 *570 ppm,* H_2SO_4 *(mean) 140 ppm . . .*

—*Selected extracts from science log*
Alya B-V
IRS *Charles Darwin*
C.E. 2541

They'd landed on the outskirts of what the DalRiss said had once been the largest of their homeworld's cities. The place was preternaturally still and quiet, with no indication that their arrival had even been noticed.

The Thorhammers had landed in full regimental force, establishing a perimeter around the big Typhoon transports, then extending a platoon-strength line to sweep through the tortured, blackened landscape in search of . . . *anything*.

The city had been alien to begin with, a vast and geometric sprawl of dwellings grown rather than built, with materials that ranged from stuff with the texture of sponge to something like a seashell's slick, opalescent hardness. Most of the DalRiss structures had hugged the ground, part of the terrain they rested on. Now, though, the nightmare shapes and surreal forms that cloaked the ruined city added layer to machine-blind layer, utterly transforming the original shape and feel and logic of the place. The surfaces were smooth, bloated . . . obscene, as though some vast and intricate work of art had been desecrated, twisted from one design of rational purpose into something irrationally different.

And that, Dev reflected as he scanned the dead cityscape through the senses of his Ghostrider, might very well be what had happened. Most of the old DalRiss buildings had been converted, eaten or mutilated or simply buried by the coal black Xeno growths that covered everything like a sea of once molten lava.

From what he'd seen on ShraRish, DalRiss architecture usually presented smooth surfaces and curved shapes that fit together in strange but aesthetically pleasing ways. Most of what he saw now, though, had the look of something *excreted* . . . organic, but unspeakably foul, and with a randomness that suggested the builders had been blind . . . or simply completely unconcerned with anything a human or a DalRiss would have called *beauty*. Most surfaces were covered with massive, tangled coils of glistening tubes that reminded Dev of heaped entrails. Here and there, bizarre forms, some smooth, some spiked and angular, rose from the organic tangle, jet black in the light of that blazing sun.

"Delta Leader, this is Delta Four," Dev called over the tactical net. "Katya? You scanning anything?"

"Kuso, Dev, this place is dead," Katya replied. "Like a tomb. I don't think there's been anything alive here for a century at least!"

Glancing to his left, Dev could see other members of Group Delta, Katya's Warlord and four striders of First Platoon. To his right, a Kani APW stilted along on spidery legs, pacing the warstriders' recon sweep.

It was eerie, and lonesome despite the presence of the other striders, with a graveyard stillness as oppressive as the obscene growths surrounding them.

"Delta Leader, Delta One," Hagan called. "I'm picking up

some interference on the radio. G and H bands . . ."

"Spooky, ain't it?" Nicholsson added. "Like the city's singing to us . . ."

When Dev shifted bands, he could hear the interference, too—not the usual hiss and crash of static, but a modulated thrumming, like the plucking of some bass stringed instrument. "Yeah," he said. "But what's doing the singing?"

They came to a gulf, a canyon with sheer walls carved through solid rock, spanned by vaulted arches and the limply hanging tubiforms of the Xenophobes, many running straight up and down the walls. The depths were lost in shadows. Dev probed with a ranging laser and found the bottom almost two hundred meters down.

"Delta Leader, Delta Four. We're crossing."

"You're covered."

Dev flexed his legs and jumped, sending the Ghostrider soaring above the chasm. Mentally he shrugged his shoulders, cutting in the strider's hotbox, feeling the surge of thrust catch hold, extending his leap across the gulf. His flanged feet struck the hard surface on the other side, striking sparks, as his knees flexed to absorb the shock.

"Down and clear!" he called over the net. Data flowed across his visual field. Jump reserves down thirty-eight percent. Full power in another twenty-eight seconds.

Dev scanned the surreal terrain, wondering if he would recognize a threat in this strange landscape of meltingly soft, malformed shapes if he saw it. Nothing looked normal, nothing looked right. Even the sky had an aching, hollow feel to it. Atmosphere readouts showed the same general composition as Alya A-VI, though it was much drier. The temperature hovered around forty degrees Celsius. Acid concentrations in the air were no worse than in a pre-nano industrial park on old Earth, the result, possibly, of the extinction of all native life. In the hours since they'd landed, in the days they'd been orbiting the planet, there had been no sign at all of biological life on this world.

His audio sensors picked up the roar of the Kani APW

touching down with a crash in a billowing cloud of superheated steam sixty meters away. Seconds later, Hagan's Manta landed a hundred meters to the left.

"I'm getting a heat plume up ahead," Hagan reported. "Three-five-oh, range forty-two hundred."

"I see it," Dev replied, catching sight of the geyser of heat on an IR scan. "Let's check it out." The cityscape was so still and dead that anything as energetic as a warm exhaust from some subsurface pocket was a welcome event, and worth checking out. Was the infrared leakage from this world a natural effect, or the result of some kind of industry?

Together, then, Dev's *Morgan's Hold* and Hagan's *'Phobe Eater* advanced, adopting a bounding overwatch through the twisted terrain that sent first one strider, then the other ahead, each covered in turn by the other. The APW followed. A kilometer to the west, Katya and the rest of 1st Platoon continued the sweep toward the center of the city.

Everywhere Dev saw the stark, bleak evidence of older DalRiss buildings dismantled . . . no, *digested* by the Xenophobe invaders, replaced by the Xenophobe excretions. Haphazard mounds of tubes, some of them tens of meters across, lay in tangled masses, some heaped into artificial mountains hundreds of meters high.

It must have taken armies, Dev realized, to so completely wreck a flourishing civilization. Where had those armies gone?

Uneasily he glanced up into the deep violet sky. The Expeditionary Force was watching all wavelengths, all radar bands. Nothing could move on this world's surface without Captain Sato's immediate knowledge.

But what about *under* the surface? Many of those obscene-looking tubes were open, gaping blindly at the sky. Tubes descended into the bowels of the planet everywhere, spreading and burrowing between and through the remnants of DalRiss foundations like the massive roots of ancient trees.

Always the Xenophobes emerged from underground. Had their armies emerged to devour the DalRiss civilization here, then returned to those black depths?

He checked his weapons system readouts again. This time he mounted a Taimatsu Type-50 on his right-arm hardpoint, a strider-sized version of the man-portable chemical flamers. A rocket pod was mounted over his left shoulder. Less than adequate if the Xenos should decide to emerge and—

"Target!" Hagan cried. "Bearing three-three-one! Firing!"

Dev turned just as the Manta opened up with its Kv-70 weapons pods. Streaks of fire sleeted like machine-gun fire across the twisted landscape, smashing into a tower a kilometer away.

There was no response from the structure, which exploded as Hagan's rockets tore through it, then collapsed.

"Kuso!" Hagan snapped. "It's already dead!"

Dev summoned an image of the tower from his Ghostrider's memory, zoomed in, enhanced. . . .

It *had* been a stalker. Hagan's first instinct had been right. It looked something like a Fer-de-Lance, round and squat and covered with spines. But the thing was an empty shell, a corroded torso as lifeless as its surroundings.

"What the gok are you shooting at, Vic?" Katya's voice said over the tacnet.

"Sorry, Captain," Hagan said. "I thought—"

"Forget it. But let's cruise easy, huh? We've got a long way to go."

They found more machines after that, hundreds of them, scattered across the city ruins. All were dead, abandoned centuries ago.

Why?

Dev stepped closer, scanning the silent ranks with his optics. "Hey Captain," he called. "You getting this?"

"Affirmative, Four." He heard her shift channels. "Starlight, this is Delta Leader calling Starlight. Come in, please."

"Starlight copies." It was Colonel Varney, still aboard the *Yuduki*, but personally supervising the deployment. "Go ahead, Delta Leader."

"I'm relaying transmissions from Delta Four. Do you copy this, Starlight?"

Dev continued to pan the derelict Xeno machines so that the mission officers aboard the *Yuduki* could see the full, grand sweep of the scene. It was eerie, like an army of skeletons, waiting to be summoned to rise. . . .

"Affirmative, Delta Leader, Delta Four. Your signal is clear."

"It's like they all just packed up and left," Dev said.

"Roger that." There was a pause, filled with the singsong cries of radio interference, the background hiss of static. "Ah . . . Delta Leader, this is Starlight. Be advised that Intel believes that the Xenos might be underground. They recommend caution."

Cheerful thought.

"We copy," Katya replied. "Starlight, we are investigating a heat source, map reference Alpha Delta One Seven Niner. Do you see it?"

"Affirmative, Delta Leader. Orbital scans show IR source, probable venting from subsurface structures. Watch your step."

"Rog."

"Dev, you heard that?"

"I copied, Captain. Vic and I are moving closer now."

The heat plume was clearly outlined against the sky under IR scan. Another chasm yawned ahead, where some ancient DalRiss structure had been cleared away all the way to its roots far underground, leaving gaping-mouthed tubes and shafts plunging down into darkness.

Dev kicked off, then triggered his jump pack once . . . twice . . . a third time, holding the jump as he aimed for an invitingly clear area on the far side. His strider's feet came down . . .

. . . and then he was falling as the ground disintegrated beneath his weight. What he'd thought was steel plate shredded like foil as his warstrider plunged through. Forgetting himself, he almost triggered his left and right weapons pods as he tried to fling out his arms and grab the edge of the pit as he fell. Warnings flashed across his vision and he aborted the accidental aim-lock-fire order, then fired his jets.

Morgan's Hold had twisted sideways as it broke through, and the thrust slammed him into an arching strut. Then he was falling. "Mayday! Mayday!" he cried, using the ancient call for help. "Delta Four calling mayday—"

The pit opened up around and beneath him, a webwork maze of girders and steel scaffolding. Dev twisted himself in midair, swinging the Ghostrider into a feet-down attitude, then mentally shrugged his shoulders, firing the twin jets. Warnings flicked through his consciousness. The fusion jets had not yet recharged; their combined thrust was a fraction of what was necessary to even slow his fall.

He banged into another projection . . . and another. He was falling down a well of some kind. . . . No! It was one of those tubes, he realized with a horrid crystal clarity, a tube twenty meters across, roofed over by a flexible sheet of metal foil too thin to support his strider's twenty-five-ton weight. The walls consisted of recognizable bits of technology fused into a random hodgepodge of organic-looking struts, girders, braces, and bits and pieces crushed together into a nightmarish tracery of interlocking jackstraws. Laser rangers probed the darkness below as he fell. Fifty meters more and he would strike bottom. . . .

Dev's attention focused on the swiftly dwindling range numbers flashing through his mind. Time seemed suspended, his senses and the workings of his brain itself working with a computer's speed. He tensed himself . . . then flexed his shoulders at the last possible moment.

This time the jets fired at full power, and kept firing, slowing him with a savage deceleration that would have been crushing had he been able to feel his body. Clouds of superheated steam billowed around him. His feet struck bottom and his torso kept going, slamming into a duralloy-hard pavement as his legs folded on either side. There was a thunderclap of noise, a spray of debris from overhead as part of the wall collapsed, and then . . . silence.

For a long moment Dev remained there, unmoving, not even daring to acknowledge the warnings flashing through his mind. The Ghostrider had been hurt—the actuator links and shock supports of both legs damaged—and a power drain from his lower right torso probably meant a bad short. For a moment he'd thought he was about to be buried alive as the weakened tunnel walls collapsed, but the cave-in had only been partial. Slowly, gingerly, he tested systems, opened circuits . . . then eased the machine into a wobbly upright stance. Pieces of tunnel wall, like smoothly rounded tree trunks, spilled to the floor in a cascade of rubble, dust, and gravel.

He was down, and he was safe, at least for the moment. The big question was . . . where?

It was pitch-dark at the bottom of that well. The Ghostrider's AI calculated a fall of 103 meters . . . a drop that had carried him well past the shell of machines and reworked buildings on the surface and into the dark, stone-walled crust of the planet itself.

Looking up, he could see the partial blockage of the well. He thought he could probably see the tunnel opening far above if he moved, but he didn't want to move yet until he was sure the strider's systems were all working.

In any case, he wasn't getting out that way. The Ghostrider's jets had been barely up to slowing his fall; they'd never lift him up that sheer drop, and he knew that he couldn't climb one hundred meters.

With escape ruled out for the moment, he decided to investigate his surroundings. Had anyone heard his earsplitting entrance? Was there anyone to hear? On infrared his surroundings took on the irregular, smooth-surfaced look of cavern walls, glowing with radiated heat. To his left, though, he could see a definite regularity to the rock. He might be standing on the foundations of some extremely old stone buildings, ancient DalRiss structures, though their architectural purpose had long ago been lost, or possibly the rock had been somehow reworked according to a different plan.

A Xenophobe plan, perhaps.

"Delta!" he called, opening the tactical frequency. How the hell was he going to get out of here? "Delta Sweep, this is Delta Four! Do you copy?"

A burst of static was his only answer, one shot through with alien twitterings and flutings and high-pitched piping sounds that set his imagination crawling. Radio interference from the surrounding walls, he decided, and the blockage overhead, possibly mixed with assorted local transmissions.

Transmissions by whom? Imagination gave texture to the heat-glowing semidarkness around him. Dev tried to pierce it, tried to resolve some sort of images from the midnight blackness. He could make out walls, but he decided that his IR feed had been damaged. The walls seemed to be moving with that vague crawling sensation one senses when focusing on shadows in the dark in the middle of the night.

No, it was not his imagination. The walls of the cavern *were* alive . . . and moving.

He tuned his IR receptors, trying for better resolution. There was almost no visible light at all, and his infrared feed gave indistinct images at best, because the walls and what seemed to be covering the walls were very nearly the same temperature.

At last, though, he was able to resolve those masses of color marking sources of heat, letting the AI filter the images in such a way as to pretend that the cavern walls were cool, with warmer masses covering them, patches of yellow against green and blue.

It was impossible to see any detail. Through linkage, Dev's senses could receive infrared data, but his brain could still only interpret input in the hunorm range. Anything else was a translation, and subject to interpretation. At first Dev thought that the walls were wet, that water was flowing across rock surfaces, but as he watched, he became convinced that he was looking at something more complex than that.

Impulsively he switched on the strider's outer lights, flooding the cavern with harsh brilliance. At visual wavelengths the walls retained their glistening, wet-smooth look, like the walls of a limestone cavern sculpted by a million years of flowing water.

But they were moving, rippling beneath the lights like the flutter of a jellyfish.

It took several minutes for Dev to understand what he was seeing well enough to even attempt to describe it to himself. There were . . . *things* hugging that wall, each a meter square or more, each rounded, smooth-surfaced, and shapeless.

He was sharply reminded of the greaseballs, the organic, sluglike creatures he'd seen before. These were similar, but each hand-sized bioform was imbedded in a gelatinous ooze, an ooze that extended across the rock wall like amoebic pseudopods, each arm touching the others around it. Each was dark-colored, almost black, but under direct lighting they turned a murky and translucent gray in which he could make out bits and pieces of debris imbedded within the jelly.

Or were they internal organs of some kind? Or lumps of undigested food? Or unborn young? He didn't know what it was he was looking at, but it/they indisputably was/were *alive*. The smooth-bodied masses were flattening, stretching as he watched, as though spreading themselves beneath the light. He wondered if it was the light that was attracting them, or his own presence.

He glanced at his readouts, checking for the nano count, but there was none. The absence of nanotechnic disassemblers was only mildly reassuring. Dev was trapped in a well a hundred meters deep . . . completely surrounded by Xenophobes.

And yes, they were definitely reacting to his presence, stretching out from the walls to envelop him. . . .

Chapter 30

At first, all the One sensed was heat, a warmly glowing mass that dropped into the One's midst, as dazzling as the ignition of a flare in the depths of a cave. Reacting with an instinct inherent within the One, individual components began closing on the object, spreading their receptor surfaces to the fullest extent to drink this bounty which had appeared so unexpectedly, at levels so far above the comfortable Depths below.

After a moment, as the One considered the heat source, emotions surfaced from somewhere deep within its being . . . surprise at this unexpected gift, and . . . curiosity.

Those ancient twistings of the Self's mind had not been lost or forgotten after all.

The One knew nothing of humans, of course, knew nothing of the oddly formed, strangely bilateral machine that was the source of so much radiant heat. In the trinary logic of the One, there was only Rock, Not-Rock, and Self. From the One's point of view, the Universe was an unimaginably vast cavern, an empty gulf of Not-Rock sealed in Rock, which was itself surrounded by an endless, semimolten sea of life-giving heat.

The One occupied one minute piece of that Cavern, between the heat-sea and the temperature fluctuations of the Gulf. Elsewhere in the Great Cavern, it knew, other Ones dwelt, parts of Self, though many were still Children of the Dark, primitive and mindless.

This glowing apparition was neither the comfortable, data-rich recognition of Self, nor the empty blankness of Not-Rock. It must be, therefore, Rock . . . but that strange subset of Rock that moved of its own volition, like Self, but which was decidedly Not-Self.

The concept was almost unimaginable, but the One had run into such paradoxes before. Among the Children of the Dark, long ago, during the first dim stages of consciousness as Children, memory was passed as genetic coding from Child to Child with each tripartite conjugation. The One possessed memories extending back to the Beginning, eons past, and within a portion of the Great Cavern far removed indeed from this place where it found itself now. It remembered the Selfs-that-were-Not-Selfs that had threatened the Children of the Dawn . . . and that had appeared in different forms during many of the Cycles since. It remembered the Selfs-that-were-Not-Selfs that had threatened this *cycle.*

Always, those Selfs-that-were-Not-Selfs had been threats.

Protection from such threats, of course, was the duty of the Children, necessary if the Cycles were to continue. The concept of "death" was alien to the One since the One would effectively live for as long as the heat sea endured. But it did comprehend the extinction of individual Children, a kind of transformation into the void of Not-Rock, a timeless hell of nonexistence.

Never in all its memories had the One itself been threatened with extinction . . . but never in all its memories had the One been threatened after the Children had become One.

This cycle, it seemed, was different, horribly so. . . .

Chapter 31

The Nihongo word for 'nightmare'—akumu—and for 'demon' or 'devil'—akuma—obviously have linked etymologies. The image is of the demons that haunt our sleep.

—*The Gods Within*
Viktor Sergeivich Kubashev
C.E. 2314

"Captain! We've lost Delta Four!"

Hagan's call caught Katya as she completed a rocket-assisted leap across a narrow chasm. Somehow she maintained her concentration, coming to a halt with a metallic clash of actuators, hydraulics, and armored flanges.

"What happened?" she snapped. Swinging the Warlord right, she acquired Hagan's Manta visually, then broke into a ground-eating lope across the tortured landscape. "Where is he?"

"Landed on a thin surface, like ceramic, stretched across the mouth of a big tunnel. Surface gave way, and down he went. Watch yourself, Captain. There may be more covered holes like that."

Cursing her careless impatience, she slowed her pace, selecting each piece of ground before she trod on it. This part of the alien city was so completely covered over with Xenophobe forms that each step was still a matter of guesswork and luck, but by avoiding flat, circular patches that looked as if they might be the masked openings of vertical tunnels, she swiftly reached the Manta's side.

Dev's Commandos were already clambering out of their Crab APW, seventeen men and women cumbersome in black armor and slung weapons. Beyond, the shattered surface Dev had landed on revealed the gaping, night-black maw of a pit, the ruin slick and smooth as though polished by wind and water across the centuries.

Katya had wondered at Dev's decision to include Cameron's Commandos in this recon but hadn't questioned him about it. He had proven himself right at Regio Aurorae: there were things men in armor could do that were impossible or difficult for a warstrider, and men and striders could complement one another on a mission.

Katya approached the pit, where troops in black and red armor were breaking out strands of monofilament from external stores compartments on the Crab. Gingerly she edged past the crunchies to peer down the open shaft. Blackness yawned half a meter in front of her feet. The singsong wailing on G and H bands was particularly strong here, but once she thought she heard a human's voice, Dev's voice, filtered by the blasting of static. She probed with a ranging laser. Eighty-five meters, a long way to fall. She shifted to her communications laser, opening the beam wide to tag the entire bottom of the well, praying for a response, any response.

Nothing. Which could mean that Dev was dead, his strider a twisted mass of wreckage at the bottom of the well.

Or it could mean that his lasercom gear was damaged, or that he was alive but unconscious or disconnected or that he'd moved into a side passage and the laser line of sight was blocked, or any of several other possibilities. If the lasercom gear was working and the Ghostrider was in the L-LOS, though, she ought to be able to establish a link with the LaG-42's AI, even if Dev was out of the link.

"We thought we might have picked up some light down

there a moment ago," a woman's voice said in her mind.

She turned her attention back from that dizzying partial circle of night, focusing instead on the armored figure standing beside her. "Who're you?"

"Sergeant Wilkins, sir. Lieutenant Cameron's team leader."

"You think . . . he's still alive?"

"He could be. If he was able to orient himself and use his jets for the landing. We're getting ready to go down and check."

"Check? How?"

Wilkins jerked a gloved hand over her shoulder, toward the Crab. "Buckythread. We have enough to lower five people down there. I'll take an armed team down, and we'll see if we can find him."

Katya swiveled her sensors back to the pit, probing the depths once more with her ranging laser. Eighty-five meters. No . . . on the far side she got a reading of one hundred three meters. Dev's crash must have caused a partial cave-in. She could imagine the descent blocked by debris hanging from one wall of the tube, tangled in the blackness.

Blackness. She suppressed a shudder.

"There could be Xenos down there, Sergeant."

"Yes, sir." She hefted her subgun. "That's why me and my four guys'll be going in armed."

"Three guys, Sergeant."

"Beg pardon, Captain?"

"You and three of your guys. I'm coming with you."

Wilkins hesitated. "That might not be such a good idea, sir."

You're right about that, Sergeant, she thought. She felt exhilarated, even a little crazy, and she could feel the terror of the blackness beneath her feet.

But Dev was down there, and she was going to get to him. If he was unconscious in a damaged warstrider, a striderjack might be necessary to talk with the AI and help pull him free. She had to go.

Into the dark.

"No arguments, Sergeant," she said. "Break out an extra subgun for me. Torolf? You've got my baby until I get back."

"Sure thing, Captain."

She began severing her link with the Warlord.

Chapter 32

Within the past century, akuma has evolved a secondary meaning born of this linguistic relationship. As researchers continue to use cephlinkage and implant technology to delve into the unfolding mysteries of the mind, akuma has come to refer to those very special, personal demons of our own creation, those that drive us from within to greatness . . . or to catastrophe.

—*The Gods Within*
Viktor Sergeivich Kubashev
C.E. 2314

Dev tensed, ready to twitch the muscles that would trigger his Ghostrider's flamer. At such close range he would kill hundreds of the monsters.

But he hesitated to fire.

First, of course, there was no escape from this cavern that he could see. The backblast would certainly bring down the crumbling tunnel walls, destroying *Morgan's Hold* as well as the Xenos.

But there was more to it than self-preservation. Never, so far as Dev knew, had Xenophobes ever been seen living within the black labyrinths of their tunnels . . . *never*. Robots and striders both had attempted to penetrate openings on various human worlds, but communication was impossible and none had emerged. These creatures, bathed in the radiance of his lights, were exhibiting behavior strikingly different from the individuals he'd seen before. Those others had appeared to be interconnected as they crawled free of their opened travel pods, but these seemed to be woven together, moving but permanently connected, a living network that reminded Dev of individual cells tied together as parts of a single, larger organism.

Was that the answer? Were the Xenos part of a group mind, one that Man had not yet learned to communicate with? That didn't seem likely. Xeno efforts, while sufficient to kick humans off eleven worlds so far, had been victorious more because of the strength of numbers and the inaccessibility of their deep subsurface nests. Individual masses of Xenos had seemed disorganized, even chaotic in their attacks. He remembered human attempts to analyze their attack plans, and smiled inwardly at a dawning truth. There had been no attack plans to analyze.

No wonder the Imperial War Staff had been baffled.

Hell, there was so much about them humans didn't know. He relaxed slightly, still watchful but unwilling to start the fight. He would wait and see what this crowd did.

Yes, they were definitely reacting to the strider's presence, sliding toward it, but very, very slowly. He cut the Ghostrider's external lights, but it didn't seem to make any difference. Dev nodded to himself. He'd begun to suspect that the creatures were reacting to heat rather than light, and his experiment confirmed that. There were no eyes on the things that he could see, no organs of sight . . . unless the whole translucent glob was photosensitive, and he did not think that that was the case.

Okay, the critters were thermovores, heat-eaters. His strider had blasted the cavern with a hell of a lot of heat when it fired its jets, so much so that his strider's AI was battling to dump excess heat into the surrounding air, which was quite a bit hotter than the strider's vents. Outside temperature . . . fifty-one Celsius.

It occurred to Dev that the heat plume he'd seen earlier was not waste heat from industrial processes, but a means of planetary engineering on as large a scale as the attempts to remake Loki's atmosphere. These creatures *liked* heat. Maybe that was the reasoning behind those giant tunnels, a system for bringing heat from deep within the planet's interior to the surface. The excretions on the surface of GhegnuRish certainly seemed designed to catch sunlight, possibly for the purpose of transforming it into heat.

He wondered if cold might be an effective weapon, then abandoned that line of thought. He'd seen these creatures blindly questing on the surface of Loki, where the air temperature hovered at thirty to fifty below. Hardly a choice environment for a life-form that lived off heat.

There was a way to find out once and for all . . . possibly.

Communication.

The DalRiss Lifemasters aboard the *Darwin* claimed that the new Translators they'd engineered would be able to bridge the communication gap between a human cephlink implant and the Xenophobes. A special, newly devised program designed to facilitate that communication had been downloaded into Dev's RAM before the drop, and his orders were to try to use it if the opportunity presented itself. This, Dev thought unhappily, was certainly an opportunity.

There was only one hitch. The Translator had to establish physical contact with both Dev and the Xeno. To use the damned thing, he was going to have to break linkage and leave the protection of his strider, walk out there, and *touch* the goking things.

That might not be as much of a problem if the Xenos were bubbling masses of grease blobs and jelly lying in the open shell of a travel pod. But this! . . .

Switching his external lights back on, he continued to scan the Xenophobes outside. There were thousands of them, stretched across every surface he could see. The one thing going for him was that none of the Xenophobes was wearing armor. If a stalker or even a Gamma appeared down here, he wouldn't have a chance.

Dev thought about leaving the relative security of *Morgan's Hold*, and shuddered inwardly. He remembered his trek across that flame-blasted battlefield on Loki, unprotected, alone. He remembered the battle outside the Warlord, and the terror and pain when the Gamma had grabbed his ankle.

"Well," he told the encircling creatures, speaking aloud. "We could just sit and stare at each other for the rest of the week while you soak up my lights."

There was no reply, of course. The amorphous forms were definitely closer now.

No choice, he thought. *I'll just have to meet them on their terms.*

Silently he ran through the list of mental commands that would break the link. Abruptly he was lying in the cramped and stifling dark, his body protesting with the usual postjack list of aches and pains and stiff-muscled complaint as he pulled the VCH from his head and unjacked the feeds.

For an instant he was deaf, dumb, and blind to the universe. Then he was awake, alone inside the cramped and ill-smelling claustrophobia of the Ghostrider's command module. The heat was oppressive. It was like sitting in an oven, and he could scarcely breathe. In seconds he was bathed in sweat, reeking of fear and exertion.

Fumbling for the pressure latch of an equipment locker, he opened it and extracted a gas mask. He wished he could wear an E-suit helmet, but even with positive pressure from his PLSS feeds, atmospheric carbon dioxide could still diffuse into his helmet air, and even a tiny rise in his CO_2 partial pressure could cause unconsciousness, then death. He slipped the mask on, pressed the seals against his face, and tested the airflow.

Good. It was easier to breathe now.

He thought about the horrors waiting just outside the strider's hull, and nearly balked.

Akumu. The Nihongo word meant nightmare, and this was Dev's own, very personal nightmare, to step outside the protection of artificial armor, exposed, *vulnerable*.

Reaching into the equipment locker, he extracted a gleaming canister. Touching the seals, he broke it in two, spilling the formless blob of gray jelly within onto his stomach. It looked very much like the things plastered over the cavern walls outside. With some distaste—he still hadn't gotten used to the feel of these things—he pressed the fingers of his bare right hand into the mass. Slowly the amoebic mass began oozing up his fingers, coating the back of his hand, then trickling around his wrist and across his palm. In a few moments his hand was encased in what looked and felt like a glistening wet, translucent gray rubber glove, with an ugly, gray-brown mass clinging to his forearm.

Careful not to bump the comel, he untangled himself from the webbing. As he lifted his arm, he caught sight of the artificial symbiont by the faint light of his console, and smiled. His hand and arm felt cooler now; the comel, like the Xenophobes outside, was a thermovore. It was feeding on the heat of Dev's body.

"Okay, fella," he said. "We're about to find out if you live up to your billing. I sure hope you can speak the natives' language. . . ."

Dev reached up and cracked the commander's access hatch.

Chapter 33

Dreams, fecund musings,
Reality in the world
I shape for myself.

—Imperial haiku,
mid-twenty-fifth century

Katya caught herself with one hand as she started to swing, the buckythread suspending her from her harness like a spider on the end of a very long strand of webbing. Buckythread—a nanosynthesized single-chain molecule made of carbon atoms linked together in a very long, geodesic tube—was immensely strong, stronger than diamond fiber, so strong that to cut it required the application of specially programmed nano to disassemble the carbon-carbon bonds. There was no danger that the thread would break and send her plunging into the well.

It wasn't the danger of falling, however, that threatened her. It was the enveloping blackness, imperfectly dispelled by the lamp clipped to her helmet, and the closeness of her surroundings, made smaller by the dark and by her own adrenaline-charged apprehensions.

Secured to the prow of the parked and anchored Crab, her cable was playing out from a small spool attached to her harness. Keeping one hand on the spool's pressure plate, she was able to control the speed of her descent. She felt clumsy, though, and the four bobbing lights below her feet proved that Dev's Commandos were a lot better at this than she was. One boot caught on a projection, knocking her sideways. She swung in a dizzying arc, returned, and crashed her shoulder painfully against the wall. Her subgun jammed against her hip and the weight of her PLSS hanging from her back. She stopped her descent, steadied herself, adjusted her harness and weapon, then began the descent again.

She was blind . . . as blind as she'd been hanging in the Dark between worlds years before. The knowledge that she could still see . . . the half circle of light overhead, the four bobbing helmet lights of her companions below . . . could not banish the fear of that palpable night.

Worse, though, was the knowledge that the Xenophobes might be all around her, hidden in the dark. Nightmares she'd had as a child, imagined monsters in the shadows, returned with vivid force and reality.

But she kept her hand on the spool's touchpoint, lowering herself steadily into the depths. She was getting the hang of the thing now, controlling her descent with gentle kicks off the wall.

Somehow, she kept the monsters at bay.

Chapter 34

Even the most alien of beings, though, must share some definite perceptual biases, understandings, stimuli, even emotions. If it doesn't, communication is impossible and demonstration of sentient self-awareness is impossible.

I wonder if that hasn't been our problem with the Xenophobes all along. Perhaps the one emotion we have in common with them is fear.

—Dr. Paul Hernandez
Hearings on the DalRiss,
Terran Hegemony Space Council,
C.E. 2542

The heat inside the strider had been bad. Outside, it was like a furnace. Dev clung to the open hatchway, head reeling, before he managed to release the ladder and start down the rungs. The Ghostrider's lights illuminated a tiny world of silver light and slick-surfaced, slow-gliding Xenos. Elsewhere was blackness.

The ground felt slick beneath his feet. Looking down, he saw he was standing on a thin layer of jelly—Xeno cells smeared by the Ghostrider's foot when he'd righted it after the fall.

Careful of each step, he approached the nearest wall, right

hand out. He could feel the comel quivering against the flesh of his forearm, as though in anticipation.

What would it be like, communicating with the Xenophobes? With the DalRiss, he'd simply heard their voice inside his head, thanks to the comel's translation and the interface through his link. But the Xenos were different enough to make DalRiss and humans look like brothers. Dev didn't know what to expect.

He placed his gloved hand against the wall, bringing the comel into direct contact with the glistening mass of Xeno cells layered across the rock in their veneer of translucent jelly.

Threat . . . fear . . . threat . . . but the invader looked nothing like the dimly remembered Selves-that-were-Not-Self that had vanished from the world so very long ago. The Self moved with crippling slowness; the speed of its thought was the speed of microelectronic circuitry and relays, of individual switching units the size of single molecules. But movement, reaction, the dim memories of old fears and drives and needs, were slowed a billionfold by the inefficiencies of the Self's haphazard design. The One could think very quickly when it had something to think about, but its reactions were painfully slow.

Curiosity. Fear. The Not-Self had approached, was touching one subunit of the Self. The One prepared to discard the subunit to avoid contamination, yet in a shock of awareness, Self and Not-Self were merging, blending, communicating *at blinding speed. The electronic currents that passed for thoughts, currents describing mode and existence and being and memory, had been picked up by the Not-Self and returned, and when they returned, they brought . . . images.*

Dev felt the alien thoughts, a flood surging through his skull, a cascade of images, concepts, *strangeness* . . . seeing heat and equating it with comfort and completeness, understanding space as the taste of Self crowded unit by unit into an unimaginable body that laced through a million kilometers of tunnels riddling the planetary crust from the chill void of the inner surface to the warm glow of the outer fires, spanning the globe . . . no . . . the *universe* . . . a hollow shell . . . inside out . . .

He struggled to understand, to comprehend, fighting a sluggish mental vertigo that threatened to turn his world inside out. It was like rebirth; worse, it was as though everything he'd ever learned in his life was *wrong, wrong, wrong* and he had to learn everything anew.

The universe is Rock, endless Rock going on forever, surrounded by warmth. Somewhere deep within the Rock and far away from the warmth, there is Not-Rock, Void, an immense bubble of emptiness pervaded by strange phenomena, by heat that fluctuates according to a seemingly meaningless pattern, a heat source that seems unreachable, violating any reasonable hypothesis of the universe.

The One would be content to remain close to the surrounding warmth, but the compulsion remains to seek the Void and the warmth beyond the Void and populate it with extensions of the One.

But from the Void come the Not-Self units that do not obey any laws at all, but that disrupt the One and seek its destruction, but these become part of the One, turned to good. . . .

Dev tried to clear his mind, staggered by the data flowing through it from outside. And there was more, echoes in the thunder in his brain.

I always wanted to be a star pilot, wanted it so bad, it hurt. I remember the summer Mom and I went to see Dad off when he went up the sky-el on his way to the Imperial Palace and his new job. The sky-el is anchored on a promontory on the north coast of Pulau Lingga, a forty-kilometer island smack on the equator a hundred kilometers southeast of Singapore proper, and you reach it by tube magtrains that run beneath the waters of the strait. Sometimes you can see the sky-el from Singapore, a thread-thin vertical scratch against the sky that catches the sun with a silver gleam just after sunrise, like sunlight on a strand of spider's silk.

The place to really see it is from the visitors' gallery close by where the magtrains unload, but the gallery was closed that day and all I could do was cling to the wire mesh fence that closed off the service access areas from the public and look up and up and up and up at that silver tower arrowing into the zenith and know that that tower is the first step on the road to the stars and that's where I want to go, into the Galaxy and out among the stars and bathed in the blue glory of the godsea and when will I see Dad again and why does it hurt so much, oh God—

Dev knew he was rambling in his thoughts but couldn't stop, as the pain and fear of years were released as though by the smashing of a dam, a cascade of feeling and memory.

His hurt when his father left, the betrayal. The agony when he learned his father was dead and that there could never be reconciliation. His frustration at losing his chance to be a starpilot, the humiliation of being consigned to the enlisted ranks . . .

. . . and the warm and easy camaraderie of yujo, *the warrior's bond, a new family, acceptance, self-mastery, victory . . .*

My God, he thought, shaken by the intensity within himself that he'd never known was there. *What's the Xeno think of all of this?*

He heard an answer, though not in words. The two sets of experiences and backgrounds and worldviews, his and the One's, were too mutually alien. But he could sense the Xenophobe's intense curiosity, could sense questions streaming through his awareness like the systems readout when he was linked to his strider. . . .

What is mesh fence?

What is island?

What is sunlight?

What is planet?

What is stars?

What is God?

And more, many more. He could sense that the Mind behind those questions was very large and very, very old, that it was cycling through what it had sensed in Dev's uncontrolled rush of thoughts with the speed of a supercomputer, matching words with images, concepts with understanding. It was fast, but hampered by its own perceptions. Dev had glimpsed some of those twists and recoiled, unable to comprehend them.

But memories continued to surface. Dev had just experienced a direct RAM feed. There was new data in his permanent memory, like the note passed to him by Katya, but containing files and files of uncounted millions of bytes of memory.

All he had to do was . . . remember.

He remembered being a Child of the Night, half-formed, knowing warmth and darkness and the taste of brothers. He remembered before that, crossing the Inner Void in a tiny sphere flung from the Rock at some unimaginably distant time in the past. He remembered . . .

Dev knew what the Xenophobes—

No, not *Xenophobes*. That was human misperception, born of fear and ignorance. They did not fear strangers; they simply did not know them, did not recognize them as a part of the universe not bound up with Self.

They, *it* . . . was the One, all there was in a universe that held no One else.

A clatter of falling rocks sounded twenty meters behind him. Dev half turned in time to see rubble spilling across the crouched form of *Morgan's Hold*, like some huge, motionless crustacean dimly visible behind the four-eyed glare of its lights and the swirling dust. Seconds later, four figures descended through the misty light and dropped to the ground at the Ghostrider's side, two men and two women in black and red combat armor hitting the releases on their harnesses and unslinging their weapons in one smooth movement.

"Lieutenant Cameron!" Sergeant Wilkins advanced on him like an avenging Valkyrie, a vicious-looking Steyr-Hitachi submachine gun in her hands. "Oh my God, what's it done to you? . . ."

Behind her, Corporal Bayer raised a hand torch as the other two unslung their sleekly vicious-looking Toshiba laser rifles, but hesitated, uncertain where to direct their fire.

Dev blinked against the light, suddenly aware that he was still standing next to the cavern wall, aware that the One had flowed down to engulf almost half of his entire body, as more and more of the One's subunits moved in to make contact through the comel. With a sudden twist of insight, he realized that he must look like part of this living wall. There was no pain, no compulsion.

Merely . . . *Oneness.*

"Hello, Sarge." His voice sounded strange, muffled by the mask over his face. Dev almost couldn't trust himself to speak. The images, the thoughts . . . Strangeness still galloped through his skull, threatening to trample him into the ground. "Don't shoot. It hasn't hurt me. I'm okay . . . *really* okay. . . ."

Reluctantly he pulled himself free from the wall with a wet, sucking sound. The comel remained with him, trembling gently against his bare skin. The One had felt cool where it touched him. The heat of the cavern washed over him again like a hot blast from an oven.

With another, louder clatter, a fifth figure descended into view, legs kicking at the wall. Dev's eyes widened with surprise. This figure was clad in black skintights and wore an E-suit helmet.

Katya.

She almost got hung up trying to unhook the spool attached at the chest of her descent harness, but she got free at last, unslung her subgun, and strode toward him, stiffly determined. "Dev?"

"I'm okay, Katya." With sudden insight, he knew what that

descent into the dark had cost her. "What . . . what are you doing *here*?"

"Looking for you." He saw her eyes go wide behind her helmet visor. Her helmet light swept past him, gleaming against the living wall. "Is that, that *thing* behind you what I think it is?"

Dev managed a smile. "This, people, is a Xenophobe." His smile broadened. "Bad name. It isn't afraid of us. Doesn't hate us. For it, life is nothing but tunneling and expanding and reproducing and growing and always, always, always seeking warmth, filling the Rock, turning Not-Self into Self. But then you meet someone who makes you stop and *think*. . . ."

Wilkins stepped closer, but cautiously, the muzzle of her Steyr-Hitachi wavering uncertainly. "Lieutenant, you are making no sense whatsoever. Maybe you'd like to start over?"

"To think," Dev said slowly, "that all we had to do was explain things. I mean, part of it died, and suddenly the universe just didn't look the same anymore." Sobering, he shook his head, painfully aware of how disjointed his words sounded as he tried to assimilate the . . . strangeness. His head hurt. " 'It' . . . that's the wrong word. Too impersonal. Maybe we just don't have the right words."

He paused, blinking as another thought occurred to him. "Better put your guns down, people," he said. "I think our war may be over."

Katya turned her full attention on Dev. "Can we trust it?" she asked. And Dev heard the unspoken question: *Can we trust you? Has it done something to your mind?*

"We can trust it," he said with careful deliberation. Too much revelation, too soon, and they would be convinced that it wasn't Devis Cameron speaking. Contact with it *had* changed him, but not in the way they feared. He took a deep breath, worked to steady his voice. "It's a machine. A very large, very complex machine made up of God knows how many trillions of computers, each the size of a bacterium. Electrochemical computers manufactured—

grown—from the equivalent of nucleoproteins."

Katya looked doubtful. "Who grew them? Where did it come from?"

Dev hesitated, choosing his words. "We have a kind of symbiosis with our machines, right? With nanotechnology, we can grow computers inside our brains, inside our skin, make them a part of us, a way for us to interact with the rest of the world. So much so, it's hard to imagine life without them.

"Okay, now imagine a . . . a life-form. I can remember a little of it, like fragments of a grainy, two-D film. Evolved on a very old planet, circling a red dwarf sun, deep underground, maybe in a pocket of water warmed by the planet's molten core. A primitive organism, but evolved to its absolute highest potential over billions of years. Imagine what it would have been like if tunicates or molluscs had evolved to intelligence on Earth.

"Locked away deep in the rock, it . . . *they* were cut off from the rest of the universe. Evolution must have been slow, slow, with nothing but the natural radioactivity of the rocks to cause mutation and change. But there would have been competition for raw materials. For warmth. They were thermovores, always seeking heat. It doesn't seem possible, but maybe that was enough stimulus for them to evolve intelligence. To become self-aware.

"Imagine how they perceived the universe. There was Self. There was Rock. There were the openings in the Rock they made . . . Emptiness. Not-Rock. Everything else—water, heat—was variations of Rock."

"Sounds like the old idea of elements," Katya said. "Earth, Air, Fire, Water."

Dev nodded. "Kind of a simplistic cosmology. But it fit what they were aware of. Eventually they developed nanotechnics."

"Whoa there," Wilkins said. "How could they go straight from stone age to nanotechnics?"

Dev smiled. "For them, their 'stone age' *was* nanotechnics.

Their first tools. They must've learned to manipulate molecules inside their own bodies, probably to get raw materials for growth from the rock. Or to tunnel out larger living spaces for themselves. Or to break hydrogen and oxygen out of certain rocks to make more water. Millions of cell-sized machines, made from minerals drawn from the rock, could be joined together into larger structures. Machines that could carry the organic components of this symbiosis, keep them wet and alive even when the underground seas dried up, or tunnel deeper as the planet's core cooled. If they worked at it long enough, for billions of years . . .

"My guess is that they evolved with the Galaxy's first generation of Population I stars, ten or twelve billion years ago. It must have been eight or ten billion years more—twice as long as Earth or any of the other worlds we know have even existed—before they finally made it to the stars.

"And when they did, they carried with them a view of the universe that was completely inside out."

Dev tried to explain what he had picked up from the One only in fragments of passed-on memory, pictures and sensations imperfectly understood, imperfectly transmitted.

For most of those billions of years, the Xenophobes had slowly developed side by side with their submicroscopic technology, utilizing tailored proteins as computers, with the equivalent of nucleic acids as records, enzymes as encoders and readers, viral bodies as packets of tightly encoded data, a mimicry of biological life but deliberately shaped and molded for ever-increasing efficiency. Separate organisms communicated with one another, exchanging data packets first by chemical, later by electrical means.

Organism and machine were utterly dependent on each other. The dual organism expanded to utilize the entire crust of its homeworld. Ultimately the original life-form that had used nanotechnics to secure its place within its world was absorbed by its own technology. Cells patterned succeeding generations of cells, and what did it matter whether the original pattern was natural or artificial? As the distinction between organic and inorganic vanished, so, too, did distinctions between individuals. Like separate neurons linked together into a vast network capable of acquiring, processing, and storing data, the multitude of individuals, linked together through the millions of kilometers of chambers and tunnels that filled the planet's crust, became the One.

As with any life-form, change forced adaptation. The underground seas dried up; the One manufactured its own water and, ultimately, adapted the subunits of its form to the harsher environment by wrapping each in gelatinous, water-filled shells. The planetary core continued to shrink and cool; the One expanded its caverns, learned to use electromagnetic fields to warp rock into easily traversable paths, learned to remake rock, atom by atom, into shapes that suited its needs.

Ultimately the One must have converted most of the planet's crust into a vast machine for collecting and transmitting heat.

"But their world was dying," Dev said. "They got some heat from their sun, but they must have known that, sooner or later, the planetary core would be cold and dead, and that would be the end of them."

"And that's when they learned how to build starships?" Katya asked. "I don't see how they could without heavy industry. You can't make K-T drives out of cells."

"The DalRiss grow their ships," Dev reminded her. "And they don't use the K-T plenum. In the case of the One, it was simpler still. Remember the travel pods?"

"*Those* are the Xeno spaceships?" Katya asked.

"Or something like them."

"But at sublight speeds, it would have taken years. . . ."

"Millions of years, Katya. They did it blindly, flinging pods filled with life into space.

"You see, they didn't know about the stars. And the . . . the living component of the symbiosis was crippled because it didn't know, *couldn't* know what the universe was really like.

"They couldn't see. They couldn't sense position the way

we can tell where our arm is even with our eyes closed. All they knew was warmth and Rock and empty space and Self. They constructed a picture of the universe that was essentially an infinity of Rock. Inside that Rock is an enormous empty space. Going out from that empty space, it gets warmer . . . and warmer, until it's too hot and the pressures are too great to sustain life."

"Like the people who once thought Earth was flat," Katya said, "balanced on the shell of a tortoise."

"Exactly. When they launched their life pods toward the stars, what they thought they were doing was launching them out into that huge central cavern they thought of as a kind of Void of Not-Rock. They were trying to reach another part of Rock, a place not yet occupied by Self. Thousands of pods must have been sent out. Maybe millions. They drifted through space for millions of years, guided—maybe—by nanotechnic machines on board that could sense magnetic fields. Nearly all of them must have been lost, out there among the stars. Lots more must have homed on stars . . . and found more heat than they bargained for.

"Or maybe they could recognize the danger, and had control enough to find cooler, more habitable pieces of Rock."

"Planets," Katya said quietly. "Like Loki."

"And GhegnuRish and all the others. Those that survived the trip landed, the pods opened, and the passengers started tunneling." He shook his head. "Other parts of the vast cave in the heart of the universe.

"I think a kind of life cycle evolved. What we call Xenophobes land on a planet, dig themselves in, and begin spreading through the planet's crust looking for heat, tunneling deep on cold planets like Loki, spreading out near the surface on warmer planets like GhegnuRish. They take the world over, fill it with life, *their* kind of life. When the crust is filled . . . they launch another generation to the stars."

"I still don't understand why we've never seen their travel pods in space," Bayer said. "They'd be easy enough to detect."

"Sure. But we haven't seen them because they arrived a long time ago. How long do you think it takes for a handful of organisms to spread through the planetary crust of an entire world? I think the first Xenos must have landed on Loki hundreds of thousands of years ago. Maybe longer."

Katya looked startled. "Like an infection. They could have spread through this entire part of the Galaxy. They could already be on Earth, *in* Earth, buried deep."

"A distinct possibility. They'd only make themselves known if they rose from the warm depths looking for heat from the sun or raw materials from our technology. We were right, Katya. They don't think in terms of, oh, refining iron into steel. Or manufacturing their own nano films or durasheathing. But if they can get at it, their nanotechnic disassemblers can take it apart and reuse it elsewhere. They found our cities to be quite useful that way."

"They never even knew we were there."

"Oh, they knew there was *something* there. They knew when they were being attacked, when parts of the Self were dying. And they adapted. They took pieces of our own equipment, modified it to fit the surroundings—"

"Alpha stalkers were never our equipment. Or magnetic travel pods. And we got the idea for nano-D shells from them! Where did they come from?"

"Katya, these . . . beings have been spreading from system to system for a long time. Hundreds of millions, maybe billions of years. The machine we call a Fer-de-Lance might be technology remembered from a war with some other species a million years ago. The travel pods were part of their original nanotechnology, capsules for moving through the rock where temperatures and pressures would be too much for unprotected organisms. The patterns are all stored in their computer memory, and passed on with each new wave of colonists. Each new world is a new One. One world doesn't communicate with another. They simply utilize their world, send another generation of colonists toward the sky, and . . . *think*.

"The tragedy was that, with their inside-out worldview, they could never conceive of another intelligence, outside of their own. As far as they were concerned, they were simply utilizing the resources of their universe. Adapting. Surviving. They could never even approach their full potential with the baggage of their old, organic philosophy.

"But by the same token, they never had the . . . intuition that would let them overcome that philosophy. They couldn't innovate, only react. Maybe, in the end, they were more like machines than organic life after all."

Dev looked at the cavern walls surrounding the little group of humans. The One, the tiny part of it that he could see, was quiescent, patiently waiting.

"Now, though, it's come into contact with a different worldview. It's learned something new, maybe for the first time in millennia. And I think . . . I think it wants to know more about the universe."

Katya reached out, touching his arm. The contact was warm. Reassuring. "It could tell what you were thinking?"

Dev nodded. "It saw, through my link, a little bit of the way we see the universe—how we see space, a Galaxy of three hundred billion stars, planets, other galaxies beyond ours. And people. Relationships. Change. Variety. I don't think it understood even one percent of what it saw. What it *felt*. But . . ."

"But what? What was it feeling?"

"More than anything else?" He closed his eyes, feeling again that alien tide. *"Wonder . . ."*

Chapter 35

Compared to what's Out There, every human culture and somatotype, from Imperial Japanese to New American Outback Ranger to !Kung to gene-tailored Freefaller, is identical. To most of what's Out There, humans, planaria, and tree ferns are as similar as makes no difference. Maybe, someday, that realization will be the salvation of our species.

—*Life in the Universe*
Dr. Taylor Chung
C.E. 2470

Dev sat in the most luxurious room he'd ever seen in his life, despite the fact that there was little furniture. The awards ceremony was over and he ached to get back to his assigned quarters and out of his dress grays, but the invitation, unprecedented as it was, could not possibly have been refused.

He sat tatami-fashion on the padded floor before the low, richly ornamented table. Katya knelt beside him on his right, with General Varney next to her. The silhouettes of guards stood motionless behind translucent walls.

Opposite, an old and wrinkled man sipped tea from a perfect cup. He did not, Dev thought, look much like his portraits. "The Empire," he said, carefully placing the cup before him, "owes you a debt of gratitude, *Chu-i* Cameron-san. A debt that can never be truly paid back. Certainly not with trinkets."

His new rank still felt uncomfortable, as did the starburst at his throat.

The Imperial Star.

The Emperor seemed to read his thoughts. "I remember your father, Cameron-san. He was a brave, an honorable man. His loss is deeply felt. I wish he could be here with us now, to share your honor, and to see how his son has brought an end to the Human-Xeno War."

Dev looked hard at the Emperor but could detect no deeper meaning beyond the simple words. Strange. A thousand years before, this man would have been revered as a descendant of the sun god. Now he was just a man . . . but an immensely powerful one, a man who could make or break an officer's career with a word. It would not be wise to contradict him.

"The war is not over yet, Your Majesty," Dev said. "All I really learned out there is that it may never be over."

That was true enough. The One of GhegnuRish knew nothing of its offspring, blindly flung against the stars, or of other Ones hidden in the worlds of neighboring suns, even suns as close as Alya A and B. Dev's discovery had proven only that each separate world-entity would have to be approached and shown the reality of the universe separately.

How many worlds did the Xenophobes occupy already? Dev had never been able to determine just how many generations of space-faring life pods there'd been, or how distant the original Xenophobe homeworld had been. Xenophobes—unconverted Ones—might inhabit every planet in the Galaxy with a molten core and a significant magnetic field.

And there was no way to tell how those other Ones would react when they were contacted. Each One was an individual, reacting to its own environment, unaware of the Ones of other worlds. Each had a long and bloody heritage, a racial memory written in the genocides of entire species, to overcome.

Genocide on a planetary scale. On a galactic scale.

The Emperor had been silent for a long time. He stirred now, as if throwing off some troubling thought. "Are you familiar with the novae of Aquila?"

Dev leaned back on his haunches, extracting data from his RAM. Yes, he'd picked up something about that, one of the tidbits acquired years before when he'd read everything that he could about the stars. There was an area of Earth's sky, he'd learned, in the direction of the constellation Aquila the Eagle, where there'd once been a higher-than-expected number of novae—exploding stars. During one forty-year period in the first half of the twentieth century, twenty-five percent of all of the bright novae observed from Earth had appeared in an area equivalent to a quarter of one percent of the entire sky; two had appeared in one year alone—1936—and Nova Aquila of 1918 had been the brightest recorded in three centuries, outshining every star in the sky but Sirius.

"I've been thinking about those exploding suns," the Emperor said quietly. "They're much farther away than Alya A and B. Nova Aquila, I believe, was twelve hundred light-years distant. But all lie in the same general direction from Earth."

True. Eagle Sector embraced the neighboring constellations of Aquila, Serpens, Ophiuchus, Scutum, Sagitarius—a tiny part of the sky lying in the general direction of the Galactic Core. Alya—Theta Serpentis—lay right on the border between Serpens and Aquila, only three degrees from the site of the nova of 1918. In galactic terms, the line from Nova Aquilae to Alya to Sol was almost a straight line.

Had someone else been confronted by the Xenophobe threat in C.E. 700 and sought to deal with it in a direct and uncompromising fashion? How many of the Xenophobe pods that had spread to worlds of the Shichiju had been fleeing the wholesale destruction of their planets' stars? The memories passed on by the One were still confused and tangled, but Dev saw there images of warfare and titanic struggle, age following age of genocidal war.

Dev saw little reason to be hopeful. The Xenophobes might be the closest thing Man had to natural enemies in the Galaxy—outside of himself, of course—and the war might go on year after year on world after world. On each planet, the resident Xeno intelligence, the "One," would have to be individually approached, contacted, and converted to a different way of looking at the universe.

"As I said, Your Majesty, the war might not be over for a long time yet. We will have to deal with each planetary intelligence one by one. Just contacting them may be difficult. Certainly it will be all but impossible on worlds where we're actively fighting them."

"True. Still, the One of Lung Chi has been at peace for a number of years now. Perhaps we could approach that world in peace, now that we know what to look for, how to communicate with it. The DalRiss have offered to help. They're already intrigued by the possibility of reoccupying their own homeworld. We may yet return to the colonies like Lung Chi and An-Nur II, to worlds lost to Man for decades. With the intelligent cooperation of each world's intelligence, terraforming will be miraculously easy."

Dev tried to imagine an organism that girdled a planet, busily converting raw materials to human-breathable air, adjusting the planetary temperature, even manufacturing entire cities to spec, all in exchange for intelligent conversation with the Not-Self organisms inhabiting the surface.

There was so much to be gained from peaceful contact. The alternative was genocide . . . and the exploding suns of Aquila.

"So you see, *Chu-i* Cameron-san, we have much to thank you for. True, communication alone will not end the war, but it is a beginning. Perhaps the most important beginning there is. That medal cannot repay what we owe you. Nothing can. But perhaps we can reward you further."

Dev reached up and touched the Star. "I am content, Your Majesty."

"Indeed? My staff has been going through your records. I gather that only last year you were seeking transfer to the Hegemony Navy. Certainly you have amply demonstrated your talents, both in linking and in tactics. According to your records, you possess that blend of psychological attributes that would guarantee your success as a naval officer. Perhaps you would consider a transfer to the Imperial Navy? A more tangible reward for your services, one that could see you with a command of your own within a few short years."

Dev grinned. Glancing to his right, he caught Katya's eye, warm with understanding, and maybe just a bit moist as well.

It was definitely a breach of protocol, but Dev reached out, taking Katya's shoulders and giving her a hug.

"Thank you, Your Majesty," he said. "But I already have everything I could possibly want."

TERMINOLOGY AND GLOSSARY

AI: Artificial Intelligence. Since the Sentient Status Act of 2204, higher-model networking systems have been recognized as "self-aware but of restricted purview," a legal formula that precludes enfranchisement of machine intelligences.

Alpha: Type of Xenophobe combat machine, also called stalker, shapeshifter, silvershifter, etc. They are animated by numerous organic-machine hybrids and mass ten to twelve tons. Their weapons include nano-D shells and surfaces, and various magnetic effects. Alphas appear in two guises, a snake-or wormlike shape that lets them travel underground along SDTs, and any of a variety of combat shapes, usually geometrical with numerous spines or tentacles. Each distinctive combat type is named after a poisonous Terran reptile, e.g., Fer-de-Lance, Cobra, Mamba, etc.

Analogue: Computer-generated "double" of a person, used to handle routine business, communications, and duties through ViRcom linkage.

AND Round: Anti–nano disassembler. Tube-launched NCM round that bursts almost as soon as it is fired, releasing an NCM cloud.

Antigenics: Nanotechnic devices programmed to hunt down and destroy disease bacteria and parasites inside the body.

APW: Armored Personnel Walker. Any of several large, four-legged striders designed to carry unlinked passengers. VbH Zo ("Elephant") can carry fifty troops. Kani ("Crab") can carry twenty.

Ascraft: Aerospace craft. Vehicles that can fly both in space and in atmosphere.

Beta: Second class of Xenophobe combat machine, adapted from captured or abandoned human equipment. Its weapons are human-manufactured weapons, often reshaped to Xeno purposes. They have been known to travel underground.

Bionangineering: Use of nanotechnology to restructure life-forms for medical or ornamental reasons.

CA: Combat Armor. Light personal armor/space suit providing eight hours' life support in hostile environment.

Cephing: Also **linking.** Derived from cephlink. To operate equipment, computers, striders, etc., through a cephlink.

Cephlink: Implant within the human brain allowing direct interface with computer-operated systems. It contains its own microcomputer and RAM storage and is accessed through sockets, usually located in the subject's temporal bones above and behind each ear. Limited (non-ViR) control and interface is possible through neural implants in the skin, usually in the palm of one hand.

Cephlink RAM: Random Access Memory, part of the microcircuitry within the cephlink assembly. Used for memory storage, message transfer, linguistics programming, and the storage of complex digital codes used in cephlinkage access. An artificial extension of human intelligence.

Charged Particle Gun (CPG): Primary weapon on larger warstriders. Including proton cannons and electron guns, they use powerful gauss fields to direct streams of charged subatomic particles at the target.

Colonial Authority: Hegemonic bureaucracy charged with overseeing government, trade, and terraforming of the human-inhabited worlds.

CMP: Cluster Munitions Package. Missile or artillery round payload. Dispenses hundreds of mines, bomblets, or nuclear-triggered plasma bolts in a destructive "footprint" across a large area.

Cryo-H: Liquid hydrogen cooled to a few degrees absolute, used as fuel for fusion power plants aboard striders, ascraft, and other vehicles. Sometimes called "slush hydrogen."

C-socket: Cervical socket, located in subject's cervical spine, near the base of his neck. Directs neural impulses to jacked equipment, warstriders, construction gear, heavy lifters, etc.

C^3, C-Three: Military term for Command, Control, and Communications, the essentials of battlefield command.

Deplur: Depleted uranium. Ultradense metal used in massive projectiles such as 8-mm hivel ammunition.

DSA: Deep Seismic Anomaly. Seismic tremors associated with subsurface movements of Xenophobe machines.

Durasheath: Armor grown as composite layers of diamond, duralloy, and ceramics; light, flexible, and very strong.

El-shuttle: Saucer-shaped pressurized chamber ferrying passengers and cargo up and down the sky-el. The passenger deck has seats for up to a hundred people, complete with jackplugs and a recjack library.

E-suit: Environmental suit. Lightweight helmet and garment for use in space or hostile atmospheric conditions.

Fabricrete: Artificial building material assembled molecule by molecule by nanotechnic constructors in Rogan Process, using dirt or refuse as raw material.

Fusorpak: Power unit carried on board most striders and large vehicles. Uses tanked slush hydrogen as fuel.

Gamma: Third type of Xenophobe combat machine, usually relatively small and amorphous. Apparently a fragment of a Xenophobe Alpha, animated by one or more Xeno machine-organism hybrids. Its surface consists of nano disassemblers, making its touch deadly.

Gun tower: Unmanned sentry outpost armed with various energy or projectile weapons. May be automated, remote-controlled, or directed by an on-site, low-level AI.

Hardware: Any physical computer equipment, but usually specifically applied to cephimplants, sockets, and other equipment surgically implanted within brain, skin, or bone.

Hegemony: Also Terran Hegemony. World government representing fifty-seven nations on Earth, plus the Colonial Authorities of the seventy-eight terraformed worlds. Technically sovereign, it is dominated by Imperial Japan, which has a veto in its legislative assembly.

HEMILCOM: Hegemony Military Command. Local military command-control-communications (C^3) headquarters, usually based in sky-el orbitals, charged with coordinating military operations within a given sector.

Hivel Cannon: A turret-mounted, high velocity rotary cannon. Similar to twentieth-century CIWS systems, it fires bursts of depleted uranium slugs with a rate of fire as high as fifty per second. Usually controlled by an onboard AI, its primary function is antimissile defense. It can also be voluntarily controlled and used against other targets.

HMC: Hegemony Military Compound. Military base supporting at least one battalion of warstriders plus auxiliary forces.

Hotbox: Strap-on rocket or scramjet booster. Small modules allow striders to softland after an airdrop or provide jet-assisted boosts for navigating rough terrain. Larger modules provide surface-to-orbit thrust for aerospace transports.

Hunorm: Human-normal. Refers to link-feed senses, especially vision, in human-normal ranges, as opposed to spectra normally invisible to humans, such as infrared.

ICS: Intercom System. Provides shipboard voice communication for unlinked personnel. Also refers to linked communications between crew members of a single vehicle.

Imbedded Interface: Network of wires and neural feeds imbedded in the skin—usually in the palm near the base of the thumb—used to access and control simple computer hardware. Provides control and datafeed functions only, not full-sensory input. Used to activate T- and C-socket jacks, to pass authorization and credit data, and to retrieve printed or vocal data "played" inside the user's mind. Also called 'face or skin implant.

Jacker: Slang for anyone with implanted jacks for neural interface with computers, machinery, or communications networks. Specifically applied to individuals who jack in for a living, as opposed to recreational jackers, "recjacks."

Kokorodo: Literally "Way of the Mind," a mental discipline practiced by Imperial military jackers to achieve full mental and physical coordination through AI linkage.

K-T Plenum: Extraspacial realm at the hyperdimensional interface between normal fourspace and the quantum sea. From Nihongo *Kamisamano Taiyo*, literally "Ocean of God." Starships navigate through the K-T plenum.

Kuso: Japanese word for feces. Not a Japanese expletive, it is used as such by Inglic-speakers.

L-LOS: Laser Line of Sight. Straight-line path clear of interfering smoke, dust, or other obstruction along which laser communications can be established.

Loki: 36 Ophiuchi C (Dagstjerne) II. World 17.8 light-years from Sol currently undergoing terraforming by colonists of Scandinavian descent. Place names taken from Norse mythology, including Asgard (synchorbital), Bifrost (sky-el), and Midgard (towerdown). Capital: Midgard. Language Norsk-Lokan.

Lung Chi: DM+32° 2896 (Chien) IV. World terraformed by colonists of Manchurian descent. Overrun by Xenophobes in 2537.

Medsystem: Any AI-oriented electronic network dedicated to monitoring and controlling biological functions during cephlinkage. Bodily functions are monitored through microcircuitry imbedded within ship or combat suits, which in turn are plugged into the AI overwatch system. All physical sensations, including pain, can be edited from the human brain's awareness.

Meteffectors: Metabolic Effectors. Nanotechnic devices that increase the efficiency of certain bodily processes, converting body fat to energy, and food to muscle tissue.

Microbion: Gene-tailored, microscopic artificial life-form designed to perform some ecological or life-support function, such as adjust a planetary ecology's tolerance to high or low carbon dioxide levels.

MJ: Megajoule. Measure of energy. The detonation of one kilogram of TNT releases approximately five MJ of energy.

Morphing: Xenophobe ability to change shape or repair itself within certain limits, made possible by flexibility of positioning and bonding between the machine's nanotechnic "cells."

MSE: Mental Stability Evaluation. Test recorded by full sensory link determining a subject's reactions, flexibility, and the presence of potentially hampering or unwanted prejudices or mental debilities.

Nangineering: Nanotechnic engineering. Use of nanotechnic devices in building or in medicine.

Nano-Ds: Nano disassemblers. Xenophobe weapon, delivered by mag-accelerated projectile or through contact with a specialized appendage, consisting of billions of submicroscopic machines programmed to disassemble molecular bonds. A high concentration of nano-Ds can cause several kilos of mass to disintegrate into its component molecules within seconds.

Nanoflage: Nanofilm on military vehicles designed to transmit colors and textures of vehicle's immediate surroundings. Selectively reflective, it does not reflect bright light or motion.

Nanomold: A semiportable nanovat used in construction. Placed on site, it uses Rogan's Process to convert dirt or other locally available raw material into fabricrete walls or prefab building sections.

Nanovat: Industrial tank used for growing nanotechnic products. Small vats can produce, on order and with proper raw materials, food, garments, disposable computers, and other small items. Large vats are required to grow pieces of large manufactured goods like vehicles.

NCM: Nanotechnic Countermeasures. Submicroscopic devices programmed to hunt down and destroy enemy nanotechnic disassemblers before they cause irreparable damage. In combat, applied as a patch or an aerosol.

Neopsychometrics: The science of measuring human psychological variables, such as aptitude, emotional disturbance, or psychotechnic disorders. "Neo" pertains to the revolution in human psychology brought about by link-assisted diagnosis and treatment.

New America: 26 Draconis IV. Frontier colony 48.6 light-years from Sol.

PLSS: Portable Life Support System, pronounced "pliss." A small and lightweight unit providing air, heat, power, and waste recycling for environmental suits and other protective garments.

Psychotechnic Disorders: General term for a group of mental disorders resulting from breakdowns in an individual's abilities to relate to high-tech, computer-oriented society. They include:

Technic Depression (TD): Feeling of inferiority to AIs, coupled with an inability to cope with speed of information transfers, virtual reality shifts, or changing styles.

Technomegalomania (TM): Delusion of godhood fostered by virtual realities. Marked by depression, anger, or hostility when subject is in the real world, by feelings of invulnerability and power when linked.

Technophobia (TP): Unreasonable fear of machines, computers, or aspects of technic society, such as analogues or cephimplants.

Quantum sea: Energy continuum reflected in "vacuum fluctuation," the constant appearance and reabsorption of vast quantities of energy on a subatomic scale. Tapped by starships operating within the K-T plenum.

Rank: Terran Hegemony ranks are based on the Imperial Japanese rank structure, though the English terminology is preferred in common usage. A rough comparison of rank in the Hegemony Military, as compared to late twentieth-century America, is given below:

Enlisted Ranks

U.S. Army/Marines	*Imperial Military*
Private 2nd class/(no equivalent)	*Nitto hei*
E-2 Private/PFC	*Itto hei*
Superior private/(no equivalent)	*Jotto hei*
E-3 PFC/Lance Corporal	*Heicho*
E-4 Corporal/Corporal	*Gocho*
E-5 Sergeant/Sergeant	*Gunso*
E-9 Sgt. Major/Sgt. Major	*Socho*
WO Warrant Officers (CWO)	*Jun-i*

Commissioned Ranks

U.S. Army/Navy	*Imperial Military*
0-0 Cadet	*Seito*
O-1 2nd Lieutenant/Ensign	*Sho-i*
O-2 Lieutenant/Lieutenant (jg)	*Chu-i*
O-3 Captain/Lieutenant	*Tai-i*
O-4 Major/Lieutenant Commander	*Shosa*
O-5 Lieutenant Colonel/Commander	*Chusa*
O-6 Colonel/Captain	*Taisa*
O-8 Major General/Rear Admiral	*Shosho*
O-9 Lieutenant General/Vice Admiral	*Chujo*
O-10 General/Admiral	*Taisho*
O-11 General of the Army/Fleet Admiral	*Gensui*

Recjack: Using implants for recreational purposes. These range from participation in ViRdramas to shared multiple sensual stimulation to direct stimulation of the hypothalamic pleasure centers (PC-jacking).

Riderslot: Opening in an ascraft or other transport's hull designed to receive striders. Usually equipped with grippers, magnetic locks, and autoplug ICS and datafeed connectors.

RJ: Military slang for free time spent recjacking.

Rogan Process: Nano construction technique, named after inventor Philip Rogan, employing assemblers and any plentiful raw material. Through "RoPro" or "RoProduction," walls, buildings, roads, any similar large structure, can be "grown" out of rock and earth quickly and cheaply.

SDT: Subsurface Deformation Track. Path through a planetary crust previously used by Xenophobe underground travelers. Rock once turned plastic by intense heat and pressure offers subsurface "highways" more easily traversed by subsequent craft.

Selfware: Jacker slang for the human mind, both the physical processes of neuronic impulses and the less quantifiable processes of consciousness, reasoning, and "self." If software is the program run on hardware, selfware is the program run on wetware.

Shichiju: Literally "The Seventy." Japanese term for the seventy-eight worlds in seventy-two systems so far colonized by Man.

Silicolubricant, silicarb: Greasy black silicon compound used to reduce friction in interior working parts.

Sky-el: Elevator used to travel between a planetary ring and the surface of the planet. A cheap and efficient way of moving people and cargo back and forth from surface to orbit. Earth has three sky-els: Singapore (Pulau Lingga), Ecuador (Quito), and Kenya (Mount Kenya). New Earth has two. Other worlds have one. Some, including New America, have none.

Slang, profanity:

easy feed: Slang expression for "no problem," or "that's okay."

gok, goking: Sexual obscenity. From Japanese *goku*, "rape."

I'm linked: I'm with you. I'll go along with that.

jackin' Jill: Girlfriend, especially as a casual RJ sex partner.

nork (also NORC or NORC-Socket): Colloquial for an idiot. From nonregistered C-socket, it refers to the common practice of illegal "back-alley" implant surgery for people who don't have the money or the connections to secure a legal (registered) implant. Many such operations result in permanent brain damage.

nullhead: Stupid. Empty-headed. By association, crazy.

odie: Let's odie = let's do it, let's move. From Japanese *odori*, "dance."

pulling strings, jerking strings: Slang expression: "You're kidding me."

scut, scutting: Worthless. A useless person. From medieval scuttage, a tax paid in feudal times to avoid military service.

staticjack: Mild curse. Expression of disgust or amazement.

static free: Easy, direct, simple, problem-free.

straight hont: The truth. From Japanese *honto no koto.*

Slot: 1) Linkage module for human controller. Warstriders have one, two, or three slots; a three-slotter strider has places for a commander, pilot, and weapons tech.

2) Space for equipment aboard transport. Ascraft have "slots" to carry four or six warstriders. (Slang) By popular usage, a place for a person in an organization, i.e., a "slot in the infantry."

Software: The programs run by computer hardware, up to and including AIs.

Stridertink, tink: Personnel who perform routine repair, maintenance, and service on striders, vehicles, and heavy equipment. Also called techs or techies.

Synchorbit: That point, different for each world, at which a satellite has an orbital period exactly matching the planet's rotation. Planetary sky-els rise from the world's equator to extensive constructions—factories, habitats, and other orbital facilities—in synchorbit.

Synchorbital: Facilities built at synchorbit.

Tacsit: Military slang for Tactical Situation.

Teikokuno Hoshi: Star of the Empire. Imperial medal for supreme service to the Emperor.

Teleop Weapons: Long-range missiles operated by weapons technicians at remote locations. Control can be by radio or—to avoid battlefield jamming—laser or a molecular fiberline unreeled behind the projectile.

Tenno Kyuden: Palace of Heaven. Seat of Imperial government, located at Singapore Synchorbital.

Thermal: Military slang for any infrared sensory device or scanner.

TO: Table of Organization.

Towerdown: The base of a sky-el tower, a busy terminus for freight and passengers.

Transplas: Synthetic building material, transparent and very strong.

T-socket: Temporal socket. Usually paired, one on each side of subject's skull, in temporal bone above and behind the ear. Used for full-sensory, full-feedback jacking in conjunction with an AI system, including experiencing ViR, full-sensory communications, and computer control of ships or vehicles.

VCH: Vehicle Cephlinkage Helmet. Allows direct human control of warstriders, ascraft, or other military vehicles. Internal leads plug into the operator's temporal sockets, while external sockets receive leads from AI interface.

ViR, Virtual Reality: Made possible by cephalic implants, virtual reality is the "artificial reality" of computer interfaces that allows, for example, a human pilot to "become" the strider or missile he is piloting, to "live" a simplay, or to "see" things that do not really exist, save as sophisticated computer software. An artificial world existing within the human mind that, through AI technology, can be shared with others.

ViRcom: Full sensory linked communication. Linker enters a chamber and plugs into communications net. He can then engage in conversation with one or more other humans or their computer analogues as though all were present together.

ViRdrama: Recreational jacking allowing full sensory experience through cephlinkage. Linker can participate in elaborate canned shows or AI-monitored games. Two or more linkers can share a single scenario, allowing them to interact with one another.

ViRnews: Also ViRinfo. Jack-fed informational programs permitting viewer interaction and questions with programmed "guides."

ViRpersona: The image of self projected in virtual reality dramas or communications. Clothing styles and even personal appearance can be purchased as a cephlink program, much as someone would buy new clothes.

Warstrider: Also strider. Battlefield armor on two or four legs, giving it high mobility over rough terrain. Generally consists of a fuselage slung between two legs, and equipped either with two arms mounting weapons or with interchangeable weapons pods. Sizes include single-slotters (eight to twelve tons), dual-slotters (ten to thirty tons), single-slotters three-slotters (twenty-five to seventy tons), and special vehicles such as Armored Personnel Walkers that carry large numbers of troops.

Wetware: The human brain, the ultimate computer.

Whitesuit: Slang for Hegemonic naval personnel. From their dress uniforms, which are white with gold trim.

Who-was: Rumor, scuttlebutt. Corruption of Japanese *uwasa.*

Xeno, Xenophobe: Human name for the life form that first attacked the human colony on An-Nur II in 2498. So-called because of their apparent hatred or fear of other life forms. Investigations within the Alya system in 2541 proved Xenophobes are machine-organic hybrids evolved from fairly simple organisms billions of years ago. They are defined by their technlogy, much of which has been borrowed from other civilizations.

Yukanno Kisho: Medal of Valor. Imperial decoration awarded in ten orders, or *dans*, for bravery in the line of duty.

Japanese Words and Phrases

Baka: Foolish, stupid, or silly.

Daihyo: Representative. In twenty-sixth-century usage, the Emperor's representative to a government or local military force within the Shichiju.

Dan: Order or ranking.

Fushi: Eternity, immortality. Era-name of current Emperor: Fushi 84.

Gaijin: Foreigner, specifically a non-Japanese.

Hema: Damned mess. Bungled situation.

Kichigai: You're crazy!

Nengo: Era-name, determined by each new Emperor, for purposes of dating.

Nettena-yo: Wake up!

Sen-en: One thousand yen (en in Japanese).

Sensei: Master. Title of respect for the teacher of a given discipline.

Sheseiji: "Bastards." Related to *shesei*, "posture" or "attitude."

Shoko: Military officer.

Tatami: Padded floor or floor mat.

Tenno-heika: Formal title of address—His Majesty, the Emperor.

Uwasa: Rumor, gossip.

Yujo: Camaraderie. It has taken on the special meaning of "warrior's bond."

Zugaikotsu: Skull.